Praise for t

"Some love stories touch you ....g after you've finished reading."
—Katy Regnery, *New York Times* bestselling author, on *More Than Words*

"There is no love story like a Mia Sheridan love story."
—A.L. Jackson, *New York Times* bestselling author

"Heartbreaking...inspiring, uplifting and raw."
—*RT Book Reviews* on *Most of All You*

"Utterly mesmerizing. An exquisite, beautifully written romance."
—Samantha Young, *New York Times* bestselling author, on *Most of All You*

"What ensues is the magnificent story of two kindred, shattered spirits finding hope and partnership and eventually love."
—*Washington Post* on *Most of All You*

"*More Than Words* is Mia Sheridan at her best! The story of love, heartbreak and second chances...each scene was beautifully written and paired with breathtaking imagery and epic love."
—Alessandra Torre, *New York Times* bestselling author

"Mia Sheridan has outdone herself with this beautiful, uplifting story of two broken souls finding themselves and each other. I savored each word of *Most of All You*. This story will stay with me forever."
—Corinne Michaels, *New York Times* bestselling author

"I love the men Mia writes. She's able to create sensitive real men with insane sex appeal."
—Renee Carlino, *USA TODAY* bestselling author, on *Most of All You*

"Sheridan explores the power of first love in a tale of childhood friends parted and reunited."
—*Publishers Weekly* on *More Than Words*

To learn more about Mia Sheridan and see an extensive list of her books, visit her website, miasheridan.com.

MIA SHERIDAN

HEART OF THE SUN

CANARY STREET PRESS

**CANARY
STREET
PRESS™**

Recycling programs
for this product may
not exist in your area.

ISBN-13: 978-1-335-42492-1

Heart of the Sun

Canary Street Press
22 Adelaide St. West, 41st Floor
Toronto, Ontario M5H 4E3, Canada
CanaryStPress.com

Printed in Lithuania

MIX
Paper | Supporting
responsible forestry
FSC® C021394

To Elizabeth, an angel and a warrior.

prologue

Tuck

Now

Holy shit. What the hell is happening?

Cold sweat broke out across my back as the lights inside the small, chartered plane blinked off and the engine went quiet. I could hear the pilot, Russell, behind the curtain to the cockpit, speaking into the radio with what sounded like growing alarm. I rose from my seat and took a few unsteady steps to the cockpit doorway where I slid the curtain open to see Russell furiously pushing buttons and moving dials. I grabbed the wall to hold myself steady as the plane bumped and jerked, sudden flares of lightning pulsing through the darkened cabin.

"What's going on?" I asked, voice as shaky as the rest of me.

"The engines and the navigation equipment went down," Russell said. "Air traffic control cut out and I can't get them back on the line."

My heart dipped along with the plane, and I heard a small squeal of fear from behind me where Emily and Charlie were sitting. "Isn't there a backup system?"

"That's out too! Copy! Copy!" he called into his headpiece, but again there was no reply. "*Shit.*"

I ignored Emily's quiet cries; there was nothing I could do. I had no idea what the hell was going on, and my own fear was mounting as the plane made another small drop. A bead of sweat rolled down the side of Russell's cheek, punctuating the fact that he was panicked as well.

"Sit down and buckle up. I'll use the manual controls," he said, obviously trying to insert a note of confidence in his tone. "We can still glide, but I'll need to get us down quickly. Brace for impact."

My heart was racing as I turned back toward my seat. "What's happening?" Emily asked, eyes wide with fear.

"Something knocked out the engine and navigation system and air traffic control isn't answering," I said, my eyes sweeping over her to verify she was buckled in. "He says to brace for impact." I glanced out the window. The sky had dimmed, and I could see zigzags of lightning in the distance. An unexpected electric storm?

Emily looked straight ahead, grasping the armrests as the plane gave a groaning shiver.

I sat down and buckled myself in just as the plane dipped and then dipped again, my stomach rising and falling quickly as a small piece of luggage went flying past my face. Then the plane took on a bumpy flight pattern and strange milky clouds streaked past my window, splintered by a spidery bolt of white lightning right next to us.

I could hear the muted blast of the wind outside, highlighting the dead silence of the engine.

Brace for impact, the pilot had said. But I didn't know how to do that other than sitting still and silent, terror pounding through my body.

We plunged yet again, the force jolting and lifting me and causing the seat belt to bite harshly into my hips. For a minute I was afraid the belt would break against the immense pressure. When I turned my eyes toward Emily, she was still gripping the armrests, her face ashen, eyes clenched tight. Next to her, Charlie had his eyes squeezed shut as well and looked to be hyperventilating. The plane began to shake, making a long, shrieking sound as though it was at risk of being torn apart by the rapid descent. My heart slammed, the hair rising on my nape and arms.

Just get us on the ground, Russell. Please get us on the ground.

We bumped and shook and for a moment, the sky went even darker, then seemed to split. The plane lowered again and this time didn't straighten out for several long seconds. My breath lodged in my throat. The aircraft straightened, and as the nose rose, the sky parted once more, and I glimpsed the ground. It was red and fiery, smoke billowing everywhere. I swallowed heavily, the bony fingers of terror gripping my lungs.

I closed my eyes, focusing on my breath, conjuring the one place on earth that had always brought peace to my soul. I was a child again, the air tinged with the scent of orange blossoms. I lifted my face to feel the kiss of dry heat upon my skin and listened for the ringing echo of my mother's laugh.

"Tuck." *Her* voice. *Emily.* Not who she'd later come to be, the woman she was now, but the girl she once was. The one I'd loved. "Tuck." That whisper again, my name floating over her shoulder as she ran through the groves of my memory, dirty knees and tangled hair, her quickened breath interrupted by bursts of giggles, spirit as radiant as the California sunshine. Another dip, another swerve, my memories dissolving in the surge of adrenaline shooting through my veins. My eyes shot open, and I leaned forward, watching helplessly out the window as we descended straight into hell.

one

Tuck

Eleven Years Ago

I hopped the split rail fence, jogging along the creek bed, bend-ing quickly to cup my hands and bring a drink of fresh, clear water to my mouth. A lizard scooted from under a rock, both of us startling each other before he darted away. Upright again, I ran the path I'd used a thousand times, toward the old stable on the east end of our property. The sun was just beginning its descent, purple streaks bleeding slowly across the horizon. Behind me I heard the shouts and laughter of my friends—the children of the farmhands and a couple neighbor kids—goofing off among the citrus groves. Normally I'd be hanging out with them, especially on a summer night like tonight, but more and more recently, I'd craved the quiet of my own thoughts, the time to focus on my dreams.

I was only fourteen, but my grandfather had come from

Mexico and settled in California when he was just about my age, and even then, began to map out and work toward his future, the results of which spread out all around me, from the logo emblazoned on the front gate, to the far pasture where our horses roamed. *Honey Hill Farm.*

The old stable, no longer in use anymore, except for storage—and a secret space I'd claimed as my own—came into view and I raced toward it. A slight breeze rustled the leaves surrounding the structure, and I pulled the side door open just enough to squeeze through into the dim interior. It smelled like motor oil, dirt, and old wood, and though the mingling scents couldn't necessarily be described as pleasant, they comforted me in some odd way. They spoke of peace, of found solitude, of safety even. This was my hideaway, a place of secret thoughts and dreams that felt as never-ending as the sky, and as bright and sweet as those oranges dripping like jewels from the trees.

There was something different—though temporary—occupying the space, however, and I thinned my lips as my gaze caught on the shiny convertible decked out in American flags and "Phil Swanson for City Council" campaign signs. The restored 1957 Ford Thunderbird was undeniably cool, the pride and joy of the owner of the orange grove neighboring ours, but I'd be glad when Mr. Swanson had backed it out of here, and this all-but-forgotten space once again belonged to me and me alone. That would be this weekend, right before the annual Labor Day parade, where Mr. Swanson planned to drive the car for his campaign. It was only being stored here because he'd washed and waxed it and didn't have a space to house it as his own garage was undergoing some sort of expansion.

I looked away from the shiny red interloper and headed for the ladder that took me to the loft area. As my head cleared the high-up floor, my eyes widened, shock halting my movement, one leg raised to step to the next rung.

Emily Swanson.

Kneeling in front of the small, round window, next to my pile of books and among the other things I'd brought here, a hardcover open in her hands as she read.

No. Way.

Of *all* the people that I never wanted to find this spot or rifle through *my* things.

The burst of anger fueled my movement and I practically catapulted over the top of the ladder, coming to my feet, my head just grazing the ceiling. "What do you think you're doing?" I demanded.

Emily whirled around, fell to her butt, and dropped the book. "You scared me!"

"I scared *you*? You're not supposed to be here. You're…trespassing!"

She scrambled to her feet and then immediately put her hands on her slender hips, one golden brow arching. Despite my indignation, I couldn't help noting how pretty she was. In fact, just the day before, I'd lain beneath that very window, my head propped on my backpack as I wondered what it'd be like to brush my lips against hers. The memory made heat flood my face like she might be able to read my mind, and my anger flamed hotter. It felt like she'd not only invaded my personal space, but somehow crept into my private thoughts as well. Thoughts about *her* that sort of embarrassed me, but mostly intrigued and excited me. *When* I was alone with them. For all my life, our parents had called us the worst of enemies and the best of friends, which I supposed was true. But now…something else was floating around the perimeter of our friendship, something I'd only begun to explore haltingly, secretly. *Alone.*

Emily stood, smoothing her sundress and brushing off her backside. "I wasn't trespassing," she insisted. "I just came out here to see my dad's car all decorated."

As if she had part ownership of this stable just because we'd allowed her dad to park his car here for a few days. To be fair, we'd always sort of treated each other's neighboring orange groves as one continuous property, but I was in no mood to be fair. And anyway, what she'd said was clearly a lie. "Your dad's car is down there," I gritted, pointing behind me as though she didn't already know that.

Emily moved her eyes slowly in the direction I'd pointed and then back to me, smiling sweetly. "I saw the books from below and was curious. I thought some homeless person might be living here. Maybe even a mass murderer or a…cannibal or something. I figured your mom and dad would want to know." She looked around at the things I'd brought into my private hangout—books, binoculars, a pad of paper and a few pens, a deck of cards—and her lip quirked. A *cannibal*? *Really*? No, the little brat had uncovered a secret of mine and could tell I was mad. She was enjoying this.

"Get out before I push you over the edge," I threatened, taking a step forward, hoping to scare her and wipe that self-satisfied smirk off her pretty face.

"You can't do that!"

"Watch me."

She glanced toward the edge, noting, it seemed, that she was nowhere near it, and therefore, not in any danger of being pushed. My baseless threat appeared to anger her more than anything, and with a huff, she bent and picked up one of my books and then held it in front of her. "I should have known these were *your* books the minute I saw them," she said, her gaze going to the title of the one she was holding. *Roman Aqueducts and Water Supply.* Her expression registered dramatic disgust. "*Boring* books." She lowered the pitch of her voice, doing a mocking impersonation. "I'm Tuck. I read boring books so I can get more boring. Boring, boring, boring." I watched, my mouth falling open as I radiated rage and disbelief, and though I wouldn't have admitted it, a small bit of curiosity. I was never quite sure what Emily was going to do from one moment to the next. She picked up another book, *A Soil Owner's Manual*, and held it up to her face, pretending to read, crossing her eyes, taking a few steps one way and then the next in a drunken sort of stagger. "Oh good," she said. "A book about *dirt*. I just got even *more* boring. Just what I was going for. Maybe I can join the Boring Olympics or start a business where I help people who can't sleep."

"Boring is better than stupid," I retorted.

Her mouth set. Her blue eyes sparked fire. Yes, I knew her well enough to know that that was her button. She had trouble in school. Her parents were always on her case about her grades. She was behind in almost everything, except her beloved *music* class. She picked up one of the hand weights I'd brought up here so I could strengthen my mind *and* my body, the same way my grandfather had done all those years ago, or so the story went.

"I'm Tuck," she said, using that same mocking pitch. "I lift weights so I can get even..." she paused to move her eyes over my body "...*scrawnier* than I already am." She lowered the weight, crossing her eyes again and pretending to struggle as she lifted it, doing it again, huffing, moving her arm faster as she grunted in a parody of *me*, attempting to workout. Part of me wanted to laugh at the ridiculous show she was putting on, but the larger part was still raging mad and hugely offended. And so, when she jerked her arm backward and the weight slipped out of her hand, flying over her shoulder and sailing off the edge of the loft, I let out a bark of laughter that died a quick death as the sound of breaking glass exploded from below.

Oh God.

The Thunderbird.

Emily yelped, and we both moved quickly to the edge, going down on our knees and peering over to where the weight had landed, smack-dab in the middle of the Thunderbird's windshield, shattering it and landing in a pile of shards on what had been the unblemished white interior.

Her father's pride and joy. The one he'd spent three years restoring to pristine condition.

Emily's sudden wail pierced the silence and she crawled to the ladder, turning around and descending in a blur of blue sundress and bouncing blond ponytail. I followed, my body still rigid with disbelief, and a fair amount of horror.

Emily's dad was going to go ballistic on her.

Good.

Emily was standing next to the car, leaned toward the shattered windshield, as though, up close, it might not have been as bad as it looked from high above. She wailed again, tears pouring down her cheeks as she hiccupped and blubbered. "He's going to *murder* me," she cried. "Then he's going to murder me again!"

I felt a small trickle of satisfaction but resisted the smile I felt tugging at one corner of my lips.

"At least it's just the windshield," I said. I didn't know much about cars, but I figured that could be replaced more easily than if the weight had fallen on the hood and dented the paint and the metal. "He might only *half* murder you."

Emily threw her head back and wailed again. "I'm supposed to go to a music camp this weekend. I'm already on thin ice because of my grades. He'll never let me go now. He might as *well* just murder me!" She let out another high-pitched sob.

God, she was dramatic. My mom called Emily a "little showboat," even if she smiled when she said it, affection in her voice. I gave her a glassy stare. "You really are a baby, you know that? You're going to have to tell him what you did and accept the consequences."

She deserved this. She really did. This was called *just deserts.*

Emily hung her head and sobbed for a minute, her shoulders shaking. But then with a shuddery breath, she nodded and looked up at me with her big blue eyes, now red-rimmed and glittering with tears. "I'm sorry, Tuck. I was mean. You're not boring. At least not all the time." Then she turned and headed slowly to the door, shuffling as she walked like she was heading for the gallows.

two

Tuck

I waited a few minutes, giving Emily time to get ahead of me so I didn't have to hear her pitiful sobs. When I emerged from the stable, she was already a few hundred feet away, her pale blue dress and yellow hair standing out against the rust-colored dirt. The sky had dimmed since I'd first entered the building, and far beyond, I could see the dancing flames of the bonfire our parents had lit, a regular occurrence on weekend summer nights. Sometimes we'd roast hot dogs or s'mores. And sometimes Mrs. Swanson would bring out the board games. Those were the nights I'd hear the adults laughing and chattering long after I went to bed.

I trudged toward the firelight, the rising and falling sounds of conversation meeting my ears as I drew closer. There was an ice bucket filled with drinks on the edge of the large brick patio, and I grabbed a soda, popping it open and taking a sip. "Tuck. There you are," my mother said, smiling and waving me over. I glanced at Emily as I passed her, sitting on the edge of the stone wall surrounding the patio, her head bent, eyes darting to where her father stood talking to mine.

She looked completely miserable. I glanced away, barely resisting rolling my eyes. She really was the most dramatic person sometimes. It wasn't the end of the darn world. The windshield could be fixed, even if her dad was steaming mad, which he would be. So she'd miss *music camp* this weekend. Oh well. I didn't feel the least bit bad for her.

My mom grinned as I approached. "Hey, handsome. Where have you been?"

I shrugged. "Just around."

"Just around," she repeated, tilting her head as she studied me in that way of hers that made me feel slightly itchy like she could pluck answers from my head whether I'd offered them or not. "Emily's always over at the house asking about you these days," she said. "She says you haven't been hanging out with her and the other kids very much lately. She says you've been *disappearing.*" My hand tightened on the can as my outrage spiked. Not only was she spying on me, but she was also ratting me out to my mom.

"I haven't been disappearing," I asserted. I glanced over to where Emily sat, staring gloomily at her shoes. Her small breasts stretched the elastic of her sundress, and I averted my eyes down to her skinned knees, mostly scabbed over. I didn't tell my mom that Emily had found me and ruined my secret hangout forever, or that she was an annoying drama queen and a snitch as well. And I especially didn't admit that I'd thought about kissing her more than once, and I intended to keep doing that, but I wanted to think about it when I was *away* from Emily, not when she was anywhere close by.

"I don't have much in common with her anymore," I said. Which was sort of true, and sort of not, but I didn't know how to describe the strange middle ground where I'd suddenly found myself regarding Emily Swanson.

My mom was quiet a moment, but I felt her eyes on me, and I sensed something in her silence that led me to believe once again that I'd revealed myself to her though I hadn't meant to. She reached out and ruffled my hair the way she'd done when I was very young. "Don't grow up on me too fast now," she said, and there was a note in her voice that almost sounded like sadness.

I nodded, concentrating on the dirt as I dug the toe of my sneaker into it. The raised voices of my dad and Mr. Swanson caught my attention and I looked up, watching as they spoke animatedly, Mr. Swanson waving his arms around as he gestured. "What are they arguing about?" I asked.

My mom sighed. "Oh, they're not really arguing, just discussing the fact that the Henleys and the O'Rourkes sold their orchards."

My head whipped back toward her, eyes widening. "They did? When?" Devin Henley and Andy O'Rourke were two of my good friends, their orchards part of the community of family-run orange groves—including ours and the Swansons'—that stretched for miles, often referred to as Citrus Row.

"Just last week," my mother said, forehead creasing. "A development company offered far over market value, and they decided to take it and retire."

Far over market value. I didn't know exactly what that meant, but if they were retiring instead of buying another farm, or going to work somewhere else, it must mean they were offered a lot of money. "Did they...did they offer us money too?" I felt funny, like the whole world had just tilted in some weird way, and while I didn't totally understand it, I felt like I was standing slightly sideways.

My mother gave a thin smile. "Oh sure. But no amount of

money could get me to sell our farm. You know that. It's my legacy. And yours."

My world righted just a bit, even if not completely. I watched my father and Mr. Swanson for another minute. Mr. Swanson was speaking, and my father was rubbing his forehead as though he was torn about whatever Mr. Swanson was saying to him. A company had wanted that land. What was going to happen to it now? I started to open my mouth to ask more questions when Mr. Swanson gave my father a companionable pat on the shoulder, their conversation obviously ending as they each turned away. I watched as Emily stood, marching stoically toward her father, about ready to ruin his day with her confession about his damaged car.

"Em," her father said, smiling and gesturing her over as he glanced at my mom. "You promised to sing for us next time Mariana had her guitar out."

My mom smiled, taking a few steps to where her guitar rested against an Adirondack chair. "I'm ready if you are. Something simple," she told Emily on a laugh. "I'm still practicing." My mom had been taking guitar lessons once a week for the past six months just for fun—*it's been on my bucket list forever,* she'd told my dad—and would sometimes strum a few chords around the bonfire, but she was still a beginner. Emily was better on the guitar, having played longer, but I knew Emily preferred to sing, and was happy to let my mom accompany her.

Emily hesitated, clearly torn between the confession she'd mustered up the nerve to deliver, and accepting the delay of a performance. She shot her dad one final, indecisive look, but then turned toward my mom, who was hooking the strap on her guitar and moving to the elevated portion of the patio.

Emily's parents, my father, and a few of the men who worked with us, along with their wives, moved closer, some taking seats on the slew of Adirondack chairs, some sitting on the low stone wall surrounding the patio. Emily and my mom murmured a few words, obviously choosing which song to play.

I stepped away from the adults, leaning against the pergola that covered the outdoor dining set. Hot pink bougainvillea twisted around the pillars and dripped through the slats, providing shade when the eating area was in use. The sun had set, stars blinking in the navy sky, but the temperature was still in the nineties at least, and the coolness under the overhang welcomed me.

Lanterns and string lights provided illumination to the outdoor area, especially bright over the portion of patio now acting as a stage. My mother sat down on a folding chair with her guitar, Emily stepping to the forefront, all gazes fixed on her. The gold in her hair glinted under the glow, the skin of her shoulders smooth and tan. I was surprised the adults hadn't noticed that her eyes looked slightly swollen from crying. Even so, she was prettier than any of the other girls from town. I wanted to stare, and so I did. Emily's gaze met mine and I startled, the back of my neck growing warm. I made it a point to yawn. Emily's eyes narrowed, but then, as my mother began to strum, Emily's shoulders lowered, and she closed her eyes, her body swaying gently.

The first note broke the night hush and somehow melded with it too. Emily's voice was high and sweet, but also held an undertone of smoke as though she'd inhaled the bonfire and it wove between the words. Everything inside me seemed to still—my thoughts, my breath, even the beat of my heart and the flow of my blood—taking up the slow melody of the song. Emily sang about rainbows and bluebirds, but it felt like more than that. A longing rose inside me, for what I had no words to describe. All I knew was that I was completely entranced. And that if she looked at me again, I wouldn't be able to hide it.

The beauty of her voice was effortless, even if there was a sad quality to it. Maybe she was feeling the loss of that music camp that would be taken from her as she sang the melody. But rather than ruin the song, her sadness seemed to add something...an extra note...another chord. I didn't understand it exactly, but I felt it, and I could tell the others watching felt it too, saw the way Emily's mother brought her hand to her heart, and a farmhand named Arleen wiped her eye.

As the song came to an end, Emily dropped her head, bending in a bow, the final note somehow still suspended all around us, though it had already faded to silence. The small audience jumped to their feet, clapping exuberantly, whistles ringing out. Emily smiled, and my mother stood, taking her in a hug. "You're a star, beautiful girl," I barely heard her say from where I stood.

The applause died down, conversation picking up, a few people heading toward the standing ice buckets where drinks were chilling. I watched as Emily took a deep breath, walking toward her father.

I moved behind a row of hedges closer to where they stood.

"Dad... I have something to tell you," I heard her say.

"What is it, honey?"

"Your Thunderbird..."

"My Thunderbird?" His eyes widened and his head swiveled toward the old barn as though he might be able to see it from where he was standing. "What about it?"

"The...the windshield is broken. Shattered." I heard the tears in her voice even though I was standing twenty-five feet away. I ducked slightly, moving behind a flowering bush.

"*What?*" He pulled her to the side of the patio, nearer to where I was listening in, and through the foliage, I saw the people who had been standing nearby turn back to their own conversations to give them some privacy. I gently moved the brush aside, watching as Mr. Swanson gripped the front of his hair in his hands, shaking his head. "How in the hell did that happen?" he yelled. Emily's shoulders curled forward, and she hung her head. I could see most of her father's face, and his expression went through several stages of anger.

"I was in the old stable," she said. "I just wanted to see your car decorated. Sorry, Dad."

His jaw clenched and he spoke through barely moving lips when he said, "Sorry? *Sorry?* You asked if you could walk out to the Mattices' old stable, didn't you?"

Her head hung lower. "Yes, Dad."

"And what did I tell you?"

"You said no."

"That's right. I told you explicitly that you weren't allowed in there. Sorry isn't good enough, Emily Nicole. In fact, this is the final straw in a string of poor choices and unacceptable grades. You will stay home this weekend and you will—"

"I broke your windshield, sir," I said, stepping out of the brush and coming to stand next to Emily, who pulled in a surprised breath as she lifted her head and turned toward me. "It was an accident, but...it was me who did it."

From my peripheral vision I saw Emily's mouth fall open.

"Tuck? You broke my windshield?" Mr. Swanson asked. "How? How in the hell did that happen?"

I stuck my hands in my pockets. "I hang out in there sometimes. In the old barn. I dropped a hand weight from the loft. It landed on your windshield. I'm sorry. Emily was only there because I asked her to come see it. She thought you'd take it better if she broke the news to you. But it was me who did it."

"What's this?" my father asked, coming up next to me.

"I broke Mr. Swanson's Thunderbird windshield," I muttered. "It was just an accident."

"An accident?" my father exclaimed. "How does an accident like that happen? What were you doing in the old stable anyway? Jesus H. Christ, Tuck—"

"Rand," my mother said, approaching my father and putting

a hand on his arm, obviously having heard what was going on. "Let's all calm down. We can figure this out."

He shook her hand off. "This is unacceptable. What's wrong with you, Tuck?"

My face burned, and for a moment I almost took back my false confession, the one I hadn't really planned on or thought through, the one that had seemed to break from my lips of its own accord. "I'll pay for it," I murmured, daring a glance at Mr. Swanson, who was massaging his temples.

"You damn sure will," my father gritted. "But that windshield will need to be fixed in the next few days if Phil is going to drive it in the parade." He looked at Mr. Swanson. "Arnold at the repair shop will fit you in," he told Mr. Swanson. "I'll pay for it, and Tuck here will pay me back. I'm sorry about my foolhardy son, Phil. This never should have happened."

I'm sorry about my foolhardy son. My dad's temper could flare at a moment's notice, and he'd said hurtful things to me before, but that one really hurt. Even if it was based on a lie I'd told about myself. My mother put her hand on my father's arm again, and this time he didn't shrug her off. In fact, he put his hand over hers, giving her a small nod. My mother had a special knack for calming my father down when his anger began ramping up. She knew how to do it with a look, or a touch, or a word or two. "There we go, then. A perfect solution," she said. "Tuck, please apologize to Mr. Swanson for the carelessness that resulted in damage to his car."

I put my hands in my pockets but met Mr. Swanson's eyes. "I'm sorry, sir."

He gave me a nod, putting a hand on my shoulder. "I accept your apology."

My father looked at me, jerking his head to the left. "You can get started paying me back tonight, mucking out the horse stalls. And don't let me catch you near the old stables again.

There are sharp, rusted tools in there. It's dangerous and I don't want you fooling around."

"It sounds like it was just an accident, Rand—"

"Even so," my father said to Mr. Swanson. "Tuck needs to take responsibility for his actions. I'd offer to take the Thunderbird to Arnold myself tomorrow, but it sounds like it might be safest to have it towed."

Phil nodded. "I need to drop Em off at the bus for music camp early tomorrow morning. I'll call Arnold when I get back."

I shot a look at Emily, still staring at me, eyes wide. I looked away. My dad tipped his chin. "Go on and get started, so you won't be up all night," he said, his tone softer.

"Yes, sir." I looked at Mr. Swanson again. "Sorry again, sir."

"Thank you for your apology, son. That shows a man of principle."

Principle.

My mother caught my eye, giving me an encouraging nod. I didn't glance at Emily again before I turned and walked away.

three

Tuck

I hefted the pitchfork, dropping the pile of dirty, urine-drenched hay into the wheelbarrow, and spearing another. It was hot in the stable, the quiet chuffs of the horses in the other stalls mixing with the distant buzz of the crickets outside.

Soft footsteps sounded near the entrance, but I didn't turn until Emily was right next to me. I gave her a quick glance, not halting my work, lifting another pile and dropping it in the half-filled wheelbarrow.

She retrieved another pitchfork from against the wall, and without a word, walked to the other side of me and began collecting forkfuls of dirty hay and dumping them on top of the pile I'd started.

When the first load was full, I wheeled it outside and grabbed a second wheelbarrow. I'd bring both out to the garden in the morning where it would be used as mulch. If you ran a farm well, nothing needed to go to waste.

We worked in silence until all four empty stalls were cleared out. Our horses were settled for the night, so in the morning, when they headed out to the pasture, I'd clean out the remaining stalls. Emily set her pitchfork against the wall and then turned to me. She was dirty and sweaty and had pieces of hay sticking out of her hair. I swiped my forearm across my own damp forehead. "You better get to bed since you're leaving early," I said.

"Why'd you do it?" she asked. "Why'd you cover for me?"

I shrugged. "I didn't have anything going on this weekend. And I don't mind the work." What I didn't say—what I didn't know *how* to say—was that after hearing her sing, it had seemed wrong in some massive way that she should miss out on her music camp. On *developing her talent* or whatever my mom had said about the program. And so, I'd lied. I hadn't even really thought about it; I'd just acted. I couldn't exactly explain my split-second decision, but I also couldn't seem to regret it, even standing there smelling like sweat and horseshit, and knowing I was facing down a long weekend of back-to-back chores under the grueling sun. Not to mention my dad's anger and disappointment.

Emily's gaze moved over my features for a moment, confusion clear in her expression and the tilt of her head. Then she took a step closer, my breath halting as she leaned in. My heart skipped a beat as she came closer, closer, her eyes closing. For several breathless moments, time stilled, the background fading so that it was only her and nothing else. Velvety skin. Flushed cheeks. Lips that looked as soft as a rose petal. A strange prickle of panic jumped inside my chest as though I had only this one chance, only now, to memorize the details of her before she moved away. As though she'd sensed my sudden turmoil, her eyes fluttered open just as her lips grazed mine and for two heartbeats…three, they lingered there, our gazes locked. And when her lips left mine, I felt a groan of disappointment move up my throat but swallowed it down. *Don't stop.*

"Thank you," she whispered when she finally stepped back. I brought my hand to the place where her lips had been as she turned and walked to the door and slipped out of the stable. My heart kicked back into rhythm, a slow grin spreading across my face. I stood there for a few minutes, reliving the kiss before I practically skipped over to the fresh bales of hay, picking one up as though it weighed nothing, and hefting it over to one of the clean stalls.

I heard the door behind me once more and dropped the bale, turning to see my mom walking toward me holding a sports bottle. "It looks good," she said, peering into the stall and then turning her head toward the others. "Was that Emily I saw heading away from here?" She held the bottle out to me.

I brushed my gloves together, a small explosion of dust creating a cloud around my hands, bits of hay and debris drifting to the floor. "Yeah," I answered, because it wasn't like I could say anything else. I accepted the bottle and lifted it to my mouth, grateful for the clean, cold water, though the hose would have quenched my thirst too, even if that water had a slight metallic tang.

"It sure was nice of her to help you out for no reason whatsoever."

I took another sip, deciding it was in my best interest not to provide a comment. I'd lied enough for one day. A small smile played around my mother's lips as she walked with me, helping to carry a second bale of hay to another cleaned-out stall.

"I went with Phil to surveille the damage to the Thunderbird," she said as we lifted a third bale of hay. "The interior is fine, which is lucky because that glass could have cut the seat."

"That's good," I said as we set the hay down and returned for the fourth and final one.

"I was curious about how a weight fell from the loft and so I climbed up there to check it out."

I sighed as we set the bale on the floor and I took the wire cutters from my pocket, snipping the binding and beginning to spread the hay on the floor. "You set up a spot very similar to the way I imagine your grandfather lived when he first came to this farm," she said. I didn't look at her, just continued spreading hay.

"I know my grandfather's story," I said. I'd heard it a hundred times. Truth be told, I never grew tired of hearing it, but I didn't say that then because I was embarrassed that she'd found my setup, like I was playing some sort of role or something, trying to pretend I was him. Guillermo Luis Castañeda, an orphan from a small village in Mexico, had come to America when he was only seventeen years old. He'd gotten a job right here on this farm, picking oranges under the sweltering sun. He'd slept in the old stable—that had been brand-new at the time—and learned English, eventually surrounding himself with books on every subject he could get his hands on. He read, and he learned, his mind growing strong, along with his body as he labored picking fruit. When he wasn't in the orchard, he worked his muscles anyway, lifting coffee cans filled with dirt as he practiced pronouncing the words he read. It came to be that when there was a problem on the farm, people went to Guillermo because he had a wealth of knowledge on everything from the animals, to the machinery, to the quality of the dirt. At first only the other farmhands and laborers sought him out, but then the bosses did, and eventually, even the owner knew his name. Guillermo worked his way up, becoming invaluable to the operation, socking away every cent he earned. He implemented a new water system that saved time and money. He came up with an original method of picking the fruit that cut cost, and he brought in hives of bees and set them up on the hillside because he'd read that they helped sweeten the fruit, and found it was true. He married my grandmother—a local girl—when he was twenty-five, and he bought the farm outright when he was thirty, renaming it Honey Hill Farm, after those bees that set his citrus crop apart from all the others.

We moved to the next stall, and I again cut the binding on the hay and began to spread it out. "You have the same yearning for knowledge that your grandfather had," she said. "And the same determination. The same work ethic. It's nothing at all to be embarrassed about, Tuck. It will open doors for you, in the same way it did for him. So many lack the grit and the heart to carry forth the legacy of those who came before them. Like your uncle, for instance," she murmured, her forehead knitting the way it always did when she mentioned her brother. But she took a deep breath, her lips curving as she looked at me. "But not you. If your grandfather was alive, he'd be so proud."

"Thank you, Mom." I felt a wash of warmth, her words giving me renewed energy as I picked up the speed of my work. I liked knowing she thought Grandpa Castañeda would be proud of me.

"Follow in his footsteps," she told me. "But also, forge your own. If anyone is capable, it's you, my smart boy."

"I will, Mom."

She smiled, stepping closer and ruffling my hair. "I know you will." She turned, heading for the door. "And, Tuck," she called, nodding to the pitchfork in my hands. "Never lose your sense of decency. It's your badge of honor." She shot me a wink, but her expression faltered as she began to turn, stumbling, catching herself, and then stumbling again.

"Mom?" I dropped the tool, rushing toward her as she fell. "Mom!" I yelled, barely catching her before she hit the ground. Panic jolted my system, my arms trembling as I held her. "Dad!" I called through the open door. "Dad! Somebody, help!"

four

Tuck

Ten Days Ago

"You're home early," my uncle said through a mouthful of turkey sandwich, setting it back down on the plate in front of him.

"I got let go." I tossed the apron I'd forgotten to leave behind over the kitchen chair. I'd return it tomorrow to the restaurant. Or maybe I wouldn't. What was another theft on my record, especially one that wouldn't be officially reported? They'd obviously expected me to steal something. Why disappoint them?

My uncle was studying me casually. "I told you—you should have disclosed your record."

I fell into the chair with a sigh. "Yeah. Well." I felt defeated, no energy left in my body to do much of anything, not even form a meaningful sentence. Alfonso obviously guessed why I'd been fired anyway, so why use a bunch of words to explain? Yeah, I should have been honest about my criminal record, but recent history had taught me that didn't go well when attempting to find employment, and so I'd lied. And I'd hoped that, if they did check, they'd let it slide that their dishwasher had served time.

Clearly, that had been a miscalculation, even though I'd worked hard, showed up every day on time, and kept my head down. Apparently, I wasn't even worthy of scraping dried food off other people's dirty plates.

"What are you gonna do now?" my uncle asked.

I looked away, tapping my knuckle on the table. *What are you gonna do now?* That was the question. The one I'd been trying to answer for the last four months since I'd been released from prison. Only, *what I did now* didn't seem to be up to me. Once...once I'd had a legacy. Now I had a criminal record and extremely limited employment options, if any existed at all.

But I pushed thoughts of *legacy* far, far away. That had been taken from me a long time ago and it wasn't something worth dwelling on. "I don't know," I murmured. But I had to do something. The terms of my probation required me to have a job, not to mention I'd racked up some serious debt before I'd been sent to prison. And adding to that, I had a responsibility to help two people who'd suffered the fallout of my failure.

Hopelessness flooded me and for a moment I felt crushed under its unseen weight. My uncle had taken me in when I was seventeen, put up with a whole slew of bad behavior over the years, and then taken me in again when I was released, but he had issues of his own and lived paycheck to paycheck as it was. He couldn't afford to help me financially, and though I appreciated the roof over my head, the thought of living on my uncle's couch for even one more month, made that weight grow heavier.

Stop looking a gift horse in the mouth. It's leagues better than the lumpy cot you slept on for six years in a windowless cell. That was true, but it did little to bolster my mood. Because in prison, I'd had an end date to move toward. Here, in the outside world, it was becoming increasingly clear that I was still stuck, even if in different ways, just as I'd been behind bars.

Strangely enough, I hadn't minded the dishwashing job. It was solitary work, and I'd become a solitary person since I'd been locked up. I'd grown used to—almost comforted by—a rigid schedule and precise way of doing things. Loading that machine, pressing the button, listening to the whir of the brushes and the gush of the water, and then unloading, separating, stacking…and then doing it all over again, was mindless work, but it fed my new affinity for *order*. There was a word for what had happened to me during those six long years where I woke at the exact same time every morning and was directed through my day by others: *institutionalized*. I was well aware, and so I recognized that the loss of the job wasn't simply about a paycheck—paltry though it was—but about having the meager sense of order I'd regained being taken away.

A magazine was off to the side, and my eyes lingered on the cover headline, "Sun's Fury." The subhead read: "Scientists Warn Solar Flare Could Hit Earth in Our Lifetime."

I read it once, then twice, finally sighing, and pushing it aside.

If only.

With one massive explosion, I'd be on common ground with every other man and woman out there.

Which was to say, we'd *all* be fucked.

Fortunately or unfortunately—I couldn't quite decide—that wasn't going to happen.

Alfonso stood and dropped his plate in the sink with a clatter. "Oh, by the way," he said, plucking a piece of mail off the top of the pile on the counter. "This came for you."

I took it, and he gave me a pat on the shoulder as he moved past, pausing. I waited for the words of encouragement he might give me before he left. "Wash those up, would you?"

I eyed the sink full of dirty dishes. "Thanks for the words of wisdom," I muttered sarcastically.

His soft chuckle drifted behind him. "You'll see the wisdom in not letting small messes accumulate. Take it from someone who's been where you are."

Sure. Okay.

The front door opened, and then closed, and a minute later I heard the growl of his car's engine as it pulled away from the curb, off to his job as head custodian at a local high school. Maybe he had a little more of his father's determination than my mom had believed, because he'd started out as a janitor there right before I'd gone to prison and was now running the custodial team. Unfortunately for me, they were currently on a hiring freeze. In any case, maybe my uncle would never live in Bel Air, but his outlook was a whole lot better than mine.

He'd been where I was, even if his time spent in jail had been for a series of shorter stints. He'd struggled with drugs for much of his youth and had finally gotten clean right before I came to live with him. He'd put up with me when he didn't have to, and while he might not have been equipped to deal with an angry, grieving, troubled teenager when he was only just getting his own life together, he'd done what he could. He'd put a roof over my head and food on the table, and I'd "repaid" his generosity by being a total fuckup.

And here I was living the consequences. I tapped the table with the envelope in my hand, my heart giving a small jolt when I caught sight of the return label. I tore open the flap and pulled out the Christmas card from the Swansons. The shiny front featured a colorful rendition of Santa, and on the inside, it had a generic printed greeting under which Mrs. Swanson had written: *Merry Christmas, Tuck. Thinking of you this holiday season and wishing you well. Let us know if you're ever in the area. We'd love to see you. Love, Jena and Phil.*

I placed the card down on the table. They'd sent me a Christmas card every year since I'd moved away, even when I'd been in prison. They must have heard that I'd been released. Shame wound through me. Jena had been my mom's best friend. It must hurt her to know how devastated my mom would have been had she lived—

The chair legs scraped across the tile as I stood and then headed for the living room. But I paused in the doorway, the kernel of an idea making me turn, my gaze landing on Santa's jolly grin. I took the few steps back to the table and picked up the card and the envelope, staring at that return address, the one I'd once known as well as my own.

five

Tuck

I stood on the other side of the road, staring at the place that had been a second home to me.

It was barely recognizable.

Swanson Groves still featured the same gate, with a white house in the distance, but instead of the seemingly never-ending rows of orange trees that had once stretched from their home to ours, there was now only a handful of trees. The rest had been mowed down to make room for square, nondistinct tract houses and what looked like a mall in the distance. A hole inside me gaped wide, an old wound made up of anger, bitterness, resentment...hate. I'd spent so many years convincing myself I'd moved on from those feelings, but I obviously hadn't, because in one unexpected moment, they poured forth.

All these years, I'd held this place in my heart as a slice of heaven on earth. Out of my reach, yes, but still there. Still proof that a *piece* of perfect, no matter how small, no matter how removed, existed. But now, I felt that hope crumble. I knew there had been changes, but I hadn't imagined this level of...carnage.

And that's what it felt like. As though invading marauders had come through my homeland and laid waste. Rationally or not, I felt personally violated.

I closed my eyes and took a deep breath. I'd received enough emotional blows in the past eleven years that I knew how to stuff the feelings back down, to keep moving. And that was what I did, looking both ways before walking purposefully across the street.

The gate was propped open the way it'd always been. If there was now more reason for security, the Swansons didn't seem to know it. Or maybe they just chose to embrace the last sliver of tradition that existed in these parts. Trust.

There was a black truck in the driveway, indicating someone was home, and I climbed the two steps to the front door and knocked. A dog started yapping from inside, followed by the sound of a woman hushing it, and approaching footsteps. The door swung open, and Mrs. Swanson was standing there, her face morphing from polite confusion into recognition and then wide-eyed surprise. "Tuck. Oh my goodness." She brought both hands to her mouth and then dropped them, stepping forward and gathering me in a hug. A smile took over my face, and the expression felt foreign. I couldn't remember the last time I'd felt air on my teeth.

"Hi, Mrs. Swanson."

She stood back, her hands on my arms. "My goodness. Oh, look at you. You're a man. Goodness, goodness, I'm going to try not to cry. Quiet, Teddy," she said to the yappy dog dancing around her legs. "Come in. You should have called—I would have made sure Phil was here and had some snacks ready. Oh, forget that. You never need to call. And who needs snacks. It's just so good to see you." She led me into the living room where there were several large bins sitting off to the side, the contents green and red and cheerful. It appeared that she'd just started decorating for Christmas. There were a few pieces of new furniture, but it looked mostly the same and something eased inside me so that I could take in a full breath. I sat down on the beige sofa, looking around at the familiar items, the family photos I'd committed to memory long ago. A studio pose of the three of them, another of Emily with dirty knees, grinning with a slice of orange rind covering her teeth like a goof. It made me smile. I knew from Mrs. Swanson's updates that Emily had been picked up by a record label and recorded an album that was garnering all sorts of success. I wasn't surprised. She'd been hugely talented, even as a kid. When I looked back at Mrs. Swanson, she was watching me as I took in the room. "How are you, Tuck?" she asked. "Really?"

I sat back, sighed. "Getting by."

A crease formed between her brows. "I wanted to visit you," she said. "I would have—"

"I know," I said. "I know you would have." She'd written to me many times over the course of my sentence. I'd appreciated the lifeline, but I'd asked that she not come see me. I couldn't bear it. Just the thought of sitting there in my state-issued uniform in a family visiting room while my mother's best friend sat across from me had hot shame creeping up my neck. I couldn't face the reality. I'd written back, though with far less regularity. There weren't many updates to convey from behind bars.

"Have you talked to your father since…"

Since. I knew very well the words left unsaid. *Since you got out of prison.*

"No."

She reached out and briefly touched my hand where it lay on my knee. "Tuck. Surely you don't still harbor resentment toward him. It's been so long."

So long. Not for me. For me it felt like yesterday that he'd told me he was selling Honey Hill Farm to the company that would later turn the panorama of orange groves that was my dream and my legacy into a subdivision. The betrayal continued to sting, like the bees my own grandfather had gathered and lovingly cared for. The memory of that moment still made me clench my jaw and want to swing at something. Anything, even if it wasn't my father. It'd felt as if he'd ripped my heart from my chest and auctioned it to the highest bidder. He didn't get it. He didn't understand because he didn't have the same attachment to it that I did. That my mother had. He associated the place she'd loved with her loss, but to me, it kept a part of her alive. And because of it, we'd had a falling-out that had never mended. Even before I'd been locked up, we'd rarely spoken once I'd gone to live with Alfonso. "He sent me a few cards over the years," I said. "He told me he was getting remarried."

"Yes." She worried her lip for a moment. "They had a little girl. She'd be...oh, five now, I guess. I tried to keep in touch, but..." She waved her hand through the air, and I took her meaning. He wasn't interested. He'd washed his hands of this place, and that included the reminders too. Maybe I didn't blame him. I'd done the same, even if for different reasons. "Anyway," Mrs. Swanson said, "tell me what you're doing. Your plans. Where you're living. You must be on your way somewhere."

I rubbed the back of my neck. I hated this. Hated asking for help. It made me feel low, worthless. "Well, actually, no... I was sort of hoping you had a job here that I might be cut out for."

Her face fell. "Oh...oh, Tuck, I'm sorry." She shook her head. "The truth is, we're barely getting by here. I'm sure you noticed all the changes," she said, waving her hand in the general direction of what had once been miles of fragrant orange trees. "We're downsizing, not expanding. To be honest, I'm not sure how much longer we'll be in business."

I winced. From what I could tell, Swanson Groves was the

very last of its kind. When it closed down, Citrus Row would truly be a thing of the past.

She watched me worriedly for a beat, then two, as I processed what she'd told me. "It's been hard, I suppose, starting fresh," she finally said.

"Yeah." I let out a small, uncomfortable laugh that died a quick death. "I've found I'm not qualified for much, and people aren't real willing to cut a break to an ex-con."

"Oh, Tuck. You're so much more than that."

"Not on paper."

She sighed, that worry line between her brows growing deeper. Then her head snapped up, eyes widening as she sucked in a sharp breath. "I can't offer you a job here, but I *can* offer you a job. Or rather, Emily can."

"Emily?"

She nodded, her sudden enthusiasm obvious as the speed of her words quickened, her voice rising animatedly. "Her career has really taken off, Tuck. She's just announced a big tour which, oh, I don't even know all the details because they're still being worked out, but it's all so exciting. Anyway, she was just telling me a few nights ago that her manager wants her to hire a security team." She sat up straighter, her smile growing. "You've obviously been working out. You're fit and strong, and well, let's be honest, you'd spot trouble before someone who hasn't had the experiences you've had in the last decade. That's an asset and a well-earned skill. It's fate that you showed up today. Emily needs you, Tuck."

I smiled uneasily. Mrs. Swanson was being extremely kind. Emily didn't need me at all.

I hadn't seen nor heard from Emily in a long, long time. She'd once been like family to me, even if we'd drifted far apart since then. And I was glad that she was well on her way to forging the life she'd always wanted. But no, she didn't need me. Not even close.

But... I needed her. Or rather, I needed the job she might have to offer.

"I'll call her," Mrs. Swanson went on. "She'll be thrilled. So relieved. Who better to have her back than someone who knows her personally? Do I have your permission?"

I opened my mouth to ask a few questions...where, and when, and what the hours might be. But then I slowly closed it. Did it matter? *Not really.* "Yes. Thank you, Mrs. Swanson. I really appreciate it."

She reached out and squeezed my hand again. "Your mom was my very best friend," she said, blinking away the tears that suddenly filled her eyes. "We once promised each other that if anything happened to the other, she'd look out for Em and I'd look out for you. I've felt so helpless over the past six years, Tuck, and so I'm grateful you came to see me now, and that I'm able to help you get on the track toward happiness. It will happen. More people than you might think believe in second chances." She stood, discreetly swiping the moisture from her eyes. "Now come help me with dinner. Phil will be home in an hour or so, and then I insist you stay here until you start working for Emily."

Later that night, after dinner with the Swansons, I excused myself early and headed to the guest room where Mrs. Swanson had put my duffel bag with the few belongings I owned in the world. The guest room had once been Emily's. It still held the white, wrought iron twin bed she'd slept in, but now featured a pale gray quilt instead of the pink frills I remembered. That had been so long ago though. Maybe her room decor had changed as she had. I wondered who she was now, and if she would seem like a stranger, or a friend.

The shade clattered as I lowered it, blocking the view that made my gut churn with that old longing. The bedding felt soft beneath my fingers, the sheets crisp and clean, but after a moment of staring down at it uneasily, I pulled the quilt from the bed and laid it on the floor. I grabbed a pillow and then made myself comfortable on the rug, knitting my fingers behind my head.

The whir of the ceiling fan above lulled me into a type of hypnosis, my eyes drooping. I'd been living on the outside for several months now, and yet my body was still programmed to go to sleep early and wake at first light. As I drifted, I swore I could hear the clank of metal and the various conversations happening around me, kept low so as not to catch the attention of the guards. Conversation, laughter, threats, both veiled and outright, personal bodily sounds that I'd never quite grown accustomed to.

I bolted upright, shaking away the slow dip into sleep at the unfamiliar noise that had roused me. My head turned toward the window as a horn blared in the distance once again. My shoulders dropped and I exhaled a slow breath. The ability to awaken quickly, even if it meant I was constantly on edge, had been a necessity for a long time. Now it just kept me from ever feeling truly rested. I wondered if I'd ever sleep deeply again.

There was a bookshelf on the far wall, and I pulled myself from the floor, walking over to it and perusing the titles in the dim light of the small table lamp I'd left on. A couple of them looked familiar for some reason, and frowning, I pulled one from the middle. *Aqueducts and Water Supply.* I turned it over, reading the description, the words coming back to me. This had been one of *my* books, one I'd been reading in the weeks before my mother collapsed and ended up in the hospital. I'd read it up in that loft in the old stable. *My secret hideout.* God, I hadn't thought of that place in a long time. I tilted my head, staring down at the cardboard cover. How had it ended up here? Something about this particular book in my hands opened up a small wellspring of peace inside me, as though the very pages contained the simplicity of that time. The innocence. The joy.

Then again, books had been bringing me a measure of comfort for my whole life. Companionship. Distraction. They'd helped me survive my time behind bars.

I returned to my bed on the floor, propping the pillow against the wall so I could read. After a few minutes and feeling much calmer, I turned my head toward the window where shifting shadows barely showed around the edges of the blinds. The outside world. One I was now a part of. Only not really. Or at least...not yet. But I felt a tiny trickle of hope as Mrs. Swanson's words from earlier filtered through my mind.

More people than you think believe in second chances. God, I hoped that was true.

six

Emily

"Tuck Mattice? Tuck *Mattice?*"

"Yes, Em, I did say Tuck Mattice," my mom repeated into the phone. "And he needs a job."

"I haven't seen him in a hundred years, Mom, and you want me to hire him?" Along with the shock of hearing my mom say Tuck's name, a strange and sudden bubbly sensation had erupted in my stomach, like an internal hurricane.

Tuck Mattice.

Or maybe I was just hungry. I hadn't eaten since breakfast.

Only, that bubbly sensation? It was familiar. My body had always reacted that way to Tuck. And despite the years, it obviously still did. But flesh was dumb. And my body didn't remember how Tuck had treated me, and how it had hurt.

It didn't know who he'd become.

"He's practically family, Emily."

"Close," my makeup artist, Sasha, said, and I closed my eyes so he could apply my eyeshadow.

"Family?" I asked. "He's as good as a stranger to me. And, Mom, *Nova*. I need you to call me Nova when I'm getting ready for an event." If I didn't get into character, so to speak, I'd forget to respond to the stage name and look clueless. It'd happened before.

"Keep still, girl," Sasha instructed.

"Sorry," I murmured.

"I know he didn't keep in touch," my mom went on as though she hadn't heard what I said about my name, "but you know what a rough time he had after his mom died."

"Open," Sasha said, tipping my chin. I opened my eyes, and he moved his gaze from one to the other, measuring. "Good. Louisa, she's ready for you," he called to my hairdresser in the living room, turning and beginning to gather his kit.

"Hold on, Mom." I leaned toward the now-unobstructed mirror, turning my face in each direction. "Thanks, Sash. You're an *artiste*," I said, making the gesture for a chef's kiss. He'd done a heavy nighttime look on me, and though it was dramatic, he'd kept it tasteful. He was truly talented, and I was lucky to have him as part of my team.

"Kisses," he called, sweeping out of the room. I lifted the phone toward my mouth again, moving my mind back to the conversation. My mom had been making excuses for Tuck Mattice.

"We all had a rough time after Mariana died, Mom. We all loved her." I took a deep breath, mentally shaking off the feeling of that time. Of learning of Mariana's—the woman who'd been like an aunt to me—diagnosis: brain cancer. We'd all been shocked and scared. Her immediate prognosis hadn't been good, and the next nine months had gone by in a devastating blur of treatments, prayer vigils, and finally hospice care. Our orchard and the Mattices', once brimming with gatherings and laughter and shared community, suddenly went quiet. When I remembered that time, my memories contained no sunshine, as if the hours between Mariana's collapse and her coffin being lowered into the ground had gone by in perpetual night. Along with Mariana and her guitar strumming, music had died on Citrus Row as well. It was too painful, I guess. But music had always been my solace, and so I sought it out wherever I could, and it eventually took me away from home for good.

Tuck had turned inward as Tuck was wont to do. And then things had taken another sharp turn when his father announced he was selling Honey Hill Farm. That's when the fighting started, the shouting matches we could hear all the way on our property. Two and a half years after Mariana's death, Mr. Mattice moved to Florida and Tuck—almost eighteen—chose to stay in California with his uncle. He'd remained somewhat close to me, distance-wise, but it might have been a million miles away. Any friendship that had remained between us at the time was suddenly and completely over.

My hand dropped from where I'd been adjusting one of the false lash strips as Louisa came in the room, smiling at me. I pointed to the phone. *My mom*, I mouthed. She nodded, bringing a finger to her lips. Then, picking up the brush, she began running it through my hair.

My mother let out a shaky exhale as though for a moment, she too had traveled back and took in a stale breath of that sadness-tinged air. "Tuck didn't only lose his mom, Em. He lost his home too, and his father as well."

For a moment, I saw Tuck as he'd been. Quiet, angry, closed-off. I'd tried to be his friend, but he'd turned away from me completely. "He didn't *lose* his home. His father made the choice to sell it and who could blame him? Everything in the area was changing and moving on. You know that, Mom." I wasn't trying to rub it in, but my mom and dad had been one of a handful of owners who had hung on for dear life to the orchards that were becoming a thing of the past in the San Fernando Valley, and instead of selling for top dollar and taking a profit, now they were barely making ends meet. In my estimation, it had been Mr. Mattice who'd made the wise choice at the right time. I'd offered to move my parents to LA more than once, but they'd consistently declined, preferring instead to hang on to a dying way of life. "And Tuck didn't lose his father either," I went on, a new energy to my words. "It was his bitterness that cost him that relationship. Tuck became a total asshole after Mariana died." Louisa sprayed my hair and used the curling iron to form loose curls.

"Oh, Em. You're being cold. It's far more complicated than that, and you know it."

I sighed, watching as Louisa moved quickly around my head, wielding the hot iron like the professional she was. My mom was right. Tuck had suffered a devastating life blow. But then he'd made *choices* that ruined his future, finally landing himself in prison. And that was on *him*.

I didn't know all the details of the crime he committed, but I did know he'd been convicted of involuntary manslaughter. Each time I tried to picture him, I still saw a little kid grinning boyishly and squinting into the sun. I heard his laughter, remembered the delight I'd felt when all his attention was focused on me. That little boy was gone. He'd grown into a troubled man who'd committed a terrible crime that resulted in a human being's life ending, even if Tuck didn't intend for it to happen. He'd once been my best friend. Now he was a stranger, and frankly, that was fine.

I did hold some good memories, however, and because of that, I wished him well. "Okay, Mom," I conceded, "you're right, people do deserve second chances, but not as part of my security team, or any other for that matter. Is he even allowed to carry a weapon?"

Louisa picked up the can of hairspray and crop-dusted it over my head, shielding my face with her hand. I resisted the urge to sputter and cough.

"I thought you were against firearms," my mom said. Louisa waved me off and I smiled, mouthing *thank you*, and headed for my closet.

"Well, I mean I don't necessarily *like* guns, but I don't make all the rules." I unbelted my robe and let it drop to the floor, and then set the phone down on a shelf so I could slip on my dress as I spoke through the speaker. "My manager might insist that I have an armed bodyguard. There are a lot of loonies out there."

"I thought you were the boss. Don't you pay those people?"

I rolled my eyes. My mom didn't get anything. "Yes, but I'm just the performer. I'm not the expert on every aspect of my career. I still need *advisors*, Mom."

"But you don't have to *take* every piece of advice they give. Tell them you'd prefer someone who's strong, rather than armed. And you should see Tuck, honey. He's so tall and broad. And he's built like Thor, all muscle. He must have spent a considerable amount of time working out in the last six years."

"Well what else was he gonna do?" I murmured.

"Again, cold, Em."

My assistant, Destanie, pulled the door open, panic written all over her face. "Take that dress off," she demanded. "Right now."

"Who's asking you to undress?" my mom asked.

"Hold on, Mom," I said, taking her off speaker. "What is it?" I asked Destanie.

She held her phone to show me an Instagram post. "Layne Beckett is wearing that dress. Or close enough." She rushed past me and started rifling through my dresses muttering, "I'm going to kill that bitch. I bet it got out that you were wearing an emerald green Ossie Francisco. Then she posts herself on Instagram wearing the exact same color dress? Trust me, it's no coincidence. Oh no, she *knew* what she was doing. Look at that satisfied smirk on her face," Destanie said, shoving the phone toward me before turning back to my collection of dresses. "She's only dating Freddie Halston so she can show up everywhere you do."

Layne Beckett was a singer, and Freddie Halston was an actor like my boyfriend, Charlie, so we did attend many of the same events, though I'd never formally met her. I wasn't quite convinced she was so wrapped up in competing with me that she'd arranged her dating life around that effort, but the dress was a low blow. And from what I'd heard, it was exactly the type of thing she'd do. And so here I was, standing practically naked in my closet with only minutes to finish getting ready.

"Plan B," Destanie was muttering as she ripped through my clothing rack. "Aha!" She pulled a red number out, holding it up. It was a gift from a newish designer that I'd forgotten about, still in the clear plastic garment bag it'd arrived in the month before. "Put it on," she said. "The shoes will still work. I'm going to spike Layne's drink with a laxative at the after-party," she said over her shoulder, an evil tilt to her grin as she breezed away.

I let out a half-hearted laugh. She was kidding of course. The laugh died quickly in my throat. *Wasn't she?*

I put my mom back on speaker and began unwrapping the red dress. "Sorry, Mom. Fashion disaster narrowly averted."

"Oh my. Sounds serious," she said. "By the way, where are you going? It's late." As if to prove it, she let out a loud yawn.

"To a premiere." I began pulling the dress on. "This is when the nightlife starts in LA."

Out in the living room, I heard a knock and then the loud buzz of multiple people entering my apartment. Charlie's entourage.

"Nightlife," my mom repeated as I slipped my foot into one spiked heel. "Nightlife here is when nature calls at three a.m."

"Gross, Mom."

My mom let out a tittering laugh, and Destanie popped her head around the corner, her gaze moving up and down my body before she gave the thumbs-up and gestured for me to hurry up.

I nodded to Destanie and then opened my mouth to ask my mom where exactly Tuck was sleeping but decided not to. He was probably in my old room, the one my mom and dad now used as a guest room. He was probably sleeping in my childhood bed. Which made me feel...weird. I pushed that hazy visual aside. "Hey, I've gotta go. Charlie's here and a car's waiting."

"Tell Charlie I said hi. And please, please consider what I said. Tuck seems...lost. A second chance, Em. You have the power to give one, and I know you have the heart."

"It's not about heart, Mom." It was about practicality. And safety, meaning not surrounding myself with dangerous criminals because my mom owed an old—*dead*—friend a favor. "But I'll think about it," I murmured as a knock sounded and Charlie leaned around the door.

"Thank you, Em. I love you."

I gestured at Charlie, and he opened the door all the way, handsome in a classic black tux, his dark golden hair combed to the side. He grinned, showing me his megawatt smile.

"I love you too, Mom. Bye."

I disconnected the call, smiling at Charlie. "Well, hello there. You look amazing."

"So do you. Wow."

I turned slightly, giving him a sultry look over my shoulder. "Will you zip me?"

"It'd be my pleasure."

Charlie kissed my shoulder before pulling my zipper. I sucked in my breath as the dress came closed, groaning as the zipper moved slowly up my back and Charlie struggled to move it inch by inch. "Do you want to hold on to the bedpost like Scarlett O'Hara?"

"I don't have a bedpost." *Or a corset. Unfortunately.*

"Damn," he said, working for a few more minutes before finally making a sound of victory in the back of his throat. "Got it!"

I turned slowly. It felt like my boobs were resting right under my chin, but by Charlie's heated stare as his eyes hung on my— decidedly high—cleavage, I must look better than I felt.

"I guess I won't be eating tonight." I half laughed, half groaned.

He raised one brow as his eyes grazed my body. "Or sitting," he said. "Or climbing stairs. Or... Can you breathe?"

"Barely."

"Does it help to know you look drop-dead gorgeous?"

The only one who was at risk of dropping dead was me. A laugh bubbled up, but I swallowed it down. There wasn't much room for that either. "It does," I said. "Breathing is overrated anyway."

Plus, Destanie would have a fit if I told her this dress wasn't working. I linked arms with Charlie, pushed the door open, and then walked out into the main room to a loud chorus of oohs and ahhs. I grinned, batting my lashes, slipping far more effortlessly into my Nova persona than I had into the red dress.

seven

Emily

My facial muscles hurt from smiling. My feet ached from the toe-squeezing, five-inch spiked heels, and the clamp of my dress had dictated only small, shallow breaths for the last two hours. I felt like I was wearing a boa constrictor. I *had* somehow managed to bend just enough to ride in the limo, wave and smile on the red carpet, but I wasn't sure I could hold on to the beaming grin one more second without a short break.

At least the premiere itself—a big-budget action movie Charlie had starred in—would take place in the dark where I could bend my spine a little, even if it meant rolls of mashed-down skin spilled out the top.

I hurried to the restroom, my shoulders dropping as I curled my spine forward and exhaled the bit of breath I'd managed to suck in just before exiting the limo.

"You've got this," I muttered to myself. This was an important night for Charlie, and I was thrilled to be celebrating him, but arriving on his arm would also garner lots of press for me. The pictures from the red carpet splashed all over social media sites tomorrow would make any amount of physical discomfort completely worthwhile. They would provide a big spike in tour ticket sales the next day. I was already sold out in LA but was hoping to sell out in the entire US before my tour started. At least I wouldn't be singing tonight. I could *exist* for the next several hours in this dress but singing would have been out of the question.

The surprising thing about finally "making it" as a singer was that there wasn't a whole lot of singing involved. It was a disappointment I hadn't considered before my popularity had begun to rise. Sure, I had recorded my album, but once that was done, the recordings had been handed over to technicians and sound engineers for the mixing and mastering. When that was done, it was time for the release of a press kit, media appearances, photo shoots and showing up at every event I was invited to in an effort to get my photo, and my name, in front of as many people as possible.

Of course, it helped that I was dating one of Hollywood's most popular young actors, not only because cameras naturally followed him, and if I was on his arm, they followed me as well, but because he'd introduced me to a new echelon of society. Half of my team had come from introductions Charlie had made, high-level professionals that never would have taken my call if not for him.

But that wasn't why I was dating Charlie. I mean, I had to admit I liked the attention, and it benefitted my career. But more than that, he was sweet and funny, and an all-around *good* guy—a rare quality in show business, I was beginning to learn.

I walked around the corner to the row of sinks, a long mirror stretched above them. For a moment I simply stood staring at myself. I looked good. Amazing even. Which was interesting considering how physically awful I felt. I'd become good at it though. Grinning for the camera regardless of whether I wanted to or not, laughing at jokes that weren't remotely funny because I knew it was expected of me, making idle chitchat and appearing engaged even though I was dying of boredom. It was all part of the job. Part of being *Nova*. Someday I'd be able to make my own rules. Someday, singing, not media buzz, would once again be my focus. But for now, I had to play the game. And I would because I'd worked my entire life for this moment.

I heard the restroom door open and close and pulled myself straight, adopting a casual expression as I leaned toward the mirror and pretended to touch up my makeup.

From my peripheral vision, I saw a swath of emerald green, my eyes moving to my right as I met Layne Beckett's gaze in the mirror. *Oh no.* I gave her a thin smile and went back to adjusting my makeup. I'd act casual, aloof, and then I'd stroll slowly out of here as if this was the dress I'd planned on all along, and whatever conniving she'd done to show me up had been a total fail.

For several beats, the bathroom was utterly quiet, tension filling the space. "I'm sorry, you probably came in here to escape all the fangirls, and now I'm going to act like one," Layne said, turning my way, "but oh my God, I love your music. Seriously, if you knew how often I listen to 'Find You in the Dark' on repeat, you'd be totally embarrassed for me."

I turned slowly toward her, narrowing my eyes slightly. What game was this? Before I had devised what to say, Layne tipped her head back and started singing a few bars. She put her hands over her mouth as though she had to physically stop herself from belting out the song, and then grinned. "Obviously it sounds ten times better when you sing it, but wow, what an emotional, heartfelt piece. You wrote it yourself, right?"

"Uh…yes."

"True depth like that doesn't come along very often in the music business."

I tipped my head, completely taken off guard. "I... Thank you, Layne."

She brought her hand to her chest and stepped back, eyes widening. "You know my name."

I chuckled. "Of course I do. I'm a fan of yours too." Which was the truth. Layne Beckett's mother had been in the business since Layne was a little girl. Her mother had passed a couple of years before, and just recently Layne was attempting to follow in her mother's footsteps. She was just as beautiful and talented and was born with an "in" which automatically opened doors for her. Of course, that meant she was currently my main competition, and according to everyone in my circle, was a back-stabbing bitch and a cutthroat businesswoman. Which was why I was presently so off-balance. I had not expected...this version of Layne. Was it real or some sort of trick?

"Wow, well you just officially made my night. And I didn't just say that because these events are tedious and stuffy, and anything might have made this night better."

I let out a short laugh, surprised by the honesty. These events *were* tedious and stuffy. And afterward, everyone would gush about how amazing and wonderful it all was, and I'd nod along.

She grinned as I cut off the laugh I'd managed. Layne arched a perfect brow, her gaze moving downward to where my hand was held on my diaphragm as I attempted to push it farther to the center of my body where it had some room to expand. "That's a Frida Valli, isn't it?"

Was that the name of the designer who had sent me this dress? When it had arrived unsolicited, Destanie said it was pushy, rolled her eyes, and stuffed it in my closet. "Um, I think so, yes."

"It's beautiful. And you probably just made her a star by wearing it tonight. I try to wear up-and-coming designers too. This one just arrived this morning and was made by a nine-teen-year-old designer. Gaia Laurent. Remember her name.

She's incredible." She smiled. "But…can I…can I show you a little trick?" she asked, lowering her voice and looking around before she opened her small evening bag and removed what looked like a sharp hook from a tiny sewing kit.

"Uh…" Was this the part where she tore my dress to shreds like in *Cinderella*? *One could only hope.* "Sure."

"Lift your arms."

My brows knitted in confusion, but I did as she said, at least as far as I was able. "Some more current designers construct their dresses with this specific stitch… Ah, yes…" She leaned in, using her tool to move down the seam.

I let out a small squeak, but rather than the dress falling apart, it simply opened a little bit, allowing me to take the first full breath since I'd put it on. "Oh my God. I might cry."

Layne smiled, moving around to the other side where she used her tool to do the same thing to the opposite seam, providing me even more room.

"Voilà," she said, and I turned to the mirror. The dress looked exactly the same, but she'd magically provided me with what felt like several inches of breathing room.

"I love you," I said. And in that moment, I really truly meant it. Or maybe it was just the sudden flood of oxygen to my brain.

Layne laughed again. "Okay, well, forget about you making my night. I think you just made my year." Layne's phone, sitting on the counter, buzzed, and she leaned toward it, reading the text that flashed on the screen. "My manager is wondering where I am. I better go."

"Thank you, Layne, seriously. It was so nice meeting you."

"You too. Enjoy the rest of the night, okay?"

I gave an exaggerated eye roll and we both laughed again. This one went all the way through my body. "Hey, Layne. Be careful about leaving your drink unattended at the after-party. I've heard…stories."

Her brows dipped, but she smiled. "Always good advice. Bye, Nova."

Layne breezed out of the room, her emerald green dress flowing behind her, and I turned back to the mirror, simply enjoying the act of breathing for a few moments. My stomach growled. Maybe I still had time to eat a few bites of dinner.

I stared into my own eyes, thinking about how absolutely wrong the rumor mill had been about Layne. She hadn't plotted to steal my fashion thunder. She hadn't plotted anything. She'd given a budding designer a gift by wearing her dress to a red-carpet premiere. And so had I, though unwittingly. It'd come from last-minute desperation, not from generosity. Maybe I'd deserved to feel like a cased sausage for the first part of the night.

Be better, Emily. My mom always said that to me when I made a bad choice as a kid. Which was often. I'd judged Layne unfairly. I'd have liked to think I'd stop my assistant from actually spiking Layne's drink had I witnessed such a thing, but...would I? Or would I look the other way and pretend not to notice? Would I have considered it fair and square for what I'd been told Layne had done to publicly humiliate me? *Be better, Emily.*

Yes, I'd judged Layne, and earlier... I'd judged Tuck. I had more reason for that. After all, the things he'd done weren't just rumor. He'd committed a crime. He'd served time. He was a felon.

But you did know him once, before everything fell apart. Before he hurt you and everyone around him.

Once, he'd had honor. I had the sudden flash of a weight shattering the windshield of my dad's prized car. The weight that *I'd* dropped while in the midst of taunting Tuck. And even so, he'd taken the blame so I wouldn't bear my father's wrath. He'd suffered both the humiliation and his dad's anger—for me.

And all I'd given him was my first kiss.

Not that he knew that that was how I still thought of it.

His sacrifice had meant I was allowed to attend the music camp where I'd met a singing coach who'd changed my life's trajectory. She'd seen my potential and taken me on as a client even though she was completely booked. She'd not only been vital in my growth as a singer, but she'd known a lot of the right people, and they had guided and mentored me, each one an integral stepping stone to my success.

And if not for Tuck…if not for that camp and everything that had occurred after that weekend… I might not be where I was today.

I sighed, removing my phone from my evening bag. There was a text from Charlie asking if I was okay and I sent a quick response that I'd be right out. As I walked toward the door, I composed a new text to my mother: Tell Tuck he has a job if he wants it. And before I could reconsider, I hit Send.

I'd only taken a handful of steps when my phone dinged with a response from my mother: You won't regret it.

I snorted softly. *Unlikely.* But what was done, was done.

I pulled my shoulders back, plastered on my smile, and once again, pulled forth Nova.

eight

Tuck

I squinted up at the steel-and-plexiglass monstrosity. Others probably considered it sleek, but I'd seen enough steel and plexi- glass to last a lifetime.

But this was Emily—or, *Nova's*—home, my new boss, so I better get used to it, even if most of my work hours would be spent at public events. Or so I assumed. Mrs. Swanson hadn't given me many details, only that Emily had been thrilled by the offer of my services, and that she'd outline my position when I arrived.

I entered the open lobby, heading to the bank of elevators and pressing the button to the penthouse level. My black jeans, black boots, and gray T-shirt looked worn and overly casual for a job interview, but it was all I had. Plus, I'd already been hired for the job, and so it wasn't as if this was an *actual* interview. I'd signed the tax forms Emily's accountant had sent to her mother's email address, and a nondisclosure agreement, promising not to leak any of Emily's personal information.

As the mirrored elevator car rose, a flutter of nerves made me feel antsy. Not only was I somewhat anxious about seeing Emily for the first time since we were kids, but I also hated feeling penned up. I'd never had claustrophobia before, but prison could do that to you. I'd had to actively work through it every day for six years, and it seemed my nervous system wasn't quite ready to let go.

The elevator dinged when it reached the penthouse level, and I stepped into a wide-open foyer area with two walls made completely of plexiglass, so the Los Angeles skyline was on full display.

I raised my hand to knock on the tall door across from the elevator, but before my knuckle made contact, the door was pulled open, and a very petite girl with bright fuchsia lips, a high black ponytail, and a flower tattoo that wound up her neck, stood there. She gave me a cursory glance and then her gaze returned to the phone in her hand, and she punched something in before again looking up. "Tucker Mattice," she said, perusing me. Her tone was unimpressed.

Not that I'd imagined I was very impressive, but most people could muster the basic social grace of a smile. *This is LA,* I reminded myself. *Everyone is unimpressed by everything. It's a whole mood.*

"Tuck," I said.

She raised her brows. "Well, you certainly look the part."

"The...part?"

"Bodyguard. Hired—" her gaze swept my body again "—muscle."

"Oh, ah, well yes, that's why I'm here..." I held my hand out, realizing I hadn't been given her name and waited for her to tell me, but she simply nodded, gave me a limp shake, and then stood back so I could enter.

Okay, then.

The inside of the apartment felt about as welcoming as the outside. Everywhere I looked was white and shiny and bereft of knickknacks of any kind, as though I'd stepped into some futuristic alien pod. *If the aliens in question were completely devoid of personality.* There was a Christmas tree by the window that looked more like a large, white pipe cleaner adorned with shiny silver balls. I looked over at the woman just to set my eyes on something that wasn't stark and mostly monochromatic. She was staring at her phone, her eyes practically bugged out. "Oh shit!" she exclaimed.

"Is everything...okay?"

"No, it's not okay. Excuse me, I'm on damage control. Nova will be out in a few."

With that, she raced out of the room, yelling something into her phone about an Instagram post.

I walked over to the couch and began to sit down but then thought better of it. I'd showered that morning, and my clothes, though old, were clean, but even so, I worried I'd leave a speck of dirt or an ass imprint in the smooth velvet. Standing seemed safer.

"Tuck."

I looked up, and every molecule in my body seemed to quicken at the same time. *Emily.* It was her, only...

She came closer, her lips curved slightly, expression pleasant, if not warm. Her hair was no longer the golden shade I remembered, but instead a pale champagne blond, the waves hanging down to her waist. Her lips were plump and glossy with long, dark lashes shading her blue eyes. She was wearing a cropped shirt, a small slip of her smooth, tanned stomach showing, and torn jean shorts that barely hit the crease at the top of her thigh. This was not Emily. This was *Nova.*

I tried to keep my eyes from wandering. I didn't recognize this woman, but she was undeniably sexy. A twinge between my legs reminded me that it'd been a long damn time since I'd touched a woman. Over six years in fact. Frankly, I couldn't even *remember* the last woman I'd touched. "It's nice to see you."

Her expression barely changed. She held out her hand, and I glanced down at her nails, silver and sharpened to blades. *Walking contraband.* I cleared my throat to hold back the nervous laughter that threatened to spill out.

"It's nice to see you too, Tuck. You look good."

"So do you."

There was an awkward silence, and a pit opened in my stomach. Emily had become something entirely different than what she'd been *then*. Just like my family. My home. The entire area where I'd grown up. All that had once been overflowing with warmth and natural beauty, had either disappeared completely, or become cold and fake.

Even her.

I felt something I could only call deep disappointment trickle slowly through me. I hadn't actively thought of Emily in a long time, but somewhere in the back of my mind I'd held her up as one of the last remaining pieces that still existed from my former life, the one I'd never been able to fully let go of. Seeing her like this felt like another unexpected loss, and one I hadn't been prepared for. But I was standing in front of this new person now, and so I pushed my emotions aside. "I appreciate the job offer," I said. "It came at just the right time." I was sure her mom had told her I'd gone to their orchard looking for work. She might be able to guess that I'd had a hard time finding employment, but I wasn't going to confirm it.

It'd also become exceedingly clear in the last few minutes that Mrs. Swanson had lied. Emily had not been *thrilled* to hire me. Not even close. She'd most likely been guilted into it. The realization was humiliating. But I supposed it was a fair trade. If *I* was disappointed in what she'd become, there was a good chance she was disappointed in me too. I wouldn't exactly blame her, but that didn't mean it didn't sting.

"I'm glad the timing worked out for both of us," she said, gesturing to the couch and then sitting in the chair across from it. I hesitated, then sat down gingerly, beginning to lean, but realizing the back was tilted at a strange angle that would force me to practically recline, and so I remained upright. "I'm sure things have been...challenging for you," she said, her eyes sliding away as though she was uncomfortable talking about my hardships.

"You've really done great," I said, turning the conversation away from me. *My challenges* were the last thing I wanted to talk about with her. I glanced around the room. Whether it was my personal taste or not, I was pretty damn certain that the decor had come with a substantial price tag. She seemed to *fit* her surroundings. All perfection and gloss and superficial beauty. "You've become everything you ever wanted to be." Had she though? Was this how she imagined her life would look once she'd found fame? Still, she was hugely gifted, and it was nice to know that sincere talent was rewarded. "You deserve it, Emily. You were always a beautiful singer."

She held my gaze for a moment as though searching for something, but then blinked and looked away. "Thank you, Tuck."

"You're welcome... Should I call you Emily or Nova?" I asked, tipping my head.

"Emily. Unless we're working." She waved her hand in the air. "It can be kind of hard to switch back and forth, but I'm sure you can manage it."

"I'm sure I can." Plus, I didn't imagine there was a lot of talking that went along with the job.

There was another awkward silence. I waited for a minute, wondering if she might bring up her parents, or the area where we had once lived, or something personal regarding the years we'd been apart, but when she remained silent, I sat forward.

"So, ah, tell me about the job," I said. "I understand of course that I'll be part of your security team, but what do I need to know specifically?"

"Well, it's not so much a team right now." She let out a thin laugh. "I have a few people who help me out with things." She made a face, which gave me the first small indication that she still had at least a tiny sense of humor and made me smile in return. "But none of them are equipped to handle any real trouble." Her gaze moved down my body, but then as though her eyes had wandered without her permission, they shot back to my face. "I know you're not trained either, but I think you can do a good job. You're obviously very fit and, you know... in good shape." I swore I saw the color in her cheeks deepen very slightly, but I couldn't be sure. "Anyway, your job will be to have my back, watch the crowd, act as a barrier between me and any out-of-control fans. Two weeks ago, someone rushed me. He just wanted to give me a letter, but it spooked me. My boyfriend has a security team, but their job is to keep their eyes on him. So, when the guy shot forward, they surrounded Charlie, and I was sort of left hanging."

Her boyfriend. "Got it," I said. It sounded easy enough. I'd learned to keep my head on a swivel in prison as a matter of self-preservation. I could certainly keep Emily safe from over-eager basement dwellers wielding love letters and reeking of desperation.

"You'll accompany me to any and all social events. If it's a party or something like that, you'll only be expected to escort me in and out of the location. But if it's a public affair, I'll ask that you guard me inside the venue."

"Okay."

"So, your work hours may be unpredictable. I'll have to ask you to be on call some days."

"That's fine."

"If at some point it becomes clear that I need to expand my team, then I'll make that happen."

I nodded.

"Anyway, some of it we'll have to make up as we go along. I've never had a bodyguard before. Any questions for me?"

I ran my palms over my jean-clad thighs. "I guess my only question now is whether you want me to wear anything specific?" Did bodyguards wear uniforms? I wasn't sure. I'd let her tell me.

She seemed stumped for a moment, looking away as she twirled a piece of ice-blond hair around one daggerlike finger, her lips puckered in a shiny pout. "All black, maybe?" Her eyes moved over me again. "Hold on." She turned her head. "Destanie?"

The petite, colorful young woman rounded the corner as though she'd been standing nearby, just waiting to be summoned. "Yes?"

"What do you think my new bodyguard should wear?"

Destanie approached, crossing her arms and examining me as though looking closely at something the cat had just dropped on her doorstep. "Gray," she said. "But not just gray. *Silvery* gray. Something with spandex in it for a bit of shine. Tight too. The spandex will give it some stretch so he can perform his duties, but definitely very tight. His muscles alone will deter most of the creeps," she said, talking about me as if I wasn't sitting right there.

And hold up. Tight? Silver? *Stretch?* They wanted me to dress like a Cirque du Soleil performer? No fucking way.

"Perfect," Emily said. "It'll differentiate him from Charlie's team too, which is important. Okay, so that's the uniform."

She stared at me, and I stared back, attempting to keep my expression as neutral as possible. With effort, I put aside the small amount of pride I had left. "Where might I find clothes like that?"

"Oh, I'll give you the names of a few department stores where I have lines of credit. They'll take care of you."

"Make sure to get some shoes too," Destanie said on her way out of the room. "And sunglasses," she called over her shoulder. "No one should ever know exactly where your eyes are focused."

Emily picked up the phone she'd set on the side table next to her. "Give me your cell phone number," she said.

"I don't have one yet. I'll have to pick up one of those prepaid phones." Not that I could afford very many minutes.

She stared at me a moment and then laughed. "Wait, are you joking?"

I slowly shook my head.

She waved her hand. "I'll have a smartphone sent over and put it on my plan. That's a necessary part of the job. Plus, I need to be able to text you, and I have to know you're available at a moment's notice."

"Okay. Thanks." I sounded like a pet dog. God, it was stuff like this that made me feel like a total loser, and I hated it.

"We leave for the tour in six weeks."

A tour. I'd barely been out of California, and suddenly I was heading out on a big tour in just over a month. I'd have to let my parole officer know. What did I need to know? Would I be provided with an itinerary? Did I need to scope out places before Emily's arrival? Fuck, I was way out of my depth. Not that I could say that, of course. My head spun at what a difference a week could make.

Emily stood, and again, I made sure to maintain eye contact, even as my mind begged me to peruse her curves. She gave me the name of a hotel nearby that I'd be staying at until the tour. "If you want to wait in the lobby downstairs, I'll call an Uber to pick you up. It will be paid for."

An Uber. I knew an Uber was a ride, but I'd never actually used one. Ubers hadn't really been popular—especially in the neighborhood I'd lived in—before I was taken out of society. But I wasn't going to ask questions. I'd wing it from there. "Thank you."

"I'll have Destanie text the information about the stores to the phone that's delivered later today."

I gave a terse nod. I was grateful for the job, but the fact that I was about to become one of these people, part of Emily's *entourage*, did not sit well. Frankly, it pissed me off because this was *not* me, and it was only due to my desperate situation that I was being forced to play along. And there wasn't a thing I could do about it, except squander the opportunity.

She walked me to the door, and held out her hand, those fingertip daggers glinting in the overhead light. I frowned but shook it.

"Thank you again," I said. "I'll wait to hear from you." And then I got the hell out of that weird spaceship and hightailed it for the lobby, eager to put the last demeaning half hour behind me.

nine

Emily

Why did I feel so damn antsy? I crossed my arms, pacing in front of the floor-to-ceiling window, the view of the Los Angeles skyline awash in a hazy orange glow.

"She said your resting bitch face is the blueprint!" Destanie exclaimed, tone aghast. I glanced at her, sprawled on the couch, punching her phone keys violently, face set in outrage. I got that I was supposed to feel irate too, and so I turned my focus more fully to my assistant, replaying her words in my head.

"The blueprint for what?"

Her head snapped up, as did her peaked eyebrows. "Resting bitch faces, I guess."

I pondered that momentarily. "That could be a compliment."

Destanie looked briefly confused, her mouth opening and then shutting again as her eyes widened. "It could be, right?" She pulled herself straight, clearly excited about the idea. "We'll make it one. That's your signature look from now on."

Will we call it blue steel? I wondered, a giggle threatening at the vision of that ridiculous expression from *Zoolander*, but I swallowed it down. Destanie was obviously enthusiastic about the idea, even if it made me feel like a parody.

The important thing though was that it had solved a problem. I didn't know who *she* was who had made the comment, and frankly, I didn't really care. What was important here was that it had allowed me—or Destanie as my spokesperson—to take back control of my image. It was always better, I'd learned, to take ownership of what could be considered an insult, rather than become immediately defensive. So much of social media was pure *strategy*. Not just in what you posted and the image you chose to put forth, but how you responded to others online as well. And though I'd only been in the spotlight for about a year, I was getting better by the day at cultivating an image.

I should be proud of that. So why did it make me feel sort of...depressed? Why did it sometimes feel like social media—instead of singing—was my new full-time career?

Destanie continued to punch keys into her phone, and I turned back to the window.

Tuck Mattice.

It'd been surreal to see him, a grown man, no longer even a trace of the boy he'd once been. Now a honed and hardened felon. Chiseled. Muscled. *Gorgeous.* He'd always had a quick smile and an easy laugh. He'd always made bubbles explode under my ribs. His eyes had hung on me then, his expression part bewilderment and part something else I'd been too young to discern and couldn't conjure now. I'd shown off for him because I'd loved his reaction. And I'd craved that inner turbulence—part off-putting but mostly exciting. We'd fought like little wildcats sometimes, but we'd also played, and chased salamanders, and explored, and gotten into trouble together. I'd thought about our old exploits as I'd gotten ready for his arrival, taking extra care with my hair extensions and makeup.

I'd expected that same old look that made me feel *fascinating*, but it would be even more blatant, more *raw*, now that I was a woman, a *star*. Instead, when I'd walked in the room, his face had fallen. He'd looked at me like I was nothing but a deep disappointment. My stomach knotted, those bubbles dissipating one by one.

How dare he?

I'd made the decision not to judge him hastily, but now that I'd seen him in person, I'd realized that I'd had every right to make assumptions. If anything, he'd confirmed exactly what I'd imagined about who he'd become. Hardened. Bitter. Still as unaffected as he'd been the last time I'd seen him. Cold.

And the knowledge not only made me angry, it also hurt. It brought back all those memories of the time after his mother died. He'd turned away from me then, and I'd felt utterly abandoned. I'd tried with all my might to be the friend he'd obviously needed. I'd even gone to that loft in the old stable and taken a few of his beloved books. I'd read one cover to cover even though it was far above my reading level. I'd had to go over some pages ten times before I understood the words. I'd thought I could engage him that way, pull him out of his emotional coma, bring him back to me. But he'd looked right through me as if I didn't exist. He'd stared at me like that earlier today too. And it'd hurt. It made me bitter that he could still illicit that reaction in me, even now, when I had everything I'd ever wanted in life, and more. When he was so far beneath me, dammit.

And yet, here I was, about to entrust my safety to him. About to bring him into my inner circle. Once again, Tuck Mattice was going to be part of my everyday life.

I looked out at the deepening sunset, troubled and antsy. I had a feeling this was not going to work out well.

"That's it. That's the one," Destanie said, grinning as she took in my face.

I brought my hand up as though whatever she was referring to might be hanging off my cheek. "Oh," I said, my arm dropping as understanding dawned. "The signature look?"

Destanie laughed, rolling her eyes. "I called your name three times, and you didn't hear me. Leon just called and said he's on his way up."

"Sorry," I mumbled, attempting to straighten out my features. "I got lost in my own head. Tell Leon to meet me on the deck."

"Will do," Destanie called as I turned and headed for the small place I considered a respite. It was off the kitchen and had a fantastic view of the hills, even if they were currently brown and parched from the ongoing drought here in Southern California. I'd brought a couple of patio plants home from Trader Joe's six months before, and they'd climbed up the privacy screen that separated this unit from the one next-door, creating a lush backdrop. I liked the opulent feel and clean lines of my apartment, but I supposed in some ways I was still a farm girl, because the untamed beauty of climbing vines and natural vistas brought me a sense of peace when nothing else did.

"Emily."

I turned to see my manager smiling, stepping through the sliding glass doors and onto the deck. "Leon." I approached, and he took both of my hands in his, giving them a warm shake. "Thank you for stopping by. I would have come into the office."

"No, I was heading to another meeting across town and your place is on the way," he said, glancing at the ivy. "Also, this is great. Especially since I've been sitting in a boardroom for most of the day." We both took a seat at the four-person glass table. Even though the sun was setting, the heat of the day hadn't quite burned off yet. But it was comfortable under the awning that covered the space. Leon sighed, gazing out to the hills for a moment, his eyes lingering on the silvery lavender sky. I turned toward it as well, the horizon a shade I didn't recall ever seeing before. How was it that I'd witnessed thousands of sunsets in my life, and yet one could still stun me? "Do you ever forget there's a world out there beyond boardrooms and recording studios?" he asked.

I smiled, and it felt like the first real one all day. "Sometimes," I admitted.

He cleared his throat, seeming to come back to himself. "So, listen, Emily," he said, tapping his open palm on the table for a moment as he studied me. "I've been ironing out the contracts with several of the team members joining the tour, and I wanted to talk to you about a few of their suggestions."

"Oh, okay."

He reached in his briefcase and removed a stack of papers. "I've approved all of these. They just need your signature. Take a few days to read them over and give me a call if you have any questions."

I nodded, sliding the stack of contracts toward me and glancing at the top one. It was for a lighting crew. Just looking at my name at the top of the page was surreal. It was hard enough to believe I had a manager and an assistant, a bona fide *team*. But now I had a lighting crew! Tasked solely with lighting my show.

And a bodyguard. Now you have a bodyguard.

I pushed that thought aside, clearing my throat and thanking Leon.

"One other thing," Leon said, and the way he paused made me tense. He looked like he was about to deliver bad news. "I'd like you to lip-synch."

Confusion made me gape. "Lip-synch? Lip-synch...what?"

"Your show."

"My show?" I let out a small laugh that died a quick death when Leon stared at me with zero amusement in his expression.

He raised his hand. "I knew you wouldn't love the idea but hear me out. The dance sequences are extremely vigorous. You're a new performer, especially in venues like the ones where we've booked your shows. There's a lot of money riding on you, Emily. Millions of dollars. People have made investments in your image, and we cannot afford your vocals not to be everything the audience expects and more. It's too risky."

"Isn't it a risk that I'll be mocked?" I asked. "That my talent will be questioned?"

"You're not lip-synching someone else's vocals, babe. You're lip-synching your own. Lots of big names do it. It's practically expected in this day and age. And the professionals get it. Very few can focus on doing ten things at once, and why should you? You're called an entertainer for a reason."

I *thought I was called a singer.*

Leon went on. "We've weighed the risks and benefits and determined this is the best way to go. A flop now would be career suicide. This is a business, babe. Business can make the dream feel less shiny, but it's also what keeps the dream alive. Do you understand?"

I nodded slowly. I understood, I did. And I was scared of risking it all too. Leon Lee was one of the very best in the business. His client list—and their net worth—spoke of a man who knew exactly what he was doing and guided his clients to success. Was I going to be the fool who disregarded what he thought was best for my career? Wouldn't I be stupid not to take Leon's advice to heart?

Yes. Yes, I would.

So why did it feel like my heart was shrinking in my chest? Yes, it was because the idea of lip-synching made me feel like a total sellout. But also… I'd chosen this career so that I could sing all the time. *That* was my dream. My passion. And I was having a hard time squaring how living my dream also meant… losing it.

ten

Tuck

The getup Emily was currently shimmying in across the make-shift stage was little more than a tasseled, rhinestone-studded bikini. The thigh-high boots added a bit more coverage and yet somehow made the outfit that much more risqué.

Risqué? You sound like a crotchety old man. Just enjoy it.

The problem? I *was* enjoying it. A little too much. I pushed my sunglasses up my nose, angling my head so it appeared I was looking off to the side when I was really staring at her. She did have an amazing body. Toned yet rounded in all the right places. Long, shapely legs. And though I couldn't see them now, I knew even her ankles were pretty. And the way she moved. Graceful. Effortless. Sexy as hell. God, the way she'd feel underneath—

"Are you all right, man?"

I turned at the sound of the man's voice next to me. The tall, blond guy was looking at me with concern. He waved his hand in front of his face. "You look like you're in pain. Too much to drink last night?" He grinned, nodding to my sunglasses.

I pushed the shades up, so they rested on top of my head, squinting as a spotlight from the stage glanced off something shiny and hit me in the eye. "No, it's just unusually...bright in here."

He laughed. "You get used to it." He held out his hand. "I'm Charlie, Emily's boyfriend. You must be her new bodyguard."

Ah, the boyfriend. I gripped his hand. The guy looked familiar, but I couldn't say why. When I glanced over his shoulder, a very large man with a buzz cut and wearing all black stood with his hands clasped casually in front of him, but obviously watchful. Charlie's security? He must be someone famous in the music industry too. My eyes returned to him. "Tuck Mattice. Nice to meet you."

"Welcome to her team. It's great to have you here. Your presence will really give her peace of mind. And me too. Especially on this tour. You never know what to expect from fans. Most of them are a hundred percent nice and genuine. But there's always that fringe, you know?"

I'd take his word for it. To my mind, anyone who followed *anyone* around town, much less around the country, was less than stable. Then again, my own judgment had been questionable—to say the least—for much of my life, so I'd work to tone down my assumptions when it came to Emily's *fans*.

Also, I didn't want to undermine Emily's talent. She was a beautiful singer. Her voice had moved me when I was nothing more than a kid. I remembered standing off to the side while she'd sung for our families. I'd always separated myself from the others when she performed, because I'd wanted to direct all my focus on her and her alone. It'd felt like witnessing a small miracle. She was a star now, or so I'd been told, but God, I'd been starstruck by her back then. Totally and completely.

Currently though? The number she was gyrating to was

overly fast, the recording making her voice sound strange and electronic, doing nothing to highlight her natural velvety soulfulness. A particularly high note made me cringe as Emily danced across the stage, ending in a dramatic pose. A smattering of applause from the small crowd went up and I let out a sigh.

Emily unclipped the microphone she'd been practicing with and then stepped off the stage, a bounce in her step as she walked toward us. She was breathless and glistening with sweat, and I had the sudden flashback of Emily running toward me during a game of tag, as we wove and ducked through the orange groves. Only this time, she was a woman and her...tassels were bouncing. I felt my blood notch up a few degrees at the sight of all that flushed, glowing skin. I looked away as she arrived where we stood, seeing her go up on her tiptoes and kiss Charlie on the lips from my peripheral vision.

"I see you took some liberties with the uniform," Emily said.

I looked back at her, one perfectly drawn eyebrow arched as her gaze moved down my body over the medium gray cotton T-shirt and dark gray jeans, down to my black boots. "Yeah, about that," I said. "I just couldn't find exactly what Destanie described. I hope this will work."

"The main point is that you're comfortable," Charlie said, clapping me on the back. "If there's trouble, you need to be able to move. And move fast. Right, babe?"

Emily gave him a noncommittal hum as her only response. "How's your hotel?" she asked.

"It's perfect. More than I hoped for. Thanks."

"Great."

"Great."

For a moment we simply stared at each other, some sort of tension swirling in the air. I wasn't sure what it was, or maybe I didn't want to look at it too closely. Didn't want to see something that wasn't there simply because I was way out of practice with women. All I did know was the hair on the back of my neck was standing up and my clothing began feeling overly tight as the seconds ticked by and neither of us looked away.

Charlie pulled Emily toward him, wrapping his arm around her waist and splaying his palm over her bare stomach. Emily startled slightly and looked up at him, her expression melting into adoration. "I'm glad to see you're lip-synching, babe," Charlie said. "Things will go a lot more smoothly that way, and you can give your all to the dance numbers."

What? "You're not really singing?" I blurted. I'd thought the recording was just being used for rehearsal purposes.

Emily's eyes jerked to me. "No," she said as she pulled her shoulders back. If she was trying to hide the defensiveness in her tone, she failed.

I remembered the sweet sound of her voice, the way her natural talent had been obvious to everyone from the time she was a little girl. "That's too bad."

"Is it? In my view, nothing about this seems bad." She swept her arm around the room, indicating, I supposed, her entourage, the spotlights, the sequins, the bright and shiny fruits of her labor. Or her luck. Or whatever had gotten her here. Because apparently, it wasn't her voice. They'd changed that into something robotic and unrecognizable.

I followed her arm, squinting into the dizzying lights, the electronic sounding track still playing, though softer now. They'd made her sound like a relative of The Chipmunks. It made me cringe. "You sure?" I asked.

"*Very.*" Her jaw was tight and if she was a bird, her feathers surely would have ruffled. That tension again. Swirling. Emily had stepped forward, and now her eyes blazed up at me, chin lifted stubbornly. I hadn't felt myself move, but apparently I had, because suddenly, we were practically standing toe to toe, chests rising and falling in tandem. Her cheeks were flushed, and we were far too close. This was inappropriate and so was what I'd said. I stepped back.

The way she looked though… It reminded me of how she'd looked when she'd been a young girl and challenged a score, or a win, or a tag, or any other small rule loophole she could find. Which had been often. She'd never been a very graceful loser. The memories made me want to smile. Almost.

I hated all these memories that kept rushing back, ones I hadn't even realized I still carried. Because they reminded me that I still held some tenderness deep down for the defiant little brat I'd once known.

But mostly, they made me dislike what she'd become.

"Uh, hey, Emily babe," Charlie said on an uncomfortable chuckle, clearly confused about whatever was going on between us, something even I couldn't exactly figure out. "Why don't we go get a bottle of water? You gotta be thirsty after all that dancing."

"I am. Thirsty," she said, addressing Charlie but still staring at me. "Grab me a water, will you, Tuck?"

"I'm your bodyguard—not your gopher."

Her mouth fell open.

Are you trying to get yourself fired, Tuck?

Maybe. Maybe I was. Because I had a recent history of being self-destructive. Reactive. Stupid. *Prideful.*

And look where it'd gotten me. I pulled in a deep breath. "It's safer if I remain where I am, guarding this entrance. It's been propped open for air all afternoon. Anyone could walk right in." I softened my voice, motioning to the door behind us.

Emily's gaze moved to the door and then back to me, narrowing suspiciously. But then she let out a slow breath as she stepped back, apparently appeased, at least for the moment.

She took Charlie's hand in hers and, without another word, turned and began to walk away.

"Nice to meet you, Tuck," Charlie said.

"You too," I murmured as I lowered my sunglasses once

more, grateful now that Destanie had suggested they be part of the *uniform*.

I watched Emily as she uncapped a bottle of water, tipping her head and drinking half of it, her slender throat moving as she swallowed. Charlie laughed at something the woman next to him said, leaning toward Emily as though letting her in on the joke, his hand resting on the small of her back and then sliding down to her ass before again moving up and coming to rest on her lower spine. She smiled at him half-heartedly. I massaged my jaw. She glanced over her shoulder at me, and I turned my head slightly so that it appeared I was scanning the small crowd. When she'd rejoined the conversation, I focused my gaze on her again, watching as she pulled at her top, grimacing and readjusting it. I saw the edge of a red welt where the sequined fabric had obviously dug into her flesh. So that was why she wanted me to wear tight spandex or whatever. She wanted everyone around her to be as uncomfortable as she was. I stretched my arms, glad I'd disobeyed the instructions.

The woman onstage who had been going over some moves with the backup dancers called Emily's name, and she gave Charlie a kiss on the cheek and headed back to join them.

When I looked back at the table laden with snacks and drinks, Charlie and his bodyguard were gone. I walked to the door, closed it and flipped the lock and then went to grab a water but when I got there, I didn't see any among the cans of soda and energy drinks.

"Can I help you find something?" I looked up at a pretty brunette wearing a lime-green sports bra and a pair of small white shorts. I recognized her from the earlier dance number.

"I was just looking for a bottle of water."

She looked over the drinks. "Oh. I guess they ran out. There's a refrigerator around the corner there in the lounge where extra supplies are kept. Do you want me to go check?" She gestured behind her, then brought her hand forward, holding it out to me and smiling. "I'm Caycee, by the way."

"Hi, Caycee. Tuck. I'm Emily's bodyguard. And no, that's okay. I'll go grab it. I need to stretch my legs anyway."

"Oh! Emily's bodyguard. That's great. I'm a member of the dance team. Welcome to the family. It looks like we'll all be getting to know each other well over the course of the tour." Her smile grew and her eyes moved down my body, giving me a suggestive stare. "By the way, a group of us are going out for drinks after this if you're available."

"Ah, maybe. I'll see. Thanks for the invite."

"Sure, catch you later."

I moved around her, heading in the direction she'd indicated. Before rounding the corner, I glanced at Emily, confirming she was onstage, surrounded by the other performers hopping around and that the door I'd shut and locked was still closed.

As I approached the lounge, I heard two male voices, speaking in hushed tones and halted. Worried I was interrupting something, I began to back away when I heard Charlie's name spoken by a man with an exceedingly deep voice. The security dude I'd seen standing behind him earlier? "What do you want?" he asked.

My muscles froze, ears perking up as their voices grew quieter like they'd turned away from where I stood. "I'll need to stock up—might not have good connects in some of these places I'm traveling over the next couple months. All the usuals—dust, bars…some molly, you know." Charlie's voice.

"Got it. I'll pick 'em up tonight."

Holy shit. I'd lived in the heart of Los Angeles. I was well acquainted with the terms used to reference drugs. I guess Charlie wasn't the golden boy he appeared to be.

Damn, Emily really knew how to pick 'em.

I heard rustling sounds and then footsteps and backed up slowly. Charlie walked out of the room, head down, putting some bills back in his wallet as he turned in the other direction. I blew out a slow breath. He hadn't seen me.

I started to turn away when the brute of a bodyguard exited the room, our eyes meeting. "Do you know if the bathroom's this way?" I asked.

He paused, his eyes narrowing for a brief second before he raised his arm and pointed behind where I stood. "That way."

"Right. Thanks." I turned and walked away.

I stopped in the lounge on my way back from the restroom, grabbed a pack of water, and delivered it to the table laden with snacks and drinks. Caycee came up next to me, disconnecting one of the waters from the plastic and grinning. "Thanks."

I smiled back. "No problem."

Charlie was standing near the stage now, watching Emily rehearse, and I took a sip of water as I thought about what I'd heard between him and his security guy. "Hey, Caycee, that guy over there, Charlie? What does he do?"

Caycee laughed, almost choking on the sip of water she'd just taken. "You're kidding right? You don't know Charlie Cannon? He's, like, one of the biggest movie stars right now."

Huh. With the amount of product I'd just heard him "order," he must be a known partier. "What's he like?"

"He's super nice. He has a reputation in the business and with his fans for being really wholesome. And he's *mega* rich." She picked up a bag of trail mix, opened it, and started pushing the M&M's aside to get at the peanuts. "He lives in this insane mansion in Bel Air. He threw this lavish party for Emily when her single hit number one, and all of us who were in the video were invited."

Wholesome? Unless my definition of *wholesome* was considered narrow, Charlie was a phony. Or maybe that was just the persona he played for the media and Emily was well aware of his vices. Maybe she even partook in some. An emotion that felt a lot like protectiveness buzzed along my ribs, but I willed it away. It was none of my business.

Having plucked out all the peanuts and a few raisins, Caycee dropped the bag of perfectly good M&M's in the trash. This woman was clearly *off*, even if she was hot.

I'd thought I was surrounded by degenerates for the last six years. Hollywood might give prison a run for its money.

The music stopped, and Charlie lifted Emily from the stage, her body sliding down his as she laughed. She wrapped her arms around his neck, and her eyes met mine over his shoulder, then moved to Caycee and back to me, her smile slipping.

Charlie set her down on the floor, cupping her jaw and kissing her. I turned, focusing on Caycee, who was saying something about the guy's three infinity pools. She laughed at some joke she'd made, twirling her hair, her eyes twinkling. I smiled back. I'd thought I didn't want company, but maybe I should rethink that. "Are you still planning on going out for drinks?"

"Yes! Will you join us?"

"Yeah. Let me make sure I'm officially off duty. I'll be right back."

"I'll be waiting," she called, giving me a small wave and a smile.

Emily and Charlie both turned as I approached. Emily's gaze slid from me to the place over my shoulder where Caycee was standing. "If you're done here for the day, I'm assuming I'm free to go?"

Emily put her hands on her hips, her lips thinning as she again glanced behind me. "Yes. You're free to go. But, Tuck, there's no cavorting with other members of my team. It gets far too messy."

"Cavorting? I didn't see anything about cavorting in the contract."

Her expression faltered momentarily. "Well... I'll add it in."

"Too late. I already signed."

Somehow, once again, without me knowing, we'd moved closer as we spoke so that we were almost standing toe to toe. "So, you're saying you are going to...cavort?"

I almost laughed, but held it in. I was irritated, but I was also slightly amused by the natural way she and I seemed to fall back into childhood bickering. Truthfully, I wasn't planning on "cavorting" with Caycee. I didn't need any complications. But I wasn't opposed to finding a willing woman at a local bar to relieve some pressure. "No. But if you're going to make amendments to my contract, I'll have to sign a new one. My job duties should be spelled out in black and white. I wouldn't want to misstep because you and I weren't clear about what was expected of me."

"That seems fair," Charlie cut in, taking a few steps toward Emily.

She looked up at him, appearing almost startled by his presence. "Sure. I'll have a new contract drawn up," she said.

"Great."

"Great."

I felt a hand on my arm, and Caycee came up next to me. "Ready?" she asked.

"Sure. See you tomorrow," I said to Emily, offering Charlie a chin tip. Just before we both turned away, something crossed Emily's face that looked vaguely like hurt. I felt a punch in my gut and for just a moment, she looked exactly like the girl I'd once known despite all the ways that she had changed. I paused, feeling as if I should say something to...what? Soothe her? Make it so we were parting on terms that weren't as strained? There were all these weird lines I kept spontaneously crossing. But it didn't matter anyway. The moment had passed, and she was already moving away.

eleven

Emily

My pillow was too hot. I sat up, turning it over, punching the middle blindly and falling back onto it with a frustrated grunt. Maybe I'd turned the heat up too high before going to bed, because my apartment was sweltering. I tore off my black velvet sleep mask and tossed it onto my bedside table. Instead of getting up right away to check the thermostat, I crossed my arms, staring up at the ceiling and watching the shifting lights from the street below.

I didn't see anything about cavorting in the contract. The memory of Tuck's words wound through my mind, the disdainful look he'd worn on his face as he'd challenged me, causing a zing of anger. Less than a week on the job and he was already pissing me off. I'd been right about this arrangement being a bad idea.

But I guess I was stuck now.

I tossed my comforter aside, feeling around for my slippers on the carpet next to my bed, and then padding out to the living room. I turned down the thermostat a few degrees and then sat down on my sofa and picked up the remote. A news program came on, and I turned the volume low, not necessarily wanting to get invested in a show but craving the noise, the voices. I felt...lonely.

Why do I feel lonely?

That was ridiculous, of course. I was surrounded by people all day long. I rarely, if ever, got any time to myself. Sitting alone like this should be a luxury. Sure, I wished Charlie hadn't had to jet off to a publicity event for his next movie, but he'd be back in a couple of days. And I'd talk to him on the phone multiple times before that.

A small sound pinged out on my balcony, and I turned in that direction, nerves jittering under my skin.

What was that?

I waited, and a few seconds later, it happened again. A shadow moved outside, and I let out a small squeal, sliding down low on the sofa and then crouch-walking to my bedroom.

It's just a piece of ivy blowing in the breeze.

But what if it isn't?

I locked my bedroom door and hurried to where I'd left my phone on my bedside table. It was probably nothing. I was sure it was nothing.

But I did have a bodyguard.

I paid him to provide me peace of mind in the event a psychopath had somehow scaled my building and was trying to break into my apartment via the patio.

He answered on the second ring, sounding like I'd pulled him from sleep. "Hello?"

"Tuck?"

"Em?" I heard the creak of a bedspring as though he'd sat up. *Or someone else had turned toward him.* My heart picked up speed. "Are you okay?"

I paused, listening for a moment. When I didn't hear anything—or anyone—in the background, I let out a breath. "I heard a noise on my patio."

"A noise? What kind of noise?"

"I don't know. Like someone—"

"Someone?" More rustling as though he was pulling on clothes.

"Or some*thing*. I don't know. It just...it made me nervous."

"Okay. I'm on my way. Go in your bedroom and lock the door."

"That's where I'm calling from."

"I'll be there in ten."

I hung up, pacing as I waited, attempting to hear through the door anything that might be happening on the patio, but no sounds met my ears. Either it really was nothing, or the person was being exceedingly quiet.

Tuck was true to his word, and a text came through my phone exactly ten minutes later, asking me to open my door.

I scurried through my apartment and opened the door to find Tuck standing there with his hair mussed and a shadow of scruff on his jaw. His chest rose and fell as though he'd run there from across town.

"Can I come in?" he asked, eyeing me as I stood and stared at him.

"Oh—" I stepped back, allowing him entrance "—yes, of course. Thank you for coming over. I...um...hope I wasn't interrupting anything..."

"Nope," he said. "I was in bed." He strode through the apartment and pulled aside the shade on the sliding glass door. I jumped behind him, my fingers on his back as I peeked out, half expecting to see some hideous clown or equally diabolical beast.

A pigeon sat on the glass table. At the sight of us, she let out a soft coo and flapped her wings before flying a short distance upward where she disappeared under an eve.

I stepped from behind Tuck's impressively large back and followed him as he opened the glass doors. "Stay inside for a minute. I'm just going to check things out," he said. There weren't many places to hide, except maybe behind the ivy, but I appreciated his diligence.

I watched as he checked each corner and ran his hand over the plants, then stood on one of the chairs and peered up into the place where the pigeon had flown. He stepped down and came back inside. "You have a nest on your balcony," he said.

I sucked in a gasp. "Baby birds? Can I see?"

"It's your space. I'd stand back if I were you. Mothers can get aggressive if they think their young are being threatened." As if I didn't know that. Had he forgotten I was a country girl?

I stepped into the cool night air, climbing carefully up on the chair and then stretching my neck to look into the nest. The mama bird was in there, busily feeding three little open, upturned mouths. I grinned with delight, turning my face toward Tuck, who was watching me with a small, confused smile on his lips. *There it is. That look. The one he'd given me...once.*

Time seemed to still for a moment, the delight I'd felt at seeing the babies eclipsed by the greater pleasure of seeing Tuck look at me the same way I'd once craved so desperately.

He held out his hand, and I took it, stepping down from the chair. I looked at his hand in mine, so much bigger, his palm rough and calloused. His skin had always been dark. He tanned so easily. He was paler now. Too much time indoors. Years. "Thank you," I said, my words emerging in a rush. "For coming over so quickly. I hope I didn't...disturb you." I felt strangely shy in a way I hadn't in...well, a long time. It was an odd feeling, but also somehow familiar.

"No," he said, and I worked to bring myself back to the conversation. "You didn't disturb me. I was just reading."

I smiled, brushing past him into the living room. He followed, and I closed the sliding glass door behind him, latching it. "You and your books."

He gave me a lopsided smile and rubbed the back of his neck. "Yeah. They got me through a lot."

A lot. Maybe he meant everything that had happened to him as a kid. Or maybe he meant serving time. Probably some of both. I shifted on my feet, feeling slightly uncomfortable. "That had to be very hard for you," I said. "Being locked up."

His eyes moved over my face as though searching, but then his expression seemed to fall in some slight way, and I sensed whatever he'd been looking for he hadn't found. "It was, Emily." He looked away, signaling that was all he was going to say about that. And I noted that it was back to *Emily.* No more Em.

Which was good. Of course. Our relationship was professional. It was confusing when it started to drift into other more intimate territory. So why was I disappointed? Not only in the fact that he obviously had no interest in opening up to me, but that the wall he'd momentarily lowered had just slammed solidly back into place? Why did I feel like I needed to save something, or defend something that I couldn't even describe? A trill of panic rushed over my skin. I hated feeling like this with Tuck. Hated feeling this undefined *want* when it came to him and hated that I suspected he'd closed himself off because of something lacking in me.

I pulled my shoulders back, smiling the smile I'd practiced in the mirror, the one that was regal and slightly aloof, the one that sought to gain the upper hand. Not Em. Not even Emily. But Nova. I reserved it for those who got too close because they thought my public image meant they knew me. Or those who made me feel less-than. It was time to say good-night to Tuck. Instead, I blurted out, "I'll have you know that my team weighed the risks and determined that lip-synching my own music was in my best interest." I knew that was at least part of the reason he looked at me with such disdain. He thought I'd tossed my standards aside for fame. I understood that, and it was the only thing I could address or defend. "The dance moves are very intense and I'm not only a singer—I'm a performer. Fans are paying for the whole package."

One of Tuck's eyebrows went up and the other went down as though he was as surprised as me over my sudden outburst. I remembered that look. He'd given it to me often, growing up. Only then, it had usually been followed by a disarmed smile. Right now, there was no trace of affection in his expression. "You don't owe me an explanation."

I resisted a cringe. "No, you're right. I don't. It's just, well, it'd be in *your* best interest to root for my success. A lot of people are depending on me for their paychecks, including you, by the way, and if I mess this up… I'll let them all down."

"That's a lot of pressure," he said. "But I hope you're not only doing this for other people."

"Of course not," I snapped. "I'm in full agreement with how things are being done."

"Good. It's your life. Your career. You have to manage it as you see fit."

The words he said didn't match the tone in his voice and I bristled. *More judgment.* "And you? Are you living your life as you see fit, Tuck?"

"Low blow," he said smoothly. "I'm trying."

I released a long breath and pinched the top of my nose. He'd come rushing over here to help me, and I was insulting him. True, he was getting paid to respond to my calls, but still. I felt emotionally out of whack and somehow completely unsurprised that of all the people who might have managed to make me feel that way, it was still only him. "We always did love to fight, didn't we?" I asked.

"Old habits die hard, I guess," he said. "And that was a long time ago."

"Yes, it was." I shifted on my feet more, and now that we weren't fighting, I felt that odd shyness once again. He just seemed so *big*. He sort of sucked all the air out of the room. "So, um, you saw the schedule I emailed over, right? We leave for fittings in New York on Monday?"

He nodded. "Yes. I'll be ready."

"Okay. Good. Charlie's coming too, so it'll be the three of us."

A troubled expression moved over his features. "By the way, why didn't Charlie come over to check out the patio?"

"He's out of town for work. He left a few hours ago."

"It must be hard," he said, "spending so much time in different cities."

I gave a small shrug. "It's worth it. And it won't always be this...intense," I said, giving a small laugh. Charlie was at the height of his career and my own was just beginning to take off. There would be a time when our lives didn't revolve around constant ladder climbing and social engagements. There would be a time when we could afford to say no to some things, and yes only to that which set our souls alight. Creatively speaking.

He was looking at me that way again, as though he heard something I wasn't saying. I didn't like it. It made me feel exposed. "So, you're pretty serious, then, I take it?"

His question surprised me. Or rather, the fact that he'd asked it surprised me after I'd just been thinking about how, up to this point, he'd seemed to avoid any personal connection.

"Yes," I said. "Very serious." We hadn't talked marriage or kids or anything, but I could see it going that way...a few years from now. Again, when life ceased to be as intense as it currently was.

Something flitted over his face once more, but before I could attempt to read Tuck's expression, he turned slightly, looking toward the door. "I should go."

"Oh. Yes. Right. Thanks again. Oh, do you need to call an Uber?"

"I'll do it downstairs. I downloaded the app."

"Oh great." I smiled as I opened the door. "Look at you, downloading apps." I cringed. *What the hell are you talking about, Em?* "Thanks again."

"You're welcome." He started walking out, and I moved to close the door when he suddenly turned back. We almost collided, and I pulled in a big inhale of his T-shirt. Soap and sage and clean male skin. God, he smelled *good*. I practically jumped away. "Don't forget to lock the door behind me. And I know this building provides some security, but it wouldn't hurt to get an alarm on that sliding glass door. You know, for peace of mind."

"That's a great idea. Good night, Tuck."

For a moment I thought he might say something more, but he didn't, simply stepping back into the vestibule.

I closed the door and flipped both locks, listening as his soft footsteps moved away, then I let my head fall forward, my forehead connecting with the wood.

I knew I was no longer in danger, so why did I still feel so shaky?

twelve

Tuck

The ride to the airport was spent listening to Charlie talk business with some director or another. Frankly, I was happy to have the time to sit in relative silence with Emily. For the first time since I'd started working for her, it felt mostly comfortable. I felt like we'd found a new understanding at her apartment a couple days before. Even if we weren't going to be friends again, we weren't going to be at odds either.

I could finally settle into my job and begin rebuilding my life. Planning. Strategizing. Thinking about where I wanted to be and where, ultimately, I might fit in.

This wasn't it. Frankly, I had no real idea where or what or how I'd finally find a sense of purpose, because in so many ways, I was still floundering. This was merely a means to an end, which was fine for now. And hopefully my presence would bring Emily the peace of mind she needed to focus solely on her job and becoming…whatever it was she wanted to become.

Win. Win.

The car pulled onto an airfield and came to a stop. I opened the door of the limo just as the driver was rounding the car. "Sorry, sir. I've got that."

"Hey, no problem," I said as I got out. I didn't want other people opening doors for me. It felt off.

Charlie climbed out, slipping the guy some cash. "Thanks, Cory," he said as the guy nodded, hurrying to the trunk to retrieve our bags.

A few minutes later I was climbing the short set of steps to the private plane as Emily and Charlie waited for Cory to unload one piece of luggage after another. I swung my singular duffel bag through the door, lowering my head as I entered the cabin.

Wow.

Now this...this I could get used to. I'd only flown once before, when my parents and I had traveled to my grandpa's funeral in Seattle. My family hadn't had much time for vacations. It was too difficult to find people to care for all the crops and animals when the three of us were a vital part of the team who ran the place. We'd gone away for a weekend here and there, but always somewhere within driving distance.

I remembered that flight well though, and these conditions were in a completely different league.

This was *class*.

This was money.

Swiveling, camel-colored leather seats that were large enough to ensure even the most sizable man was comfortable. Polished mahogany paneling that made up the walls of the cabin. A glass-cased beverage/snack bar along the back wall that held all manner of in-air sustenance.

The pilot ducked out of the cockpit just as I was sitting down in a seat on the left side of the cabin. There was an empty seat next to me, and across the aisle, two more seats for Emily and Charlie. The pilot took the few steps to where I sat, shaking my hand and smiling. "Hi, I'm Russell Martin. I'll be flying you to New York today. It looks like it'll be a smooth flight."

"Nice to meet you. I'm Tuck, Emily's security."

"Ah, great. Well, I don't expect any trouble in the skies today, but you never know," he said on a laugh.

Emily and Charlie bustled in, Cory behind them draped in garment bags and holding a suitcase in each hand. Russell stepped aside and I looked out the window at the airfield as they got situated across the aisle and then greeted the pilot.

"Want me to toss that up into the overhead bin?" Cory asked, nodding to my duffel bag at my feet.

"Oh, ah, sure," I said. I removed my current paperback from the side pocket before handing it to him. "Thanks."

Cory wished us a good flight and headed out the door, and Russell closed it behind him and returned to the cockpit, only separated by a short, navy blue curtain.

"Tuck, I'm going to grab myself a beverage. Would you like anything?" Charlie asked.

"A water would be great. Thanks."

Charlie stepped to the back of the plane and returned a minute later with a water for me and Emily, and a soda for himself.

"Buckle up," Emily said, turning her head my way as she stretched the belt across her body, her arm accentuating her breasts. I looked quickly away, clicking my own seat belt into place.

We taxied to the runway, and as the plane started lifting into the sky, I glanced over at Emily, who was staring straight ahead, eyes wide, knuckles white as she gripped the armrests. Next to her, Charlie calmly sipped his drink, completely oblivious to the fact that she was clearly a nervous flyer.

Which was confusing since he had to have flown with her at least a few times before this. And he'd never noticed what I could see in a single glance?

I turned my head and looked out the window. I already knew that Charlie was more than met the eye. And not in a good way.

The plane rose, and then leveled out, and though it was a small aircraft, the ride to cruising altitude was mostly smooth.

It was a beautiful day, the sky powder blue and dotted with silver-tinged clouds. I felt strangely free, as if all my problems were still on the ground, and up here, I was only *me*, completely washed clean of all I'd left behind.

Part of me wanted this flight to last forever. Nothing would take away what I did or who it affected, but racing through the clouds, it felt as though none of that existed. As if I'd never fucked up anything. As if I didn't have a past that would be a proverbial manacle for the rest of my life. I'd been somewhat unwilling to "go there" in my head as of late when there were more pressing matters to address—namely, the ability to eat—but I knew I'd have to, eventually. I knew I *should*, eventually. But up here, the temporary sensation of freedom felt more than welcome.

I sighed, glancing over at Emily, and her eyes widened slightly as though whatever was on my face had surprised her. She gave me a small, wobbly smile.

Charlie said something to her, and she leaned into him, laughing softly and then taking his hand in hers, squeezing it. I turned toward the window again, removing my paperback from the pocket on the wall and cracking it open. For the next couple of hours, I buried my nose in my book, tuning out the soft murmurs and occasional laughter from Emily and Charlie.

"Darn, I left my lip gloss in my purse," I heard Emily say from next to me. "My lips always get so chapped on flights."

"Do you want me to grab it for you?" Charlie asked.

Emily unbuckled. "No, it's fine. I'm right here. I think my purse is near the front." She stood, opening the overhead bin, her ass in my face as she began rustling through the bags overhead. I dog-eared the page I'd stopped on and placed the book on the seat next to me. "Shoot," she said just as a number of items fell to the floor and rolled beneath my seat. I leaned down to start gathering them.

Emily bent too, and our heads bumped, both of us letting out a sound of surprise, and then laughing as we pulled back.

"Sorry," we both said at the same time. She laughed again, shaking her head and picking up a bag that was at her feet. It must have been upside down because as she lifted it, a pile of small baggies fell out, fluttering to the ground.

Emily gasped, squatting and bending toward the contents. "What is this?" she asked, her hand hovering over what I could now see were baggies of pills and powders. *Oh shit.* Charlie had brought the drugs I'd heard him discussing aboard this flight. And the shocked look on Emily's face answered any questions I might have had about her knowledge of Charlie's drug use.

Charlie had finally leaned forward to see what all the commotion was, and when he caught sight of the baggies, I saw the panic that altered his features. "What *is* this?" Emily asked, waving her hand over the scattered contents.

I met Charlie's eyes just as he masked the panic that had quickly flared. He tilted his head, appearing very suddenly baffled. "Tuck," he said, "answer her question. What is this? Are you dealing?" he asked, gesturing to the baggies still littering the floor.

I jerked my head back and then came to my feet. "Are you kidding me? You know very well those are yours."

"*What?*" Emily said, her voice rising an octave as she too rose. "That's not possible. Charlie isn't into drugs. He'd have nothing to do with them." She looked so distraught, clearly very upset by the mere idea of her perfect boyfriend having anything to do with illegal substances. As she should be. But he wasn't only a drug user, he was a blatant liar.

Charlie stood up and put his hand on her arm. "Emily, babe,

you know I'd never be involved with drugs in any way. I don't even drink alcohol."

I reached up, massaging my jaw. Charlie shook his head as he regarded me, the look of disappointed sorrow on his face almost making me question his guilt. He *was* an actor after all. "Tuck though, well, his history speaks for itself."

"You piece of shit," I said, taking a step toward him as I realized he was really going to go with this angle.

Emily reached up and placed her palm on my chest. "Stop it," she said. "You are not going to physically intimidate Charlie."

"Physically intimidate? He's *lying* about me."

Charlie made a sound of disgust in his throat. "Please. I have no reason whatsoever to lie about you."

A scorching flame of anger ignited inside me. His lies sounded sincere. The innocent expression on his face looked genuine. And worst of all, even I knew that it made more sense that someone like me was involved in drugs.

But Emily *knew* me. At least she'd known me once.

But she also knew what I became.

I felt a bead of sweat drip down my spine. This was not just some silly accusation. Possession of this many illegal drugs was a felony. Charlie was making an accusation to get himself out of hot water with his girlfriend, but to me, this was life or death. If they went to the authorities and they were believed, I could go back to prison. "Emily," I said. She turned her face toward me. "I'm not a part of that world anymore." I looked at Charlie, shooting daggers at him.

A tear coursed down Emily's cheek. "I get you needed the money, Tuck, but—"

"That. Is. Not. Mine," I said. It felt like frustration and fear had me in a chokehold. The plane gave a little bump and Emily took a small step toward me. "Em," I said, trying to appeal to that part of her hopefully still there. My friend. The one who might know I'd made some really bad mistakes, and that I'd run with a rough crowd, but that I'd *never* let someone else take the fall for me. "You know me better than that." I met her eyes. "I'm not that person."

"Oh please," Charlie inserted again. "You're exactly that person. You're a *felon*. Emily, come on, he served time. It's part of the lifestyle." He met my eyes. "She gave you a second chance, and this is how you repay her?" He made a sound of disgust in the back of his throat. "Sorry to say, but this was obviously a bad idea, babe."

My blood simmered, temperature rising. I was thirty thousand feet above the earth where it'd seemed that, for a short time, I'd left all my problems behind. But that wasn't true. It'd never be true.

Still, I tried one more time. "Look at me. I'm not lying."

Emily looked back and forth between me and Charlie and for a moment, I held my breath, daring to believe that she'd see in her heart that, above all else, I'd never put her in a position like this. No matter who was suggesting I had. "Please, Em, you know me."

She looked down, shook her head. She seemed so torn, and it hurt me. It hurt me to my core. "You're different, Tuck. You're not that kid anymore." She pointed to the baggies. "Clearly."

The simmering frustration boiled over. It mixed with anger and pain. Because part of me knew she was right. I *wasn't* that kid anymore. I didn't need the reminder. I'd done a lot of bad things, highly regrettable choices I'd be paying for, for the rest of my life. But I'd never dealt drugs. And more important than that, I would never put Emily in a position that might jeopardize her safety in any way. And I'd never lie and let someone else take the blame for my actions.

For a few minutes there at her apartment, I'd thought we connected. I'd thought she looked at me the way she had once because she remembered our friendship. She remembered *me*.

The important parts. But I was wrong. It didn't matter. In the end, it didn't matter at all.

"You've given me no choice but to fire you," Emily said, pulling herself straight. "I can't have a drug dealer on my security team. When we land, I'll arrange a flight back to LA for you and a driver will take you to the hotel where you'll gather your things."

My gaze landed on Charlie once more, and I saw the minute twitch of his lips. He was really going to stand by as I paid the price for this. A part of him was *enjoying* it. If I tried to fight it, to plead my case, it would be my word against his. I didn't stand a chance against Hollywood's golden boy. It wouldn't only get back to my probation officer, it'd be all over the tabloids. I'd be connected to this forever. If I thought I'd been ruined before…

Charlie wrapped his arm around Emily's shoulders and pulled her to him. A united front. A red haze filled my vision.

"You wanna know who *you* are?" I said to Charlie. "A lying phony with zero honor. And you," I said, my gaze moving to Emily. "You're nothing but a caricature of what you used to be. A cheap knockoff."

Her face blanched, and she gasped, a sound that sent satisfaction shooting through my veins, bolstering me. "There's not one thing about you that's true or authentic. No wonder that piece of shit likes you so much. You deserve each other."

"How dare—"

"How dare I? I've been wanting to say this since the moment I walked into your apartment and saw you. You're a sellout. They could have picked up any pretty girl off the street and created *Nova*. Your producers didn't need talent. They needed compliance. And you bought into it, hook, line and sinker. And you'll think about what I'm saying long after I'm gone, because deep inside, you know it's true."

"That's enough," Charlie said. "Don't say another word to her."

My gaze hung on Emily, whose face was set in frozen shock. "Happily," I gritted. And with that, I turned, sliding into the farthest seat from them and turning toward the window. I was vibrating with rage and injustice, and I sat in stony silence, the anger festering as they retook their seats, whispering to each other from the other side of the plane. Under any other circumstances, I would have gotten up and left. Too bad doing that would mean plunging to my death thirty thousand feet below.

It almost seemed like the better option.

As if in response to my thought, the plane jolted, causing two of the bags overhead to tumble out of the open compartment.

Emily let out a little squeak, and alarmed, I stood and shut the compartment. Emily had obviously tossed the drugs back in the bag or somewhere else while I'd been turned away, because they were no longer on the floor. The curtain to the cockpit remained closed. I assumed the pilot, Russell, had a headset on, which was a good thing for him, as he hadn't had to endure the tense exchange between the three of us.

I sat back down in my seat and strapped my belt on. Just some turbulence.

"My Wi-Fi isn't working," I heard Emily mutter to Charlie.

"That happens," Charlie said. "Give it a few minutes."

Emily sighed and I turned more fully to the window just as the nose of the plane dipped, foisting me suddenly forward.

Holy shit. What the hell is happening?

thirteen

Emily

Now

I screamed, terror a hot buzz beneath my skin as the plane tilted and the ground rose up. I clawed at my armrests, hanging on tight as there was another jolt and another tilt. *Pleasepleaseplease.* I had no idea who I was begging, but it was the only word that raced through my mind. I squeezed my eyes shut, but not before I caught sight of a large fire burning in the distance out the window, and several smaller fires spread out all around it.

The earth is on fire. Why is the earth on fire?

My stomach lurched as the plane bucked and then began to nose-dive. My squeal mixed with Charlie's yelp—a horror-filled duet. We were both pitched forward, jerking in tandem against our lap belts. "Holy *fuck!*" Charlie yelled.

Brace for impact. Brace for impact. The words Tuck had relayed from the pilot pounded in my skull.

I turned my head to see Tuck gripping his armrests too, his gaze focused straight-ahead, jaw clenched tightly, brows bunched severely. I remembered that expression. It flashed in my mind, blooming large, the clock turning back.

I jerked forward again, the memory melting as though the flames from below had reached up and licked into my reeling mind, the lightning flashing in the sky, scorching my frayed and fearful nerves.

My back slammed against the seat as the plane righted, my gaze fixing on the portion of cockpit I could see through the wide gap in the blue privacy curtain. The pilot's hand gripped a lever or a gear or whatever it was. He was holding it so tightly his knuckles were white. For several minutes, the plane soared and dove, the small plunges seeming somewhat controlled as though the pilot was lowering the altitude the only way he was able. I dared a glance out the window, the ground much closer than it'd been before. "We're going to crash," I sobbed. *Brace for impact. Brace for impact.*

"No," Tuck said, not turning his head but raising his voice. "We're going to land. It's going to be bumpy. Hold on."

Okay. Okay. We were going to land. He sounded so sure, and his instruction gave me hope. We weren't going to crash. We were just going to experience a very rough landing. *Okay. Hold on. Okay.*

Next to me Charlie had his eyes clenched shut and a low humming was coming from the back of his throat as though he was barely holding back a scream. I reached over and grabbed his hand, linking his fingers with mine. He didn't open his eyes, but he gripped my hand tightly.

We broke through the cloud cover and the lightning diminished, the sky brightening. The ground grew nearer, but then the plane turned, heading in the other direction. An open field appeared, and the plane dipped, my stomach rising into my throat, vomit threatening. *Breathe, Emily. Breathe.*

Hold on.

I hadn't heard any landing gear come down. We had no wheels. How were we going to—

The plane hit the ground with a violent bang, and my body bounced, an intense burn spreading from my hip across my stomach as I screamed.

Glass breaking. Screeching metal. Pain.

We were on the ground, but the plane was still flying across the earth. The tail tilted, and for a moment I was suspended forward, held in place only by my belt, a horrible crunch exploding in my ears before the plane once again slammed backward.

Groaning, both human and machine. Labored breaths. Settling metal.

"Are you guys okay?" Tuck. It was Tuck's voice. I managed to turn my head and meet his eyes. His gaze jumped over me, and then looked to Charlie. I realized one of my hands was still linked with Charlie's and the other was holding Tuck's. I didn't even remember reaching for him. I let go of them both, assessing my body, moving my limbs, shaking so hard my teeth were chattering. My hip burned, and my head ached, but I seemed to be mostly okay. I nodded, a jerky movement of chin to chest. I couldn't find my voice.

"We have to get out of here," Tuck said. "There's a fire somewhere. I smell the smoke. And I smell jet fuel too. There's probably a leak." Fire. Jet fuel. Leak. *Danger.* I felt numb and still shaky, and it took me several tries to reach down and remember how to unlatch a seat belt. My thoughts were disjointed, my body nonreactive. Suddenly, Tuck was standing in front of me, leaning in. I felt his warmth, and I smelled his sweat. It was familiar and somehow comforting, and I pulled in a gasping breath, not realizing I'd practically forgotten to breathe for a minute.

"Shit," he swore, struggling with the belt across my lap. "It's stuck. I'm going to have to pull hard. This might hurt."

"I don't care," I said, suddenly desperate to be free. To get out of this death trap. He met my eyes, thinning his lips before he yanked the latch and pulled the strap away. I flinched, feeling a burning pain where the belt must have cut into my skin, but I stood shakily.

Next to me, Charlie was standing too, already having unbelted himself. He looked glassy-eyed and shocked. He lunged toward the door and pulled the lever, wrenching the door open and then practically hurling himself through the opening. A blast of cold air hit me, working to bring me from my semi-stupor.

"Go," Tuck ordered. I did as he said, sitting on the edge of the opening and then jumping down. My legs buckled, and I landed on my knees, prickly grass biting into my skin. My breath came in white pants, and I reached down, taking fistfuls of grassy earth in my hands and gripping it, the cold dirt falling through my fingers. Sobs racked my body, and distantly, I heard the sounds of retching. Charlie.

When I finally raised my head and looked around, taking in several deep, cleansing breaths, I saw that we were in a massive field, nothing but trees and grass for as far as the eye could see.

"Help me out here!" Tuck said. I turned toward his voice and saw that he was standing in the plane's doorway, holding the unconscious pilot under his armpits. The pilot. God, we'd left the pilot. Blood was dripping down the man's face and there was a large gash on his forehead. I stood, trembling but swallowing my sobs. Charlie was still retching, so I took several steps back toward the door where Tuck turned the pilot's body so that I could hold his legs while Tuck supported his upper half, sitting down and then sliding off the edge with him. The pilot's head lolled, and I noticed the front of his shirt was soaked in blood too. *Oh God.* The cockpit had taken the brunt of the impact. It was a wonder Tuck had been able to get him out.

"We need to move away from the plane," Tuck said. I walked

with him, supporting the pilot's legs. I wasn't even sure how I managed it, except that Tuck was instructing me. If he thought I was capable, then I guess I was. When we got about fifty feet from the plane, we laid the man down on the grass. Tuck supported his head, setting it gently on the earth before placing two fingers on his throat.

"Is he...okay?" Charlie asked, coming up next to me and wiping his mouth with a shaking hand.

Tuck's fingers fell away from the pilot's neck, and he hung his head for a moment before standing. "No," he said, turning away from us. "He's gone." He shifted his head so I could only see his profile. "But he saved our lives, and he deserves our gratitude."

Gone. Oh God. Oh no. He was dead. I couldn't even remember his name. I'd barely paid attention to him, and he'd saved my life. Our lives. Another sob rose in my throat, and I brought my hand to my mouth so it wouldn't escape. I turned away from the dead pilot and closed my eyes. He'd given his life and we were standing here, banged up, but alive.

Tuck was striding back toward the plane. I could now see the fire and smoke Tuck had smelled. It was small, but if it was near the fuel tank—which I really had no idea if it was—then we needed to stay far away. "What are you doing?" I yelled to Tuck.

"Gathering what I can," he called back. I started to follow him, but Charlie stopped me with a hand to my arm.

"There's no reason for all three of us to put ourselves in danger," he said. "Grab our phones!" he called to Tuck. "And some water!" He lowered his hand. "I'm thirsty as hell." Tuck either didn't hear him, or ignored him, hopping back up through the open door and disappearing into the cabin. A minute later, a suitcase came flying out, landing on the ground with a thud. I debated joining him and helping to grab whatever we could but hesitated. Charlie was probably right. Tuck was obviously willing to take this risk. If something happened to him, we'd be available to help. We had a good visual of the fire and could shout at him if it started to spread.

I jogged forward and picked up the suitcase and then delivered it several feet away, under a small, bare tree. Tuck continued to toss things out of the door, Charlie and I "rescuing" them and putting them in the pile we'd made at a distance I'd deemed safe.

"You're shivering," Charlie said as we stood waiting for Tuck to toss something else from the door or emerge to join us. "And your teeth are chattering."

Where is he? Charlie ran his hands up and down my bare arms. "Do you have something warm in your suitcase?"

I nodded, my eyes glued to the plane. *Come on.* What was taking him so long? I startled when the fire at the back of the plane jumped, a burst of sparks exploding as though it'd encountered something flammable. "Tuck?" I called. My eyes darted past the windows, trying to catch sight of him inside. I took a step forward just as he appeared in the doorway. My breath released, my shoulders dropping. He was holding a blanket that obviously contained a pile of stuff, his fist gripping the gathered fabric that held it closed. He jumped from the door and started walking toward us just as the fire leaped again, causing another small explosion. Tuck picked up his pace, walking quickly and then jogging as the fire surged and spread, whooshing toward the cabin and blooming large behind him.

I let out a small scream, turning my cheek as the warmth billowed toward us. "Grab the stuff," Tuck said, foisting the loaded blanket at Charlie and then turning toward where the pilot lay. "I think the plane's about to blow."

I could smell the fuel now, closer and more pungent as though Tuck had stepped in a puddle of it. I bent, grabbing the handle of my suitcase.

"Did you get the phones?" Charlie asked.

"Yeah," Tuck said. "Maybe we can get some service but I'm not hopeful."

"What if we can't?" Charlie asked. "It's cold as fuck out here."

Tuck ignored him, heading over to the dead pilot.

"What are you going to do?" Charlie asked.

Tuck didn't answer him. He seemed to be in some zone, or on a mission only he had been given. He bent and picked the dead man up under his armpits. His jaw was set, muscles bunched, dirt smeared across his cheek, the pilot's blood on his clothing as he adjusted his weight and began dragging him across the ground. Charlie and I stumbled along behind him. "I'm going to get his body a safe distance away from the fire and then figure out where the fuck we are," Tuck murmured almost as if to himself.

Seconds later, we all hit the ground when a giant boom filled the air, an explosion creating a whoosh of heat. I screamed, covering my head as flying debris crashed to the ground with a thud. *Close. Too close.* Breath sawed from my lungs as I lifted my head moments later, taking note of Charlie and Tuck just rising as well. Flaming pieces of what had been the plane were scattered on the ground nearby. Behind us, the entire body was engulfed in fire. Tuck's eyes met mine. "Are you okay?"

I nodded jerkily. *Yes.* But he almost hadn't been. Thirty seconds longer in the plane, and he'd have gone up in flames.

fourteen

Tuck

Day One

I hated the thought of leaving behind the body of the man who'd saved our lives and given his own in the process, but there was really no other choice. He now lay between two massive evergreens in the middle of the field we were in, his body covered in the rocks I was able to gather, hopefully offering some protection against scavengers. *It's the best I can do for you. I'm so sorry, man.* My hope was that we could find help and send a crew in to recover his body.

From the corner of my eye, I saw Charlie and Emily rummaging through their suitcases and changing into warmer clothes. Wherever we'd crashed was frigid. As I arranged the rocks around Russell's body, I tried to determine how far we'd flown and where we might be. I'd been angry and stewing and because of that, my internal clock was likely off. But my best guess was that we were either in Indiana, or Illinois. Had we traveled far enough to be in Ohio or even Pennsylvania? Maybe, but I didn't think so. I'd never been to the East Coast, but it was early December, and it was cold as hell, maybe even on the verge of snow, and so we definitely weren't in Arizona or Colorado. Plus, no mountains or desert. Maybe Charlie or Emily would have a more accurate guess. I assumed they'd flown this route at least a few times. But frankly, I didn't much feel like talking to either of them. They hadn't so much as offered to help grab what we could off the plane. They'd stood aside and watched me do it. They were clearly useless. Unless one of them could get their phone to work.

I placed the final rock on Russell's cairn—the best one I could manage anyway. I had balanced larger ones on top, so he was mostly covered. I turned away, the lump in my throat making it difficult to swallow. I didn't even know the dude, but he deserved better than this. I made a mental note of the landscape here, and the direction of the sun, so as soon as possible, I could send the authorities to collect his body and bring it home to his family. He'd been wearing a wedding ring that I'd removed and put in my pocket to return to his wife.

"Nothing," Charlie was saying, staring down at his phone and pressing buttons and then holding it up to the sky as he turned in circles. He'd done the same thing thirty minutes before when he'd taken his and Emily's phones from the blanket I'd used as a sack to collect what I could from the plane. "It won't even turn on."

"Same with mine," Emily said, staring down at hers. I'd looked for my own phone but hadn't seen it anywhere. It'd likely rolled under something in the mayhem of the descent and the crash, but since we had two phones and the smell of jet fuel was strong and worrisome, I had decided it wasn't worth the risk to search for mine.

"They weren't low in charge, so maybe they got banged

around in the crash," Emily suggested, turning hers over as though there might be evidence of damage on some part of the device.

"Even if it starts working, we're probably too far out in the middle of nowhere," Charlie said, his expression glum as he put his phone in his pocket.

The blanket from which they'd retrieved their phones lay open on the ground, the water bottles, snacks, and other items I'd deemed useful still inside. Of course, I hadn't had any idea where we were or what we might be up against, so who even knew if I'd gathered anything useful, other than food provisions.

All I did know was that we seemed to be in the middle of nowhere, the sun was lowering in the sky, and Charlie was right about one thing: it was cold as fuck.

Emily had put on a white jacket with a fur collar and a pair of tight black leather pants, but she was still shivering. "Do you have anything warmer than that?" I asked.

She looked down at her outfit and shook her head. "I have a pair of pajama pants."

"I'd put them on. Layer up."

She appeared ready to argue, but then nodded, bending toward her luggage. Charlie had put on a jacket too and was sitting on his suitcase, fiddling with his phone again.

I opened my duffel bag and pulled out a jacket and some boots, and then tossed the useless clothing items on the ground and began transferring the things I'd gathered from the plane into the bag.

"What are you doing?" Charlie asked.

"It'll be easier to carry this," I told him, zipping it closed.

"Carry?"

"Yeah. Carry. I'm going to start walking."

"Walking?" Emily balked. "Why would you start walking?"

"Because there's probably some sort of civilization within

a few miles, and it's better than sitting here and freezing our asses off."

"But...but air traffic control must know our plane went down," Charlie said. "Help has to be on the way."

"Didn't you hear Russell?" I asked.

"Who's Russell?"

"The *pilot*."

"Oh," Charlie said, his gaze skittering toward the place where his body lay and then away.

"He was trying to contact air traffic and couldn't get through. No one was answering. That was right before the engines failed. It's very possible no one knows where we are, or even that we went down." Plus, something weird had happened. Everything on the plane had very suddenly shut down. And I had wondered about an electric storm because of the lightning. But would that have caused fires on the ground too? I couldn't see any now, but I'd seen them from the airplane window. It was like something specific had happened to both the sky and the earth. Whatever it was had knocked out all the plane's systems. And if that was the case, no help would be coming. We were on our own.

"I don't know," Charlie said, "waiting here seems like the smarter option. Who knows what's—" he waved his arm around the mostly empty field save for a few scattered trees "—that way, or that way. We might get lost."

"We're already lost," I said, picking up my duffel bag. "But suit yourselves. Good luck."

"Hey!" Emily said. "You have all the food and water."

"I'm the one who got back on that plane and collected the food and water," I said, my jaw tight. Still, I wasn't going to leave them to die, even if Charlie had lied about me and Emily had willingly believed his lies. That stuff seemed insignificant at the moment. I opened my duffel bag and tossed them each a bottle of water and a handful of the individual-sized snack bags from the minibar on the plane. Then I rezipped my bag and headed away.

"Wait!" Emily said. I halted, turning again. She shot a glance at Charlie, hesitating, as though she was waiting for some form of permission from him.

"I'm losing daylight," I gritted out, anger suddenly warming me like an internal fire. Good, I'd stay angry. My nose felt like a damn ice cube.

"It's just..." She shifted from one foot to the other. I glanced down and noticed that she was wearing a pair of hot pink heels. "I think we should stay together," she said in a rush of words punctuated by puffs of white vapor. "Strength in numbers. There could be predatory animals out here." Her eyes darted around and then back to Charlie.

Charlie's gaze shifted around too. "Maybe you're right," Charlie said. "There could be a town or something over that hill. It's impossible to see from here."

I'd honestly been looking forward to ditching them. But... God. What if she died out here? What would her parents say if they knew I'd just left her to fend for herself? I looked down to Emily's heel-clad feet once more. "You can't walk in those."

She followed my gaze. "Oh...well, these are my most comfortable heels and all I brought."

Christ. They were already holding me back and we hadn't even started walking yet. I glanced at Charlie's feet. They appeared about the size of my own. She wouldn't fit in either of our shoes. "Do you have a pair of slippers?" I asked.

"Slippers?" Her brow dipped. "Um...yes. Hold on." She bent to her suitcase and dug through it, retrieving a pair of pink fuzzy slippers.

I reached out and took one, turning it over. There was a thick layer of rubber on the bottom. "These'll work," I said. I took a pair of socks out of my duffel bag and tossed those and the slippers at her. She caught them against her chest, her mouth

opening slightly. "Put these and the slippers on and let's go."
She clutched the socks and slippers, her expression morphing
into confusion. "Sixty seconds," I said, "and then you can catch
up." I wrapped the duffel bag's strap around my body, balanc-
ing the weight on my back. "Or not."

I looked away, out to the horizon, planning my route and
silently counting the seconds. When I'd reached sixty, I started
walking. I heard lots of movement and huffing behind me, and
then the sounds of their footsteps following, but I didn't look
back. If they couldn't keep up, that was their problem. And yet,
the way my ears perked up and my steps slowed the few times
I didn't hear them behind me made me suspect I was lying to
myself about not giving a shit about leaving Emily alone in the
wilderness. Either way, however, the minute we hit a farm, or
some other form of civilization, remote or not, they were on
their own. They could call their *people* to arrange a pickup, and
I'd be on my way.

Where, Tuck? Where will you go now?

I had no answer to that question, and a hollowness opened
up between my ribs, where the lump of terror and confusion
from the plane crash had been. I wasn't sure which one I preferred. I picked up my pace, stepping over rocks and brambles,
my eyes focused on the faraway hill that I hoped would make
it clear what direction I should travel.

fifteen

Emily

My lungs burned and my thigh muscles ached as I practically jogged to keep up with Tuck. Next to me, Charlie looked winded too, although he was clearly struggling less as his legs were as long as Tuck's.

Tuck hadn't managed to retrieve all of our luggage from the plane, but he'd tossed out two of my pieces, and two of Charlie's as well. We'd both condensed those into one small rolling suitcase each. However, the "rolling" part didn't exactly work in our current terrain. So, while Charlie was strong enough to hold his piece of luggage in one hand—while switching it back and forth—I was carrying mine in two arms against my stomach, making sure to avoid the spot on my hip that still burned. When I'd put on my jacket and then removed my shorts, I'd noticed that blood had seeped through the material at my flank where the seat belt had cut into my skin. I'd used a pair of my undies as a makeshift bandage to stop the bleeding. It would work for now and then I'd have it looked at when we got back to civilization.

Please let that be soon. An hour, hopefully less. I didn't think I could take any more than that.

Ahead of us, Tuck stopped suddenly. For a moment, we did too, then with a burst of hopeful excitement, rushed ahead. Had he spotted something? We came to stand on either side of him, looking out to the valley below, bathed in a magnificent sunset.

The peachy waves stretched over...absolutely nothing.

"It's...woods," Charlie said.

"Fuck," Tuck swore.

"Oh," I breathed in disappointment.

Tuck glanced over at me, his eyes moving from my face to the suitcase in my arms, his lips thinning. Instead of commenting, he turned around, stepped forward and looked in each direction from our higher vantage point.

"Well, this is fucking great," Charlie muttered. He dropped his suitcase and sat on it before removing the water bottle from his pocket that he'd been drinking as we walked. He downed the rest of it before setting it on the ground and then leaning his elbows on his knees and letting out a long-suffering sigh. I felt a burst of annoyance. But that wasn't fair. This was just a really shitty situation.

Beyond shitty.

The shittiest.

For a moment, my mind spun. How had I ended up here, standing in the middle of nowhere in a pair of leather pants and slippers, holding a carry-on suitcase like it was my baby? It felt surreal. Maybe I'd fallen asleep on the plane and the combination of altitude and the turbulent emotions from the fight we'd had with Tuck had tossed me into a strange dream I was finding it hard to wake from.

I set my own suitcase down and then pinched my wrist. *Ouch.* No, it was real. We had survived a plane crash. How?

I couldn't say. I knew I should feel thankful, but I was still shocked and terrified. And cold, so, so cold.

"Look," Tuck said, and the hopeful tone in his voice made me whip my head his way. He was pointing off into the distance. "I see smoke. Do you see that?"

I jutted my head forward and squinted my eyes. "Um... I think so! Yes!" I said excitedly. It was definitely a trail of smoke coming from what looked like a few miles away past a thick forest. "Let's go," I said. Whoever's home it was would have heat and a phone and a bathroom with a door.

Tuck's arm jutted out, stopping me in my tracks. "In the morning," he said.

"The morning?" My mouth fell open. "Why spend the night out here in the dark and the cold when there's a house right there?" I pointed at the wispy trail of smoke.

"Because for one, it's not right there. It'll probably take us a couple of days to travel that distance. It'll be slow going through those woods and it's not safe when we can't see. It'll be dark any minute now."

"A couple *days*?" *Oh. God.* Then my estimation of a *few miles* was definitely off. This nightmare just kept getting worse.

"And for another," he went on, "if it *is* a house, we have no idea who lives there. It seems like a strange place for a singular home with nothing else around. It could be dangerous. But at least we have a place to shoot for. We'll bed down here tonight and get up with the sun."

"*Bed down?*" Charlie asked, his tone as incredulous as mine had been. "What exactly should we bed down on?"

"The ground," Tuck said. He glanced at the suitcase Charlie was sitting on. "With all the clothes you brought along, you can drape them over yourselves and be nice and toasty. There's a tree right there that will provide some shelter from the wind. We'll be fine."

I didn't like the thought of sleeping on the cold ground under a tree either, but Tuck mentioning sleep made me realize how exhausted I was. It wasn't just the hours of walking while carrying a heavy suitcase with improper footwear. It was the toll from the adrenaline that had been bursting through my body as our plane went down. I suddenly felt so tired I wanted to drop to the ground right there, press my cheek to the dirt and close my eyes.

Tuck adjusted his duffel bag and started walking toward the tree. Its leaves were gone, but it was massive, and its branches alone provided cover.

"Come on," I said to Charlie, pointing over to the tree, which was only about three hundred feet away.

"Can we just sit here another couple of minutes? My feet are killing me."

We? *We* weren't sitting anywhere. I was standing. In my slippers. "If I sit down here, I won't be able to move again, Charlie," I said.

Charlie glanced at Tuck and then away. He obviously didn't want to allow him to be in charge. Part of me didn't blame Charlie after what we'd discovered about Tuck. I was still in shock over all that, if I was honest. The Tuck I'd known as a kid would never get involved with that stuff. He'd changed. But I had to do my best to put that aside and simply trust in Tuck for the moment. He was more qualified when it came to "roughing it," and so for now, it was wisest to follow his lead. Soon we'd be back in civilization. Soon everything would be back to normal. Soon everything would make sense again.

Charlie huffed but then nodded. "Come on. You're right. We all need to rest." He stood and picked up both his suitcase and mine and walked with me toward the protection—meager though it might be—of the massive tree.

There was no quiet like the quiet of a winter night outside in the middle of nowhere. And there was nothing that made you feel smaller than staring up at a star-studded sky, your back against the earth before you drifted to sleep.

I'd dozed a little, but the cold, and the sting of the wound on my hip, had roused me fully awake, and I was having a hard time falling back to sleep even though I hadn't gotten nearly enough. An hour? Maybe less. I had no way to tell. I pulled the pile of clothing I'd draped over my shoulders tighter, turning away from Charlie, who lay next to me snoring softly. At least he was managing to sleep.

A small sound made my eyes fly open, and I saw Tuck, sitting up, leaned against the wide tree trunk, his knees bent, feet flat on the ground. I blinked though my vision needed little time to adjust to the brightly moonlit night as I tried to figure out what he was doing. Was he…sharpening a stick?

I leaned up on my elbow, and his head lifted. His eyes glittered in the silvery light, the angles of his face more sharply defined. A strange shiver tightened my stomach muscles. "What are you doing?" I whispered.

"Making a weapon."

"A…stick?"

"A spear," he said. "Not ideal. But better than nothing."

I glanced around. "What are you anticipating?"

"Nothing specific at the moment but it's always best to be prepared."

"I guess you're right," I murmured. He flicked his wrist, and a small piece of wood went flying off the stick, landing somewhere next to him. "What are you using to sharpen it?"

"The knife on a wine opener," he said. His voice was quiet, sullen. *A wine opener.* He must have snagged that from the plane with the other things he'd collected. We were lucky he had. Because of him we'd had water to drink and a bag of crackers each for dinner. Not exactly a feast, but better than the nothing we'd have had if we'd simply sat and watched the plane be incinerated.

"You didn't happen to snag any wine with that opener, did you?"

"The liquor was locked up. I didn't think it was worth breaking the glass."

I'd put a teasing note into my tone, but Tuck had responded with flat coolness. He was obviously still angry that I'd fired him. But what choice did I have? And he was the one who had not only engaged in something criminal but had flung hurtful words at me because of my completely justified reaction. I wasn't going to think about those words, however, because frankly, I had enough on my plate at the moment without also dwelling on Tuck's unfair opinion. Also... I knew his words had been spoken out of anger, a reaction to being exposed. And I would give him some leeway—and try to put myself in his shoes as much as possible—because he was helping us find our way back to civilization.

I bit at my lip for a second. "Tuck...listen. I... I understand why you might have done what you did. It must be hard, not having any money. No direction..." Was that how he felt? I didn't want to put words in his mouth, but I also wanted to let him know that despite what I had learned about him, I appreciated that he was helping us now. "But you understand why I can't have you working for me anymore, right?"

His expression didn't shift, but I felt the weight of his stare, and for some reason, I felt guilty. I dismissed the feeling. How many chances did one person get? I wasn't the one who'd messed up. "Sure, Emily."

I stared, a heavy sinking feeling in my stomach. He didn't care at all. Who had he become?

I suddenly wondered if he'd taken a moment to hunt for those little baggies among the mess inside the plane. Were they in his duffel bag now? He'd need the money they'd bring in more than ever now, wouldn't he? Well. That was no longer my business.

He went back to sharpening the stick, obviously not interested in any further conversation. I sighed, glancing up at the glowing orb overhead. The sky was streaked in shades of gray, from dark to platinum, and though it was somewhat eerie, it was also incredibly beautiful and made our surroundings surprisingly light. Had the moon always been this luminous? Had the city lights dimmed it so much for me in recent years? I started lying back down, but pressure on the wound on my flank almost made me yelp. I pressed my lips together to hold it back as I sat up. Tuck's head rose, his gaze meeting mine. "I have to use the bathroom," I squeaked, rising stiffly but quietly, careful not to wake Charlie.

I noticed Tuck's hands halt in their task as I moved past him toward the denser section of trees and brush off to the right. "Don't go far," he said.

I didn't answer. I'd go as far as I wanted. Yes, he was helping us. But he wasn't the boss of me. Truthfully though, I had no interest in going far anyway. I was creeped out and had this odd weight sitting on my chest that felt like it was about more than just the fact that we were basically lost in the wintery wilderness. I just needed to privately investigate this wound that was getting more painful by the hour.

I stepped behind a section of brambly bushes that hid me from view and lowered my pajama bottoms and then unbuttoned my pants, hissing as I peeled them down slightly and the leather scraped over my skin. I'd stuck a pair of ankle socks in my jacket pocket to wear on my hands and I took one out and dabbed at my wound which was now oozing and angry red around the border. *Great. And ick.*

The edge of the seat belt had obviously sliced into me pretty deeply in this spot, but it'd also abraded and burned from my waist to halfway down my ass. I hadn't gotten a good look at the gash as it was in a spot that was difficult to see unless I simultaneously twisted and bent. But even in this dimmer section of woods and from my awkward vantage point, it didn't look good. And dabbing it with a sock was doing nothing except getting small fibers stuck to the open flesh.

Tears pricked my eyes, frustration and fear and sadness and a slew of other emotions hit me all at once as I stood there alone in those cold woods, uselessly attempting to treat my own wound. I straightened as I dropped the sock and brought my hands to my face, giving in to the quiet sobs that racked my body. Maybe I just needed a release. I'd been doing my best to hold my emotions at bay and do what needed to be done since the crash and they simply wouldn't be contained any longer. The sight of that angry wound across my skin had opened the floodgates, in a sense representing some inner part of me as well. Ripped open. Exposed.

"Emily." I jolted, letting out a tiny shriek as I dropped my hands from my face and whipped my head around. Tuck was standing behind me as though he'd materialized out of thin air. His gaze moved from my tear-streaked face down to my rear. "Are you okay?"

"Obviously not! God, you scared me! What the hell? What if I was doing my business?" I said, attempting to calm my racing heart after he'd practically given me a stroke.

He stepped forward, his jaw set. "I could hear you crying. And I could tell you were injured by the way you were moving." He nodded toward my wound. "That doesn't look good."

"No kidding?" I sputtered, swiping at my tears and starting to bring my pants up. "It's the least of my problems right now."

"Not if it gets infected," he said. "Don't move. I'll be right back with something to treat that with."

I crossed my arms over my chest, aware that I was standing still in the woods with my pants pulled down because Tuck had told me to. But the promise of something that might lessen the pain was too tempting to pass up. Tuck was back in thirty seconds with a small first aid kit in his hands, one he'd obviously tossed in that magical duffel bag of his. He set the kit on the ground and knelt down, leaning in and examining me. "It's not so bad you need to cry about it," he murmured as he opened the kit and took out a few items.

"I'm not crying because I'm injured," I snapped, annoyed by his suggestion that I was still a dramatic baby. What I'd said was honest, but I hadn't necessarily planned on admitting it. What did I care if he thought I was crying over my injury? I didn't want to expose myself further to someone who thought I was a *sellout.*

Tuck leaned closer and used a cotton ball soaked in alcohol to clean my wound. I grit my teeth, squeezing my fists as he tossed one cotton ball back in the box and then soaked another.

"Then why? Why the tears?" he asked, and I swore his voice had gentled. I felt Tuck pause in his dabbing as though waiting for my answer and I again wished I'd lied. I wasn't even exactly sure why I was crying and wasn't prepared to discuss it with Tuck of all people. But the woods were dim, the night folded in around us. I was too spent to spin falsehoods.

"It's just…everything. I'm cold and scared and I keep picturing Russell's dead body under those rocks in the middle of nowhere." A shudder moved through me. "His family doesn't even know he's dead." I held back another torrent of tears. I'd been trying so hard not to think of the man who'd welcomed us onto the plane earlier that day, likely expecting to be home for dinner. How could I cry over a cut in my skin when he'd lost his life? When right that moment, someone might be waiting for him and didn't yet know he'd never be home.

Tuck was quiet for a few moments, his hands continuing to attend to my gash. "I know," he finally said. "It's a lot to handle. When we get to a phone, we'll notify the authorities about Russell and send someone to pick up his body. It's the best we can do for him, Em."

Em. "So you're sure we can find our way to civilization?"

"Yes. I am."

My shoulders lowered, that invisible weight lessening just a little at the confidence in his voice. I believed him, not only because he'd sounded sure, but because he'd known enough to collect food and water and medical supplies while Charlie and I had stood there watching him with our mouths hanging open. Useless.

He turned me slightly with light pressure on my hip as he assessed the abraded skin, and I took in a shaky breath. Despite the issues between us, just being cared for was making me feel better, and I appreciated that he'd been willing to put that stuff aside, at least temporarily. He let out a small grunt as though satisfied that the gash he was cleaning was the worst of it.

"So, I guess this makes you the resident medic now, huh?" I asked, shooting him a small smile to let him know I appreciated what he was doing. And also, to distract myself from the weird bubbles popping between my ribs at the feel of his warm, calloused fingertips running over my hip.

"Hardly," he said, looking back down and giving the wound one more swipe. "Although I did used to read lots of veterinary medicine books when I was a kid," he said, his gaze rising to meet mine again.

I let out a surprised laugh when I saw a glint of amusement in his eyes. "Are you comparing me to a horse now too?"

He gave me a small tilt of his lips and his fingertips exerted the barest bit of increased pressure. "Not even close," he murmured. The moment stretched as our gazes held, one of his hands still on my lower back where he'd held me steady as he'd treated the wound. He released a breath, looking away as his hand dropped. My smile faded. I immediately missed the warmth of his palm on my skin and the way that, for a moment, I'd felt held together by his touch in some way I couldn't describe. And I felt strangely rejected too. I gave my head a miniscule shake. That, however, was a ridiculous thought. There was no rejecting going on because there was no offer. Quite the opposite, in fact. "You always did have a book," I said. *You and your damn books.*

"Some things never change." He reached for a tube of oint-ment or cream or whatever was contained in the emergency kit.

Some things never change.

But others alter drastically. *Like you.*

So why did I suddenly feel unsure of that? Why did he con-fuse me so much? Still?

Because everything is on shaky ground right now. Nothing is cer-tain. Of course you're confused and off-kilter.

And the moon is strange, its pearly glow filtering through the trees and making this moment feel like the vestige of a dream.

As though he'd heard my inner turmoil, or maybe felt it too, he glanced up quickly before focusing back on dabbing the cream on my wound and spreading it over the red outer por-tion. I watched his hand as it moved over that small section of my body and a shiver went down my spine. I tried not to react physically but saw his eyelids flutter as goose bumps broke out on my skin. The skin he was currently up close and personal with. "Does it hurt?" he asked, and I released a silent breath of relief that he'd assumed my reaction had to do with pain and not... *What, Emily? What did that reaction have to do with?*

"No," I said, the word emerging in a rush, the volume not quite appropriate for the lack of distance between us and the quiet of the night. I pulled in a deep breath and let it out. "I mean, a little. But it's manageable."

He tipped his head back and our eyes met again, and for a moment, he looked confused too and...almost vulnerable. My breath caught. *What are you thinking?* I wanted to know. I'd al-ways wanted to know, and with Tuck, I'd never figured out how to ask so that he'd answer me honestly. He'd always been so secretive, held his emotions so close to the vest whereas I'd worn mine on my sleeve—and belted them out using the songs I sang. The ones that were usually about him. *God.* I hated thinking about that. I hated it. Especially now when I had to rely on him in so many ways.

Especially now, after he'd disappointed me so deeply. All those drugs...

And yet still, our eyes held.

"Emily—" Charlie suddenly appeared over Tuck's shoulder, and I gave a small jolt as Tuck turned his way. Charlie's gaze went from Tuck to me, down to the exposed wound. "What's going on?" he asked, his tone suspicious.

I started to pull my pants up as though we'd been caught doing something salacious but halted before I got antibiotic cream all over my clothes. But I did hold my hand in front of the sore, so Charlie didn't have a good view. "Tuck was helping me treat my wound," I said. "It might be infected."

"You should have told me," Charlie said. "Does it hurt?"

"No. It's fine."

Tuck picked up a bandage and stood. He started to turn to Charlie to, I assumed, give him the bandage so he could finish the job, but I stopped him before he did. "I'll take that," I said. Truthfully, I didn't want Charlie to see it, because I could just picture the way his face would scrunch up with distaste like it'd done as he'd glanced at Russell's dead body.

Or the way I'd seen it do when he got any small injury.

Charlie wasn't good at keeping his reactions at bay. Part of his job was using his face to express his emotions, and so maybe he had a hard time turning that off. In any case, I preferred to keep my oozing sores away from him.

Tuck turned back toward me, hesitated, but then put the bandage in my outstretched hand. He seemed careful not to touch me. "Make sure to cover the whole thing," he said. "And reapply the cream and change the dressing every few hours." He nodded down to the medical kit.

"What do we owe you, doc?" Charlie asked as I unwrapped the bandage and removed the surgical tape.

Tuck gave Charlie that unimpressed, thin-lipped look again, obviously choosing to ignore the rhetorical question.

I quickly secured the bandage with two pieces of tape and then gingerly pulled my bottoms back up before Charlie and I followed Tuck to the tree where we were camping. I lay down next to Charlie and Tuck retook his position against the tree trunk. My wound felt better, but my inner turmoil increased. I scooted closer to Charlie, my brain buzzing with questions of what the next day would bring. And the day after that... The moon shimmered, the hoot of an owl sounded, wind whistled, and eventually, the soft sound of Tuck's carving lulled me into a restless sleep.

Day Two

The morning dawned clear and crisp, a few snowflakes swirling in the air, but not sticking to the ground. Just like the evening before, Charlie and I trekked behind Tuck, holding our respective baggage.

Unlike the day before, however, we had a goal, a destination, and that gave me a renewed burst of energy. The smoke had been visible again this morning, which meant there was warmth ahead. And electricity. We would use their phone and call for help. I could be in a hotel room basking in a hot bath with a glass of wine in my hand...well, *soon*. It was going to be the best bath of my entire life.

The forest became dense, but I could still catch glimpses of the sunrise, the sky painted in shades of orange, from deep pumpkin to pale tangerine, all bleeding together. It was magnificent, even under the cover of trees, and made the woods around us glow with this ethereal light.

The woods grew ever thicker, and though the sun was still rising in the sky, the farther we walked into the forest, the dimmer it got. There was no way to track time now without either a working phone or the ability to see the position of the sun. The only measure that we'd walked for hours and hours was the pain of my muscles, and the number of blisters I could feel forming on my feet. And we could no longer see the smoke from this lower ground. "Are you sure we're going in the right direction?" I whispered to Tuck, not exactly certain why I'd lowered my voice. He'd begun walking much more slowly since the visibility had decreased, so it was easier to keep up with him. I realized how right he'd been about waiting until we had at least a little light to travel through these woods.

"Yeah," he said. "Pretty sure."

Pretty sure. "What are you basing that on?" I asked. Because I was all turned around, and it definitely seemed like we'd passed that exact tree an hour before.

"Emily. If you want to head in a different direction, no one's stopping you."

Charlie swung his suitcase to his other hand, and it hit the side of my thigh for the ten millionth time, and I barely held back a hissed curse. He was going to treat me to the biggest and most expensive steak dinner to make up for what had to be a massive bruise as soon as we got back to civilization. Champagne too. And a flaming Baked Alaska for dessert. We'd laugh as we fed spoonfuls to each other. I'd try my best not to choke him with it.

"You should ditch those," Tuck said, stepping over a rotting log.

I snapped back to reality. "Ditch what? Our suitcases?" Charlie and I exchanged a wide-eyed look.

"Yeah," Tuck said. "Keep a few warm pieces of clothing around your neck and ditch the rest of it. I doubt there's anything useful in there, even if we end up having to spend the night in the woods again."

"My shoes are in here," I sputtered. Did he have any clue

how expensive a pair of Louboutins were? "And some jewelry too. I can't just ditch it all in the woods."

He was quiet a moment. "Put the jewelry in your pockets, then. Leave the rest."

"You're talking like we're going to be walking for days. There's help up ahead. We saw it," I said, and even I heard the plea in my tone.

"It's hard to say how far ahead that smoke was. But even if we make it there before the sun sets, what's the point of struggling for a few pairs of shoes?"

"Maybe Tuck has a point," Charlie said, surprising me. I whipped my head toward him as he set his suitcase down. "I can easily replace all of this," Charlie said, nodding at his luggage. I didn't miss the small glance he then aimed at Tuck's worn duffel bag, the message clear: *unlike him.* "Why waste the effort over some clothes and shoes I can just buy again? Let's leave this stuff here."

"But…this is a Louis Vuitton suitcase," I said, tightening my arms around the designer luggage I was carrying, the one that seemed to get heavier by the footstep. I realized how materialistic I sounded, but the suitcase was one of the first things I'd bought after signing my record deal. I'd been so proud to walk into that store on Rodeo Drive. The luggage purchase was a tangible sign of my hard work and success. Every time I looked at it, it reminded me that I'd *made* it. I'd already left several of my other hard-earned designer items behind, and now I was being asked to abandon the last of them in a cold forest where rodents would probably come to nest?

Charlie had opened his suitcase and was removing several items of clothes and draping them around his neck. "Babe, you know I can buy you another Louis," Charlie said, kicking his suitcase aside and giving me a charming smile. "Heck, I'll buy you the whole store. We'll go on a shopping spree to celebrate this ordeal being over. We'll sip Champagne and give my credit card a workout."

"I'm suddenly glad I don't have anything in my stomach," Tuck said, beginning to turn.

Charlie's head snapped up and he glared at Tuck. "Watch your tone when you talk to us."

Tuck stopped, turning back, a muscle tightening in his jaw. "I'll use any tone I damn well please," he said, his voice low and even, locking eyes with Charlie.

My heart doubled in speed at the look on his face right before he turned again and began walking. That was a side of Tuck I hadn't seen. That was the *don't fuck with me* Tuck, maybe the one he'd developed while locked in a cage with other more dangerous men. And why it made me slightly breathless I didn't know and didn't want to think about. "Cut it out, guys," I said, clutching my suitcase and moving past Charlie. "Let's just find that house, or campground, or whatever and—"

"There it is," Tuck said, stopping. "Right through the trees."

Excitement made me want to run toward the house and the muted light it was casting through the thick wall of pines. Was that the sound of…chickens? Yes, I thought it was. If there were chickens, there were people who tended chickens. People who had *eggs*. And hopefully some cheese too. Coffee would be *fantastic*.

"Let's go," I whispered.

Tuck nodded but held his arm out. "We will," he said. "But I want to check it out first. You stay here."

"I'll come with you," Charlie whispered.

"I'd prefer you didn't."

"If there are people inside, and the light says there are, they'll recognize me," Charlie said. "I'm a ticket inside any door in America."

Tuck was facing the other direction, so I couldn't see his eye roll, but I swore I heard it. "You're also a prime robbery victim if the people inside are so inclined," Tuck pointed out. "I've been considering taking you for ransom myself."

"What?"

Tuck ignored him, inching a few more steps forward. He'd been joking about the ransom. But he wasn't wrong about Charlie—and me for that matter—being vulnerable to robbery should we stumble across the wrong people. Despite the strange combination of clothing I'd been forced to wear to keep warm, our attire was clearly expensive, and I was currently cradling a very high-end suitcase.

Charlie and I watched as Tuck carefully removed his duffel bag, set it on the ground, and then moved slowly and stealthily toward the break in the trees where the light was shining through.

He stopped, and then reached up slowly and moved a tree bough, before leaning forward. Through the larger gap, I could see the edge of concrete on the ground. A driveway?

Tuck let out a heavy exhale, dropping the branches back into place and turning toward us. "It's not a house," he said.

My heart plummeted, and I walked to join him. "What? No. What is it?" I'd take any kind of shelter at the moment. Any kind of *civilization*.

Charlie came up next to me and Tuck glanced at both of us before stepping through the trees. We followed, the flock of birds I'd made myself believe sounded like chickens rising into the sky in a sudden flap of wings. "It's a substation," Tuck murmured, walking forward. "Or it was."

I blinked, looking around at the smoldering equipment that had been surrounded by a chain-link fence that now lay charred on the ground. "A substation?" I asked, a lump of deep disappointment settling in my gut. No house. No electricity. No shower. No chickens. No eggs or coffee. Just a smoldering pile of metal and concrete. I felt like crying.

"This was probably one of the fires we saw from the sky."

His eyes met mine. "There were lots of fires burning though," he said, his expression deeply troubled. It startled me because Tuck rarely looked troubled. Even in extreme situations like running back into a plane to collect valuables, he'd appeared nothing but completely resolute.

"What does that mean?" I asked.

"I don't know exactly." He paused. "Except that there's no way this didn't affect the electricity in this area. It must be down for miles around." He moved forward. "The one silver lining," he murmured, nodding to a dirt road, "is that that road has to lead somewhere."

sixteen

Tuck

"That road might go on for thirty miles," Charlie whined. "What the hell do we do now?"

I didn't attempt to provide an answer, instead turning my back and taking a slow walk around the station that had once been part of the electrical grid.

This situation disturbed me. I considered what it might mean. What if instead of an electric storm, some other, more monumental natural event had occurred that brought down our plane? The lightning might have been a result, not the originating factor. And then whatever it was also hit a bigger station in these parts and then spread? Were substations connected? I thought I'd read somewhere that they were, but I didn't know exactly how. What if this had been caused by a...meteor or a comet or something? I glanced up. Because the sky was still *off* and it had been since we'd crashed, streaky and strange-colored which had to mean something. Or was this targeted?

Some type of bomb or attack? Jesus, for all I knew, we were at war right now.

Maybe we'd emerge somewhere and immediately be drafted. At least then I'd have some direction.

Stop. Stop being dramatic and full of self-pity.

The truth was accidents happened all the time that sparked localized catastrophes. My mind was spinning, attempting to work through what I knew so far. But at this point, I could only guess.

"What are you thinking?" Emily asked, coming up beside me.

My guard went up, slamming into place. "What do you care what I'm thinking?" I blurted as though she'd read my secret, pitiful thoughts about the backward direction of my life.

Her head turned toward me as she blinked, and I was pretty sure I saw hurt mixed in with the confusion in her expression. But then she pulled her shoulders back and held her head higher. "I was only asking if you had any ideas about what might have happened to this place," she said. "I'm standing here too, Tuck, among the ashes. The least you can do is talk to me." Her voice shook on the final few words, and she whipped her head forward again so I could only see her profile.

The least *I* could do? *The least you could do is give me the benefit of the doubt over Charlie.* But why should she in all honesty? My life choices hadn't exactly made it easy to trust my judgment. I let out a slow breath. Whether I was justified in my bitterness toward her or not, I didn't have to be rude. I'd already determined that I owed it to her parents to get her to safety, and since that was my decision, I could act cordial until then. Emily and I were at odds, but she also surprised me sometimes with her depth of feeling, like the night before when she'd stood crying in the woods over Russell's death. As I'd cared for her wound, the moment had felt…almost intimate and maybe I was extra irritated because I wanted to stay mad at her, but there were these times where protectiveness and affection and unwanted emotions regarding Emily snuck up on me. And some part of me welcomed it. But another part wanted to growl with frustration.

I glanced over my shoulder to see Charlie with his phone raised to the sky again, walking in circles. I almost rolled my eyes. He hadn't even gotten it to turn on. How was raising it to the sky going to do anything? But...hell, it couldn't hurt to keep trying. Maybe the dirtbag would end up getting reception somewhere along the way and have the last laugh.

In this case, I hoped he would.

I turned back to Emily, who was staring out at the dirt road in front of us and the sky that stretched beyond. I seriously hoped Charlie wasn't right about this road going on for thirty miles—or more—but it was definitely possible. I didn't see any tire tracks whatsoever, so either weather had erased them, or no one came out here very often at all.

It was well into the evening now and though the vibrancy of the sky had dulled, the orange hue still remained, just like the day before. I'd never seen anything like it, and it kept making me wonder if my internal clock was off. The moon had been different too, unusually bright so that the nighttime hours seemed like eternal dawn. "I don't know what to think about what happened—" I waved my hand around "—here or to our plane. I'm not even sure they're connected, although...it'd be a big damn coincidence if they weren't."

"Any guesses at all?"

I shrugged. "I thought about an electric storm, or something bigger like a meteor that worked to alter the weather in some way."

"The sky *is*...odd," she said, voicing the same thought I'd had. "It's like a forever sunrise." *Eternal dawn. Forever sunrise.* Despite the somewhat romantic wording, a strange chill wound through me. I didn't like the idea of the sky remaining in any state permanently. It meant the natural order of things had been severely interrupted at the very least. By *what* was the question.

"I also considered an attack of some sort."

"Like a bomb?" she asked, eyes widening as her lips formed an O. I looked at her, taking her in more closely. The full face of makeup she'd been wearing had started rubbing off and one of her false lash strips was sort of hanging crookedly. "What?" she asked, obviously noting my gaze not moving from that spidery-looking thing clinging to her eyelid.

"Your lash..." I said, tipping my chin toward it. "It's coming off."

She went sort of cross-eyed as she tried to look at it, color rising in her cheeks. She reached up and used two fingers to try to straighten it. Instead, it stuck to her fingers when she pulled them away. Her lips thinned, and she looked briefly angry, and a little embarrassed. She huffed out a small breath and then removed it entirely and then peeled the other one off as well, tossed them both on the ground and then brushed her hands together as though she'd just won a mini battle and was proud of the achievement. My lip quirked against my will. What was it about this damn woman that had my emotions swinging so dramatically moment by moment? And why, despite my best efforts, was I still thinking about the feel of her satiny skin beneath my fingertips?

I cleared my throat, moving my mind back to her question about a bomb. "We won't have any way of knowing what happened until we make it somewhere."

She nodded slowly. "Where do you think it goes?" Emily asked, pointing out to the road.

"There's only one way to find out," I said. I dropped my duffel bag on the ground. "But not tonight."

"What? We're going to camp here?" she asked, her voice rising into a whine.

"I'm not walking into anything unprepared in the dark,"

I said. "We have a road in front of us now, and all roads lead somewhere. But it's warm here from the residual fire, and so we might as well take advantage of it."

She sighed and turned her head, her eyes meeting mine. "All we have left are a couple packs of crackers. And some chocolate."

"It'll do. We still have water, which is the most important thing. We'll start out fresh at first light."

"More walking," she said. "How far do you think?"

"I don't possess an internal map, Emily," I said. "I'm just going with my gut."

"Oh, your gut. Great."

My jaw tensed at the insinuation that my gut was less than trustworthy. Again though, maybe she wasn't wrong—if the state of my life was any indication—so I chose to bite my tongue.

She glanced back at Charlie still doing his little circle-dance and then gestured to the remains of the station. "This is a power station, right? But our phones should have satellite service. So it must mean our phones just aren't working. Unless the satellites are down too?"

Or both. I squinted up at the sky as though I'd be able to see one of the satellites she spoke of. Because we might be too far out in the wilderness right now but the phones should at least turn on. I was beginning to think that whatever had affected the plane, had affected a lot more. "There's no way to tell right now," I said.

Charlie came up beside Emily, stuffing his phone in his pocket and taking her suitcase from her so he could place it on the ground and sit on it. I saw the irritation flash in her eyes as she watched him and stifled the laugh that threatened. The weird thing was, he didn't seem to notice her emotions or reactions. Or maybe he just didn't care.

Not my problem.

He scooted over slightly and patted the suitcase in invitation, and she let out a breath on a smile, perching herself next to him as best she could. I turned away. Those two deserved each other, and they could curl up together with their useless designer shit.

I needed to start turning my attention to myself because the road in front of us led to the destination where the three of us would part ways. I had an actual visual of the beginning of the end of this unpleasant threesome.

seventeen

Emily

Day Three

Once again, we set out at the break of dawn. I'd actually slept decently next to the smoldering substation that cast off enough heat to ward off the winter night chill. That and my exhaustion had meant I hadn't stirred and for that I was grateful.

There was also a buzz of hopefulness inside because of the fact that we were setting off on a road. A road that, like Tuck said, led somewhere, and I hoped to God that somewhere arrived quickly. I wasn't sure how many more blisters I could sustain and still walk. My slippers and socks were brown from the mud and dirt we'd been trampling through, but I refused to utter a word about the state of my feet and allow Tuck to look at me like I was the greatest burden that had ever been foisted on his broad shoulders.

We shared the last pack of almonds and then Charlie and I

fell in line behind Tuck. The sky was again cast in tangerine the way it had been the day before and gave off that same hazy glow that was both beautiful and bizarre. *Haunting.*

I hefted my suitcase higher, attempting to rest some of the weight on the front of my hip without disturbing my bandaged wound. "Here, babe, I'll carry that," Charlie said. I resisted, but not overly much because, God, it really was heavy and cumbersome and when Charlie took it, I sighed with relief. But when he transferred it to his other hand, I caught the fleeting expression of annoyance.

We continued walking, my guilt increasing with every step. Because what was the point of holding on to something that was supposed to represent independence, if it was causing my boyfriend to have to suffer under the weight? How was *that* independent? How did that signify girl power? *You're a sellout.* And how long were Tuck's angry words about me lacking talent going to repeat in my mind?

I stopped and so did Charlie, allowing me to grab the suitcase from his hand. "You know what? Fuck it," I said, as I tossed it to the side of the road. "I can replace my stuff too. And I'm sick to death of lugging that stupid thing along."

I brushed my hands together and began marching forward, Charlie caught up and slung his arm around me. "Being rich is freeing, right? Like I said, when we get back to LA, we'll go on a shopping spree."

"Sounds dreamy."

Tuck had stopped and turned toward us when I'd chucked the luggage. Before he turned back, he pressed his lips together, and I swore I saw a tiny flicker of amusement move over his expression. *Laugh if you will, Tuck. I'll show you. I'll show everyone.* I had beat all the odds so far and I'd continue to do so.

We traveled, and walked, and walked some more. The sun rose higher, a yellow swath across the orange sky. At some point we ran out of water and so we stopped and gathered snow in our water bottles and then pressed the plastic against our bodies as we walked to melt it.

As I trailed Tuck, my mind roamed freely. And it was the weirdest thing because I realized that my mind hadn't done that in...well, probably *years*. It was a sort of panicky sensation not to have anything to reel me back in. I kept reaching for my phone to distract myself, and each time I looked at its blank screen, a trill of fear would vibrate inside me. I saw Charlie doing the same thing, patting his pocket intermittently and then flinching.

The lack of search engines, and online maps, and the ability to call for help made it clear that, at the moment, the only things I could count on were the strong lines of Tuck's body moving smoothly in front of me, leading the way.

Tuck looked back at me, and I realized suddenly that I was humming, snippets of song lyrics weaving through my brain, arranging and rearranging and then forming tunes. I went quiet.

"I've gotta take a leak," Charlie said. I halted too and he stepped off the road and walked toward the woods. Tuck, just a few feet ahead, looked back and then came to a stop as well, opening his backpack and removing a bottle of water and taking a long swallow. I walked the short distance to him, honestly surprised he'd stopped. Over the past few days, he'd kept walking each time we'd needed a bathroom break and we'd had to hurry to catch up. We'd been walking for what *had* to be close to three hours now, and perhaps even Tuck needed a break once in a while. "You used to hum like that during those harvest mornings," Tuck said, his gaze focused on his hand screwing the cap back on.

For a second, I was confused, but then his words brought forth a memory, the picture blooming so suddenly and so vividly that I swore the scent of orange blossoms infused the winter air. The workers at our grove had risen at the crack of dawn to avoid the heat of the day, and so had we, running outside in shorts and bare feet, with bedhead and sleep grains still stuck in our eyelashes. The oranges were so fragrant. If I closed my eyes, I could feel one in my palm, heavy with ripeness, and hear the small snap as it broke from the branch. It'd felt like a gift, the way the tree had so easily let go of its fruit with only the smallest twist of my wrist. A blessing. "I did?" I asked. I'd hummed as I'd picked? I didn't remember that.

Tuck nodded and then took another swig from his bottle.

I tilted my head. I remembered the picking. I remembered following along behind Tuck. But I didn't remember humming. It was because my mind had been free to roam, I imagined, like it was now, my body moving from tree to tree, reaching and plucking, reaching and plucking. Daydreaming as I worked. I wondered if that was when I'd first started composing "Find You in the Dark"—the melody, if not the lyrics—which became the single that had catapulted my career into the stratosphere. Because the thing was, when I wrote that song, and the others on the album too, they'd all felt so effortless, like they'd lived inside me all my life, and had just been waiting to be set free.

They could have picked up any pretty girl off the street and created Nova. *They didn't need talent. They needed compliance.*

I sucked in a breath, once again shoving aside the words Tuck had volleyed at me on the plane. He'd said them out of resentment at being exposed. The problem was…they hit hard because it was a vulnerability. He must have known that and that's why he'd said it. To hurt me back.

I hadn't written anything nearly as inspired since "Find You in the Dark." My *deepest* fear, the one I didn't like to think about, was that that was all I had. The well had run dry. I was a one-hit wonder and nothing more.

Maybe it was why I pushed myself so hard to milk every drop I could from all the recent opportunities I'd been given. Because there wouldn't be more after this. The Louis Vuitton I'd tossed aside really was the last luxury item I'd ever own, the final sign of my once shooting star that had fizzled to the ground. A part of me wanted to run back and snatch that suit-case from whatever animal was now burrowed inside of it.

A void opened inside me as words attached to the fear that had been skating at the edge of my brain for years, the one I'd refused to *really* think about. The one Tuck had clearly seen and thrown at me.

I massaged my temples and looked at Tuck. He was watch-ing me, a look of curiosity on his face as though he was mes-merized by the shifting nature of my thoughts. He'd noticed I was humming too, and *I* hadn't even realized until Tuck had mentioned it. A cascade of emotions tumbled through me: bit-terness, fear, happiness, uncertainty, hope. I couldn't grasp any of them, because they were all fleeting, and I didn't know what to attach them to.

I cleared my throat and looked away briefly. There was no need to think about any of this now, during this harrowing, yet temporary circumstance. "What do you think it's going to be like when we get to civilization?" I asked.

He paused for a moment. "No idea. It'll depend on how far the outage stretched and whether their infrastructure is back up. But they'll at least have some information about what's going on and how long before things are expected to be working again."

Before I could respond, Charlie came stomping noisily out of the woods and breaking me from my worried thoughts. "Goddammit," he said. "I think I fell in some poison oak." He was wiping his hands off, his jacket covered in dirt and pieces of brush.

"I'm sure it wasn't poison oak." Charlie had never com-muned with nature—he probably had no idea what poison oak even looked like. He'd grown up in Bel Air. "Are you okay?"

"Yeah. I'm fine. Let's go." I plucked a piece of leaf out of his hair before we both turned back to the road.

Tuck was already walking. We fell in line behind him just as we had before, continuing down the dirt road.

Eventually the dirt road turned into a stretch of gravel, which seemed like a good sign even if the only thing surrounding us were derelict fields. But as day turned to evening, Tuck slowed, and then came to a stop. I shielded my eyes from the bright horizon, squinting as something up ahead caught my eye and I saw why he'd halted. "Holy shit, it's a gas station," I said. My heart lurched toward that beautiful beacon of hope. And of people. And even one of those gas station sandwiches that I would have never touched with a ten-foot pole a week ago. But now...now, I was going to devour every bite of it and lick the wrapper. I'd kiss it before I put it in my mouth. I'd say a prayer of gratitude. Then I'd buy a bottle of cold water and drink every drop. They might have shoes there. Those canvas ones that hang on a rack near the ball caps and playing cards. Neosporin!

"Oh my God, Tylenol," I almost sobbed.

We all started walking again more quickly than before. We turned onto the paved road that led to the gas station a quarter mile or so up ahead, and I never thought I'd be so excited about asphalt, but I was. Oh, I was. I grabbed Charlie's arm. "We did it," I said. "We made it, Charlie. The nightmare is over."

He grinned at me, but then took out his phone and raised it to the sky as had been his habit since the crash. He was like a man who'd been tossed into the ocean, reaching for an invisible lifeline.

"Don't worry about that," I said. "They'll have a landline there. Or some other way to call for help."

We were hurrying toward that beautiful piece of civilization that would offer a way to reach the outside world. And a toilet! I could pee in a toilet rather than squatting in the woods. "Never again!" I shouted to which Charlie glanced over at me in alarm. I laughed and squeezed his arm again.

A quarter mile felt like twenty as we limped toward our destination, turning onto the paved entryway to the lone gas station. With each step, however, my hope diminished. "It looks closed," Charlie said.

Tuck was already walking slowly, and we caught up to him, all moving at the same pace now. "Maybe the power outage extends all the way here," Tuck murmured. "There could still be people inside. The lights might just be off."

·There was a vehicle sitting in the middle of the road, and Tuck leaned over to look in the window and then stood straight, his head turning toward another car sitting to the side of the road.

"Why are they just sitting there?" I asked, as Charlie and I came to stand next to him, shading my eyes as I looked farther down the road where I could see another car seemingly abandoned near the center as well. It was like all the vehicles that had been traveling on this road had just...stopped. So where were the people? Why hadn't they been towed? It was eerie.

"I don't know," Tuck muttered. "But it makes me think the station might not be open if these cars are just sitting here like this."

"Wouldn't a gas station have a generator though?" I asked. "I mean, usually businesses, especially crucial ones like gas stations, have generators, right?" Charlie looked at me and nodded hopefully. Honestly though? I had no idea who had generators or even how they worked. But it...sounded right.

"Let's just stop guessing and wait and see," Tuck said before he started walking again.

We all stepped into the lot and came to a stop as we looked around. There was an ice machine out front of the tiny store, and a lotto sign in the window that was obviously meant to be lit—but was as dark as the rest of the place.

Tuck started walking first, moving slowly and cautiously as he glanced around like we might be ambushed at any moment. We walked past the singular gas pump and came to stand in front of the store. The sound of the door of the ice machine opening broke the silence and made me startle. I looked over at Charlie, who smiled sheepishly and shrugged his shoulders. "The ice is gone and what's left is mostly melted," he said.

There was a handwritten sign on the door of the store that said, "Sold Out."

"What do you think that means?" I asked but received no answer from either Charlie or Tuck. I cupped my hands against the glass and peered inside, my gaze roaming the small space. "There's nothing in there," I said. The refrigerators along the far wall were empty, as was the case that would have held sandwiches near the register. I wanted to cry.

Worse than that, there was no person manning the register who might have called for help.

"They must have cleared the food out so it wouldn't go bad," Charlie said.

"Or people bought it all," Tuck said, gesturing to the sign again.

"It's just…weird," I said. And I was so disappointed and hungry that I felt like I was going to lose it.

"Let's fill up our water bottles at least," Tuck said as he took his empty bottle from his bag and dipped it into the ice machine that was now a water machine. I was sure the water would be less than clean now that it had been sitting in a metal freezer, but still safer than scooping water out of a stream, and I had finished the last of mine hours ago, so I did as he suggested, drank half the first bottle I scooped, and then refilled it again.

Tuck pointed off through the trees. "Look. I think I see a highway there. It looks like a portion of overpass. See that?"

I squinted in the direction he was pointing, but my eyeballs must have been as tired as the rest of me because I didn't see it. "Come on," he said. "A highway definitely leads somewhere. We're back to civilization. We just have to find someone who can help us make a call now."

My shoulders curled forward. I'd convinced myself this was

the end of our trip out of hell, and I just couldn't go on. I'd done my best. This station was out of fuel and so was I. I couldn't take another step. Tears spilled from my eyes and tracked down my cheeks. Tuck looked at me, his expression blank. "I can't walk anymore. I'm sorry. Just send someone for me. I'll be here."

"You're not staying alone at an abandoned gas station in the middle of who knows where," Tuck said.

My shoulders shook as I gave in to my exhaustion and misery. "I'll wait. I can't move."

"The sun is starting to go down, Emily," Charlie said.

"Yes!" I waved my arm around at the sky that was dimming by the moment. "And still no lights! Anywhere. Look!"

"We'll be able to see better from the highway," Charlie said. "I don't want to walk more either, but it's just ahead. See? There have to be restaurants and hotels and all sorts of businesses close by."

"What if they're all out of power?" I cried. "We've walked for days and the power's out here. It probably is there too. Maybe it's out everywhere. Maybe the whole world is dark." I let out a high-pitched sob. "We were expected in New York *days* ago. You know how tight the schedule was! They've probably replaced me by now."

"No one replaced you, babe," Charlie said. "You're irreplaceable. They know our plane went down. Lots of people will be worried about us. They're probably having a candlelight vigil. Oh my God, we've gotta be front-page news…everywhere." He looked briefly elated as his gaze zoned out somewhere behind me, probably picturing his fans sobbing uncontrollably in social media posts. The whole imagined scenario seemed to perk him up, but all it did was make me more miserable.

The world was dark, and my career was fading by the moment. No one waited around in the music business. Not even for tragedies. Not even for things that weren't your fault. Charlie was established. They wouldn't give up on Charlie. But me? I *was* replaceable. Everything was crumbling. *Everything.*

"For the love of Christ, get it together," Tuck said.

My head came up as anger raced through me. "*You* get it together, you smug asshole."

"I have it together," he said smoothly.

"Do you?"

His eyes flashed, and another bolt of indignation pinballed through my body. How dare he? I'd been miserable for days and I hadn't complained at all, despite being the smallest of the group and wearing improper footwear. I reached down, picked up a handful of gravel and hurled it just because. The resulting sound was soft and scattered and mostly unsatisfying, even if both Tuck and Charlie leaned to the side so as not to get hit by a rogue pebble. "I don't have your muscles and your…stupid long legs," I shouted, waving my arm in the general direction of his sturdy thighs and well-muscled ass I'd been staring at for days now. "But I've been keeping up anyway! And I'm wearing fucking slippers and leather pants!" I practically screeched.

"Are you done?" Tuck asked.

With a loud growl, I elbowed him aside, moved past him, and started marching down the road, Charlie catching up after a moment.

My general rage kept me moving for the next thirty minutes until we made it to the base of an on-ramp at which point I sagged against the guardrail. The sky had turned a gorgeous shade of deep mauve, and despite the dwindling sunlight, not a single light had blinked on over the highway. It was confirmed: we'd walked for miles and miles and were still in the dark.

And beyond that, it was quiet. We were standing right beside a highway, and not a single engine could be heard.

"Damn," Tuck said. "There are cars up there, but they're all stopped, just like the other ones we saw.

"What the fuck is that about?" Charlie asked as we followed

Tuck up the on-ramp to get a closer look. We'd see more from up there. Maybe a hotel... I didn't need power. Just a bed. A pillow. Oh my God, carpet beneath my feet.

Vehicles littered the highway, dark and abandoned like the few we'd passed at the gas station. We stood there, looking in both directions. "Whatever happened disabled all these cars and trucks," Tuck said.

"I saw this movie once where a comet vaporized most of the people on earth," I said. That explanation seemed ludicrous, but then again, this whole situation felt bizarre and inexplicable. What *if*? At this point, I might even be willing to consider aliens.

"This isn't a movie, Emily," Charlie said, gripping the front of his hair and screwing up his face, clearly at risk of having a breakdown too now that we'd arrived at another disappointing location.

"Yes, I'm aware, *Charlie*," I retorted. There wasn't space for both of us to fall apart, but of course, Charlie couldn't abide by that simple, unspoken rule.

"Kids," Tuck warned. "No one got vaporized."

"How do you know?" I demanded.

"Because we'd see their empty clothes where their bodies used to be. I saw that movie too."

"That doesn't make a lot of sense though, right?" I said as he moved around a big rig blocking our way and I shuffled behind him. "I mean, if a comet vaporized human hair, wouldn't it vaporize cotton too?"

He shot me a look and then pointed. I followed his finger to a sign up ahead that told us Springfield was eleven miles away. "Oh," I breathed, even if in that moment, eleven miles felt the same as eleven feet—I could walk neither. Also, which Springfield? I looked from one license plate to another. If these cars were all local, then we were in Illinois. Tuck hesitated for a moment and then climbed up onto the side of the truck, making it to the roof in mere moments. He stood up and peered off into the distance, in the direction where there was apparently a metropolitan area.

It was then that I noticed the logo on the side of the truck we were standing next to. "Charlie," I said, grabbing for his arm and gripping it.

"Ow. What?"

"This truck." I pointed to the large red logo that I'd seen on every box of breakfast cereal I'd eaten growing up. We locked eyes for only a moment before we both headed for the back.

eighteen

Tuck

I craned my neck, trying to see as far as I could from the roof of the big rig I was standing on, but I didn't even see so much as a flickering light. Not one. The power was out for as far as the eye could see. At least now we knew where we were—eleven miles outside Springfield, Illinois. And the highway in front of me was littered with vehicles of all types. Some had made it to the side of the road, but the majority had come to a standstill in the middle of a lane. What in the hell type of event would cause that? This was far from a mere power outage. Of course, our plane practically nose-diving from the sky had clued me in that *something* took place to cause that, as had the fires burning on the ground. But this was even bigger than I imagined. Something much more widespread was going on, and the mild buzz of trepidation that had been rumbling in my gut since we came up on the gas station and the abandoned cars there, intensified.

I hopped down and looked around. Where the hell were Charlie and Emily? I heard some scuffling from the rear of the truck and headed in that direction, stopping when I came upon the two of them. The rear door of the truck was wide-open and a glance inside showed it to be mostly empty except for a few scattered boxes of cereal, two of which Charlie and Emily had snagged and were currently shoveling handfuls into their mouths.

Without ceasing to gorge herself, Emily reached next to her and picked up a third box of cereal and tossed it at me. I caught it and she grinned, her teeth filled with brown cereal flakes and pink dehydrated strawberries. I held back a laugh as she said, "Truce?"

She'd saved me a box. I was momentarily touched. "Slow down," I muttered. "You'll make yourself sick."

Then I tore open the box, tipped my head, and poured the stuff straight into my mouth, trying not to follow Charlie and Emily's leads, but mostly failing. God, I was so hungry I could feel my stomach eating itself. The crunchy cereal and the tart, chalky fruit were so good I moaned, my jaw working to grind the mass quantity of food enough that I could swallow without choking to death.

"Slow down," Emily said with a cheeky smile. "You'll make yourself sick."

"Touché," I conceded as I tossed back another handful. "Good find," I said, nodding to the truck. We'd need some protein eventually, but this "meal" was going to allow us enough energy to make it to our next stop, wherever that might be. I saw movement a little ways down the highway and paused, squinting and craning my neck forward.

"What?" Charlie asked.

"I think I see someone in a car right over there." I pointed, and Emily and Charlie stood, turning in the direction where

I'd seen someone sit up in the driver's seat of a compact car. "I'm gonna go talk to him."

"We'll come," Emily said, brushing the crumbs off her jacket and following me.

We wove through the abandoned vehicles and the man sitting in the car spotted us and gave a small wave, opening his door and getting out. "Hey. Hi." He looked sort of rumpled, like he'd just been sleeping and when I glanced in his vehicle, I saw a few boxes of the same cereal we'd just scored.

"Hi. I'm Tuck." I pointed behind me to where Emily and Charlie were approaching. "That's Emily and Charlie."

"Neil. Hi. Damn, it's good to see a few faces. The last of the folks around me gave up and left yesterday. There might be one or two back that way, but I haven't walked in that direction because there's a pileup and I hear there are bodies." He turned and pointed behind him and drew his shoulders up in a shiver.

"Bodies?" Emily asked. "No, no that can't be true." But the look on her face said that she knew very well that it could be. The three of us might have been casualties of whatever event this was too if Russell hadn't had the skill to land the plane like he did.

But I shook off the thought of Russell. "What do you mean, 'gave up'?" I asked Neil. "Can you tell us what happened? From the beginning. We were in an accident, and it's taken us three days to get here."

"Oh man. Shit. Yeah, uh, I was just driving along when this bright white flash almost made me crash. Other cars veered sideways. Most of us managed to stay on the road, but our cars died. Just…died. All at the same time. After waiting for a couple hours for some help to come, most of the people here decided to walk home. A group of us from out of town walked to the closest exit where there are some businesses, but there was no power there. No one's phones were working either. Luckily, I had a little cash and went to a liquor store in a strip mall and bought some snack food and water and brought it back here. Once the truck driver took off—" he inclined his head toward the now empty cereal truck "—others who were waiting broke into the back and took the product. I was out of food by then, so I did too. There's nothing else to do. That liquor store is boarded up now, but I'd bet that the food and water is all gone and only the liquor remains anyway. Yesterday, people started getting real nervous."

"So, there were people in these cars?" Charlie asked. "They walked away? You saw them?"

Neil looked at him strangely. "Yeah."

Charlie had clearly decided Emily's theory about a people-vaporizing comet had some merit. "And no one you talked to has any guesses about what happened?" I asked as I stepped in front of Charlie.

"No. Some are saying it's just a widespread power outage. Some guy said this happened in Detroit in the two-thousands. Other people say an EMP or a meteor."

"EMP?" Charlie asked. "What's an EMP?"

Neil shrugged. "I don't know. Like a sunspot or something?"

An EMP. What was that? I'd heard the term before. An electromagnetic pulse maybe? That sounded right, but I couldn't recall much more than that.

I looked around at all the abandoned cars. "And in the three days you've been here, there haven't been any police officers or other first responders that have come through?"

"No. Not one. I haven't even heard any sirens from anywhere. I live in Ann Arbor. I'm hundreds of miles from home. It's not like I can just start walking."

I glanced at that empty food truck. "You might have to."

He looked bleakly up the highway. "Seems safer here. The authorities are bound to come. It's not like they can just stop working. I have some food and water so… I'll just wait."

"Okay. Hey, good luck."

He nodded and got back in his car. I saw him pick up the box of cereal next to him before I stepped away from his vehicle.

"Where are you going?" Emily asked as I walked ahead. The stars had blinked to life and soon it'd be too dark to do anything other than hole up and get some rest. I would bet that a number of these cars were still unlocked. It wouldn't be the worst place to sleep.

"There's a tower that way," I said. "See it?"

"What are you going to do? Climb it?" Emily asked. "Oh my God, you would, wouldn't you? Are you out of your mind?"

"No. I want to know how far this outage extends. If it goes all the way to the city of Springfield, then we need to figure out how to get to the next one."

"The next what?"

"The next city."

"You cannot be serious. There is no way in hell I'm walking to *the next city!*"

I turned. "Listen, Emily, I didn't create this situation, okay—"

"What's that smell?" Her face was wrinkled up, and she was sniffing at the air.

I paused. I smelled it too. Death. I turned toward the odor, noticing the remnants of a crash on the road a ways ahead. A tire rim. Some shattered glass. I pointed. "There it is. The pileup Neil mentioned." *Shit.* It was true. There were dead bodies in at least one of those cars. And they were decaying.

"What's going on?" Charlie asked before tossing back a handful of the cereal as he trailed behind us.

"Car crash," Emily said from behind me. "Someone obviously died. Tuck! Come on, let's go back."

But I needed to see. I needed to understand what we were dealing with. Because if the authorities had made the call to leave a slew of abandoned vehicles on the highway for now, because there were more pressing issues in a major blackout, that was one thing. But if there were literal dead bodies rotting in the road for three days, then that was something different entirely.

I began walking and heard Tuck and Emily follow. The crash involved five vehicles in a pileup that occurred when the truck at the front came to a halt, likely after slamming its brakes—though I was no insurance adjuster. The dead woman was in the fifth car, her bloated body slumped over the dashboard, the driver's side door having been torn from the car. Her airbag had clearly not deployed.

I put my forearm over my nose and turned back to Emily and Charlie, who were lingering behind. "Go on back," I said. There was no reason they needed to see this. I paused as my gaze landed on one of the woman's sneakers that had come off during the wreck and was sitting on the floor of the car. I hesitated only briefly before holding my breath, reaching in and grabbing the one shoe and then pulling the other one off the dead woman's foot. "Thanks," I mumbled, feeling foolish for talking to a dead person, but also a little guilty for taking her shoes.

The fact was, however, she didn't need them and Emily did.

Emily and Charlie were standing stoically next to an empty SUV when I approached, holding out the shoes to Emily. "Put these on."

She gave them a look of horror and stepped back. I felt a raindrop hit my cheek, and then another. "I'm not wearing shoes that you took off a corpse," she said, disgust in her tone. "I'm not wearing corpse shoes," she asserted more loudly.

I grit my teeth as several raindrops hit my head and began sliding down my cheeks. I felt irrationally rejected, which was stupid on several levels, but what did she think? That I'd wanted to pull shoes off a dead woman's body for her? "Stop being a baby, Emily." I nodded down to her grimy slippers. "Those things are about to fall off."

"I don't care," she ground out, and now the rain really started coming down, drumming on the roofs of the cars all around us. "That's disgusting and—"

"God, you really have zero survival skills, you know that? I'm surprised you didn't complain there was no milk for your cereal on that truck."

"Who the hell do you think you are anyway?"

I stepped forward. "The guy who got you out of a field in the middle of nowhere to—"

"A deserted fucking highway with a bunch of dead people!" She practically screamed, her voice rising over the pounding rain. She stepped forward too. Her cheeks were flushed, eyelashes glittering with raindrops, shoulders jutted back, and fuck if she wasn't beautiful, and *fuck* if it didn't piss me the hell off. "And now we have to walk again!"

"Yes," I snarled. "We do. So put. The. Fucking. Shoes. On." I held them between us and pushed them against her chest.

We stood toe to toe, staring angrily, both breathing heavily as rain streamed down our skin. Her hands came up and she took the shoes, her eyes narrowed, as she pressed her lips into a thin line and hissed, "I'll never forgive you."

"Likewise," I hissed back.

I felt Charlie's hand on my chest as he pushed us apart. I stepped back and so did Emily, and then I grabbed Charlie's hand and threw it off me.

When the hell had it started raining like this? It was already cold, and now it was freezing, and we were soaking wet. I moved quickly to a nearby black Sedan and was elated to find it unlocked. I slid into the front seat, while behind me, Emily and Charlie were clamoring in the back. Both our doors shut with twin *thwacks*.

I took off my coat and used the inside lining to dry my hair and my pants as best as I could, and I heard them doing the same thing. From behind me, Emily's quiet sobs took up again, mixing with the steady drumbeat of rain and making me feel trapped. It was either get out of the car and get soaked again or sit in here and listen to her crying. When the rain let up, I'd try to find another open car in the immediate vicinity, so I at least had my own space. But for now, I knew it was important to get dry. I was already chilled from removing my jacket and sitting in soggy jeans. "My God. I'm really trapped in a car with these two," I murmured, mostly under my breath.

"Stop acting like you're better than us," Emily muttered from behind me before letting out a soft whimper.

"This isn't about who's better." And that was really what both she and Charlie hated, wasn't it? In many ways, this situation had completely upended our roles. Case in point: I wasn't the one crying because I was wet. "It's about who's most equipped to lead us through this. But if you don't agree, you're welcome to go your own way."

"Quit throwing your help in my face. If you don't want to be here with us, then go! Leave me here in this car on the highway with corpse shoes! You think I haven't survived you leaving me behind before? I'll be *just* fine."

I glanced back to see Charlie peeling her socks off, and got an eyeful of her blistered, bloody feet. "Damn, babe," he said. "These are bad."

I swiveled my head before cringing. *Fuck.* I closed my eyes. I'd figured her feet were hurting, hence the corpse shoes, but I hadn't realized how injured she was. Regret twisted. I dug in my duffel bag and pulled out the first aid kit I'd used on the sore on her hip. That had been far less severe than her feet, and she hadn't had to put pressure on that for miles. I suddenly felt like a total dick. She *had* been in pain but sucking it up, and I hadn't realized it. She'd finally broken down, but not because she was a baby like I'd called her. I handed the kit to Charlie, including an extra pair of my socks. "Put some antibiotic ointment on those blisters and then bandage them up before putting on the dry socks."

He took the items and then I heard the sounds of him attending to her. "You know, Emily," he said quietly, "that comet thing?"

"Yeah," she murmured.

"I know I said we're not in a movie, but maybe we pretend we are. It might sound sorta silly, but if this is all just an acting job, it'll make it easier to handle, you know?"

"I don't know if I can do that," she said.

"You can. You have me here to play your hero, okay?"

She sighed. "Okay."

Charlie nudged my shoulder and I turned to see him handing the kit back. I took it and put it away and then glanced back at them to see him holding Emily in his arms and stroking her hair. I turned quickly, facing the rain-streaked windshield, a feeling settling in my stomach that I refused to name. I was exhausted. I just needed a night of sleep in a dry car where we were relatively safe, and I'd be ready to problem-solve again in the morning. I closed my eyes, finally lulled by the rainfall into a fitful slumber.

nineteen

Emily

Day Four

I woke alone, sitting up gingerly and groaning as my sore muscles protested my odd sleeping position in the cramped back seat of someone else's car. The sun hit my eyes and I squinted as I climbed out to see Charlie and Tuck walking toward me. "Where were you guys?"

"Searching the vehicles. A lot of them are unlocked. When the comet hit and the drivers—" Charlie gave me a pointed look "—dissolved, they obviously couldn't lock their doors," he said, delivering the line smoothly like the professional actor he was.

He continued to stare at me when I didn't respond. Finally, I shook my head. "Yeah, no, I'm not going to be able to do that." Playing make-believe in this situation was going to be more work than anything and I was too tired and uneasy for that.

Charlie sighed. "It was worth a try."

I looked around at the cars. Obviously whatever electrical situation had occurred to cause this mass breakdown also meant they could only be locked manually or not at all.

He grinned, then handed me something from his pocket.

I looked down. "A granola bar?"

"Yup. I had one too."

"I don't have to pretend that you're my hero," I said with a smile before leaning up and kissing his cheek.

Tuck pulled open a car door to our left and rummaged through it for a moment before heading our way. I leaned against the car and stretched before peeling open the granola bar and taking a bite. It was stale and delicious and once I got back home, I was never going to take food for granted again.

"Hey, I gotta go to the bathroom." Charlie pointed off the side of the highway where there were some bushes right before a steep incline. "Be right back."

I nodded just as Tuck made it to where I was standing. "Good thinking about searching the cars," I said, holding up the granola bar before taking another bite.

He looked back over his shoulder. "That dude Neil is gone, and he packed up the last of the cereal."

"Oh. Well, I was sick of that anyway."

Tuck gave me a wry smile before opening the car door, grabbing his duffel bag, and beginning to unload his pockets of the things he'd collected. I spotted beef jerky and protein bars, some candy and a few packs of gum that I really hoped wouldn't become a necessary meal at some point. When he stood again, I wiped my hands on my pants and stuffed the now-empty wrapper in my coat pocket. "What's the plan?"

He stood next to me, leaning against the car like I was. "We set off again. It's all we can do. There will be a point where we'll get some answers and know where exactly to go for help. We just have to keep pushing forward until then. I think it's best, however, if we get off this highway and take more of a back road." He looked around at all the stalled cars, his expression morphing into a worried frown.

My gaze followed his and I wondered if there was more wreckage up ahead...wondered if we'd smell that scent that had told me people had died. A tiny chill made me draw my shoulders up. But while highly upsetting, dead people were no threat to us. "What type of danger are you worried about?"

He met my eyes again. "I don't know, none necessarily. But it's still unclear what happened. I want to be able to see what's in front of me, and what's behind. There are too many parked cars here. I'm thinking it might be best to avoid the city where we already know the power's out and look for a smaller suburb. Or anywhere we can tell has electricity."

I nodded, squinting in the direction the signage told me was Springfield, wondering what was happening there, and if the people piled up in apartments were helping each other, or... panicking. I felt mildly numb at the thought of more walking, but I knew Tuck was right. Sitting here on this highway full of abandoned cars wasn't going to help us. We had to search for people who were managing this obvious catastrophe, whoever those people were.

At least now I didn't have to do it in tattered slippers. "Thanks for the shoes," I said. I looked over at him and our eyes met, something passing between us that I wasn't sure what to call. It was an understanding, but of what, I couldn't exactly say because it wasn't just one thing. It felt complex and tangled. Then again, how could it not? My emotions for this man had always been deep and convoluted.

"Better?" he asked, glancing down at my feet, and I swore I saw true concern in his eyes.

I shrugged. "Yeah." They were better, and they felt more supported in the sneakers I was now wearing that were mostly my size. But it would take time for the blisters to heal, and more walking wasn't going to accomplish that.

"Hey, by the way," he said. "Not only did we find food in these cars. I found something else." He took a small bottle out of his pocket and handed it to me.

I pulled in a breath. "Tylenol. Oh my God. Oh my God." I looked up at him. "I love you, Tucker Mattice." I grinned, but then it slowly dissolved as we stared at each other, the moment thick with that complex tangle of history and bitterness and other things I just didn't want to think about and served no one. And so I looked away. "Thank you."

He handed me his water, and I took two of the tablets, washing them back and sighing as I recapped the bottle.

Charlie came stomping out of the bushes, and I had to pee, but I'd wait until we were in a spot a little farther away where there was more cover than some brambles. I was also eager to put some distance between me and the dead woman whose shoes I was now wearing. I refused to wonder if there were people at home waiting for her, having no idea that she'd lost her life on this stretch of highway.

It was a couple of hours later as we hiked through a rural area that clearly didn't see a lot of traffic, as indicated by the few broken-down cars in the road, that I heard the very distant rumble of an engine. I stopped, putting my hand on Charlie's arm and meeting his eyes. "Do you hear that?" We'd seen a few people as we'd walked, but they had all been quite a distance away and it was clear they were locals, likely as lost for answers as we were.

"Yeah."

"Tuck!" I yelled. He'd traveled a short distance ahead, but now he stopped and looked back questioningly, and I saw the moment he heard the sound too. He walked quickly back to us and took my arm, pulling me to the side of the road just as a green vehicle came around the bend and started moving toward us.

Tuck stepped out into the road and started waving his arms

and the car came to a rumbly stop before the driver's window was cranked down. A man in a flannel shirt and a ball cap leaned out. "Howdy, folks. Where you headed?"

"California," Tuck said.

The man laughed. "Quite a ways from home, eh? I'm Leonard." He looked beyond Tuck and peered at me and Charlie.

"Tuck. And that's Emily and Charlie."

Charlie stepped forward. "You probably recognize me," he said before running his hand through his hair and offering a large, toothy smile. It faltered, then dipped as Leonard looked at him with zero recognition. Charlie cleared his throat. "I'm an actor," he said. "A...movie star?"

"I don't get to a lot of movies," Leonard said.

"Oh," Charlie said. "Right. Hmm... Well..." He trailed off, obviously at a loss and deciding not to follow up with whatever he was going to say in the wake of Leonard showing absolutely no recognition.

"How is your car running?" Tuck asked. "All we've seen are disabled vehicles. They're all over the highway."

"Not sure, other 'n Bridget here don't got but one electric component in her. I rebuilt the old girl myself, so I should know." He smiled, showing a large gap where one of his teeth was missing, apparently exceedingly proud of Bridget. As well he should be as she was currently the only working vehicle for miles around. Apparently. "Got a buddy whose car works just fine too. A sweet Caddy. Course it's been hard to find roads to drive on with all the broken-down cars and big rigs. It woulda been easier if this thing happened in the middle of the night instead of nearly rush hour."

"Any idea what this thing was?" Tuck asked.

"Few guesses," Leonard said. "But listen, I gotta be goin'. Traveling by night isn't the best idea and I got a trek in front of me."

I eyed his back seat. I could practically feel those soft cushions beneath my rear rather than the asphalt under my blistered feet. I stepped forward. "We can appreciate that, Leonard," I said. "If you'd be so gentlemanly as to give us a lift, we could chat while you drive." I smiled, showing him my teeth, which, even despite all the hardships I'd been through in the last few days, could be counted on to maintain their attractiveness. "I sure would love to hear your theories. Being that you were wise enough to build one of the only cars currently running, I'd imagine your guesses are pretty darn accurate."

He let out a chuff, his cheeks coloring slightly as he looked away. He tapped his steering wheel for a moment before saying, "Aw, what the hell, you look harmless. Hop in and we'll chat. I can't give you a lift all the way to Cali, but barring any blockades, I can get you to Missouri."

I held back my giddy squeal, grabbed Charlie's hand and raced around the other side of the car to get in the back seat before Leonard could change his mind. Oh, sweet heaven. A vehicle. A ride. A break from walking.

Tuck appeared less enthused than me, but he still walked around the front of Leonard's car, eyeing it suspiciously, before climbing into the front seat and pulling the door closed with a loud squeak.

"If we make it somewhere closer than Missouri where the power is on, we can get out there," Tuck said.

"I don't imagine that'll be the case, but okay," Leonard said before he gunned the engine and then took off.

"Is there a reason you're heading to Missouri?" Tuck asked.

"Yup. I'm going to my brother's place. He has a trailer out by a lake. I figure I'll sit this one out."

"This one?"

He glanced over at Tuck. "You realize we might be at war, right?"

"I'd considered it," he murmured.

I leaned forward as Charlie mumbled something about a comet. "You did?" I asked. "You think we're at war? Why?"

"I didn't say I think we're at war," Tuck said. "I said I'd considered it."

"It's worth considering," Leonard said as he avoided a car sitting in the middle of the road. "The government done wargamed this. You wanna know the quickest and easiest way to take over a country? You set off an EMP, right? A real big one high up in the sky using a couple nukes. That high up, they don't affect humans but what they do is shut down the entire grid. Whole country goes dark. Even the majority of generators get knocked out. No gas. No water. Eventually, no food. The attackers simply wait for the majority to die and then they move in and finish the job."

"An EMP. An electromagnetic pulse, right?" Tuck asked.

"Another man we talked to mentioned an EMP as well," I said, worry making my skin feel itchy. But Leonard had to be exaggerating about the rest of it, right? He was clearly more than a little kooky.

"Yup. It's a wave of energy that knocks out grids and other electronics. Musta been powerful as hell, because I'd never heard vehicles would be affected, but here we are." He gave a small laugh and patted Bridget's steering wheel affectionately. He looked over at Tuck. "The thing about warfare like that? It's not bloody. No one has to look a person in the eye and pull a trigger or drop a bomb that means instant death. All you do is launch a missile from some ship out in the sea, straight up into the sky. There's a certain distance from a crime like that, you know? Even though it's one of mass extinction. Because the blast doesn't hurt anyone, it's too far away for that. It's the aftermath that does the damage."

"You think that's what happened?" Tuck asked. "That's your theory?"

"No idea. Like I said, I'm gonna wait this one out at the lake.

Do some ice fishin'. See what's what. If you're smart, you'll do the same."

Tuck glanced back at me. "Our people are farther away than that," he murmured.

Our people. Only what he really meant was my and Charlie's people. Not that my parents didn't care very much for Tuck; I knew my mom had written to him religiously even when he was locked up, though he rarely wrote her back. But old friends—even loyal ones—weren't the same and it suddenly struck me what a kindness he was really doing. He was taking me and Charlie home, but where did that leave him? He had an uncle in LA, but he'd left his house and gone to my family for help when he really needed it. And should I even wonder about Tuck's future plans anyway? He was doing me a kindness, but he'd also betrayed my trust, and put me at risk. And himself. And he was so damn reactive and...ornery. God, he spun my mind around and right now, there were too many other things spinning my mind as well.

"...you gotta do what you gotta do," Leonard was saying when I tuned back in. "What I can tell you is all those minivan moms in their fancy electronic vehicles are shit out of luck." Then he let out a guffaw.

The loud noise made me cringe, and a chill moved over my skin. I glanced at Charlie, but he rolled his eyes and brought his finger to his ear and made a gesture that clearly stated he thought Leonard was less than stable. I gave Charlie a weak smile and looked out the window.

Tuck and Leonard chatted as we drove past farms and exits for what looked like small towns. Several times, Leonard had to pull into a field or section of brush as abandoned cars blocked both lanes of the road we were traveling. And we also saw a few cars heading in the opposite direction, the drivers slowing and peering at us with wide eyes as they moved past.

It seemed obvious that they were out looking for answers,

or maybe supplies, lucky like Leonard that they had never up-graded their old vehicle to something more modern with all the newfangled bells and whistles that had promptly gone kaput right when people really needed them.

God, I sounded like my mom. Those were words she would have used. And with the thought, a swell of grief expanded my lungs and made it difficult to breathe. Was she okay? Were she and my dad safe? Did they have enough food? *Calm down, Em. They're all the way in California. They're fine.* But they were probably worried sick about me. Distraught with no way to get answers because there was no power where I was.

I lay my head on Charlie's shoulder, the rocking of the car lulling me into a fitful sleep where I dreamed of bomb blasts and seas of screaming people. I woke with a start and Tuck looked back at me, his brow dipping as he took me in. Next to me, Charlie let out a soft snore. Then Leonard said something, and Tuck turned around, focusing back on their conversation. I tuned it out as best I could. I was already deeply disturbed by the fallout of this power outage and knew that at least in two cases, it had resulted in death. The shoes currently on my feet were a continual reminder of that. I didn't need to let my mind spin toward war and mass starvation.

From what I'd heard Leonard say to Tuck, a drive that should have taken three hours, had so far taken us closer to five be-cause of the slow nature of having to weave through broken-down traffic that became heavy in some areas. But I was deeply grateful for the ride, and though the lack of working traffic lights all the way from Springfield, Illinois, to the middle of Missouri, told me that we hadn't escaped the power outage, we were closer to home than we'd been.

And I hadn't had to walk.

The rocking of the car made me realize that I hadn't emptied my bladder since right before we'd flagged down his car. "Uh, sir, would it be possible to stop for a short bathroom break at the next convenient spot?"

Leonard glanced in his rearview mirror, and I gave him a smile. "Sure thing. I could use a stretch myself." He drove for a few more minutes until we came upon a wide area on the side of the road that was easy to pull off on.

A section of pine trees provided a spot to find some privacy, and Tuck got out and pulled the seat forward so I could exit too. Next to me, Charlie sat up and yawned. "Bathroom break," I told him. He nodded and followed me from the car.

Charlie and I began heading toward the trees when I looked up to see a man emerge from the brush to my left. My heart seized, and I grabbed for Charlie, both of us stumbling back toward where Tuck was still standing. The man waved the weapon in our direction and then pointed it toward Leonard. "Show your hands and move away from the car," he said.

My pulse spiked, heat blasting under my skin as my gaze darted to Tuck, who was watching the man with narrowed, wary eyes and then to Charlie, whose mouth was hanging open. We all raised our hands and shuffled to the side of the road, Tuck positioning his body so it was mostly in front of me.

"I only want the vehicle," the armed man said as he moved toward Leonard's car. "I got family I need to get to, and I need that car now. Step out," he demanded, and Leonard did, standing slowly and moving around the open door.

"Her name's Bridget," Leonard said. "Rebuilt her myself. Put a lot of time into her." He raised his hand and ran it along the top of the open driver's side door and then leaned against the body. "And a lot of love."

Then before I could even blink, he leaned into the car, stood back up with a rifle, and fired it at the gunman just as the man yelled, "Hey!"

The word was cut off as the man's body jerked. I sucked in a breath that got lodged in my throat as the man's chest blossomed red, his eyes bugging as he made a choking sound, dropping his gun and falling backward to the ground. I let out a scream, and Tuck stepped more fully in front of me. *Oh my God, oh my God. What the hell just happened?* I felt like I was suddenly floating, that heat spreading along my nerve endings, making me feel like I might pass out. *I can't breathe.*

"Which means," Leonard said, staring down at the man who was jerking, blood leaking down his chin, "that I'm not giving her up without a fight."

"You murdered him. Oh my God, you murdered him." Had that been my choked, incredulous voice?

"I saved myself," Leonard said, looking up at me and letting me know that indeed the words had come from my mouth. "And I protected my best girl. You think I was just gonna let this sonabitch rob me?" He waved his rifle in the air. Where had he pulled it from? Under his seat?

The man had stilled now, the front of his jeans dark with urine, blood already spreading far beyond his body.

"Get on back in the car," Leonard said. "We'll take a bathroom break down the road."

"Uh, we, uh…might—" Charlie stammered.

"I think we're good here," Tuck said.

I kept staring, trying to understand what had just happened. It felt like my eyes might bug right out of my head.

"Nah. Get in. We was having a nice time. Don't look at me all scared. I'm not gonna harm any of you unless you're planning on trying to steal Bridget."

Tuck pointed at the sign up the road. "It looks like there's a town close by. This seems like as good a stop as any."

Leonard peered down the road and then shrugged. "Well. I'm not gonna kidnap you. If this is where you wanna get out, fine by me. I still got a ways to go."

He sighed and took the few steps to where the man's handgun had fallen, picked it up, and put it in the back of his jeans.

"I'm gonna take this," he said. "You'd be wise to find yourself a weapon too if possible." He put his rifle back in the car, then he leaned on the doorframe and looked at us. "The world's gonna be different for a while," he said. "You either adapt, or you die." Then he smiled and gave us a salute. "Good luck." We watched as he got in Bridget, pulled back onto the road, and disappeared around the bend.

I let out a squeak, and Tuck's breath released on a whoosh. "What the *fuck*?" Charlie said.

"Should we…" I pointed at the man. My voice was shaking. My whole body was shaking. And I had no idea where to go with that question. Should we what? The man was clearly dead. There was a hole the size of a baseball in his chest, and he was staring blankly at the sky.

"There's nothing to do for him," Tuck confirmed. "Let's get out of here." He looked at me. "Walk off the shakes. It's just adrenaline. You'll be fine in a few minutes."

I gave him a jerky nod. I couldn't even think straight. We'd just watched a man die in front of us. He'd been shot point-blank over a car and now he was dead on the side of the road. What the hell was happening? I couldn't get a grip on this reality I'd suddenly found myself in. I was mentally flailing.

"This is *fucked*," Charlie muttered. He linked his arm with mine and we held each other up as we walked past a sign that told us we were headed toward Silver Creek situated somewhere in a world I no longer recognized.

twenty

Tuck

I glanced back at Emily and Charlie. I was shaken by what had happened, but Emily looked like she was barely hanging on. As much as I wanted to stop and let her come to grips with what she'd just witnessed, I also knew that moving her body was going to help. And unfortunately, even if it was unlikely, taking the time to process also meant risking Leonard returning with his rifle blazing, deciding that three witnesses to the murder he'd just committed was unacceptable. Regardless, Leonard was right on one count—the world had changed in the last four days. And it was only going to get worse the longer the power stayed off.

Charlie took his phone from his pocket and lifted it toward the sky. "Any sign that it's working at all?" I asked. It seemed plausible now that it wasn't just that the power was out, or cell towers were down, or even that satellites weren't working, but that the phone itself was fried just like the hundreds of cars we'd passed by.

Charlie shook his head dejectedly. "No."

We passed another sign for "Silver Creek, Missouri, Population 2,700," and continued in that direction.

I still hadn't gotten used to the quiet. I could hear birdcalls, and the sway of trees, and the shuffle of our feet over the ground. But other than that? Silence. No planes flew overhead, there were no distant engine roars or whatever other sounds I was used to, even in the country. And the sky was still that pale orange color with odd waves of lavender.

"It's weird, isn't it?" I heard Charlie say from behind me. "It's like the whole world fell asleep."

"We know that's not true," Emily murmured. "There are men with guns hiding in the trees."

"Look," I said, pointing ahead, and trying to distract Emily from thoughts of men who might ambush us at any moment. "The town."

We all squinted into the muted sunlight at the distant outlines of a few buildings. There were some signs up ahead as well. "I don't see any…movement at all," I said.

"It looks like a ghost town from here," Charlie noted.

"Maybe that man came here first and killed everyone," Emily suggested.

I gave her a look. "One armed man didn't kill a whole town of people. Come on. We know the power is out. People are probably holed up in their homes, waiting for things to get fixed. It's pretty damn cold out."

"Maybe we'll see more signs of life as we get closer," Charlie said hesitantly.

We walked the remaining quarter of a mile in silence. I kept my ears perked for the hum of an engine, or the laugh of a child, or *something*, but I didn't hear a sound. The fraying of my nerves continued. Charlie and Emily moved closer as we passed through the town limits, the buildings before us sitting dark and seemingly empty of all human life.

There was a small crash that made us all turn quickly toward the sound, and a cat came running from an alleyway, leaped over a short bush, and darted out of sight. Emily brought her hand to her chest, letting out a small, nervous laugh. Charlie released a breath, and I slowly straightened from where I'd braced for some sort of impact, my hand going to the short, whittled stake that I'd made a few days ago and stuck through one of my belt loops.

"Listen," I said, stopping when the sound of what I thought were voices hit my ears.

"People," Charlie said. "There are people up ahead."

We walked another block, the voices getting louder until we saw a drugstore with the door standing open, the heated conversation obviously emanating from there.

We stepped through the doors of the dim store. "It's been four goddamn days," someone said. "My boy needs a new inhaler."

"I understand the situation, Jeb," another man said. "But we don't keep much stock here and even if we did, I can't dispense medication."

"My mom needs her pills," a woman said. "What are we supposed to do?"

We all walked farther inside, and I took in the state of the store. Most of the shelves at the front were bare.

We turned down another aisle—makeup and skin care—and that one was almost completely stocked. And yet the refrigerators along the wall a few aisles over were dark and empty. People had obviously bought—or taken—things in a hurry.

More people started shouting about the items they needed from the pharmacy, voices rising in pitch, obviously scared and desperate.

"Enough!" the man with the deepest voice yelled. "This is

not my doing. My own boy's arm is broken and all we've got is Tylenol. I'm working around the clock to try to keep this town safe, but there are some things that we're going to have to do without."

"Do without, Sheriff? Brent's not gonna die of a broken arm, but that's not true of everyone who needs medication. Doing without some things is a matter of life and death!" a woman said.

We continued through the store, and I looked at a shelf at the end of the aisle that was completely empty of product, only the logos remaining. *Batteries.*

"Lorena, like I said, your mother's medication isn't stocked here, and the last shipment was a week ago. I'm sorry. Jeb, when Kari gets back, I'll ask her if she knows anyone else in town who might have an inhaler to loan you," the man who'd been addressed as "Sheriff" with the deep voice answered.

"When's Kari getting back?"

"I don't know. She's doing what she can at the hospital. Things there aren't good."

"Things here aren't good," someone else said.

As I turned the corner, I saw the group of people gathered near the pharmacy. Like the shelves at the front, the ones back here were virtually empty too. I read the price tags under the barren spaces. *Pain relief. Bandages. Eye care. Vitamins.* All but wiped out.

A man in a sheriff's uniform caught sight of us, his expression registering surprise. "Who are you?" he asked as the others turned to peer at us.

I looked among the people, their worried expressions morphing into curiosity and some wariness.

"Hi," Emily said, beginning to step around me. But I stopped her with a hand on her arm. She glanced down at my hand and gave me an impatient look. I was glad to see that, at least for the moment, she'd shaken off Leonard's showdown. But I wasn't certain yet that that was a good idea. *Leonard* had been a good reminder that societal rules had recently changed. These looked like a group of normal townsfolk with their sheriff, but who knew how they felt about strangers walking into their midst?

I let go of her but stepped in front of both her and Charlie. "My name is Tucker Mattice, and I'm traveling with Charlie Cannon and Emily Swanson," I said, gesturing behind me.

The sheriff stepped forward as well. He was an older man with close-cropped salt-and-pepper hair and a short beard that was more salt than pepper. I noted that the man's hand had gone to the holster on his belt and was now resting there, and that, like me, he'd stepped in front of the people he was with. I held my hand out. He looked at it for a beat before reaching out and shaking. "Sheriff David Goodfellow. Where are you traveling from and why?"

"Sir, if you have a way to reach people—" Charlie started to say, but the man held up his hand, his gaze still on me as he waited for the answer to his question.

"We were in a plane crash," I answered. "It was a three-day walk to the outskirts of Springfield, Illinois. From there we hitched a ride and were dropped off at the exit to Silver Creek."

"Then a man who gave us a ride shot and killed a…a bandit who tried to take his car," Emily blurted. "It was murder. But it was also self-defense so, yeah, we should report that because there's a dead body lying out there near the turnoff to your town."

"Christ," someone muttered from behind the sheriff. "The world has lost its mind."

Sheriff Goodfellow looked at Emily. "I'll have you write out a statement. But there's not a lot I can do right now."

"Okay, well, his name was Leonard and he's driving a green car named Bridget. His brother has a trailer somewhere near a lake in—" she waved her hand backward "—that direction somewhere, and and—" She stopped talking, pulling in a big breath as an older woman came over to her and put a hand on her shoulder.

"Breathe, honey."

Emily sucked in a big breath and nodded as Charlie stepped forward.

"You probably recognize me," he said, glancing around hopefully before running his hand through his hair and offering a large, toothy smile. It faltered, then dipped as the people standing around looked at him with zero recognition. Charlie cleared his throat. "I'm an actor," he said. "A...movie star?" I almost laughed at his timid, questioning voice. Despite the tense situation, I still managed to enjoy seeing him knocked down a few pegs.

"There aren't too many movie theaters out our way," the woman with her hand on Emily's shoulder offered, "but our children might know who you are."

"Oh," Charlie said. "Right. Hmm... Well..." He trailed off, obviously at a loss and deciding not to follow up with whatever he was going to ask for in the wake of absolutely no one recognizing him.

The sheriff addressed me. "Are you the pilot? Of the plane you were on that went down?"

"No. Our pilot was killed."

"I'm sorry to hear that."

I gave a succinct nod, a knot forming in my stomach as it occurred to me that Russell had been the first body we'd seen, but certainly not the only one between that moment and this one. I wondered vaguely if we'd see more death before we reached our destination and hoped to fuck not, but knew it was clear we'd have to be prepared for anything. "We haven't been able to get any cell service, and the power's been out everywhere we've been." I looked around at the people, then back to the sheriff.

The sheriff relaxed his stance. "It sounds like you've been

through a lot. I imagine the stories that are going to come out of this situation will range from interesting to catastrophic."

"I imagine so. Do you know what caused this? We've heard a few theories."

One of the men behind the sheriff took a step forward. "Roger Land, who used to be a science professor at the University of Missouri, thinks it was a solar flare. Others say it was a cyberattack that took our grid offline and knocked out our satellites. Lots of buzz from all directions. No one knows for sure."

"But you're a sheriff," Emily said, coming to stand next to me. "You haven't received any official word?"

"Not a peep," he said. All three of us looked between each other and a whirlwind of unease rippled through the group. That was really bad news. Not only was the grid down, as well as cell phones, but all official channels had been lost?

The woman who'd comforted Emily addressed the sheriff. "Are we meeting at the community center tonight?"

"Tonight, and every night until this is resolved," the sheriff said.

"And Kari's gonna be there so we can ask her about medication?" the woman asked.

"I doubt it," he answered. "But I don't have an update on what it's like at the hospital today."

"Several of the older folks are on medications that are keeping them alive," a young woman interjected.

"And there are a number of diabetics in town too," a man said. "A few of them are kids."

"I know, Harold. We're going to discuss all that tonight and pool what we can until official word comes in, okay?"

Harold gave a frustrated sigh and turned away and the rest of the small crowd began following as they talked amongst themselves.

"Sorry I can't be of more help," the sheriff said, turning his attention back to us. "Unless you need something on these shelves. I can't run the cash register, but folks have been leaving money in an envelope behind the counter and I've been collecting it for the Redmonds, who own the place. They left yesterday to get to their pregnant daughter who's in another part of the state."

I looked around. About the only things left in this store were makeup and magazines. I respected that these people were operating on the honor system so far. It was nice to see after what we'd witnessed just before stepping into this town. "Do you know if there's a sporting goods store anywhere in the area?"

The sheriff had begun walking toward the front and we turned and followed him. "Yeah, there's one off the next exit. But one of our residents rode his bicycle up that way yesterday once enough snow melted to see about buying some ammo, and he came back to say it's completely empty. Not even a pair of sunglasses. Apparently, folks got a little out of hand in a few places."

I hoped that turned out to be true. That their behavior was unwarranted and needlessly *out of hand* and they'd look back and regret panicking.

But it'd been four days. Four days with no official word was *not* good.

We followed the sheriff from the store, stepping out into the chilly but sunny day. The streets were still deserted, even the few people who'd been at the pharmacy were now out of sight. "Why is everyone hiding?" Charlie asked.

"They're not hiding. Just laying low or gathered together at the church or community center. And quite a few, who could, left to be with family in other areas," the sheriff said. "We're not sure what to expect. There's been some buzz on the ham radio about what might have happened, but no official confirmation of any kind. All just guesses at this point. Whatever happened, electrical systems all went haywire."

"Any news from surrounding towns? You mentioned one a few exits from here," I said.

"Other than the short distances a few residents have traveled to and then returned from, no. Like I said, I haven't been able to contact anyone." He looked from one of us to the other, Charlie offering a wide smile when the sheriff's gaze landed on him as though he was waiting to be recognized and his Hollywood grin would make it easier on the man. But the sheriff only offered him a confused frown. "I walked to the main interstate yesterday and saw all the abandoned cars whose electronics are fried. I talked to as many people as I could wave down or were walking. Most were from other areas in the state, all trying to get to family. But one man was right outside Pennsylvania when the lights went out. He said there were mass fires in Pittsburgh, and he barely made it out. He had an old Buick that still worked, and some extra gas in his garage that he took with him but was running low on fuel. From what he told me, all the stations between there and here are closed."

I felt a clunk in my stomach as though something heavy had dropped. "So, it does stretch east." I said, my mind spinning. At least as far as Pennsylvania, but that might mean it also affected states farther than that. I raked a hand through my hair and looked away, not wanting to consider how big this might truly be.

Charlie heaved out a breath, his phone clattering to the ground. "It goes all the way to Pennsylvania?"

"And possibly beyond," the sheriff said.

Charlie brought his hands to his head and gripped his hair. "How the hell is that possible?" He paced one way, then pivoted and took a few steps in the other direction. "No power grid? No satellites? No *phones*? *Anywhere?*" He stopped, gaping down at his phone on the ground. He let out a loud gust of breath and shook his head. "No, no, that can't be right. That's impossible."

We all stared at him for a minute. It was very clearly possible. We had at least some proof, notably the fact that our plane had fallen from the sky, and also, the useless phone currently lying on the ground. Add to that the highway jammed with broken-down cars, the corpses, and the killing we'd witnessed, and you'd think Charlie might have already grasped some reality. He turned and resumed pacing a few feet away.

Emily let out a nervous laugh, her eyes slightly glazed. "That's only the report of one man," she said. "Maybe he got it wrong. Maybe he was lying. Maybe you misunderstood," she said, pointing her finger at the sheriff and then quickly dropping it. He just looked at her, but not with anger. With understanding. He'd clearly been dealing with people having trouble accepting an onslaught of bad news since this had all started.

My heart was speeding, and I felt slightly clammy all of a sudden, despite the cold weather. Mass fires? No gas stations open? Across multiple state lines that we knew about?

"Why no gas?" Emily asked, turning back to the sheriff. "If most vehicles aren't working at all, then why did gas run out so quickly?"

"They can't pump without electricity," I said, turning my gaze back on the sheriff. "So, this outage stretches east at least as far as Pennsylvania, but what about in other directions?"

"I couldn't tell you. I haven't had a lot of time to go out to the highway and I don't feel comfortable being gone for long. My boy broke his arm right after the lights went out—tripped down the damn stairs. There's a hospital twenty miles from here, but even their backup generator is out of commission. They managed to find a couple of working vehicles and moved their critical patients to a hospital a few hours away with a generator that's running. That one will be operational as long as they can acquire gas, but only for critical needs. Even so, it's a total catastrophe there too, from reports I've gotten."

Christ. Who was making the determination about who was

critical and who was not? I didn't even want to think about what was going on in a hospital after days without any electricity whatsoever. How many had already died? "There are no medical personnel in town who could help your son?" I asked.

"They're at the hospital. It's an all-hands-on-deck situation there. Not only do they have the regular patients, many of whom are dependent on machines, to deal with, but there were burn victims from the fires that broke out, and some serious injuries from falling infrastructure. From what I've been told by those who've tried to seek help and been turned away, staff is being asked to sleep there for now and take shifts. So medical professionals who live in town haven't been home in days. And unfortunately, that leaves anyone contending with what's considered a minor injury out in the cold, literally and figuratively. I'm hoping that changes in the days ahead, but for now..." He sighed. "Anyway, we've got my boy in a sling, but he's in pain and all we can do is dose him up on Tylenol for now."

"Shit," I said. "I'm sorry to hear that."

"Shit, shit, *shit*!" Charlie swore, picking his phone up from the ground. It appeared mostly undamaged. "You're telling me there's no form of communication in the entire *world*?"

Apparently, the pacing and muttering hadn't helped much.

"I never said that," the sheriff said. "Highway traffic was a mess in *both* directions, but I only managed to talk to people who were traveling from the east. Several I tried to wave down didn't stop—people are less than reasonable when they're trying to get to loved ones. Can't blame 'em. What it did make clear was that we need to set up a patrol at the borders of our town. That starts this evening. You three were the last unchecked visitors here. We simply don't know what's coming and can't be complacent."

My head was reeling. I was having a hard time grasping this. But the sheriff was right. There was no room for complacency in a situation where the scope might be...too colossal to imagine. He was right to protect his town in whatever way he could.

"How are we going to get a ride out of here?" Charlie asked. "Do you have a vintage car we can use? I'll purchase it from you." He dug around in his pants, pulling out his wallet, and holding up a credit card. "You can write down the number and charge it once the power's back up."

The sheriff's gaze held on him a beat. "Sorry, son, I don't have a vintage car and anyone in town who does is gonna want to hold on to it. You can understand that, I'm sure."

Son. Under other circumstances, Charlie's offended expression would have made me want to laugh. But I couldn't muster so much as a chuckle at Charlie's expense. And hadn't he just heard what the sheriff said about dwindling fuel and the main highway at a standstill? Even if we *could* find a car like Leonard's, we'd be out of gas after a couple of hours. Not to mention that it'd been made clear to us that a vehicle was in high demand and quickly becoming a dangerous possession. My thoughts halted and then sped, moving in every direction randomly.

Emily's gaze darted from Charlie to me, hanging there as she blew out a huff of breath. We could ask the sheriff if we could stay here. The town seemed like it was making do and banding together in the ways they were able. Maybe they'd allow us to stay, especially if we had something to offer. I was strong and fit and suddenly realized that all the workouts I'd done in prison to keep myself occupied could be put to a greater use. A small trickle of purpose made me straighten my spine. A disaster. This was a clear disaster, perhaps of epic proportions. Sharp minds were necessary to figure out how to get by until normalcy was restored. Able bodies would be needed. I could barter with my physical and mental assets.

But...the idea of staying put, staying safe, also meant that Emily's parents would be left to wonder where she was and what had happened to her—a torturous prospect for any parent. I understood why even the people the sheriff had mentioned who owned a home and a business here in this town had left it to get to their daughter. Even before I'd understood the scope of this, I'd planned to get Emily home safely. And as for me personally, *safety* had never been a strong motivation. I craved purpose.

I held my gaze to Emily's and paused as I brought my bottom lip between my teeth. She seemed to be waiting for me to say something, as though she knew that I was making a decision about our next move. "Your parents will be panicked when they don't hear from you, Emily. I bet they're already panicking."

She blinked. Nodded. "Yes, my mom is probably climbing the walls." Her throat moved as she swallowed.

I glanced to my left, out to the horizon. "I think we should stick to our original plan and get on the road."

"To California?" Emily asked.

California felt like a universe away. So many bad things had happened to me there. I'd made such terrible mistakes within its borders. But I couldn't help remembering what Mrs. Swanson had said about my mom the last time I'd seen her: *We once promised each other that if anything happened to the other, she'd look out for Em and I'd look out for you.* My mom wasn't around anymore to look out for Emily, but I could do what she would have done if she'd been able. Right now, I was the only one who could. Plus, my uncle was there, and I wanted to make sure he was okay too. Not to mention the other people in the neighborhood, two in particular. "Yeah," I answered.

"Get on the road to California?" Charlie blurted. "Using what?"

"Our feet," I said. "We have no way to know from here what's up ahead. I think we should find out. The alternative is do nothing, and I'm not cut out for that."

I also had this deep sense that we needed to get on the road now before things really crumbled. The longer the power was off, the more desperate things would become. At a certain point—one likely approaching fast—it wouldn't be safe to travel at all. Either we set off pretty immediately, or we hunkered down here. Again, I wasn't cut out for sitting in place—I'd done far too much of that for too many years. But also, whether I could barter with my willingness to work and chip in or not, I didn't feel entirely right asking these people to put us up when basic supplies might become extremely stretched. "It'd be best if we get a night of sleep and some food, if possible, and take off in the morning. Do you think we might buy some basic camping gear somewhere in town?"

The sheriff considered that. "I'd imagine we can collect a few sleeping bags and some backpacks. That's not the type of stuff that's going to be valuable to us here in our homes."

"Great. Thank you so much. Is there anywhere we might rent a room?" I had a little bit of cash in my wallet, but not much. Still, I had to offer something and hope for the best.

The sheriff scratched his head. "Unfortunately, no. The nearest motel is about ten miles up the highway. And I have no idea if they've remained operational."

"Would a family be willing to put us up? Like, I said, just for a night and we're willing to pay, of course."

"Money won't do us any good right now. None of you work in the medical field, do you?"

"No," I said. "But I can look at your son's arm if you'd like me to. In exchange for a room for one night. If your son's injury is a dislocation, or even a simple break, I can set it." It was a risk. It'd been years since I'd set a bone, but it was also very straightforward. I remembered what to do and was willing to try. "If I deem it to be more serious than I can handle, I'll leave it be, I promise."

"You just said you didn't work in the medical field," the sheriff said.

I glanced at Emily, who was looking at me with some amount of alarm. "I don't, but we lived on a farm. I watched the vet set many bones over the years. It's a simple process that will immediately alleviate his pain."

The sheriff's gaze hung on me. "A farm?"

I released a breath. "I know animals aren't humans, but there are enough similarities that I believe I can help. Or at least try."

The sheriff was silent for so long, I was sure he was going to say no way. "Okay. You look at my boy's arm. But unless you're sure you can do more good than harm to him, then it goes no further than a look. Either way, one night in our home is all I'm going to be able to offer but it wouldn't be right not to do at least that." He gave the three of us a look in turn. "And I wouldn't expect that everyone's willing to do what's right, once you get out there so be prepared for that. More to the point, the notion of right and wrong is going to shift the longer the power's out. Frankly, there's no telling what's going on beyond Silver Creek." An expression of something akin to torment passed over his face before he glanced away.

Charlie let out a sound that was somewhere between a grunt and a whine.

"Understood," I said. "And thank you." Then I looked at Emily and Charlie. "We leave first thing."

twenty-one

Emily

The sheriff lived on a tree-lined street about a fifteen-minute walk from the downtown area. We followed him up the path toward the white Craftsman-style house with smoke trailing from the chimney, and for a moment, the sight of that house looked so normal that I was able to pretend the world hadn't completely fallen apart around us.

Had it really been four days since we'd survived a terrifying plane crash? Four days since we started off through the wilderness with a handful of supplies and no knowledge of what lay beyond the field where we'd landed in a fiery heap of steel? I was both shocked by the thought of all we'd made it through since then, and grateful that we'd arrived here, even if *here* was temporary. Night was coming, and I was exhausted out of my mind, and yet afraid I wouldn't be able to rest. Worried that the dull fogginess I felt was shock at witnessing a point-blank murder an hour before. Or had it been two? I had no concept of time, and reality was a strange ebb and flow that seemed drawn in harsh, black lines one minute, and wavery, blurred paint strokes the next.

The sheriff had used a walkie-talkie to call his teenage daughter and let her know we were coming, and though I was grateful to be given refuge even for one night, it felt odd to be staying in a stranger's home.

Before the sheriff could unlock the door, a pretty teenager with long, dark hair pulled it open, stepping forward immediately and wrapping her arms around him. "Hi," she said, stepping back and standing aside to look at the rest of us. "Come in. I'm Katelyn."

"Hi, Katelyn. I'm Emily," I said as I entered the home.

Her mouth dropped open and her eyes widened. I could see that they were slightly swollen as though she'd been crying. "Oh my goodness. Nova. Wait, you're Nova."

I smiled as Charlie and Tuck stepped inside and the sheriff closed the door. "I am," I said. Although I currently felt about a million miles away from *Nova*. Right now, I didn't even really feel like Emily. Rather, I felt like I was waiting for someone to introduce me to myself. Charlie had offered me a role, hadn't he? He'd told me the part I could play if I was willing. Damsel in distress with him as my hero in a world where a comet had hit the earth and dissolved most of humankind. And I wanted to play that part, to *pretend*. I did, because I really had no clue who to be. And yet, as much as I wanted to reject the reality of our current circumstances, I apparently wasn't talented enough to make believe this into a fantasy.

"And you're Charlie Cannon. Oh my God. Dad! You didn't tell me you were bringing Charlie Cannon and Nova home." She gave a small laugh and brought a hand to her mouth for a moment. "Hi. Are you part of their security?" she asked Tuck as she lowered her arm.

"No," he murmured, but didn't follow that up with anything. I'd noticed he'd been extra quiet as we'd walked here, his expression more troubled than it'd been thus far. And I wondered if that was because of the murder we witnessed, or the fact that this outage might extend way farther than we'd originally thought. But of course, I knew very well Tuck would be stingy with his thoughts even if I asked and so I didn't.

"Well, um, can I take your coats?" Katelyn asked. She gave me another nervous glance. "The last couple of days have been crazy and now this. I wish I could get a selfie. Will you autograph something for me before you leave?"

"So, you're really celebrities, then?" Sheriff Goodfellow asked as we took off our jackets and gave them to Katelyn, who hung them on a nearby coatrack. Tuck set his duffel bag by the door.

"Don't mind my dad," Katelyn said, gesturing for us to follow her past a living room off the entryway where a crackling fire was jumping in the hearth. I thought I saw movement from the couch, but it wasn't facing us, so I didn't know for sure. "He doesn't get out much. Or if he does, it's in the middle of the wilderness to hunt elk." She looked over her shoulder and rolled her eyes but then gave her dad an affectionate smile.

I glanced at Charlie to see he suddenly looked almost relieved. *Because he'd been recognized.* I could see that the reminder of Charlie's stardom had done the opposite for him. It had reaffirmed his identity.

Why didn't it do that for me?

I needed some solid footing. I *wanted* solid footing. Something to cling to in this new world of uncertainty. And yet, the mention of Nova had made me feel even more lost.

Katelyn craned her neck as we walked by, obviously getting a look at what had to be a person sleeping on the sofa. The boy with the broken arm, I assumed.

I saw a family photo on the wall, including an older woman who was obviously their mom. But she didn't appear to be here. Was she gone somewhere? Or were she and the sheriff divorced?

We followed Katelyn and the sheriff into the kitchen. "Are you hungry? Dad's going to grill some dinner out back," she said, nodding toward the window where I could see the side of a barbecue. "We're trying to conserve the gas, but we also need to eat the meat we have before the last of the ice melts and it spoils."

"We really appreciate the hospitality." I smiled. "We can't thank you enough."

"People have to come together in a time like this," Katelyn said.

"It seems like your town is doing that," I said.

"We are. But Silver Creek is small." She glanced at her dad worriedly. "It's the bigger towns that might be scarier."

There was a stilted moment that I didn't really understand as her gaze hung on her dad before he looked away. "Tuck has a little medical training and is going to take a look at Brent's arm," he said. The sheriff cleared his throat and clapped Tuck on the back. "I appreciate you being willing, but like I said, if it's above your training level, you tell us truthfully."

"Yes, sir," Tuck said. "I will."

I leaned against the counter, wincing when it made contact with the back of my hip, where I hadn't had the chance to change my wound dressing since the day before, causing it to split. *Great.* Back to square one. The flash of Tuck's warm hands on my skin several days before came back, but I pressed my hip against the counter again so the pain would move my mind away from that particular memory.

There was a soft cry from the direction of the living room, and Katelyn started moving toward the door. "I'll be right back," she murmured. "Dad, will you get out some Tylenol and a glass of water?" she asked, hurrying out of the room.

"Dammit to hell," the sheriff muttered, rifling through a cabinet behind him and pulling out a bottle of Tylenol.

I looked over at Tuck as he watched the sheriff shake a couple pills into his hand. I felt a burst of sympathy. It must be miserable to watch your child—and your little brother—in pain and not be able to do anything.

"If you're ready to take a look at that arm, now seems like a good time," the sheriff said to Tuck.

If Tuck was nervous, he didn't show it. And why he wouldn't be nervous, I didn't know. It'd been ages since he'd set a bone. And like he'd admitted to the sheriff, those had all been animal bones. But Tuck nodded. "Absolutely."

Charlie made a noise in the back of his throat that sounded like pessimism put to sound. And though I saw a muscle in Tuck's jaw tighten, he didn't look Charlie's way, nor did he address him.

"Thanks. Follow me."

Tuck and the sheriff left the room. I glanced at Charlie, and he rolled his eyes. "He's a doctor now because he watched a vet a few times? What could possibly go wrong?" he murmured once they'd left the kitchen. "Seriously? The sheriff is a lunatic if he's going to let some stranger who used to live on a farm touch his kid."

I was a little skeptical as well. I'd lived with farm animals too, and I remembered the vet being called out now and again to set a fracture or...whatever, but I sure as heck couldn't have performed one of the procedures myself. Then again, Tuck had always been much more interested in that sort of thing than me. I stood, gesturing for Charlie to come with me as we joined the rest of them in the living room.

The young boy was lying on the couch, his face contorted in a grimace as his sister supported him so he could sit up slightly and take the pills with a sip of water. His eyes widened when he saw Charlie. "Professor Tecton."

Charlie's grin was instantaneous. "At your service." He looked at the sheriff, who was staring blankly. "I can create earthquakes. Or...you know, the character can."

"Brent," the sheriff said, ignoring Charlie and placing his hand on Tuck's shoulder, "this is Tuck Mattice. He's going to take a look at your arm and see if there's anything he might do to ease your pain." Katelyn gave her younger brother a reassuring smile, and Brent leaned his head back on the propped-up pillows. She smoothed his hair away from his face and then stood straight and reached for a short stool just behind her. She pulled it next to the couch and gestured for Tuck to take a seat.

"Thank you," Tuck said as he sat down. Charlie and I moved just a bit closer so we could see over the couch, but still stood in the doorway. The sheriff and Katelyn moved behind Tuck as they observed.

"I'm going to press very gently on your arm," Tuck said. "It might hurt just a little, but I'm going to try to feel what's happening with your bones." The boy nodded and held his arm toward Tuck, who took a minute to remove the sling it was in. "Are you able to bend it?" Tuck asked.

Brent shook his head. "No."

Then Tuck held the boy's forearm, his gaze shifting away as he used his hands to assess, moving his fingers around the elbow area. His hands were large, but seemingly very gentle as his thumbs pressed here and there. Brent's expression was pained, though he didn't pull away.

I had this sudden flash of Tuck hunkered down next to one of the vets on our farm as the man checked one of the goat's legs. I had no recollection of how the animal had been injured or what the treatment had been, but that was because I hadn't been watching the vet—I'd been watching Tuck, taking advantage of him being so focused on something that I could let my eyes linger on him to my heart's content. Tuck had asked question after question, wanting to understand, wanting to help. And I'd been glad for the chance to watch him, but also, unreasonably jealous of that damn injured goat he'd been so interested in.

The memory hurt in some way I couldn't exactly explain, an old scar suddenly pulled tight.

"When you fell, did you catch yourself with your hands?"

"I... I think so. Yes."

Tuck set Brent's arm gently back onto his chest and turned to the sheriff. "His arm isn't broken, it's just dislocated. You can feel where his elbow is out of alignment if you'd like."

"You're sure?"

"Very. Listen, like I said, I'm not a doctor." His eyes moved away for a brief moment. "My training is limited. But I do know that if the bone isn't set right, it won't heal properly, and it will continue to cause pain. Getting it back in place should reduce the pain almost immediately. And then it will heal correctly so that he has full use."

Katelyn's eyes widened, and she looked up at her father before addressing Tuck. "Can you do it?"

"Yes, I believe so."

The sheriff gave a reluctant nod. "Brent," he said, "are you willing to let Tuck try to align your bone? It might hurt for a few minutes."

"Only a few minutes?" the boy asked.

"Yes," Tuck said. "I'll try to be as quick as I possibly can. You're going to have to be brave though, okay?"

"I can be brave."

"Great." Tuck turned toward Katelyn. "Do you have more gauze?"

"Yes. I picked up what supplies I could from the drugstore. I even got some plaster cloth."

Tuck met my eyes, and I startled slightly as though I'd grown invisible for a few minutes there and suddenly reappeared under his gaze. "Emily, will you go grab the supplies? And a bowl of water?"

"The supplies are in the bathroom," Katelyn said. "The second door on the right. And the kitchen sink is filled with clean water."

I blinked, the words registering as my feet moved. "I…sure. Okay." I walked quickly to the bathroom and opened a few cabinets and found the unopened supplies and gathered them and then returned to the living room. I walked to where Tuck was and placed the supplies at the end of the couch.

"Thank you," he murmured distractedly. He had picked up Brent's arm again and was using his thumbs to press into his flesh. I stood straight and headed for the kitchen to get the water. Charlie wasn't standing where he had been, and when I turned out of the living room, I collided with him, the bowl of water he was carrying splashing over my shirt as I let out a small screech and the bowl clattered loudly to the floor. Behind me, I heard Brent let out a yelp and when I whipped my head around, Tuck shot us a glare, pulled in a deep breath, and focused back on what he was doing.

I cringed. "Sorry. I'm sorry," I said as I bent and picked up the bowl. God, I felt like a clown. Katelyn had looked starstruck when Charlie and I entered the house. But in reality? We were mostly useless. Recognizable faces and nothing more. Tuck should have gotten the celebrity treatment. He'd recalled setting a few animal bones and now was currently attempting to fix their family member's injured arm. Not only that, but he seemed confident that he could do it.

Charlie bent too. "Sorry about that."

"It was just an accident," I said in a hushed whisper. "You get a towel and clean this up and I'll get another bowl of water." He gave me an annoyed look that he quickly covered with a small smile before standing and heading for the bathroom.

When I came back in the living room with the water a minute later, Charlie was mopping up the mess and Tuck was seated just behind Brent on the couch, as he held Brent's arm straight. I watched as Tuck put his own elbow in the bend in the boy's inner arm and gripped his hand. Then he used his other hand to hold Brent's wrist and made a quick movement that caused Brent to cry out as the clear sound of a bone popping into place met my ears. Katelyn gasped and the sheriff gave a small jerk as Tuck let go of Brent's arm and scooted back onto the stool. "That should do it," he said. "Try to bend it and see how it feels."

Brent was quiet for a minute, his eyes closed, pained expression slowly smoothing out. Then he lifted his arm gently and bent it up and then down. "Better," he said.

Katelyn let out a small sob and brought her hand to her mouth. "Oh my gosh, Tuck. That's it? It's all fixed?"

"Yes, that's it. But I'd like to put a cast on him, so he won't knock it out of alignment again before it mends itself. I don't know that that's what's typically done to be honest, but you have the materials, and it certainly can't hurt."

I walked carefully and purposefully over to Tuck and set the bowl of water on the coffee table that was pulled away from the couch to make room.

Tuck wrapped a piece of gauze around Brent's arm. He was efficient and calm. "Do you want to wet the strips of plaster cloth and hand them to me?"

My breath hitched, nerves fluttering. But I nodded as I knelt, making a point not to grimace at the pull of the wound on my hip. That was nothing compared to the pain this little boy had been enduring for days. Plus, I could at least try to make up for being a klutz earlier and causing Tuck to lose his focus. He finished with the gauze and then reached his hand out for the first piece of plaster cloth. I dipped it in the water, squeezed lightly, and then handed it to him. "This might not be the prettiest cast," he murmured as he began laying the pieces on Brent's arm. "But it'll do the job."

Brent's eyes had drifted closed, and he was breathing evenly as though he was beginning to drift to sleep. "It doesn't hurt anymore, Dad," Brent said, his words slurring. The poor kid probably hadn't slept well in days. Tuck and I worked quietly, getting into a rhythm. Dip. Squeeze. Hand over. "Put a piece over the edge of this one, would you?" Tuck murmured, inclining his head toward a strip he'd just placed down. I nodded and leaned closer to him, reaching my arm across his to lay the strip on Brent's arm. I felt the heat of Tuck's body and smelled the scent of his skin, my heart rate jumping as my hand jerked slightly and my fingernail scraped across Brent's exposed hand. The boy startled, his eyes flying open as I dropped the piece of material and withdrew my hand quickly. "I'm so sorry," I whispered.

Tuck sighed and rearranged the strip himself. Brent's eyes drifted shut again, but I cringed as I saw that one of my intact nails had drawn a small bit of blood right above his thumb. Mostly, they were ragged and broken from all our hardships. Once these nails had been the height of fashion, and now they not only looked awful, but they also seemed ridiculous. Because they were the fingernails of someone who was expected to do very little, physically speaking. And *doing very little* was currently not much of an option.

Tuck lay Brent's arm gently on the now-open sling across his chest. "It'll dry quickly," he whispered, standing and stretching his neck. I picked up the bowl of water and stood too as Katelyn stepped toward Tuck and threw her arms around him. "Thank you. We got so lucky that you're here." For a moment Tuck looked stiff and awkward, but then relaxed, accepting the physical gratitude. And I couldn't help wondering just how long it'd been since he'd received an embrace of gratitude. Or an embrace of any kind, truth be told.

"I'm glad I could help," he said when she stepped away. "It's funny what hangs around in the cobwebs of your mind." He smiled, and it was sweet and slightly bashful. My heart gave a strange bump, and I turned away to go dispose of the water, careful to avoid Charlie, who was leaning against the doorway looking bored.

Behind me, I heard Brent let out a soft snore. He was sleeping deeply and peacefully. And now he could heal.

We ate dinner with Katelyn and Brent while the sheriff went out to check on the men who'd taken first shift at the roads leading into their town and to stop in at the community center. The grilled chicken, canned green beans, and store-bought rolls were one of the most delicious meals I'd ever eaten, and that was saying something considering I'd eaten in some of the finest restaurants in America, if not the world. We'd been existing on snack food since we walked out of that field, and while I was grateful for what we'd managed to find, the small amount of it had ensured we were practically starving. Less than a week, and food had taken on a whole new meaning. I didn't want to think about where we'd get our meals from here on out because I was well aware that "practically starving," was very different than actually starving. The truth was, I didn't want to think about a lot of things and thus far, that'd been somewhat easy as the goal had been simply to find civilization and figure out a way back home.

But now, it'd become abundantly clear that the way back home was filled with a whole slew of questions, and, if Leonard was any indication of the general philosophy out there, quite a bit of danger.

Charlie was in the kitchen happily telling Brent a story from one of the movie sets he'd been on, upbeat and animated and obviously feeling smack-dab in his comfort zone. *Good.* Let him have it because I had a deep feeling there wasn't going to be a lot of comfort of any kind moving forward. At least in the immediate future.

Tuck had finished first, thanked Katelyn for the meal, and excused himself, off to who knew where. Brent had sat up eating, shoveling the food into his mouth as he shot questions at me and Charlie. And I couldn't help noticing the relieved look on Katelyn's face as she watched her younger brother, obvious that the pain he'd been in was now manageable. Because of Tuck.

I'd helped with the cleanup, and then Katelyn had asked that I follow her upstairs where she took a canvas backpack from her closet and handed that to me along with a pile of clothes with a pair of short, lace-up hiking boots sitting on top. "The boots are size eight," she said. "Close enough? These will protect your feet better than those." She pointed down to the canvas sneakers that a woman had died in, which were better than the threadbare slippers, but not nearly as good as a warm pair of hiking boots.

I took the items from her. "Yes. Thank you. I wear a seven and a half. These will be great. I really appreciate it."

"There's a thick pair of socks under the flannel shirt. The flannel is my mom's. I don't think she'll mind though. She's the most generous person I know." Tears shimmered in her eyes, and she pulled in a sharp breath. "She's going to be so mad that she wasn't here. She likes your music too."

"Where is she, Katelyn?" I asked quietly, apprehension causing me to go still.

"Vegas. She's a teacher and she was invited to an aspiring educators conference." A tear rolled down her cheek. "She was excited, but nervous. She's never traveled much at all...and then this. We don't even know if she's okay."

"Oh my God." I set the pile of clothes down and brought my hand to my forehead. "But she wasn't on a plane. Just at the conference?"

"Yes. She was at her hotel. My dad had just talked to her before the lights went off. He says maybe the power isn't even out there. He says maybe she's on her way home right now." Katelyn swiped at her eyes. "My dad's thrown himself into his job protecting the town. I think it's keeping him sane. Along with Brent and everything else, it's been a lot." She sniffled. "I'm so sorry. I can't believe Nova walks into my home, and I start crying like a baby about my mom."

"Your reaction is totally normal. But you have to keep believing she's okay. I'm doing the same with my mom too. They're okay. They are."

Katelyn nodded. "They are. And you'll be okay too. It's going to be hard but you're Nova. You can do anything."

I nodded and then I stepped forward and wrapped Katelyn in my arms and she hugged me back. "Everything feels so uncertain right now. But we're going to be okay. And when this is over, I'm going to send you front row tickets to my concert."

She let out a soggy laugh. "Okay. I'm going to start planning my outfit now."

I smiled. And something about the offering of comfort to a girl who was younger than me, comforted me as well and boosted my confidence. Tuck was cool under pressure. He was strong and he knew things. And Charlie cared about me. But I wasn't totally useless the way I'd thought of myself earlier. I could "adult" now and again if it was necessary. I'd become *Nova*. I'd risen from virtually nothing. And I was going to cling to the fact that though I was scared, I would face this challenge with grace. And I'd be proud of myself when I looked back on this traumatic time.

After a moment, we both stepped back and Katelyn walked over to her nightstand where she opened a drawer and removed something. When she held it out to me, I blinked down at it. A switchblade.

"It's been scary at night. Everything's totally dark and silent and I, well, I took this from my dad's collection. He has other knives too, don't worry. Here. You press this button," Katelyn said, demonstrating so that the sharp blade swung out. She closed it and set it in my palm. "I'm not saying you're going to need this, but..." She frowned, pausing for a moment. "My

dad says a woman should always be prepared to protect herself." She glanced out the window to our right where the pink
sunset shone through the blinds. "Promise me you'll use this
if you need to."

twenty-two

Emily

Day Five

As the town disappeared from view, I had this panicked desire to drop my backpack and run back to the Goodfellows' house and beg them to let me stay. To hole up in that room upstairs with the handmade quilt and men already guarding the perimeter of the town. There had been a modicum of safety there, and now, though we were headed home, we were also headed out into a world where I had no idea what to expect. On our feet.

"This fucking sucks balls," Charlie said. The sun still hadn't fully risen, but the streaks of color in the sky were plenty bright to light our way.

"Let's think of it like a hike," I said. "When this is all over and we're back home, we'll be in the best shape of our lives." I'd show up for my tour looking fantastic. And okay, maybe the tour would be postponed for a few months considering the catastrophe that would have taken place for a large part of the country, but I could not allow myself to believe that it wouldn't happen at all. I'd worked so long and so hard for my dream to come true and I wasn't going to let it go that easily. I wasn't able to *pretend* like Charlie had suggested we do to cope, but positive thinking wasn't a bad thing. In fact, I thought it was necessary.

"Yeah. A hike. Okay. It's not a bad idea," Charlie said. "I just signed on for that movie where I play a superhero. It starts filming this fall. I'll be ripped."

I nodded. "I was thinking last night about how I want to help too," I said. "There's going to be so much to do, you know? So much money to raise for the people affected by this disaster and maybe driven from their homes. I can only imagine the terrible stories we're going to hear, right?"

"True," Charlie agreed. "Hollywood and the music industry will go all in the way they always do. There'll be dozens of telethons."

I perked up at the thought of all the opportunities in front of me. "And marathons."

"Walkathons."

"Exactly. We should be on those phones, Charlie. We should cross finish lines for the cause and maybe even—" I drew in a breath as I looked over at him, a new idea suddenly coming to me "—perform a benefit concert!"

"That's a great idea, Emily. With great privilege comes great responsibility."

"Exactly." Maybe I'd start writing a single for it while we were out on the road.

Up ahead, Tuck's smooth gait didn't change, but I swore I saw his shoulders move as he pulled in a long-suffering sigh and then let it out slowly.

He hefted the backpack higher on his shoulder and I did the same with mine. Along with the backpack Katelyn had given me, the sheriff had provided two more for Tuck and Charlie, including sleeping bags to roll up and strap beneath. He'd also given Tuck several other items they could spare: some food to get us through a couple of days, a canteen of water, a first aid kit, some matches, a map... They'd been very generous, and I knew it was in large part because Tuck had helped their son and brother who was now pain-free and on the mend.

We followed in his footsteps like we'd done when traveling from the plane to Silver Creek, speeding up when he did, and stopping when he took out the map to study it for a moment before refolding it and returning it to his backpack.

And honestly? I appreciated being led in this situation. Tuck had very naturally assumed the job of leading me and Charlie. Taking charge. Forging the path ahead. And despite that I was grateful for his role, part of me also felt irrationally resentful about the fact that Tuck was happier walking solo.

He was such a damn loner. Always a one-man show. It'd started when he was a teenager and compounded by a million when his mother died.

But he hadn't always been that way. And that was the part I hated. Once, we'd been a pair. Once, he hadn't shut me out. And sometimes, when my mind was quiet, and I was thinking about Tuck, like right now, all I could wonder was what I'd done wrong.

We passed abandoned cars and trucks here and there, some that had their front hood open, the insides black with the evidence of a fire that had since burned out. Tuck leaned inside one of the vehicles and dug through the glove box, grinning when he stood up, holding what looked like a couple of food items. Charlie and I walked closer. "Three Fruit Roll-Ups!" I said, my voice rising with excitement.

He tossed one to me and one to Charlie. "Someone threw these in their glove box for their kids and forgot about them. Lucky us."

I tore the wrapper open and peeled off a piece of the red

sticky sweet, my mouth puckering with the taste of it before I'd even put it in my mouth. "Oh, that's good," I said, sucking on it as Tuck and Charlie opened theirs as well. My eyes met Tuck's as he peeled off a piece of his and set it on his tongue. His eyes seemed to soften as he looked at me and I wondered if he too was remembering how we used to eat these as kids, rolling them into balls and then popping the entire things in our mouths.

The sound of Charlie ripping the dried fruit from the wrapper brought me from my childhood musings and I glanced around to all the empty vehicles. "All these people are gone. Where did they go?"

"Home, I'm sure. The vehicles we've passed have almost all had Missouri plates. I'm assuming the majority of these people walked home when their car or truck died," Tuck said.

The morning was cold but bright, and I shaded my eyes to look out beyond the paved back road we were walking. "It looks like there are farms out there," I said.

"Maybe one of them will have some lunch," Charlie offered as he joined us. "Because a Fruit Roll-Up isn't going to cut it."

"Maybe one of them will know something more," I said.

Tuck shook his head. "We've only been walking for a couple of hours. There's no sign that there's any power here and we haven't come across one operational vehicle. I think it's safe to say circumstances here are the same as in Silver Creek. These people are hunkered down and waiting. We'll take things as they come."

"Should we check the glove boxes for more food?" I asked.

"Not now. It'll just slow us down and the Goodfellows gave us enough for the next little while. If we start getting low, we'll find some cars and search for snacks."

Unless other people were already raiding the abandoned cars. But Tuck was Tuck, and I was sure he'd already considered that. Plus, the hope was that the farther we walked, the fewer abandoned cars we saw until all the cars we came upon were *running*. And then we'd negotiate a ride home.

"I'd also love to find a weapon, if possible," Tuck was murmuring. "If you spot a rifle rack in an abandoned truck or anything like that, let me know."

Right. Because of characters like Leonard. I thought it was pretty unlikely that someone would leave their weapon in their vehicle, but I guess you never knew. But in any case, I wasn't totally helpless. "I took a self-defense class at my gym last year," I told him. "I can hold my own, you know, if I need to."

Tuck turned toward me slowly, his face neatly blank. "A self-defense class isn't going to do much against a firearm," he said. "Plus, people tend to forget all that type of training with a flood of adrenaline."

"I'm not saying self-defense moves could go up against a gun, Tuck, but they might help me get out of a bad situation, should something arise. I was the star of the class," I said, bristling with offense. "I didn't *forget* anything." The coach had told me that in all his years, no one had caught on as quickly. Even if he'd made a pass at me later, he'd accepted my polite "no thank you" with seeming grace, so I didn't think his compliments were contrived. I'd felt strong and…capable.

Tuck's lip quirked and he appeared deeply amused. I lifted my chin, offense increasing. I bent my knees, taking a defensive stance. "Come at me."

One eyebrow shot up. "Emily. If I *come at you*, you're going to get hurt."

"Put your money where your mouth is, then. Scared, Tucker?"

His gaze grew dark, and a thrill shot through me.

Tuck very slowly took off his backpack, letting it slide to the ground, then strolled purposely toward me. I dropped my own gear and right before I went to grab him and flip him the way we'd practiced in class, he went low and picked me up off the ground. He flipped me around with a quickness that made me squeal and then laugh, his strong arms locked around my waist. I screamed and I flailed, but he only squeezed me tighter. "Who's the star of the class now?" he demanded, breath hot at my ear.

"Put me down!" I wiggled wildly, and Tuck let out a grunting noise that sounded far more pained than it should have, considering my useless squirming.

Instead of following my command, his arms only tightened as I scrabbled to get free from his iron grip. "Surrender and I'll let you go."

"*Never.*" I lifted my knee and then kicked backward, mostly missing as my foot slid past his shin into open air. But despite my poor aim, he let me go with a startled laugh and my feet landed on the ground. I faced him and then immediately ducked left. He mimicked my movement, and I let out a tiny shriek as I dipped in the other direction, and he hooked me around the waist as I let out a sound that I feared gave away the fact that I was less than upset by this little game and that my class-star status had been tested and found severely lacking when it came to real-life role-playing.

"Hello? Children? This is really embarrassing. Can you stop?" Charlie's voice came from a great distance away. But I couldn't stop. Or maybe I just didn't want to.

Tuck spun me around with one arm, and I hooked my leg around his thigh, pushing my heel into the back of his knee as he grunted, knocked off-balance so that we both tipped forward. He twisted his body around at the last minute so that his shoulder made first impact with the snowy ground on the side of the road where we'd landed. "Ow," he grated.

I rolled over, taking both his hands and raising them above his head where I pressed them to the ground. "Say uncle."

He let out a bark of laughter. "You say uncle."

"Why should I? I'm the winner here."

And then as quick as that, I was flipped over so that I was flat on my back and Tuck was over me, bringing my hands above my head and pinning me with seemingly no effort at all. I wiggled and bucked, and Tuck let out that same pained hiss, jaw clenching as he stared down at me. "You were out of control then, and you're out of control now," he stated, voice gravelly.

Then? I stilled, setting my hips on the ground and going slack beneath him. He meant when I was a kid. And okay, I *had* thrown things at him then as well. I'd attacked and tormented and done anything to get his attention. He wasn't wrong about that. Because no one, *no one*, spun me out of control like Tuck. And I supposed it was still true, because I didn't seem to be able to stop myself from knowingly pushing his buttons and then enjoying the result.

My indignation drained completely, leaving a strange void. "You're right," I said. "I haven't changed. No wonder you still hate me."

He let go of my other arm, getting off me and pulling me up with him in a single movement so that our bodies slammed together when we reached our feet. His expression was a mix of things I wasn't sure I could read. There was some anger there, but also a bit of confusion, and maybe even the shine of what I now recognized as dwindling excitement. Or perhaps that was a description of my own emotions, and I was projecting them onto him because I never had been able to read this maddening man.

"Hate you? I don't hate you."

I sighed, stepping away from him and straightening my jacket, all bluster gone. I felt as deflated as if I were a balloon and he'd stuck a pin in me. *You're a sellout. They could have picked up any pretty girl off the street and created Nova.* The insult echoed in my head like the whistle of the last of the escaping air. No, he didn't hate me now and he hadn't hated me then. He'd been indifferent, and just like the old days, my instinct was to incite a fight—even a fake one—in order to get a reaction. Any

reaction. And I did. I always did. But then it was over and if
I wanted his attention again, I'd have to find something else
to provoke him with. My God, I was pathetic. And my stupid
class had turned out to be useless after all.

He watched me for a moment longer, seeming to be working out some puzzle, before Charlie's voice made us both look
to the right where he was sitting on a guardrail on the side of
the road, eating a stick of beef jerky from his backpack. "Can
we go?" He tore off a bite of dried meat, his expression miffed.

I nodded to Charlie and then mumbled something to Tuck
that even I couldn't interpret, and then picked up my backpack
where I'd dropped it and walked over to Charlie.

Tuck had moved ahead again, and I waited as Charlie stuck
the jerky wrapper back in the front pocket of his backpack and
met me in the middle of the road. "That was weird."

"I know. Uh, sorry."

"What's up with you two, anyway?"

"Nothing. He hates me. And I hate him."

"Doesn't seem like it," he muttered.

I gave him a look and slowed my walk so the distance grew
between us and Tuck. I didn't want him to overhear what we
were saying. "What does that mean?"

"You seemed to be enjoying yourself. Same with him."

"We were just messing around, Charlie. Not enjoying anything. He pissed me off. He treated me like a child and...well,
I admit I acted like one. All that comes from growing up together, you know? It's old habit to fight like siblings."

"So that's how you feel about him? Like a brother?"

"What? No. Or...yes! Yes, like a long-lost brother who disappointed the entire family and...brought shame on our name."

"Your name?"

"Metaphorically speaking. We don't have the same last
name."

"Which means he's not your brother."

A breath gusted from my mouth. "You get the point." But when I looked over at Charlie, his expression told me he did not get the point. "Anyway, listen, Charlie." I took his hand in mine. "This situation is bound to bring up heightened emotions. I think we should all acknowledge that none of us are going to be on our best behavior during this journey, even though we'll try our best. There's no rule book for what we're experiencing, right?"

"You're right." He gripped my hand tighter. "We just have to make it through this journey and get back home. And then everything will go back to normal. We'll go back to normal."

I smiled, but it felt forced. What about that statement rubbed me the wrong way? I didn't know, and so I wrote it off as the heightened emotions I'd just spoken of. Tuck and I had always been up and down and all over the place and that was only going to get worse now.

Tuck rounded a bend a few hundred feet ahead and for a couple minutes was out of sight. When we reached the turn, I saw him hunkered down behind some bushes on the side of the road, holding a pair of binoculars that the sheriff must have given him. He looked over his shoulder and gestured for us to hurry to where he was. "Get down," he said quietly when we caught up. "I hear horses up ahead."

"Horses?" Charlie asked. "Are they dangerous?"

"Not the horses, but the people riding them might be. I think we should wait here and see who they belong to."

"What if no one's riding them?" Charlie asked. "What if they're...abandoned horses?"

"Then we might have our next ride," Tuck said.

"Can I see?" I asked. He lowered the binoculars and looked at me, his lips thinning so that I thought he was going to say no. But then he handed the binoculars to me and moved to the side so I could look through the foliage like he'd been doing.

I put the lenses to my face and moved the binoculars from

one side of the road to the other. The road we'd been traveling had been barren of businesses for the last few miles, save
for a few empty, unmanned vegetable stands, only farms visible
way out on the horizon. But several businesses were situated up
ahead, including a few streets that stretched in other directions.
It appeared to be the outskirts of a small town.

And Tuck was right about the horses. I heard them too, and
now I could see the front hoofs of one from behind a roadside diner.

I started to hand the binoculars back to Tuck when two men
wearing black and white exited the diner, the door opening
in our direction so that I could see the front glass had been
shattered. I watched as the men let the door swing closed behind them and then stood talking. I stared for another second.
"They're Amish," I said. "Oh my Gosh. They're Amish. Maybe
they'll give us a ride." The Amish were…harmless. The Amish
didn't just have horses. They had buggies!

"Let me see," Tuck said, taking the binoculars from me. I
watched him surveil them, his mouth turning down into a
frown.

"What's wrong? The Amish are nonviolent. We don't have
to be afraid of the Amish."

"We have to be wary of everyone right now," Tuck said
without lowering the binoculars. "Also, we're in Missouri."

"So?"

"I've never heard of Amish in Missouri."

"What are you, the Missouri census bureau?"

He did lower the binoculars then and trained a steady gaze
on me. "Are we starting again?"

I smiled. "I'm joking. There could be lots of reasons they've
traveled here from…" I waved my hand around. I had no idea
where Amish people lived.

"Pennsylvania. Ohio," Tuck said.

"Maybe they wanted to see how far the outage extends. You know…get the lay of the land."

"Why would they? The Amish have no problem living without electricity. For them it's business as usual."

"True, but they do use services in the outside world, right? Like…banking and, I don't know, like mail and stuff? They have to have noticed what happened."

"I suppose you're right…"

"Did you just say I might be right about something." I brought my hand to my chest and pretended I couldn't breathe.

"Guys," Charlie broke in, "there's only one way to find out. Let's go talk to them."

I glanced over at him as though he'd appeared out of nowhere. Why did I keep forgetting Charlie was here?

As Tuck continued to look through his binoculars for another minute, I took the switchblade from my backpack and stuck it in the inside pocket of my jacket. I wouldn't admit it to him, but Tuck had quickly schooled me on the fact that my self-defense skills weren't going to save me if I *was* attacked. And though I wasn't overly worried about the Amish, it was better safe than sorry, wasn't it?

Finally, Tuck sighed and lowered the binoculars. "Fine. I think it's safest if I keep watch and you go talk to them. Wave to me if things seem okay. Scratch your head if things seem off in any way."

I pulled at Charlie's arm, and we ducked as we backtracked a bit, dipping around the corner before immediately turning and rounding it again. As we drew closer, I made sure not to look in Tuck's direction, instead, raising my hand and waving at the two men who'd spotted us. "Hi," I said. "How are you?"

I plastered Nova's smile on my face, the one that said I didn't have a care in the world and was completely untouchable. It felt stretched and uncomfortable, but that might be because the two men were not reciprocating with friendly expressions. "I'm…

Nova and this is Charlie," I said when we got to where they were standing, staring at us suspiciously.

The man on the left slowly extended his hand and shook mine. When I looked down, I saw that he had tattoos on his fingers. I felt my brows rise but quickly adjusted my expression. I didn't know a lot about the Amish, but finger tattoos didn't seem on-brand. We waited for them to offer their names, but when they didn't, and instead looked back and forth between each other, that feeling that something was off increased. What was the signal? Was I supposed to give a thumbs-down to let Tuck know things were off? God, why hadn't I listened to him?

"Hi there," the man on the right said, his smile growing in a way that looked decidedly predatory. *Uh-oh.*

Charlie and I started backing up in tandem, and I shoved my hand behind my back, making every gesture I could think of.

"Leaving so soon?" the other asked.

Then before I could take another step, they both swooped in, one pulling a firearm from his jacket pocket and putting it to my head as he spun me around and started marching us both toward the rear of the closed diner.

twenty-three

Tuck

"Mother fucker!" I hissed as I watched the two Amish men—
who were most definitely not Amish—wrangle Charlie and
Emily behind the diner. Even while being practically dragged,
Emily continued to move her hand furiously behind her back
in every gesture possible except the one we'd discussed.

Even so, the fact that the men were holding a gun on Emily
and Charlie and manhandling them up the street told me all I
needed to know.

I wanted to kick myself. I'd known there was something off
about those two, even from several hundred feet away. I hadn't
been able to say exactly what and so I'd talked myself out of the
feeling, but I should have listened to my instincts. I couldn't
take credit for a lot, but I knew I had two things going for me:
honed muscles and honed instincts. And because I'd dismissed
my gut, now Emily and Charlie were being abducted.

As soon as the four of them disappeared behind the building, I came to my feet. I quickly considered what I had in my backpack that I might use as a weapon but there really wasn't anything. Even the small knife on the wine opener I'd used to sharpen the stick in my belt had dulled and eventually fallen apart and so I'd discarded it. I set my hand on that stick now as I exited the bushes. It wasn't much, but better than nothing. I made my way swiftly across the street and then plastered myself to the side of the diner, moving my head inch by inch until I had a visual of the area in the back.

There was another road behind a parking lot at the rear of the building that ran parallel to the main road. And there were two horses pointed in the other direction, each hitched to a buggy. The buggies appeared to be more compartments than the typical riding carts, perhaps used to transfer business materials. But because of that, I couldn't see what—or who—was inside.

I peeked out farther and saw one of the men with his back to me peeing at the side of the lot. I considered whether to take advantage of his position, but I didn't have a visual on the second man and didn't want to risk getting shot in the back of the head.

At the thought, the second man exited one of the buggies and jumped down. "Hurry up!" he yelled to his partner, who then turned and jogged over to the other buggy and climbed up into the driver's seat. Emily and Charlie were nowhere in sight, so I could only assume they were in the compartments and if the men were leaving them back there, they had to be either incapacitated or tied up.

"Shit," I murmured, heart speeding as my mind flew from one rescue possibility to another. My best bet was to ambush them once they'd begun to move. Surprise was my best weapon at the moment as they didn't yet know I existed.

I turned and ran back around the front of the diner, past another business next door and moved along the side. I could already hear the *clop clop* of the hooves moving closer on the road behind where I was and listened intently, knowing timing was going to be everything and hoping that the man with the firearm had put it away to handle the reins of the horse.

I waited, holding my breath, muscles tensed as the sound of the horses drew closer. The horse's face appeared next to where I hid, then its shoulders, and I let out a gust of breath as I darted from behind the brick. I raced for the buggy, ducking low, and then grabbing onto the side of the seat and hopping up. The man holding the reins let out a short yell of surprise, reaching for what I was sure was his gun. My heart slammed against my ribs as I drew in a quick breath and kicked him hard in his shoulder. He jerked to the side, recovering quickly as he too came to his feet on the seat, the gun he'd managed to retrieve firing in the air right before he dropped it.

The horses let out shrieks of fear, the one in front of me rearing up and sending both me and the man slamming into the wall of the compartment behind us. The horse let out another shriek, and the man and I both grabbed on to what we could as the horse's hooves hit the pavement, jarring me so that my teeth clacked together and my ears rang.

A scream sounded from inside and though it was muffled, I could tell who it was. *Charlie.*

As I began to turn, I spotted the gun the man had dropped on a small ledge near the wheel. *Holy shit.* I attempted to go low and reach for the weapon, but the man grabbed the back of my jacket and yanked me up, spinning me around and flipping me so that now we were on opposite sides of the seat, and I was farther from the gun. *Mother fuck!*

From the corner of my eye, I saw movement from the other buggy where the horse was exhibiting equal fear, shaking its head and emitting ear-piercing shrieks as the driver tried to get it under control. Then Emily appeared, eyes wide, mouth open, a switchblade clutched in her fist and ropes hanging from her wrists. I gaped, and that momentary pause caused the man

I was fighting to get his bearings and lunge at me, his fist connecting to my jaw with a crack.

Emily climbed around the buggy as the man at the helm gained control of the horse, but then she let out an ear-piercing shriek as she lunged forward and lodged the knife in the side of the man's neck and then just as quickly pulled it out, ducking away from the sudden spurt of blood. I let out another jolt, my stomach dropping and my focus on Emily allowing the man I was struggling with to get in another solid whack on my cheekbone. *Fuck!*

The man Emily had stabbed let go of the reins and brought his hand to his gushing wound as the horse took off running.

It all happened in less than thirty seconds.

I pitched forward with the man I was fighting as we both grunted with the effort of the struggle while simultaneously attempting to stay on the small seat of the buggy. From my peripheral vision, I saw the man Emily stabbed jerk back and lose his balance. I turned my head in time to see him crash into Emily, each of them tumbling off the buggy on opposite sides.

"Em!" I yelled, grasping the stake at my waist and then using the strength brought on by my sudden panic to gouge the eye of the man I was fighting. He screamed with pain as he reeled away, taking the sharpened stick with him. "Em!" I leaned around the side of the buggy to see that Emily had stood—and so had the man she'd stabbed, still gripping his neck, a look of murderous rage on his face. The horses had both picked up speed, running alongside each other, the buggies bouncing in their wake. "Emily! Run!"

She only paused for half a heartbeat, looking behind her at the man who'd begun to stagger forward, before she began sprinting after the runaway buggy.

I heard the man on my buggy pulling himself up and felt the weight shift as he moved closer. But my heart was in my throat, and I couldn't turn from Emily, who was quickly gaining on the buggy, even as both horses increased their speed. I could attempt to jump off, but I'd almost certainly break something, and I'd also be leaving Charlie, who was tied up inside.

In that moment, I decided that if Emily wasn't able to catch up to the other buggy, I'd jump—come what may—so as not to leave her behind. If it was a choice between her and Charlie, I chose her, without a singular doubt.

But she could do this. She could catch the buggy and take control of the horse. I knew she could. "Run!" I yelled before turning quickly toward the man who was almost on me, his eye bleeding profusely, teeth bared. I raised my fist and surprised him with a right hook to his jaw. He went flying backward, and I looked behind me to see that Emily had made it to the buggy, reached for it with a yell of effort, her grasp falling short as she let out another sound of frustration and increased her speed.

Spooked by the slams and bumps and yells coming from behind it, the horse raced faster. We'd passed the scattered businesses on the edge of whatever small town we'd entered and were now speeding through what looked like the center of town, buildings more plentiful and closer together. And though we were one street over from the main drag, cars were appearing, some parked, and a few abandoned here and there, pulled to the side of the road, or standing in the center of it, causing the horses to veer around them.

I looked over my shoulder to see that the one-eyed man had regained his balance and was gearing up to lunge at me, his partial blindness no deterrent for his rage. I looked around the buggy, ready to jump, reminding myself to roll when I hit the ground in order to minimize injury, but saw Emily push herself forward, a look of intense concentration on her face as she reached forward and grasped something on the back of the buggy. "Yes, holy shit! Emily! Climb up!"

Fingers dug into my shoulders, and I was pulled backward before hands wrapped around my throat, my air halting. I kicked backward, vision blurring as I brought my hands to the man strangling me, prying them off just enough to gasp in a breath before he tightened them again. Emily had found purchase with her feet and was now moving around the side of the buggy. For a moment, I floated, sure I was going to pass out, and in that dreamy moment, I was so fucking proud of her. I almost laughed. She was climbing next to the wheel, pressing her weight on the buggy, mindful not to drag it over. *That's it, Em. You've got this.*

She looked over her shoulder at me just before she hopped up to the driver's seat. "Tuck," she yelled, as the horse pulling her buggy broke into a gallop, now neck and neck with the one I was on, down the center of the street that I blearily hoped to God wasn't blocked by a stranded car that left no space to move around. "The light!"

Dark spots appeared before my eyes, my head pounding as I pulled the man's hands, kicking backward but with dwindling strength. *The light. The light.* Then my eyes caught on something reflective on the side of the buggy. A red reflector light was attached. The sight of Emily in the driver's seat of the buggy, now careening wildly, and the horses running at a full-out gallop, gave me the burst of strength I needed to let go of the man's hands, grab for the light, and pull it toward me.

Thankfully it came off with a twist and then with the dark spots melting together before my eyes, I slammed it backward into the side of the man's head.

His hands unclenched, and I sucked in a gasping breath, pivoting around, the world swaying and blinking as I faced the man whose face was scrunched into a grimace, his hand holding his head as he let out a wild howl.

I turned back toward Emily, the wind whipping my face, buggy shaking and tilting and rocking side to side, Charlie's sobs increasing in volume from inside the compartment. Emily was on her knees now, leaned forward as she tried to grasp the reins that had fallen forward and were draped over the side of the out-of-control horse.

Oh, shit! There was a car in our path ahead, and my horse was going to have to veer left into the horse Emily was currently draped over as she tried to catch hold of the reins, or right where there was—hopefully—just enough room for the horse and buggy to fit between the car and a large brick building. My eyes darted between the man—now leaning toward me, hands reaching for my neck again—to the upcoming car and building.

Instead of leaning away from the man, I leaned toward him, but ducked so his hands came up empty, throwing my body down so that both of our weights were on the right side of the buggy. The horse followed the tilt, racing right around the car, and then with a mighty roar, I stood and used all my strength to sweep the man's legs out from under him and then push him off the buggy, grabbing on the side as the man was flung out, his yell cutting off abruptly as he hit the side of the building with a loud crunch.

I cringed even as I pulled myself back and quickly clambered into the driver's seat and grabbed the reins.

I didn't slow, not yet, but instead steered the horse around another car and then came up on Emily's right just as she pulled herself up onto the horse, the reins clenched in her fist. *Holy fuck.* "Hold on!" I shouted. Emily scooted backward as carefully as she was able on a galloping horse attached to a careening buggy.

I looked ahead to see that this street dead-ended in a grouping of trees, and my heart lurched. *Come on, Em.* I kept pace with her, and if the horses saw the trees ahead, they didn't make any attempt to slow. They'd likely turn at the last minute and the buggies would tip, all of us smashing into the trees in a heap of splintered wood and cracked bones.

Four hundred feet…

Emily lifted her head to look in front of her, her eyes widening as she began moving more quickly now, losing her grip once and freezing as she gripped the horse and got her bearings.

Three hundred feet...

"You're good, Em. You've got this," I repeated. She did. I had faith in her. She was going to get control of the horse, I knew she was, even if my heart was beating so hard it felt like it might slam through the wall of my chest. How many games had we played growing up where we'd encouraged each other? *Faster! Run! That way!* And she'd always come through, the mighty little thing with the skinny legs and will of iron. She'd pushed and pushed, surprising everyone because she was so full of heart that her size didn't matter.

Emily gave a nod, right before she flung herself forward, landing awkwardly in the driver's seat, the horse shaking its head in response to the sudden jolt and speeding up again. *Shit, shit, shit.*

Two hundred feet...

Emily sat up, holding the reins and looking ahead. "Gently, Em," I said, pulling slightly on my own reins. "Take control. That's it. They're tired. They want to stop."

I pulled harder, but not too hard, and both of our horses went from a gallop to a canter. I glanced over at her and met her eyes, both of us leaning back slightly as we pulled harder.

A hundred feet...

The horses slowed, going from a canter to a trot and I heard Emily let out a sound of relief as the horses bounced to a stop, the trees a mere twenty feet in front of us. For a moment I sat there in stunned shock, blinking at the reins held so tightly in my hands my knuckles were white. Then my head pivoted, and I looked over at Emily, who was already looking at me, her face bright red, eyes shimmering with shock and fear and victory as one emotion after another shifted over her expression.

I propelled my body forward, leaping off the driver's bench

and racing over to her. She was already standing, and I reached up as she practically flew into my arms and I lifted her down, her back against the side of the carriage.

My palms were slick, blood pumping furiously. Heart skittering and slamming as my breath came in rapid pants. I ran my hands over her hair, her face, smoothing her tears away and tracing the tremulous smile on her lips. "You were fucking amazing. God, Em. You did so good. Holy fuck. Come here." I pulled her to me, and she wrapped her arms around me as well, holding me tight and then running her hands up and down my back as she let out a small sob.

I pulled back and looked at her again. I couldn't stop taking stock of her, making sure I hadn't missed some injury or another, ensuring she hadn't been harmed and I didn't know it. She was shaking, but also laughing, little bursts of what sounded like shock and awe, and we were both breathing heavy as we ran our hands all over each other. "I was so scared. Oh my God. We did that. Tuck. You and me."

"We did. You and me."

"I thought I was going to die for a minute there—"

"But you didn't. We didn't. You should have seen yourself, Em. I'll never forget it."

"Me neither. Oh my God."

She breathed out another startled laugh and I smiled, but it quickly dropped. My face felt as out of control as the horses had been moments before, my emotions just as runaway.

We stood, our bodies pressed together as our chests rose and fell with our quickened breath. Sweat gleamed on her skin and her eyes were still shiny with tears, but also with victory and she was wild and brave and beautiful, that same bright spirit I'd always been so enamored by shining before me.

Her lips parted and she brought her hands up between us, gripping my jacket in her palms as I leaned in, our breath mingling, lips—

"Hello? *Hello?*" Charlie yelled, a sob punctuating his call, the sound of his voice and memory of his existence causing me to jerk away from Emily. "Help!" he yelled. "Someone help!"

The world cleared, Emily blinking at me as I stepped away and ran my hand through my sweat-drenched hair. "Shit, Charlie," we both said at once, her eyes widening.

I turned, rounded the back of the buggy and pulled the door open, before peering into the interior. Charlie was right inside the door, hands and feet bound and tied to the steel bar that connected the seat of the bench to the backer. His expression was wild, face red, eyes darting everywhere.

And next to Charlie sat a young woman wearing a traditional Amish dress and an unbuttoned coat, bound, but also gagged, her expression very similar to Charlie's. *What the hell?*

"Oh, thank God," Charlie said. "I couldn't see what was going on. It felt like we were riding into hell!"

"Here," Emily said, nudging me from the side where she'd come to stand as she too peered into the buggy. She brought the switchblade from the back of her waistband and held it out to me. "Katelyn Goodfellow gave this to me," she murmured. "I'd almost forgotten it." She'd wiped it on something at some point because only a trace amount of blood remained. Our eyes met as I took it from her, and I glimpsed her barely contained shock—perhaps at the memory of what she'd done—before I leaned in and cut Charlie's bindings.

I moved aside as he practically threw himself through the door. I didn't look back, but I heard the sounds of what I thought were him embracing Emily and murmuring jumbled words that blended together.

I cut the girl's bindings too and when they fell to the floor, she pulled the gag from her mouth, sputtering before drawing in a big breath of air. "My papa?" she asked.

"He's in the other buggy," Emily said from behind me. "I knew I had to catch it. I knew he was in there."

"Oh shit. Okay," I said. We helped down the young girl, who looked to be about fifteen or sixteen, and then we all hurried to the other buggy where I could now hear moaning from inside. I pulled the door open, and the girl let out a sob, ducking under me and climbing up into the compartment where an older man with a long beard was slumped against the wall, a large bruise on his head where he'd either been hit, or the injury sustained during the unexpected bumpy ride we'd all just gone on.

I stepped up and leaned inside to cut his bindings too and then the girl removed his gag and helped him out. He blinked as he obviously got his bearings and now that the gag was out of his mouth, I could see that he had a bloody lip making it obvious that he'd been beaten.

"Those men came to our farm," the girl said. "They stole clothes off our line and food from our house. They tried to take me, and my papa fought them and so they hit him with their gun and tied us both up and stole our horses and buggies." She sucked in a deep pull of air, appearing like she might start crying. Emily stepped over to her and put her arm around her shoulders. "You're okay now. What's your name?"

"Lavina. This is my father, Abram."

"I'm Emily, and that's Charlie and Tuck. Where is your farm?"

"Indiana. We've been traveling for four days." The girl wrapped her arms around herself, her expression bleak as she looked away. I bit back a curse. I could imagine what had happened in those four days in the back of that buggy.

"You have a community there, in Indiana?"

"Yes," Abram said. "A small community. There's a prison a few hours from us, and I believe those men came from there. They were wearing prison uniforms. It's why they needed our clothes. But then they put a gun to my head, and they took us too."

"I've gotta sit down," Charlie moaned.

"Oh," Emily said, putting her arm through his. It looked like the guy was going to pass out. My gaze lingered on the place where their arms were linked, and I tightened my jaw so hard I bit my tongue. He hadn't even asked her if she was okay. Didn't even care to know what she'd experienced. "Here, there's a curb over there," Emily murmured.

I rubbed at my jaw, just beginning to notice that my throat felt sore from where the man had attempted to choke me out and almost succeeded. A shiver went down my spine as other scenarios—ones where he'd killed me and taken Emily—raced through my mind. "Were there other men or just the two who abducted you?" I asked Abram.

"They were the only ones that came to our community that I know of. Unless more have showed up since we've been gone."

"You'll want to get back to them. I'm sure they're worried sick. And you'll need to come up with a plan to protect your people." At that thought, I turned, bending down so that I could see beneath the buggy where I'd watched the handgun slide. *Yes!* There it was, wedged between two sections of the under-carriage. I reached in gingerly and hooked it with my finger, sliding it toward me and then pulling it out. When I turned and stood straight, both Lavina and Abram stepped back, their gazes on the weapon. "Do you have any guns at all? Hunting rifles?"

"No. Guns are a form of violence and inconsistent with our beliefs."

"Okay, then," I said, glancing at his daughter staring at her feet, expression blank. Abram glanced at his daughter too, his troubled eyes returning to me. He obviously got my point but chose not to comment. "If not," I said, "then it's time to get creative."

"What do you mean?"

I squinted off into the distance for a moment. "Off the top of my head? I've heard you can build a barn in a couple days."

"One."

"One what?"

"One day."

"Badass. Okay. Think barriers, trenches, traps." I looked over to Lavina, who seemed to be fading emotionally by the moment. "Get her home. Start building right away."

Abram nodded, seeming bolstered by the plan. He extended his hand, and I clasped it. "You're traveling, right? Take the other horse and buggy. We only need one to return in. I use the compartments to deliver goods for my business, but I don't think that will be necessary for a while," he said, his voice tinged with sadness. "I trust that you'll take care of our horse." I looked over at the horses, both of which were nibbling the grass in front of them and drinking from the puddles of melted snow as they recovered from their run-of-terror.

"I'm grateful for the offer. Thanks. We will. We'll take care of her." The beautiful thing about horses was that there was food everywhere for them. Hell, maybe we could travel all the way to California by horse and buggy. It'd take a while, but it sure would be nice not to have to walk.

Abram helped his daughter up into the seat of their buggy, and then climbed up and sat down next to her. I waved good-bye as he turned and began trotting out of sight.

That's when I noticed several people on their porches, peering curiously at us. I gave a tentative wave, wondering if we'd walked into more trouble, but the people waved back, one man giving us a thumbs-up. Emily and Charlie stood as a man crossed the street and headed our way.

"You rescued them, didn't you?" the man said as he approached. He held out his hand, and we shook in turn. "Tim Cramer. Word traveled that those men were breaking into businesses. Never seen Amish do shit like that. I knew we had some bad apples in our midst."

I gave Tim our names. "You were right to be concerned.

They were prisoners who must have gotten free when the electricity went off. They abducted a father and his daughter and... weren't treating them well."

His gaze held mine for a moment before he thinned his lips and nodded. "More and more of that seems to be happening. I suspect it'll get worse before it gets better. If prisoners are escaping...damn."

I nodded in agreement because what that likely meant was that not only had the power and generators failed, but guards had deserted their posts. "Any word at all from local officials around here?"

"Nope. Radio silence. Even the officers who live in town are home taking care of their own."

"Mr. Cramer—"

"Tim."

"Tim. The two escaped convicts are back that way, likely gravely injured if not—"

"I'll send word that they need to be picked up." He gave me a resolute nod. "I'm grateful we didn't have to contend with more than that. They were armed and headed this way."

I glanced back the way we'd come. "We'll need to backtrack to collect our gear." As much as I didn't want to do that, I wasn't willing to give up the precious possessions we had.

"Stay put," Tim said. "I'll use the walkie-talkie and have a couple of the kids bike your things to you. Where'd you leave it?"

"I appreciate that."

I described where our packs could be found and Tim gave me a fist bump. "You did us a solid and we're grateful to you."

I mustered a tired smile. The adrenaline was leaving my body and taking my energy with it. Even so, we'd need to get back on the road. Despite that I wouldn't want to live through the terrifying, precarious moments on that runaway buggy as I fought for my life, because of the experience, we now had a horse and a firearm. And being in possession of a gun—especially—was damn lucky because no one was going to be willingly parting with any right now.

twenty-four

Emily

I was still attempting to come to terms with what we'd just experienced as we'd careened through a small town on runaway horses. And now Charlie and I were collapsed in the narrow compartment that featured one bench seat while Tuck assumed the reins.

Only a few days before, heck, maybe the day before, I'd have preferred it. Now I felt annoyed and antsy sitting in the buggy with Charlie when what I really wanted to do was climb onto the seat next to Tuck and talk about what had happened. Charlie seemed intent on telling the tale from his perspective again and again, droning on about how he thought he was going to die, his life flashing in front of him, all the good he'd done for the world, and the knowledge that if he died, he'd leave behind dozens of films and television cameos that would bring joy to the world for generations to come.

He wasn't necessarily wrong. Art did bring joy, movies and

television shows provided necessary distraction and comfort too. Families gathered to watch them, and positive messages were relayed through stories. I got all that, and maybe I'd have said something similar a few weeks before about what I hoped my legacy would be. But now? Now I was confused and off-kilter, all my priorities shifted and rearranged so that I didn't remember exactly the order they'd been in and why. And Charlie... Charlie still seemed unfazed by the things he'd seen around him. If he loved stories so much, why was his the only one that seemed to move him?

There was something else floating around the corners of my mind, but I was too exhausted to delve into my vague thoughts and foggy feelings. And who even knew if all the stress hormones and surges of adrenaline that had released earlier had fried a few synapses.

But when Charlie fell asleep midsentence a few minutes later, I got up quietly and opened the small door with a nervous glance backward. When I saw that Charlie hadn't moved, a snore rattling from his open mouth, I climbed around the slow-moving buggy and then plopped in the seat next to Tuck.

He looked over at me, his expression mildly surprised for a moment before he raised a brow. "I thought you'd prefer to be chauffeured."

"I am being chauffeured. I'm just sitting in the front seat. Unless you want to hand me the wheel?" I nodded to the reins in his hand.

"Nah, I got it. Couldn't nap?"

"I didn't even try. I'm wired."

"I'm not surprised." He gave me another side-glance. "You really should be proud, Emily. You were brave. Amazing, actually."

"If I knew all I had to do was chase down a speeding buggy and then hang off a horse for a few death-defying moments to win your approval, I'd have done that at the start and saved us a lot of bickering." I elbowed him gently.

"Ha. I prefer the bickering over the death-defying stunts, but...we worked together when we needed to."

Warmth traveled along my skin. Why did Tuck's approval make me feel so damn glow-y inside? All the applause, all the accolades, and at the moment, I wasn't sure if any of that had felt much better. Which was concerning, honestly, but...another of those vague thoughts I simply wasn't going to deal with now.

"Do you think Lavina is going to be okay?" I asked after a moment.

He was quiet for a few beats. "I don't know her, but I hope she's strong enough to put whatever happened behind her. And I hope she has a mother or a mother figure who can help her through it."

"Yes," I agreed. "That's going to be important."

"How are you doing regarding the man you..."

"Stabbed in the neck?" I sighed. "I feel oddly...okay. I mean, maybe other emotions will come. But after seeing how they victimized those two people. After seeing the helpless anger on Abram's face and looking into Lavina's haunted eyes... And knowing that what I did, what *we* did, stopped it from continuing... I'm not going to feel guilty about that, because if given the chance, I'd do it again."

He looked over at me, pride clear on his face, along with a bit of surprise, and that same inner glow infused me. His thigh rubbed against mine and inspired a different kind of heat, and I cleared my throat and looked away. *Your boyfriend is sleeping behind you, Em. Stop getting turned on by Tuck.*

And maybe this was a byproduct of the adrenaline surge too, but I suspected it was not because I'd responded to him this way before, though until this moment, I hadn't wanted to acknowledge it.

"Speaking of good deeds, I didn't get a chance to tell you

that what you did for Brent in Silver Creek, that was good work too. The Goodfellows were obviously so grateful and... you were generous without knowing it could benefit you as much as it did." He'd taken the lead with us, ensured we had food and water and were safe, and he'd taken the opportunity to help others along the way too, whenever he had the skills.

"Thanks, Em." We were on a quiet stretch of road where we hadn't seen travelers on foot in a while and we swayed along, the surroundings made dreamy by the pink-hued sky. We were both quiet for a moment, our thighs touching as the horse moved steadily in front of us. "You want to hear something kinda funny?"

I glanced at his profile and nodded.

"The reason I knew how to set that bone in particular was because I performed the same maneuver in prison."

I gave him a confused smile. "What? Why?"

"A buddy of mine, this dude who'd had my back a few times, had gotten injured in a fight out in the yard and dislocated his elbow. Going to the infirmary would have raised questions and he only had a few months of his sentence left. So, I got this medical book out of the library and learned how to pop the bone back into place."

"Oh my gosh, of course you did."

He chuckled. "I didn't tell Sheriff Goodfellow that. I thought the felon thing might concern him more than letting someone with a small amount of veterinary experience touch his son."

The felon thing. That phrase echoed. But I could see why the coincidence of the dislocation pleased Tuck. I liked it too, the idea that even if the knowledge one acquired was due to a negative or painful circumstance, it was still knowledge and it might come in handy when you least expected it. Even the hardest parts of our lives provided positives from which to draw.

I wondered what this whole experience would leave me with. And beyond that, I wondered what Tuck had done to end up in prison, wondered if he'd tell me. But knew that if he did, it would be because he'd decided to trust me for more than just a fleeting moment. I was surprised he'd brought up his time behind bars at all and sensed it might be some small surrender that perhaps he didn't even realize.

But in any case, for the first time, it felt like I was talking to *Tuck*. Not the man I was hiring to be my bodyguard, or the stranger I'd once known but didn't any longer. Tuck. *My friend.*

There you are. You're still in there. Something about that made me want to smile. And cry. Because it made me realize just how much I'd missed him.

"Anyway," I said quickly, attempting to move my complicated, disconcerting thoughts aside, "we're lucky we have you on our side." I hadn't seen it because I'd been tied inside the compartment, but I'd heard his running footsteps coming and could still picture him as he must have looked storming toward the buggy at a dead sprint and practically flying onto it in order to rescue us. "You'd be an asset in any situation right about now," I said. He was strong and smart, and he had an obvious comfort level in this new precarious situation that not many others likely did. "People everywhere could use your help," I said. "So…thank you for being…here for us. Charlie and I are really grateful."

I smiled over at him, but his face seemed to harden minutely before he said softly, "It's nothing." And then he looked away.

That evening, we came upon an old, dilapidated barn that had clearly been abandoned long ago. If there had once been a house nearby, it'd long since been torn down. We unhooked the horse and Tuck tied her near the side of the structure that provided her some patchy grass to munch and a few puddles of water from what must have been a recent rain. Then we slipped through the gap in the double doors and entered the space, pearly light filtering through the multitude of gaps in the wood. I watched Tuck move through, his head tilted back as though he was assessing whether or not the ceiling was likely to fall in. And though it had obviously gone unused for what must be decades, it seemed sound enough to sleep in for one night.

I dropped my backpack on the cleanest-looking portion of flooring and began clearing some refuse to make a big enough space to lay out our sleeping bags, when Tuck said, "Stay put. I'll be right back."

I watched as he ducked through an opening between some missing boards in the rear wall and then headed off into the trees still wearing his gear.

"Why does he need his backpack to take a piss?" Charlie asked as he dropped his stuff and started bending his neck from side to side.

"What?" I had a moment of intense fear, like he'd leave us and never return, and for a flash, I felt as helpless as a child, but I also experienced a wave of something I could only call grief overcome me. I reached out for the wooden post next to me, the rough grain of the wood bringing me back to the moment, a splinter stabbing my skin but also serving to pierce the odd fugue state that I'd slipped into momentarily.

"Hey, you all right?" Charlie asked. "Earth to Emily."

I looked over at Charlie, the sight of him standing there almost confusing me for a second. He seemed all out of place, like he'd breached some time barrier, and I was standing in the middle of two different universes. "Yeah. I'm just... I think all the events from earlier today are catching up to me. And I'm hungry. And exhausted."

His eyes did a sweep of my body, and then he walked over to where I stood, bringing his hands to my waist and squeezing. "We have a few minutes while he's gone," he said, giving me a suggestive smile.

Seriously?

For a moment I considered punching him in the face. Instead, I mustered a smile, but then shrugged him off and turned toward the area where I'd been preparing to bed down. I wasn't even vaguely in the mood for him to touch me, and it wasn't only because he hadn't even asked me if I was okay after stabbing a man in the neck. "I'm too starved and exhausted to think about anything other than food or sleep," I said. "I can't believe you have the energy for anything else either. This day feels like it's lasted for a hundred hours."

Charlie sighed. "I could've mustered some energy," he muttered, but then he unhooked his sleeping bag and started laying it out.

It was probably a good idea just to go to sleep even though the sun hadn't fully set. We'd eaten a can of tuna the Goodfellows had so generously given us earlier and would have to forgo dinner tonight and search for something tomorrow. The last couple of days had been warmer than when we'd started out, and so at least there was plenty of melting snow to fill our water bottles.

I startled when I heard the muted crack of gunfire. "What was that?"

Charlie stood straight and walked over to the break in the back wall, peering out at the woods. "Tuck has the gun with him. Maybe he came up on some trouble."

My heart dipped then rose, giving me a momentary head rush. "Trouble? What kind of trouble?"

We both stood at that gap in the boards, looking out into the dwindling light like two children peeking out from under the bed, waiting for a monster to arrive. And so, when the foliage rustled and it was Tuck who stepped through the trees, the relief that overcame me was sudden and fierce. I released an exhale, my gaze going to his hand where he was carrying a dead rabbit by its ears, his other arm filled with branches. "He shot a rabbit," I said.

"Gross," Charlie muttered.

Tuck stopped outside the barn where he began setting up a

campfire well enough away from the structure that I imagined would go up like kindling with so much as a spark.

I stepped through the boards and Tuck looked up when I approached. I bent and picked up one of the rocks he'd gathered and set it next to the others he'd already placed. We worked in silence to build the makeshift firepit, and then Tuck situated the branches in the center and went through the process of building the fire using the box of matches the Goodfellows had given us.

"I never thought I'd be sitting around another bonfire with you in this lifetime," I said to Tuck.

He looked up and smiled at me and again, for just a moment, he looked like the Tuck I knew, and it felt like a sharp poke to a tender spot. "Make that two of us," he said.

There were some old wooden crates off to the side that Tuck brought next to the fire and then he took a seat on one, removed the switchblade he'd stuck in his backpack, and began slicing into the rabbit. I looked away. "Ugh, how are you even doing that?"

"It's this or eat dirt tonight. Rabbit sounded more appealing. A gun and this switchblade made it possible. I'm going to give this back to you after I clean it though. It's yours."

I thought of Katelyn who'd given the knife to me and knew she'd be happy that her gift had come in handy at just the right moment. I thought of Mrs. Goodfellow too and the fear in Katelyn's eyes when she spoke of her mother and I hoped to God they'd be reunited.

I watched Tuck's face as he focused. "Thanks for doing the dirty work. Literally."

His gaze remained on his hands, but he gave a nod. I felt a new peace between us. We'd seemed to have made an unspoken agreement to cease the bickering after working together so well earlier that day. Even so, he didn't have to split a small rabbit with us. He could have killed the thing, gutted it, cooked it, and then eaten it himself and Charlie and I wouldn't be able to say a damn word. Because neither of us was willing to hunt down small animals and prepare the meat and we all knew it. But I wasn't going to feel too guilty about it, because despite whether our relationship was good or bad or in-between, when we got back home, I'd make sure Tuck had enough to get on his feet some way or another. *Happily.* And he'd have something with which to start fresh.

I felt a weird emptiness in my stomach that I wrote off as hunger, even if for whatever reason, it didn't feel like food would fill it.

"Anyway," I said, as if he'd been following my disjointed inner dialogue, "are we planning on stopping at a house tomorrow to ask if they can spare some food?"

"Maybe. We'll play it by ear. We'll be heading into more populated areas over the next few days, so I'm hoping there'll be an opportunity to purchase some necessities. I have a little bit of cash in my wallet."

Charlie still had his wallet, but probably didn't have a lot of cash as he always used credit. The thought of cash made me picture the baggies of drugs that had rained down on the plane when I'd discovered Tuck's illegal activity. I supposed because cash had been the point of it.

At the memory of that moment, emptiness gaped, but so did a niggling feeling that something was off. Or maybe it was just that today, more than ever, it hadn't only felt like we were a team, but it'd felt like he was my old friend. And though I couldn't deny the passion that had sparked to life between us, it was probably a momentary reaction born entirely from the wild circumstances. It would be wise for me to remember that to Tuck, this was a job. I should stop thinking of him as my old friend, or even a savior who would have done what he was doing now for any reasons other than at least some amount of decency, and loyalty to my parents. That was what I found so confusing, and why I kept stumbling emotionally when it came to him. There were parts of him I still recognized, even if, otherwise, he was completely different. "Right," I said. "Yes."

He did look up at me then, his gaze assessing. "If you want to make yourself useful, you could sharpen some sticks."

We roasted the rabbit on sticks over the fire and ate it sitting under the low light of the lavender sunset. And though the meat wasn't nearly plentiful enough, it remedied the ache of hunger that had burned since we'd eaten hours and hours earlier that day.

I looked over at Charlie sitting next to me, dragging his teeth along the stick in an attempt to get every last piece of meat on the skewer. In the glow of the fire, and with the addition of the stubble on his jaw, he looked like he was playing the part of a sexy mountain man. And I had the feeling I was watching him on a screen, some act that was in no way part of who he really was. Maybe I'd look down and see a bucket of popcorn in my lap, and when I left the theater, I'd think about how incredible it would be if I ever met Charlie Cannon and how I'd die if he even spared me a glance.

And I knew in that moment, I didn't want to be with him anymore.

Because Charlie Cannon was in no way the dream I'd imagined him to be, and if I'd ever really been attracted to him, it'd been a version of him that he could only maintain under certain conditions.

Ironically enough, the lights went out, and I finally saw Charlie Cannon clearly. He was an actor through and through, and he relied on a specific set to be the person he'd decided to play.

When the set went away, so too did his role, and Charlie no longer knew who to be.

Maybe every man I'd ever cared for was destined to show their true colors eventually.

But that thought was interrupted when the form of a man staggered from the trees.

twenty-five

Tuck

At the look of alarm on Emily's face as she stared over my shoulder, I grabbed the gun next to me, stood, and whirled around to face whatever threat she'd obviously seen. A man had just stepped through the trees and was heading toward us, his gait slightly staggered as he held his arm across his chest. "Stop!" I shouted. "I have a gun and I'll shoot."

The man did, raising one arm. "I'm injured," he shouted back. "I'm n-not armed. I don't mean you any harm. I just need to get w-warm. Please. I saw the fire…"

"Tell him to fuck off," Charlie hissed.

"He's hurt," Emily said. "He needs help."

"So he says," I muttered. Or it was a tactic to get us to trust him and let him get close. "Walk slowly and keep your arm raised. Spread the fingers of your other hand."

The man did as I asked, spreading his fingers but keeping his obviously injured arm bent across his chest. He had something wrapped around it and a pack hanging on his shoulder. "Stop," I commanded when he got close enough that I could see him well. He looked to be in his twenties, his clothes filthy, feet clad in muddy running shoes.

"I was sh–shot."

"Show me."

"Tuck…" I heard Emily say from behind me, but I gestured my hand low to tell her to shush. She might think I was being harsh to an injured man looking for help, but I wasn't going to take chances.

The man hesitated but then lowered his arm slowly and un-wrapped whatever fabric he'd used as a bandage, showing me the bloody portions of material underneath, and then exposing the wound in his bicep.

"Where are you coming from?" I asked.

A shiver racked the man. "St. L–Louis. It was hell t–trying to get out." The man was shivering so badly, he was having trouble speaking. I lowered the gun.

"Come on over and get warm," I said. I had no way of read-ing his mind to know his intentions, but it was clear he was weak and freezing, at the very least, and posed little physical threat. Plus, he'd come from St. Louis. He'd have some infor-mation. "What's your name?"

"Isaac."

"I'm Tuck. And that's Charlie and Emily." I moved aside as he stumbled forward, the sole of one shoe flapping, each step making a squelching sound so that it was obvious his foot was soaking wet. He sagged down on the crate I'd been sitting on. I moved around the fire and pulled another one over and set it next to Emily. She and Charlie had stood as I'd had the ex-change with the man, but now they were seated again too.

We waited a few minutes as the man reached his good arm out to the fire, his shoulders lowering as the warmth calmed his shivers. After a minute he closed his eyes and exhaled a breath. "Thank you," he said weakly.

"You need to get those wet shoes off," I told him. "Let them dry before you start walking again. Where are you headed anyway?"

"No fuckin' clue," he said. "I just fuckin'…ran. Lots of people did. I was walking with several others for a while but… I don't know, we got split up. I hitched a ride yesterday and then walked some more… It's just, a blur."

"I wish I could offer you some food—"

"Thanks. It's okay. I had some food with me. Finished it off, but I ate a few hours ago. I'm not so hungry, just thirsty if you have some water?"

I reached down and picked up the half bottle of water near my feet and handed it to him. He tipped it back, finishing it in three swallows. "Thanks," he murmured.

"What's happening in St. Louis, Isaac?" Emily asked, before she pulled back slightly as though bracing for news she didn't want.

He shook his head, gaze focused on the fire, expression slack as though he was mesmerized by the dancing flames. "The first day the power went out and all the cars stopped working, we knew something was very wrong. The sky, man. First it was like everything turned bright white overhead. And then it melted into all these crazy colors… Well, shit. You had to have seen it too. No one knew what the fuck it was. A bomb? Aliens? Some strange lightning strike? All we knew was the whole damn city had shut down. People ran to the stores. They couldn't take cards, only cash. A lot of people didn't have cash, so they went home to make do, but even so, the store around the block from me was out of water and lots of other things within an hour."

Emily rubbed her head. "My God."

"The air started smelling like smoke from fires burning in different parts of the city. Someone said they'd seen a plane practically fall from the sky and that the wreckage landed in the Mississippi. Apparently, the whole area around the Gateway Arch was burning and people were jumping in the water to get away from the spreading flames." He looked up and met my eyes. "As the city grew dark, we could see all the fires, still burning. But there were no sirens, not a single one."

Emily, Charlie, and I all exchanged looks, obviously in silent agreement that there was no need to bring up our own plane crash. But our experience certainly added merit to what Isaac was telling us. My head spun. How many aircraft were in the air at any given time? And how many of those had "practically fallen from the sky" like ours had? The number of lives lost both on the aircraft and on the ground as a result was too staggering to even imagine.

"My neighbor had a few of us over to his place to use the meat in their freezer, so it didn't go bad. We each brought something to share. The water stopped running soon after the six of us gathered though and the mood, it just…got real somber. We knew this was nothing like other blackouts and it was only the first day. Cars littering the streets, blocking roads, no way for emergency vehicles to get through if those were even still running at all. But like I said, we couldn't hear any…even far away. It was eerie as fuck. Then this dude, he said he'd heard from someone else that the MetroLink had come off the rails and people were injured and dying inside the wreckage in one of the tunnels. Everywhere, all over the city, people were *stuck* and no one was coming for them." He gave another small shiver, which I thought was more from whatever he was picturing in his head than from the cold. "Anyway, the next day, people started taking what they needed from the stores. Then others started taking what they wanted. By the third day stores were empty. Fuckin' empty. The neighbors weren't sharing anymore by then. Restaurants started being looted too. And still no sirens, no National Guard, nothing. People panicked and that panic spread faster than the fires. Everything…it all crumbled fucking fast, man."

"Who shot you?" I asked.

"I don't even know. I had some canned food, but I didn't have enough water to stay put." He lapsed into silence for a moment. "I never knew how quickly things could break down. I figured if people were looting restaurants for whatever food they had, pretty soon they'd be busting down any and every door. I saw others packed up and walking out and knew I had to too. Things were only going to get worse. It was already starting to stink. Garbage piled up in the street, the toilets weren't flushing. And that damn smoke that was only getting thicker. I packed up what I could carry, and I started walking. Met a few people who only knew they were getting out, and then formed a small group. We got robbed before we'd even left the city. I tried to run and got fired on. The guy next to me got shot in the head."

"Jesus," Charlie muttered.

"Luckily, I'd stuffed some beef jerky and protein bars in my pants pockets," he said, pointing down to his filthy cargo pants. "I've lived on those for the past few days."

My head was swimming. This was the worst possible scenario I could have pictured. I'd been worried at the gas station near Springfield, Illinois, and now I was downright scared by what was happening in St. Louis, Missouri.

Society was collapsing.

And if it was happening in those places, it was happening in other towns and cities too.

"Do you want me to look at that wound?" I asked. "I have a first aid kit and some essentials. I'm no doctor, but I can at least clean it up for you." I needed to do something with my hands, and I might as well be helpful. The guy had just talked for fifteen minutes when he probably barely had the energy to do so.

"Yeah, sure. Thanks. Thanks a lot."

He grimaced as he slowly removed the flannel shirt he was wearing.

I walked the short distance to the barn, ducked through the opening, and retrieved the first aid kit from my backpack and then once outside, picked up the crate I'd been sitting on, and moved it next to Isaac.

It only took me five minutes to clean the wound and apply antibiotic ointment. As I did so, I thought back to doing the same thing to Emily's wound in that clearing in the forest the night of our plane crash. We'd been lost and cold and shaken to our cores by what we'd experienced, but we'd had no idea what was happening to other people not that far away. In fact, despite the circumstances, I'd momentarily gotten lost in the satiny feel of Emily's skin under my fingers and the way goose bumps had risen when I'd touched her.

I yanked my mind from those thoughts and back to the present. Isaac was lucky in that the bullet appeared to have gone straight through his arm without hitting bone. But the wound was swollen and red around the edges and if it wasn't infected yet, it was dangerously close. I slathered it with antibiotic cream and pressed a bandage over it. "You'll need oral antibiotics too," I told him.

He let out a huff. "Where the fuck am I gonna get those?"

"I don't know. But you've gotta make it a priority." This kid was young, probably in his early twenties, and he was obviously alone and directionless, but I was already tasked with taking care of myself and two other people. I couldn't collect more along the way if the three of us were going to survive. As it was, tonight we'd only had the meat of one rabbit between us, and still had thousands of miles to travel. It'd get warmer the farther west we headed, but for now, it was winter and cold as hell, at least at night.

"Maybe one of the farms around here has some medicine

they'd give you," Emily said. "Even animal antibiotics would help, right, Tuck?"

"Farms," Isaac murmured as I picked up the crate to move it back where it'd been, and he started putting his heavy flannel shirt back on. "Lots of people will be coming from the cities looking for farms," he said. "I'm sure many who left sooner than me have already made it to some."

"Too many, and those farmers will have to start shooting," Charlie said. Charlie could be a real useless dick, but he wasn't wrong on that count. And what this meant was that we were far from the only nomads on the road, looking for food, shelter, and any help that might be extended. We were competing now for limited resources.

And we still didn't know exactly what was unfolding everywhere, but now we knew enough to understand that this was a big fucking catastrophe.

Conditions had just gotten a hell of a lot more dire.

twenty-six

Emily

Day Six

When we woke in the morning, the winter sun streaming through the wide slats and broken sections of the barn, Isaac was gone, and so were our horse, Tuck's map, and Charlie's shoes.

"What the *fuck*?" Charlie yelled, picking up the soggy sneakers that had replaced the ones he'd set next to his sleeping bag before bed, and then threw them against the wall. They met the wood with a slap, the sole of one coming off completely, a dark water spot showing exactly where they'd hit.

"He seemed *nice*!" I said, my disbelief clear in my tone. He'd stolen from us after we'd offered him warmth, and water, and medical help?

Tuck had paused the folding of his sleeping bag, but now began moving again, wrapping the tie around it and pulling tight. "He *was* nice," he said. "But he was also scared. And alone. I heard him get up and leave this morning, but I thought it was for the best. He must be good with animals, because the horse didn't make a sound when he led her off. I can only figure that he swiped the map last night while I was discarding the animal guts." He glanced at Charlie's feet. "And I obviously didn't see him switch out the shoes before he left."

I groaned. "Abram expected us to take good care of the horse. I hadn't even named her yet." Which was obviously for the best now as she was no longer ours. "Do you really think Isaac will take good care of her?"

"As well as he's able. But horses, like cars, attract attention. That attention isn't always good." Tuck swung his backpack over his shoulder. "Honestly, she was slowing us down. We can walk faster."

Charlie let out a bark of laughter. "We can *walk* faster? Oh great. We can walk faster. Except that I have no fucking shoes! Because of you!" He jabbed his finger at Tuck, and I stilled at the look on Tuck's face, worried that Charlie was pushing him too far. In a minute he was going to walk out of here and leave us behind. "This was your fault," Charlie said. "You wear those—" he pointed at the ruined shoes on the ground "—and give me yours."

"I'm not giving you my shoes."

"Give me your shoes and I won't report you for the drugs."

Tuck laughed bitterly, his eyes narrowing. "Go ahead and tell the authorities. In fact, be my guest and go right now." Tuck's voice was cold and even, and I detected a warning in it.

I was tempted to step between their argument like I'd done each time, but I didn't. I'd already decided Charlie and I didn't have a future after this journey from hell was over, and likewise, I'd never see Tuck again once he delivered me to my parents, so what was the point? Let them solve their own issues like men if they needed to.

Tuck walked straight up to Charlie's outstretched finger, his chest bending it back so that Charlie dropped it. "The only reason you care about that horse being gone is that you want a free ride," Tuck said, his voice as steady as his gaze. "Most entitled piece of shit I've ever met."

Oh. My eyes darted to Charlie.

"Excuse me?"

"Things have changed, Charlie. And I know you don't like it. But there are new rules, and if you don't want to play by them, then you can fuck off."

"Tuck!" burst from my mouth. I was willing to let them work this out, but no one needed to get nasty.

"I've been wanting to say that for a week," he said.

I watched as they had a stare-down. So *much* passed between them in those few tense seconds. The understanding that Charlie's position had been drastically downgraded was his foremost struggle, that was clear. And apparently, he wasn't sure what to do when his status alone didn't guarantee he got his way, and another man called him on his bullshit.

I wasn't going to step between them. But I was also getting annoyed and ready to go. What Isaac had told us the night before about St. Louis had spooked the hell out of me, and I wanted to get far away from here. I pushed Charlie aside and grabbed my own stuff. "Come on. We'll find you some shoes, Charlie."

Charlie's false bravado deflated, and he stared morosely down at the—frankly—gross shoes. I didn't blame him for being angry and not wanting to put them on his feet, but it also wasn't anyone else's problem. And there was really no choice other than to walk barefoot. Tuck was right. Charlie had been perfectly fine to let Tuck take the reins while he slept in the back of the buggy, not even offering to let Tuck rest for an hour. It was the accumulation of all these small moments over the last week that had given me a clear picture of who Charlie really was.

"Fine," he muttered, turning away from Tuck. "Let's just go."

"Tie those on with this," Tuck said, tossing him a balled-up pair of socks. "They're no worse than the slippers Emily wore those first few days. The priority is replenishing our water, then food, then we'll find you some shoes."

"Where the hell will we find shoes?" Charlie muttered, but he unballed the socks and started pulling on the shoes. I thought for sure he was going to start crying when he put his foot inside the one with the intact sole, but he managed to hold it together.

Tuck shot another rabbit for us a couple of hours later, and we built a fire, and again roasted the meat on sharpened sticks. He'd waited until we were on a completely deserted stretch of road, not one disabled car anywhere in sight. At first, we'd looked forward to seeing people to ask if they knew anything, then we'd come to expect the same wide eyes and vacant stares that we were probably wearing as people approached in cars, rolling slowly by. No one knew anything, that was clear. But now we had reason to be wary, and whenever we heard a vehicle approaching, we stepped off the road and hid in the brush along the side. "What would we have done for food right about now if we didn't have that gun?" I asked as I chewed the tough, weird-tasting meat.

Tuck ripped a piece off the stick with his teeth and met my eyes. He chewed for a minute before answering. "I'd thought about snares. But those take more time. We'd have to stay put for longer. There are other things we can try to find...pine nuts for example. I was hoping that by the time we'd walked this far, we'd have more options, but unfortunately..."

I let out a humorless chuff. Yeah. *Unfortunately.* Only, that word didn't seem big enough to encompass what we were dealing with here.

"I saw some mushrooms back there," Charlie said, nodding in the direction from which we'd come.

Tuck paused as if considering his comment. Finally, he said,

"Mushrooms aren't a great idea. I'm not well-versed on the different kinds. They might feed you, but they also might kill you."

"*You* not well-versed on something? Wow, hard to believe," Charlie said sarcastically, pressing down on his shoe so that water leaked out. Despite the fact that the shoes were still soggy, and he'd had to tie the sole on one, he didn't seem to have too much trouble walking in them, especially since we were on pavement. I could smell their stench but decided commenting on it wasn't worth more of Charlie's sulking.

"Are we just going to keep following this road indefinitely, then?" I asked. While I still found myself randomly reaching for my phone, and I could see Charlie doing the same, Tuck seemed to be having withdrawals from the map. I kept seeing his hands moving toward the pocket of the backpack where he'd kept the one Isaac stole, stop mid-reach, and fall to his sides. Whether Tuck would admit it or not, that map had been a source of comfort. Maybe it'd kept his mind occupied with roads and routes and was the only certainty regarding the future that we had. And if he felt lost now, then I guess I did too.

"Following this road indefinitely could be dangerous," Tuck said. "It might lead us directly into large groups of desperate people." He squinted out at the road stretching beyond me, as if he could see those hordes of people walking toward us now. "No, we need to find another map."

"Then we have to find a store or a gas station, right?"

"Maybe."

"Even on back roads like this, there'll have to be gas stations nearby. Surely, they'd give us a map."

He was quiet for a minute as he slid the last bit of meat off with his teeth. He'd always had beautiful teeth. Always had such a beautiful smile. Sweet but secretive. I suddenly remembered how his mom had given mine one of his school photos when we were about fourteen, months before Mariana was di-

agnosed with cancer. Such a golden time. I'd taken that photo
that my mom had stuck to the side of our fridge and slept with
it under my pillow. Sometimes I'd take it out and allow my gaze
to wander over every detail of his face. It'd made my heart beat
faster as tingles had spread all over my body. The first sexual
awakening I'd experienced, and it had happened from simply
staring at a photo of Tuck's face.

I looked away, feeling a remnant of those tingles now, which
was really embarrassing considering I was dying of hunger in
the middle of nowhere and still couldn't shake the last vestiges
of that teenage crush.

"A house might be safer," Tuck said, his mind clearly miles
away from where mine was. Hadn't that always been the case
though?

He used the stick to break up some hardened dirt, then put a
handful on the fire. As he smothered the flames, Charlie and I
stood and both begrudgingly turned to face the road. "We could
go grab a handful of those mushrooms," Charlie suggested.
"Swallowing poison might be the less painful option here."

I gave a surprised laugh and looked over at him. Maybe I'd
been judging him too harshly. He was as out of his element as
me. Of course he wasn't going to be functioning at his best.
Perhaps I should save any definitive plans for…later. "I'm not
ready to give up just yet. You?"

"No, not just yet." He grabbed my hand and when I looked
up, I saw Tuck glance at our joined hands before quickly turning away.

As we walked, Charlie leaned toward me and said quietly,
"We don't need him, Emily. Let's just ditch him as soon as we
get to the next town."

I looked up with surprise. "Leave? We need him to protect us."

"Do we? I mean, look where we are!" He swept his hand
around, indicating the empty road and miles of nothing sur-

rounding us, and then down to his shoes wrapped in socks to hold them on.

"We're alive," I told him. "Not everyone is."

"Our lives have been in danger several times. Is that a reason to stay attached to that psycho?"

I felt a bolt of defensiveness. Tuck was the one who'd saved us more than once, be it by jumping on a moving horse-drawn buggy and fighting a man with a gun or hunting for scarce food that he'd shared with us. Charlie was threatened by him, and honestly…he should be. Not only was Tuck far more equipped to lead us on this journey, but over the last six days, my feelings for Tuck had only grown, while my feelings for Charlie had soured, almost completely.

twenty-seven

Tuck

Several hours later, the sound of a clattering engine met my ears and we all turned, the sight of a white pickup coming toward us. We stepped out of the road, and I waved, the older truck with an emblem that advertised *Elrod Coltrane, General Contractor* surprisingly slowing and then coming to a stop. I reached out, signaling to Emily to stay back until I'd determined the people inside were safe. A young man rolled down the window, another guy his age in the passenger seat leaning forward to see around him. "Professor Tecton! Holy shit!"

I could practically feel the glow of Charlie's grin from next to me. He moved past and reached out to the driver for a handshake. "At your service."

The guy laughed and as Emily and I approached the window, I saw that both men were wearing sweatshirts with the University of Tennessee logo. "Damn, this is crazy as hell," the driver said. "Charlie freaking Cannon is just walking down the road all normal-like." The young man laughed again, a sound of both amusement and disbelief. "I'm Emilio and this is Wells," the driver said, hitching his thumb over to the guy next to him.

I introduced myself and Emily did too, and then Emilio leaned his arms on the window frame. "Wait, Nova, right? Charlie's girlfriend?"

Emily nodded and mumbled something that sounded affirmative.

"You're coming from Tennessee?" I asked, gesturing to Emilio's sweatshirt. I glanced at the logo on the truck. I was going to assume that whoever Elrod Coltrane was, he hadn't given these two young men permission to borrow his work truck.

"Yeah. We're engineering students there. We all got evacuated because of the flood. A dam upstream of the Tennessee River broke and the entire campus was knee-deep in water. The wreckage from homes was floating past. We didn't want to wait and see what else was gonna be in that water."

"A dam broke?" Charlie asked, his voice incredulous.

"Yeah. The hardware and software systems that control everything from pipelines to chemical processing plants to dam operations had to have gone down with the power surge or whatever it was," Emilio said. "There's not much in modern society that those systems don't control. We're fucked." He leaned back and gestured to his friend. "We mostly get how it works but have no idea how long it'll take to get fixed over such a large area. All we know is we gotta get home where the lights are hopefully on. Our folks have gotta be freaking. What about y'all?"

We're fucked. I swallowed, overcome again by yet another piece of information that sounded too big to truly grasp while we were standing in the middle of nowhere on the side of the road. "We're trying to get home to California," I said. "From what we've been told, the power is down from Pittsburgh,

Pennsylvania to here." And now we knew it extended down to Tennessee too.

"Pittsburgh? Damn," Emilio muttered, looking down for a moment as he obviously digested that. He glanced over at his friend. "We were hoping it was more contained...maybe a couple states. We're double fucked." He gave himself a small shake, obviously choosing to think more about that later too. "We're headed to Nebraska but we could drop you near Topeka before we continue north. Hop in," he said, nodding toward the bed of the truck and then winking at Charlie. "Any friends of Professor Tecton are friends of ours."

"Thanks," Charlie said, his posture and radiant expression speaking of his new lease on life, despite the additional bad news we'd just received. He paused at the driver's side door, perhaps measuring whether or not there was room for him up there or whether he'd have to ride in the back with the second-class citizens.

Regardless of having to endure Charlie's self-important smile for hours, or whether this was a stolen truck or not, I wasn't going to turn down a lift by a couple of college kids who appeared trustworthy enough and could cut several hundred miles from our trip. "That'd be great," I added.

We climbed up to the bed of the truck and sat down, Emily and Charlie on one side, me on the other, before the truck jolted forward, bumping along the road.

After about half an hour, Charlie's smug smile drooped and his head landed on Emily's shoulder, and I heard him let out a rattly snore. The man was constantly tired and wound up. And that could very well have to do with the situation at hand, but I was pretty sure it also had to do with the fact that he wanted a hit or a pill and could no longer get one. Maybe he hadn't been enough of a user that he was going through withdrawal, but he was probably pretty darn antsy with not being able to take the edge off with his regular coping mechanism.

I stretched my legs out to the right of Emily and crossed them at the ankles. I'd have liked to get some shut-eye too. I'd tossed and turned the night before, still keyed up from hearing Isaac's account, my mind churning with thoughts and horrible visions of what downtown St. Louis had looked like in the aftermath of the event. And now I could add the picture of colossal dams overflowing as trillions of tons of water washed out entire towns in their wake.

But beyond all that, I didn't feel safe not keeping guard. By necessity the truck was moving pretty slowly and at certain points, if someone had wanted, they could have chased us down and waged an attack.

As we drove, we saw more broken-down vehicles, and also a few groups of people who lifted their arms and attempted to wave down the truck. But Emilio and Wells didn't stop for them like they'd stopped for us. Perhaps the information we'd given about the extent of the outage had heightened their rush to get home, or maybe they realized if they pulled over for everyone trying to hitch a ride, they'd be filled up and weighed down in short order.

I saw Emily turn her head as a couple who'd shouted a plea, disappeared behind us. "I guess we got lucky that we have the professor with us," Emily said, tipping her head toward Charlie with a wry, if slightly shaky, smile. I nodded. I had to give credit where credit was due. We were also lucky that Emilio and Wells had slowed down when we'd waved, enough to notice Charlie at all. Isaac had mentioned that he'd gotten a ride too, which meant drivers had responded to his obvious need, but I had to imagine that certain kindnesses were going to end rather quickly.

"Yes, it was fortunate in this case that Charlie is recognizable and considered safe. They're perfectly justified in driving right past anyone trying to get them to stop," I told her. "Not everyone on the road is going to be well-meaning. We've only gotten a small taste of it."

"More Leonards and fake Amish?"

"Yes. But mostly it's wise to remember that the worst sides of people come out when they get scared and desperate. People who might not be predators under normal circumstances will do really fucked up things to survive."

She seemed to deflate a little. My eyes lingered on her. If she'd been bothered that Charlie's stardom outshined hers with the two men in the front of the truck, she hadn't shown it. I allowed my gaze to run over her now as she focused on the road ahead. Since we'd left the Goodfellows' home, she'd been wearing jeans and a thick, quilted jacket over a flannel shirt and a pair of boots. The whole ensemble was warm and practical and made her look vaguely ridiculous and kind of sexy too. A few days ago, I would have blamed that unwanted—and inconvenient—reaction on the fact that I hadn't had sex in over six years. But now... I could admit that it wasn't just that Emily was beautiful, it was that she was fiery and spirited too and that was the quality—above all else—that had always drawn me to her and still did.

Her hair was braided this morning, loose strands framing her face. She raised her hand to scratch her cheek and I saw that the talons she'd had at the start of the journey were now mostly gone. Then Charlie sighed in his sleep and moved his head more snugly into the crook of her neck and I felt an unwelcome zap of jealousy. Ever since Em and I had worked together getting the horses under control, I couldn't help thinking of her as more of a partner than an old friend I was doing a favor for. But Charlie kept reminding me exactly why that was ridiculous and foolhardy.

I looked away, off in the direction we were heading. That feeling of partnership had been brought on by the high emotions of what we'd experienced together—and the thrill of victory. It would wear off sooner rather than later and I could go back to—happily—being annoyed by her.

Next to her, Charlie stirred, blinked, and sat up. He bent his neck one way and then the other. "Are we there yet?"

The truck pulled over to the side of the road several hours later and we climbed down from its bed. Emilio leaned out the window and said, "This is our turnoff. You'll probably want to stick to this road." He extended a piece of paper and a pen. "Do you mind autographing this?" he asked Charlie. "No one's ever going to believe we gave a movie star a ride."

Charlie seemed all too delighted, signing with a flourish and then handing the pen and paper back over. We thanked them again and Charlie waved as they drove away, standing there even after their car had disappeared from view.

"You're welcome," Charlie said to me and Emily when he turned our way.

I resisted an eye roll, deciding to give Charlie his moment instead.

"My feet thank you kindly," Emily offered.

Charlie smiled. "So... Kansas," he said, looking around. "It really does exist."

Emily laughed. "Did you think it didn't?"

"Have you ever heard of anything that came out of Kansas?"

Emily chewed at her lip for a moment. "The Wizard of Oz," she finally said.

Charlie grinned and I turned up the road to get a visual of what was ahead.

I could see the distant skyline of Topeka, smoke rising in the air from various points. There'd been fires here too. And likely more death than I wanted to think about as large groups of people in a small area of land fought over limited resources. I also noticed several clusters of people walking on the edge of the highway, away from the city. I'd have preferred Emilio and

Wells drop us off near more wilderness, but beggars couldn't be choosers and I also didn't want to end up lost somewhere.

On the bright side, civilization did mean more chances to find food that didn't have to be hunted and skinned and honestly, another cereal truck would be fucking fantastic.

"A highway," Emily said as she joined me. "Is that bad?"

"It's not ideal, but we might be able to score some snacks again from a broken-down car. And we can use one of them to sleep in again. It's going to be dark soon enough and there's nowhere around here I might hunt."

Until I could find a map, being in a location with signs was important even if populated areas worried me and I'd have to be much more vigilant about being ambushed while we slept.

We traveled under the overpass, a few fires already lit beneath the massive structure with groups of people hunkered down around the flames. I moved behind Emily and Charlie, prepared to pull my weapon out should someone approach us, but no one did. I smelled the roasting scent of meat and saw a few of the people lift their heads and watch us as we moved past, likely ready to defend their food should they need to.

"What are they cooking?" Emily asked quietly, turning her head and barely moving her lips. "There are no woods around here."

"Probably rats." Maybe other more domesticated animals too, though I didn't say that, and I refused to think too much about it. All I knew was that it'd been six days since the power went out in what I now knew was a multistate outage, if not the entirety of the United States, and desperation was setting in everywhere, some locations more than others. And for those who had been vagrant or homeless even before this started? Maybe they had a leg up, or maybe they had it worse than anyone.

Charlie made a gagging sound, and we stepped out from the dimness under the overpass out into the light of the setting sun.

We walked past a large warehouse, and then a few dark businesses, the roads that led into this city growing more congested with abandoned vehicles the farther we traveled. I saw a gas station several blocks up ahead and gestured to Charlie and Emily to follow me in that direction where I might find another map to replace the one Isaac had stolen.

The buildings were closer together here—we passed a printing company and a taco shop, an insurance agency, and a photography studio.

When we got to the gas station, we found it completely looted. We stepped among the wreckage of overturned shelves and broken glass, not so much as a pack of peanuts in sight. And if any maps had been here at some point, there weren't any now.

"Great," Charlie hissed. "Not a damn thing here. And I still have no fucking shoes!"

We stepped out of the store, the sky deep orange streaked with blue, and growing dimmer by the moment.

The sound of an engine caught me by surprise, and I looked up the street to see a vehicle just turning the corner and heading toward us. "Tuck!" Emily breathed. "A truck."

"Come on," I said, and ducked as I ran along the side of the gas station, going low along the fence and then stopping. I looked around the corner to see an old-fashioned truck that looked like it had once hauled produce or something trundling toward us, a fabric cover obscuring the bed and featuring an extra-wide back bumper. There were two broad-shouldered men in the front, staring ahead resolutely, and call it a gut instinct, but I didn't think this truck would stop for a couple of hitchhikers. But it was heading in the direction we needed to go. I turned toward Emily and Charlie, who were behind me. "Follow me."

The truck drove slowly past us and then I came from behind the fence, hunching low as I ran behind it. Reaching up, I easily grabbed onto a bar and pulled myself onto the bumper. I moved over as Emily and Charlie came up next to me and did the same thing I'd done. Thankfully the truck was heavy enough that our weight didn't seem to rock it too much, and we simply hung on, squatted down as we watched the hollowed-out industrial section of town go by. Then we turned onto a long stretch of dark road, the truck avoiding stopped cars, its large tires easily carrying us through the weedy overgrowth on the side of the road.

What sounded like a window being cranked down met my ears, and then I smelled cigarette smoke. I thought I heard the crackly noise of static from the front as though the driver was changing the radio stations, perhaps searching for one that worked, but after a moment, the window was rolled up again and I could no longer hear the sound.

We traveled for about half an hour, moving between a squat and a kneel so as not to tire our legs, and I came to enjoy the lull of the engine, and the gentle rocking of the truck, taking the small break to try to remember the order of states we'd need to pass through to get home. We had the remainder of Kansas, and then we'd head to New Mexico, Arizona, and finally to California.

"Oh my God," I heard Emily whisper and when I looked at her, I saw that she was peeking under the canvas flap. She turned toward me, eyes wide as she pulled the flap open so I could see inside.

I looked in, several pairs of sleepy eyes blinking back at me. "Kids," I said, looking from one child to another. "It's a truckload of kids."

twenty-eight

Emily

We hopped off the truck just outside what looked like a military facility, with barbed wire stretched around at least several warehouses. There were milky lights positioned here and there that must be running off a generator, and so we followed Tuck through the shadows to the side of the entrance, crouching as we moved. "What is this place?" I whispered. "And why are they picking up kids?"

"I don't know," he murmured. "But it doesn't look good."

"Can we leave now?" Charlie asked. "I get that you're trying to make amends for your past by pretending to be Batman or some shit, but—"

I elbowed Charlie in the side.

"Oof."

He shot me a glare, and Tuck ignored him, moving farther along the fence to better see inside, past the spot where the truck had turned. He looked concerned, and I agreed that anyone who was scooping up kids right now should be considered highly suspect and likely dangerous. "What do you think they're doing in there?" I whispered.

Tuck gave me a thin-lipped stare. "If I knew, would I have my face pressed against a fence? I'm trying to figure it out. Maybe you could help."

"Okay, Snappy. I am helping," I said, leaning forward and widening my eyes to glare at him more fully.

He leaned in too, our noses almost touching. "How is asking obvious questions supposed to—"

There was a cracking noise behind us, one I'd heard before. It was the sound of a gun cocking. "Don't make a fucking move." A breath lodged in my throat, my heart jumping as my muscles froze. Next to me, Charlie and Tuck had gone still as well. I only dared to move my eyeballs, right to Tuck, and then left to Charlie, and back to Tuck.

"Stand up nice and slow and show your hands."

Tuck gave a small nod and then began rising, Charlie and I following suit. We all raised our hands in the air. "Now turn around and face me." *Oh God, oh God.* We were going to be shot by the men tossing kids into a truck and carting them to these fenced-off warehouses. My true nightmare was about to begin. I clenched my eyes shut and turned to face the maniacs who were threatening us. With the light behind the fence, I couldn't see the three men's faces, just their shapes. They were big and muscular, and they had rifles that could mow us down if we tried to run.

"Hello, sir," I squeaked. "Sirs, that is. We only—"

"As I live and breathe. Tucker Mattice? Is that you?"

My head whipped toward Tuck, and he shielded his eyes, squinting toward the biggest of the men who was standing in the middle. "Hosea Hardy?"

What the hell?

"Are you shittin' me?" The man apparently named Hosea

lowered his gun, and then gestured for the other men to do the same before he took a step toward Tuck. He let out a gruff laugh and then he grabbed Tuck, wrapping his arm around him as he gave him one of those man hugs that looked more like an attack than anything. But Tuck didn't seem to mind, his laugh relaying delighted surprise.

"How the hell are you here?" Tuck asked.

"Man, I got transferred to Leavenworth, remember? It's not far from here."

"Yeah, hell yeah, I remember, but I thought you had a few years left."

"I did. Come on in and I'll tell you about it." Hosea paused, scrutinizing me and Charlie, who were standing there frozen with our mouths partially open. "These two okay?"

Tuck's eyes landed on Charlie for a moment, and I thought he might throw him to the wolves, which honestly, maybe I couldn't have blamed him for, but Tuck just nodded, and then Hosea put his arm around Tuck's neck and we all took up behind them, the man's deep laugh floating to us as he and Tuck chatted.

They walked us back to the front gate, where another man with a rifle opened the latch and waved us through. The lights were a little brighter in here, the first illumination other than the moon or stars that I'd seen in six days, and I blinked around, trying to understand what this was. The warehouse buildings had obviously already been here, but along with those were a few large tents, and a row of portable toilets far back to our left. We followed Hosea and the other two through a door of one of the warehouses and walked into a large open space with what looked like fifty cots or so on one side, and cafeteria-style tables with attached benches set up on the other.

"Come on, you hungry? There's some food left."

As if responding to the word, my stomach let out a loud growl. Tuck's head turned in response to the noise, and I gave him a weak smile. We sat down at the end of a table, and Hosea stepped away and said something to a woman standing nearby who nodded and walked away. Hosea came back and took a seat on the opposite side of the table where Tuck was sitting and turned to face us. "Who are your friends, Tuck?"

"Emily Swanson and Charlie Cannon," Tuck said. The woman Hosea had spoken to came through a door carrying a tray. She brought it over to us, setting it down with a smile. There were three plates with covers piled on top of each other and Hosea doled one out to all three of us. I opened the lid to see what looked like some chicken salad, a few canned pears, and a slice of bread.

"Oh, thank you," I breathed, picking the slice up and inhaling the yeasty scent. I tried not to cry, but tears sprung to my eyes and I blinked them away before taking a bite and moaning as I chewed.

"Tell me about this place," Tuck said after he'd swallowed a mouthful of food. "Who's running it?"

"A few scattered military units were able to join up by using ham radios and are out trying to help. But it's been overwhelming to say the least."

Tuck eyed him. "You broke out of Leavenworth when the power went down?"

"Yup. It was fucking crazy, man. I was out in the yard when the event happened. The guards started scrambling to herd us inside. Only a few generators powered up, and so we were all ushered into one area. To make a long story short, fights broke out. Two guards were killed, and things got really ugly. We could hear men yelling from their cells where they were locked inside in other sections of the prison that had no power. After about twenty-four hours, it became clear this was bigger than it seemed at first and that no one was coming, not even to pick up the bodies. The rest of the guards had already started deserting their posts. After that, finding a way out wasn't too difficult."

A shiver crept over my skin. I thought of the prisoners in those locked cells. Had anyone helped them to get out? Or were some of them still there, sitting in the frigid dark, slowly dying of starvation? They were inmates, there because they'd hurt and victimized others, but they were also human and it was a very cruel way to go.

"Anyway," Hosea went on. "I switched out my clothes at a Walmart that was already practically stripped bare, and then ended up hitching a ride with a couple of the men who set this operation up when they realized emergency services were down. They figured out pretty quickly which vehicles were running and sent crews out to hotwire cars sitting on streets or in dealerships or wherever they could be found. They told me about what they were doing and said they needed muscle." He smiled and flexed his massive bicep, his teeth extra white in the midst of his deep brown skin.

"You do have those in spades," Tuck said.

"I'm sure they'd find a place for you too. We need people with special skills, somewhat outside the norm," Hosea said with a wink.

Tuck's gaze flicked to us, then away, and though my stomach was currently being filled by blessed bread, it dropped slightly. "Can't. I have responsibilities at the moment," he said. "But... maybe once that's done..."

Responsibilities.

Hosea nodded and then smiled. "Tucker Mattice. I never imagined I'd see you again. What happened to you three to bring you here?"

"Our plane crashed when the grid went down."

"Well shit."

"That's about right."

Hosea looked at Charlie and me and put his hand on Tuck's shoulder. "This is a good man right here. Taught me to read.

Taught plenty of others how to read too. Changed some lives for the better."

I swallowed. *Oh.*

Tuck looked away, his cheeks coloring. My heart thumped. Of *course* he'd taught people to read while in prison. *You and your damn books.* I had this intense desire to hug him, to throw my arms around him and squeeze him tight. I wondered what he'd do if I did. "Man, I was bored," Tuck muttered. "What else was I gonna do?"

Hosea chuckled. "Still full of shit, I see."

"What's the plan here, going forward?" Tuck asked, obviously changing the subject.

"For now, without communication, the units here are acting outside any official capacity. These warehouses are food facilities. Got a whole stock of canned and boxed food. They secured this location right away. They're problem-solvers, man. They've been out gathering whatever they believe might come in handy, they moved in the portable toilets from the baseball field and fencing too. Others have been out siphoning gas from otherwise useless cars so we can keep powering working generators for as long as possible. It's been a bona fide operation for the past week."

"Why are some generators working and some not?" I asked.

"Most aren't working, even with fuel," Hosea said. "The electronics inside are fried like everything else. But we've found a few that were in basements or other storage locations that seemed to have protected them from the surge. They'll work as long as we have gasoline and then those will be useless hunks of metal too."

We were all quiet for a moment before Tuck asked, "What's the long-term goal?"

"That changes day to day. It's a fluid situation. But for now, other than collecting necessities, we're focused on picking up kids who were left behind for one reason or another—parents never came home from work, got separated… You know how it goes. There are already predators out trolling. Hell, some of them escaped the same place I did."

Oh, we knew about predators. We'd learned plenty about them in the past week. But we'd also learned how many generous people there were too. I stuck the last bite of bread in my mouth and then licked my fingers.

"We're getting a medical tent set up too, but right now, don't have any medical staff. Like I said, it's fluid."

"You're doing good work," I said, glancing back at the cots where several teenagers were sitting and reading or chatting. God, how many people had been stranded alone in all this? How many children and teens, and heck, women like me? What if Tuck and Charlie had died in that plane crash along with Russell and I'd found myself out in the middle of a cold field with no idea what to do or where to go? I wrapped my arms around myself to ward off the growing chill, even though it was warm enough inside because of all the body heat, and I had a full belly.

"Thanks," Hosea said. "It feels good to be useful." He smiled. "And you wanna know something funny? It feels good to be one of the good guys. Never thought I'd say that. Never thought I'd be given an *opportunity* to say that."

Tuck squeezed Hosea's shoulder. "They're lucky to have you."

"Do you have intel about what's going on? What caused all this?" Charlie asked. "Everything we've heard so far is just speculation."

Hosea took a swig from the water bottle he'd set down on the table next to him. "The military, at least what's left of it, is saying it was a massive solar flare that took out our grid." He looked from Charlie to Tuck. "Apparently, it wasn't only one. Several hit, and over the span of about a day."

"A solar flare," I murmured. I remembered that Sheriff Goodfellow had said a professor in town had guessed that too.

"So, we're not at war." Which was a relief and one I'd take. Because while this had obviously created a colossal disaster, it was one that could be fixed soon. *Right?*

"We *are* at war," Hosea said, dashing my hopes. "In some ways anyway. But not from an outside army, at least not yet."

"Are there repairs being made?" Charlie asked, and I detected that note of shrill panic in his tone that made me worry he was about to have another meltdown.

But the truth was, I felt a little shrill as well. "*Can* the grid be repaired?" I asked, thinking of the college kid who'd said an electronic system ran most of society, even *dams*. "It can be, right?"

Tuck was staring off behind me, his brows knitted. Hosea's steady gaze hung on me as he answered, "Eventually, yes."

Eventually. The word rang in my head, an ominous echo.

"Some of the parts needed aren't even made in America anymore," he continued.

"That seems like a recipe for disaster," Tuck said.

"You think?" Hosea met each of our eyes in turn. "We all just got a crash course in how vulnerable we were to the system. Too bad it came too late. Hasn't quite been a week and already so many have died. Plane and automobile accidents. Fires. Floods. Those who needed life-saving machines or medicine are gone or will be very soon. Elderly living alone and kids who got abandoned are next. Disease might wipe people out in large numbers. There's already a cholera situation in Topeka. Sicknesses that have been all but eradicated for decades will start to return. Violence is going to erupt everywhere."

My God. I stood up. "Can I go use one of those Porta Pottis?" I asked. I needed a second. I needed air. Plus, I'd been squatting in the woods as of late. A Porta Potti was going to feel positively luxurious. I almost laughed but held it back, worried it'd come out sharp and crazed. My, how a handful of days could alter a person's perception.

"Is that water over there?" Charlie asked, perhaps needing a moment too.

"Yup to you both." Hosea turned. "Kelvin, do you want to escort the lady to the powder room?" The man named Kelvin wearing military fatigues nodded and gestured for me to follow him.

"And help yourself to a bottle of water. It's been boiled and filtered."

Charlie stood and headed toward the water, and I followed Kelvin out the back door and around the building to the row of toilets. I did my business, deciding that despite the appreciation for the toilet paper, I preferred the outdoors to a smelly, windowless cube.

It'd made me think, again, of the prisoners locked in dark cells, my mind reeling to all the people who were probably trapped right now. Coal miners in lightless caverns under the earth…families on tiny cars at the peak of a roller coaster ride… I gasped out a breath and stumbled toward the light. *Stop, Emily. Stop.*

There was a table set up with a number of bottles of hand sanitizer and I doused myself liberally, the sharp scent of alcohol serving to still my careening thoughts. I pulled in deep breaths, calming as I stared up at the yellow moon, nestled in the deep-purple sky, a light breeze lifting the hair around my face.

When I reentered the building, my eyes landed on Tuck, who was looking my way. His shoulders seemed to lower subtly, and I wondered if he'd been tense while I was out of his sight. I felt a small tickle between my ribs and raised my hand as though I could scratch it from the outside. A hand latched on to my arm, and I startled, looking up to see Charlie. "Hey."

"Hey," he said, glancing around. "I just talked to a girl over there." He surreptitiously pointed to a pretty blonde teen chatting near the door. "She recognized me too." He flashed me a self-satisfied grin. "Get this. Her dad has a classic car collection and she's thinking about taking off. Her parents were in Asia when this happened, and obviously didn't make it home. Anyway, her house caught fire and that's why she's here, but the garage is untouched. Em." He reached out and moved a piece of hair off my cheek. "She said she's willing to head west and we could go with her."

"Charlie, I'm not leaving here with some random girl who barely looks old enough to drive."

"She's nineteen. And she's got a good head on her shoulders. You should hear the way she recites my film lines from memory…"

Charlie droned on, my gaze going to his mouth as it moved but my brain tuning out the sound, his face blurring as my mind wandered. Instead, I pictured Tuck dragging Russell's body from the burning plane, that vision morphing into him bandaging my wound, and then gently examining Brent's arm. More memories danced through my mind, one after another… Tuck fighting the man on the buggy in order to save us, returning with food gathered in whatever way was necessary, ministering to Isaac's injury. I clenched my eyes shut, shame engulfing me, Charlie's useless drivel continuing on and on and on.

Suddenly my whole body felt hot, like I was boiling inside, and I had this urge to dig my fingers into his eye sockets and watch that fake expression crumble. My balance wobbled and for a moment a weird silence filled my head before reality came crashing back.

Tuck, Tuck, Tuck. Tuck hadn't cared about the drugs on that plane, certainly hadn't tried to dash back into the fiery cabin to retrieve them, clearly only concerned with collecting items that would ensure our survival. Tuck had only shown bravery and kindness and heroism on this journey where everyone's real nature revealed itself. He'd proved his character moment after moment in every high-stress situation imaginable. *Charlie* was the one who'd been selfish and weak and mostly uninterested in the suffering of others.

What I'd learned was that when push came to shove, Charlie looked out for number one.

I felt like I'd swallowed a razor blade, and it was moving slowly through my system. It was so clear to me now, and I wondered how I'd ever been so blind.

"Charlie," I said, cutting him off midsentence as his face came back into focus. "Those were your drugs."

He paused as if going over my words once and then again. "What? What are you accusing me of?"

"Don't try to lie, Charlie. I already know."

His expression became placid, and he blinked in that way that he did when acting the part of the wrongly accused. "What is it you think you know, Emily?"

"Stop. Enough. Enough lies." I glanced over at Tuck, who was watching us across the space. Even from here I could tell he was tense. I knew he'd spring up and rescue me if I so much as gave the smallest indication I needed him. *All* he'd done since we'd started on this journey was help others and rescue those being victimized in ways few others would. Tuck hadn't dealt drugs that would hurt people and maybe even kill them, and he certainly hadn't lied and blamed his own sins on Charlie. The very idea seemed ridiculous now. Whatever Tuck's mistakes, he didn't purposely hurt others, and he took responsibility for his misdeeds.

And me? I was a blind fool who'd fallen for Charlie's lies.

Charlie ran a hand through his greasy hair, pausing as if deciding whether or not to be truthful. His expression was so earnest, the one I'd seen on the screen so many times, the one that made him look both innocent and wise. But he'd been acting then, and he was acting now. Charlie was a good actor, but not as good as he thought he was. "Okay, listen, Emily. You know the pressure of being a star as big as me. It's so damn intense. Sometimes I feel like the world's on my shoulders." He looked off to the side, and then met my eyes, beseeching. "And yeah, so I took the edge off with a few pills. All those crowds, the legions of fans screaming my name, the expectations to be *on* every minute of every day." He let out a staggered breath as if releasing all his pent-up stress. "But all that's in the past. If this last week has taught me anything, it's that I don't need that stuff. Maybe it took this situation for me to realize how strong I really am."

I gaped, almost tempted to laugh. If I wasn't trembling with anger and shame, I might have. "Strong? You think you're *strong*? You're the weakest man I ever met. You threw Tuck under the bus and blamed him for what *you* did. My God." I put my palm to my forehead. "You were willing to watch Tuck go back to prison rather than take responsibility for those drugs. He called you out and you *still* continued to lie." I felt nauseous at the thought of what might have happened if our plane hadn't gone down, if we'd landed and I'd watched as Charlie reported Tuck for the drugs Charlie knew very well were his. But Charlie wasn't the only one to blame. Yes, he had fooled me, but I'd let myself be fooled. And maybe, in some sense, it had been easier for me to believe Tuck was now a bad person, because otherwise, I'd have to admit my deep, and apparently unrelenting, attraction toward him. Not that any of that even mattered now. The point was, Charlie was a dishonorable, lying dick and it was over between him and me. "How could I ever look at you the same way again, Charlie? You make me sick. When we get back, we'll go our separate ways."

Anger flashed in his eyes, another crack in his armor. "Jesus, Emily. You're making too much of this. None of that even matters. Those drugs are now ash in some field. No one's going back to prison. Just let it go."

But I couldn't because it wasn't the drugs themselves, it was his character I wanted no part of. If he could do that, what else was he capable of? "Tuck is going to help us get back to California, despite the fact that you lied about him and blamed him for what you did."

"You're the one who fired him."

His words felt like a punch because they were true. I had. I'd fired Tuck based on lies. I'd believed Charlie even though Tuck had begged me not to and I felt overwhelming guilt now because of that. "You're right, I did. I should have seen through you, and I didn't. I take responsibility for that."

Charlie huffed. "Whatever. Listen, they have cots set up for us next door, including a locker and some clothes. I'm wiped and we're both saying things we don't mean. I'm going to get out of this bullshit—" he pointed down to his dirty outfit and disgusting shoes "—and get some sleep." He leaned toward me. "Think about what I said, Emily. We can start fresh. Leave him behind and get back on track. I know we can."

"Not a chance. Good night, Charlie."

He paused but then turned and walked away.

I began strolling along the far wall, just needing to move for a few minutes before I faced Tuck again. How was it that he didn't despise me? Or…well, maybe he did, and if so, he had every right to. I flashed back to that moment on the plane, the way his eyes had beseeched me, the words he'd used. *You know me, Em.* And I felt even sicker.

And yes, I did know Tucker Mattice. Or I had. He was the boy who'd broken my heart. And all these years, all this time and it still wasn't completely healed. It still ached for him. And I'd do anything to make that stop.

Had I believed Charlie's lies in part due to self-preservation? Had I wanted to think Tuck was capable of unforgivable misdeeds because it was easier for me?

I let out a groan, massaging my temples. I'd made such a huge mistake, and here he was, still protecting me—and Charlie!—as he guided us through death and danger. I didn't even know how he'd done it after our betrayal. But what I did know was that I was deeply in debt and had no way to make amends or to repay Tuck for what he'd unselfishly done.

twenty-nine

Tuck

I headed back inside from the portable toilets I'd visited after asking Hosea to keep an eye on Emily. She and Charlie had had a fight, and he'd stormed off over to the building across the way. I itched to see if she was okay, but it was pretty obvious she wanted to be alone by the slow walk she'd been doing around the perimeter of the room when I'd ducked out of the building.

Now she was stopped and chatting with a couple of young women. By the animated way they were gesturing and Emily's smile, I thought they might have recognized her and were expressing their appreciation for her music. I couldn't help the admiration I felt as I watched her, noting the way she reacted with equal enthusiasm and then said something that made them laugh and bring their hands to their cheeks, like she'd just paid them a compliment in return. So many of the things Emily did reminded me of the girl she'd been. But since we'd set out on this journey, I'd also been struck by the woman she'd become, the one I'd been unfamiliar with until recently. I hadn't given her a fair shake when I'd first arrived at her apartment. I'd shown up on defense, expecting her to judge me and yet I'd judged her too. And I saw now how much of that judgment had been undeserved.

As if she had heard my thoughts from across the room, she glanced over at me, and I swore I saw a fleeting expression of what looked like sadness before she returned her attention to the two young women.

"Your first love is the hardest to get over, huh?"

I looked over at Hosea, who'd come up next to me. "Emily?"

"No, the hairy dude in the corner. Yeah, Emily. You told me about her in the joint, remember?"

"Yeah, I remember." We'd talked about a lot as I taught him to read. The truth seemed safe there in that prison library— locked behind bars just like us. I guess I hadn't thought about how the truth was actually inside of my heart, and there was really no leaving that behind.

I gazed at her for another moment, completely mesmerized the same way I'd always been when watching her from across a room. Talking or sitting, but especially singing. And I suddenly felt guilty for disregarding her grief at what was basically the end of her career...at least for quite some time. I felt the hollowness of yet another way the world had been robbed. "We were kids when all that started," I said to Hosea. "And nothing ever really came of it. She's different now. So am I." *Another if.* "And then there's Charlie," I added.

"The dude with the nasty shoes?"

I laughed. "Yeah, him. But to be fair, we're all pretty nasty right about now."

"We'll get you all some new clothes and shoes," he said. "It's one of the things we've been collecting. Good footwear, especially, is going to become very important over these next few months."

"I know. I thought about that. I've been making lists in my head of what will become vital and what used to be important but isn't anymore."

"I bet you have. That's one of those special skills I was talking about."

"Yeah, I guess it is."

"The world's become so damn soft," Hosea said with a sigh. "It's going to need folks who have already learned how to do without. All that hard living under your belt is going to serve a purpose, man. Think about it, okay?" He put his hand on my shoulder. "I've got some stuff to do so I'll see you in a bit."

"Do you need any help?"

"Nah. You rest your body. You might not have much more of an opportunity to do that if you're getting back on the road in the morning."

I met his eyes. "How many do you estimate will die?"

Hosea paused, shifting his mouth from side to side. "I'm only saying this to you because I know you can handle it. We got a guy here, real knowledgeable about politics and whatnot, who said there was a commission mandated by Congress last year who studied this exact thing."

"The grid going down?"

"Yeah. Apparently, they put their big 'ol brains together and found that 90 percent of Americans would die under the conditions I do believe we've just found ourselves in."

"We're talking total devastation, then."

"Maybe. No way to fact-check such a claim at the moment. Could be a load of BS. All I'm saying is there'll be a spot for you here."

"Thanks, Hosea. Oh hey," I said, and Hosea turned back my way. "Those big brains who determined 90 percent of society could die off with a grid collapse, what'd they do about it?"

"Nothing, man. They didn't do nothing."

Hosea turned away again and I watched him go. *Nothing.* But I guess I hadn't needed him to tell me that. We were all living it.

I turned back toward Emily, her grin wide as she looked over at me, our eyes meeting. Something gripped me, a protective instinct so strong it nearly brought me to my knees. *Ninety percent. That can't be true.* It had to be an exaggeration or a mis-remembering, or something else, but either way, I vowed that the woman I was locking eyes with would not be among that statistic. *I will get you to safety.*

At the sight of her lingering smile, my heart did a strange dip and swerve. I swore she could see it on my face, the way she slayed me, the way she always had. *Dammit.* In a way, I wanted to continue feeling disdain and disappointment for who she'd become. I wanted to keep those feelings in place because underneath them was the deepest attraction I'd ever felt for any woman and the knowledge that I'd loved her my whole life, and no matter what she did or who she was with, I always would.

I turned, walking on legs that felt slightly shaky all of a sudden, and not because of the mind-boggling topic Hosea and I had been discussing—one that I hoped wasn't true but that was terrifying all the same. I headed out the door and took in a lungful of air. There was, frankly, so much to feel shaky about. That had been true before we arrived here, and it was even more true now that I'd spoken to Hosea and learned the scope of the overall situation. And yet, for some inexplicable reason, it was meeting Em's eyes across a room that had swept the rug out from under me. *Fuck.*

I wandered over to a picnic table and sat down. The night was chilly but not cold, and this spot was blocked by the side of the building, so it was comfortable. I needed the fresh air to clear my head, or my heart, or whatever it was that was making me feel so damn dazed.

"Are you hiding out here or can I join you?"

I looked up to see Emily, her coat pulled around her as she

stood at the corner of the building. She glanced behind her and gestured. "I can go if—"

"No, don't go. I was just taking a breather."

She approached the table and sat down. "A breather. Yeah, it's nice, isn't it? Just a few hours where we don't have to worry about food or safety. I almost forgot what that felt like." She looked up at the star-filled sky. They were still clear here, but not as clear as they'd been in the unlit blackness of the places where we'd made camp along the way. She closed her eyes for a moment. "The air feels nice."

I let my eyes linger on her profile, her skin luminous in the moonglow. After a moment she sighed, opened her eyes, and looked at me. "I'm sorry, Tuck."

"For what?"

"For believing Charlie's lies. For firing you when you didn't deserve it. You asked me to trust you and I turned away."

A lead weight dropped in my stomach, even as my heart lifted. I hadn't expected that. "He...admitted it? About the drugs?"

"Only after I confronted him and broke it off. When we get to California, we'll be going our separate ways."

I didn't want to acknowledge the swirl of happiness at that news, but there it was. "What made you realize Charlie was lying?"

"Well, let's see, maybe the fact that you've gone out of your way to help people for the last week in every way you possibly could, sometimes to your own detriment, while Charlie's first priority is obviously himself. I should have listened to you. I should have at least heard you out. I'm so, *so* sorry."

I scratched at the back of my neck. Okay, yes, I was still hurt that she hadn't believed me, even after I'd begged her to. And I could also admit that part of my hurt was that she'd chosen Charlie over me. But could I blame her completely? "I made mistakes. People are going to judge me for those. I understand. I have to carry that."

She reached out and put her hand over mine on the table, the warmth of her skin causing my stomach to tighten. "That's the thing, Tuck. You get to start over. You're so needed right now, not just by me, but by so many people. I... I wouldn't blame you if you sent me off on my own from here."

I squinted at her. "I made a commitment to you."

She bobbed her head and slid her hand away. I immediately missed the soft press of it on mine. "I know, but like Hosea said, this is a fluid situation and—"

"I'm getting you home, Em, and that's that."

Her gaze ran over my face as though searching for something. "Okay. Thank you."

I looked over her shoulder. "Where's Earthquake Man anyway?"

"He left to get new clothes and shoes and go to bed. I don't think we're going to talk a lot on the remainder of this journey."

"Sounds awkward."

She made a sound of agreement in the back of her throat. "You seem to have perfected the art of ignoring him, so I'll just take your lead."

We sat there in companionable silence for a moment before she tilted her head and looked at me, pausing for a moment before she asked, "Will you tell me about it, Tuck? What were you convicted of?"

I felt a stab of shame, stomach twisting. But she'd just humbled herself and apologized to me. It didn't feel right not to answer her. "I did a lot of stupid shit when I moved to my uncle's, Emily. I was grieving. My mom, the loss of Honey Hill." *You. Everything I held dear to my heart. All gone.* "I wanted to lash out at anyone and everyone."

"I remember," she said softly, and I heard the hurt in her voice.

I met her gaze. "I never lashed out at you."

She looked away so I couldn't see her eyes. "No, you didn't."

I paused, sensing something unsaid, but then she looked back at me, her expression placid. "Anyway, none of it is any excuse, but I'm just trying to set the scene. When I moved to LA to live with my uncle, I fell in with other guys like me, ones who felt cut off from their families, or ones who had no family at all. In some ways, it was me rejecting everything I'd been before. If that life was no longer mine, then I'd make a new one—be someone completely different than the Tuck I'd always been. So, me and these guys, we banded together. We drank. We partied. We stole cars. It was a challenge to get them running in seconds."

"You always did catch on quick. And that might be one of those special skills that Hosea mentioned coming in handy now."

"Maybe. But even so, I regret it all. But back then…in some ways it felt like howling at the moon, screaming about the injustice I felt by pretending nothing mattered." I shook my head. "But that was all such selfish shit. The world didn't owe me anything. I just wish I'd learned that sooner.

"Anyway," I went on, unexpectedly wanting to get the rest of this out, now that I'd started. In some ways, it felt like I was laying down a great weight, unloading it word by word. "I swear to you, I was growing out of it. All that, it hadn't helped, and I felt guilty about it. I knew it wasn't right and I just couldn't justify it anymore. And any thrill it had originally provided was gone."

"It wasn't you."

"No, it wasn't. I still didn't know who the hell I should be, but that wasn't it. I'd picked up this course catalog from a local community college. First, I just tossed it on the coffee table, then I started leafing through it, then bringing it places. I think I was gathering the courage to turn down another road, but it felt so risky, you know?" I was silent for a few moments. This was the hard part, but it was also the heaviest to bear. "And then…this one night, this kid named Abel who was part of the crowd I hung with but was a few years younger than me showed up at my door and asked if I could borrow my uncle's car to drive him to get some beer. I could see he'd already had a few and he probably didn't need more. His girlfriend was pregnant, and he was nervous about the responsibility, and honestly, he should have been. He was only eighteen and he'd been raised in the system, didn't know a thing about being a father and didn't even have a GED. But he was a nice kid. Troubled, quiet, but still a good person. You know you meet some of these kids who've grown up in shitty situations, and with some of them, the light has just died. You can see it. You can feel it. It's hard to explain. But not Abel…he still cared. He would have been okay. I think he would have gotten it together… I know he would have." I pictured him standing there on my uncle's front porch, hands in his pockets, asking me for a ride to a nearby convenience store where they didn't give a shit about ID. It was *that* moment. That was the one where I could have changed everything. Prevented everything.

But I hadn't.

"I drove him to the store. What I didn't know was that Abel didn't have any money for beer or anything else. What he did have was a loaded gun. And a kid coming any day."

"Oh God. He robbed the store."

"He tried. But the clerk had a gun too and he was a lot faster. I don't think Abel had any plans to shoot him or anyone else. He'd never been violent before. He was just scared and desperate and had chugged some beers for liquid courage. He thought he could get a couple hundred bucks from that register and give it to his girlfriend, so she didn't look at him like he was a worthless piece of shit." I shook my head. "Meanwhile, I was out in the car looking through that stupid catalog when I heard the shots. Abel came staggering out, his hand on his chest... The blood. God, so much blood. The clerk was at the door, yelling and waving his gun around and I didn't know what the fuck had just happened. All I knew was that Abel needed a hospital. I threw him in the car, and I drove like a bat out of hell, all the while Abel is just gurgling and making these awful sounds."

"Tuck. It wasn't your fault."

"I was there. I drove him to the store, and I drove him to the hospital even if he was dead by the time we arrived."

Emily grimaced, shutting her eyes briefly. "You were convicted for...what? Being the getaway car?"

"Accessory to armed robbery."

"But you didn't even know."

"No one was going to believe that. After all the shit I'd already done? Even if I'd been a minor for some of it, and the rest was mostly petty crime. And I wasn't even sure I believed it either, Em. I saw the way Abel looked when he came to my door that night. He needed *help*. And maybe Abel thought he needed a ride or money or whatever, but what he really needed was for someone to lean on. Someone to tell him things were going to be okay. And he came to *me*. I could have been that person, Emily. Instead of driving a desperate, drunk kid to the store to buy more beer, I could have invited him inside and given him some encouragement. But I was involved in my own stupid-ass plans, and I didn't want to be bothered." I'd done to Abel something pretty damn similar to what my father had done to me. I'd disregarded his pain because it'd been inconvenient. And yeah, I wasn't the kid's father, but he didn't have one of those and I could have at least tried to steer him in a better direction, even if it meant not getting drunker that night instead of facing his fears. "I could have followed my gut and *talked* to him."

"Oh, Tuck. All those *could haves* will do is torture you."

"Good. Don't I deserve that?"

"I don't think so. But regardless of my opinion, you did your time. You paid the price that wasn't even yours to pay."

"There is no adequate price for that, Em. Not one set by a judge anyway. Abel's kid is six years old now, and he doesn't have a dad either. I'll regret what I didn't do that day forever." *That moment. The one where I failed.* "And rightly so. I might have been the one to prevent his death, and I didn't."

"So you took the blame, not *for* him, because you couldn't do that, but *with* him. You gave his girlfriend and son someone else to focus their anger on instead of only him."

Her voicing that idea hit home even if I'd never exactly put it into words for myself. But yes, it'd brought me some kind of relief to know I could do *something*, no matter how small, in the aftermath of my mistake. But before I could comment, a voice came through what sounded like a bullhorn, announcing that the generator and lights were going to be shut off in twenty minutes. "I guess that's a not-so-subtle hint to go to bed."

I smiled. "I think you're right."

She studied me for a minute. "Thank you for telling me what happened."

Our gazes held. And even though it had been hard to put the night Abel died to words for the first time, and difficult to dredge up all those emotions, I also felt unexpectedly glad that I'd not only told the story but told it to Emily. "Thank you for listening."

She placed her palm over my knuckles and laced our fingers together. And even when we parted a few minutes later, I swore I could still feel her hand in mine.

thirty

Emily

Day Seven

In the morning, Charlie was gone. I wasn't exactly surprised, and maybe I was even a little relieved that I'd no longer have to travel with someone I'd lost all respect for. But I *was* a little worried for him. There was no future for us as a couple or anything more, and I was fully aware of all his shortcomings—to put it mildly—but Charlie was no match for the state of society right now.

He'd made his choice, however. And perhaps whatever happened to him was well deserved. Hosea told me he'd seen him leaving that morning with the young woman who apparently had access to a usable vehicle—and the desire to head west with a stranded movie star.

Tuck emerged, wearing new clothes and sporting a freshly shaven face, his hair slicked back. And I didn't want to swoon like a schoolgirl, but I did. No one could affect me like him, no one ever had. And I suddenly felt vulnerable to it, a twist of fear funneling through me. Because until now—and despite Charlie—I'd used the judgment of what I'd deemed Tuck's flawed character as a shield against my attraction. I no longer had that defense, flimsy though it had become the more time I spent with him. And I had to admit my attraction didn't stop at his chiseled jaw, or his perfectly formed features. It went deeper than that. He just *did* something to me that no one else ever had. And I didn't know how to describe it. I certainly didn't know how to ignore it. And I wasn't even sure I wanted to fight it anymore. Hence the fear.

But I didn't have the luxury of dwelling on all that anyway. Tuck and I had far bigger fish to fry and the continuation of our journey home in front of us.

"Morning," I said with a smile.

He looked me over, smiling back. "Feels good to clean up, doesn't it?"

"I'll never take shampoo for granted again," I said. The women's barracks had a hose running off the back of the building and an array of hair products and soaps on a ledge. I'd stepped behind the wooden partition that provided privacy and taken full advantage of them, shivering in the cold morning air but not caring a whit. Then I'd pulled on the clean clothes given to me and almost cried at the absolute joy of feeling clean again.

"Charlie's gone," I told him. *Headed west with a nineteen-year-old fangirl in her daddy's car.*

"I figured," Tuck said. "So is the gun. I left it in my backpack in the locker when I was showering and shaving. He must have taken it then."

My mouth dropped along with my heart. "What?" *That rat!* Our weapon was gone? Our protection? And if so, of *course* it was Charlie—only the three of us had the combination to the locker Hosea had given us to store our things. I closed my eyes for several moments. When I looked back at Tuck, he appeared grim but not angry. "You're not mad?" I asked, surprise clear in my voice.

"I was, earlier when I discovered it. But...there were only two bullets left and honestly, it might be the only way Charlie survives."

I shook my head slowly. I'd even thought about the fact that I was concerned for his welfare just a few minutes before. But now things would be harder for us. More proof of Charlie's selfishness. If I'd had any niggling doubts about his character—which I really didn't—this would have squashed them entirely.

I almost inquired about Hosea possibly replacing the gun Charlie had stolen but changed my mind. Weapons were precious right now, not only as a means of protection, but as a means of food. We'd needed both on several occasions. Now we'd have to do without.

Tuck helped me loop my arm through the other strap of my backpack, eyeing me. "Are you okay?"

"Regarding Charlie? Yes. More than okay. Our parting is for the best. Although I'd like to kick him in the teeth for taking the gun."

He stood there for a moment as if adjusting to this new reality. "Okay, then," he finally said. "Hosea has arranged for us to ride with a couple crewmen heading to an army base near the border of Kansas and Oklahoma."

"Oh. Do they think the government is operational there?"

"They have no idea. Someone here happens to know about that location and it's in driving distance, so they're going to sacrifice some fuel and check it out."

I thought about that. I supposed Hosea and the rest of this crew would check out all possible locations where the military might still be stationed and able to provide some answers if they had a way to look up locations. But as of now, they had to go off guesses and memory. "Life really sucks without Google and GPS."

Tuck let out a small chuff of agreement.

We traveled in the back of a Jeep for the next six hours, the noise of the vehicle and the wind in our faces making it mostly impossible to talk without yelling. But I found it a good opportunity to come to terms with our new normal. It was just me and Tuck now, a duo where we'd once been an awkward threesome. But more than just a duo, I hoped we could find a way to settle into a partnership.

Both the driver and the gruff older man in the passenger seat carried weapons and though they were armed, I still felt exposed in the open vehicle as we passed by people on foot who waved their arms and attempted to get us to stop.

As we skirted around what I assumed were more populated areas, I could see the smoke rising in the sky. And when we moved more slowly around stalled cars, I heard distant wails that could have been dogs, but also might have been human and I began humming to block the sounds that sent shivers down my spine.

When we arrived at the army base, it was completely deserted. "Damn," Tuck muttered as we stepped down from the Jeep.

"A dead fucking end," the older man muttered.

"Thanks for the ride," Tuck said to the two men in the front who looked as disappointed as I felt. I'd allowed myself some hope that when we arrived, there would be some official organization happening, or perhaps some information.

But at least we were a little bit closer to home.

Hosea had located a map for Tuck and so again, we followed along specific routes, walking out of rural Kansas and into Oklahoma, with New Mexico in our future.

"It's pretty here," I said, gazing off into the distance where farmhouses could barely be seen beyond spans of yellow fields, giant rolls of hay dotting the landscape. The cows would have plenty to eat anyway. I thought back to the folks Tuck guessed had been roasting a rat under the city overpass and didn't let my thoughts wander to the possible fate of these cows. Instead, I hummed some more and occupied my mind with music. It had always been my sanctuary, and that was certainly true now.

The idea made me think about what Tuck had told me the night before, his description of spinning from the loss of his mother, the farm, and life as he'd known it. I'd been so bereft during that time too, and especially when he'd turned away from me, but in the midst of my pain, I'd still had music. What if I hadn't? What other choices might I have made? Where might I have gone for meaning, perhaps taking wrong turns along the way?

The same way Tuck had. And it opened up a wellspring of understanding in me. And a new level of forgiveness.

It also added context to his deep hurt when I hadn't believed him on the airplane. Tuck had never hesitated to take blame for something if he thought someone else would suffer more in the fallout—I knew that all too well. He'd done the same thing when Abel died, not declaring his innocence because he saw it as throwing Abel under the bus—again. But he had denied any wrongdoing when it came to Charlie's drugs, and I hadn't believed him. How terribly that must have stung.

We'd walked on the outskirts of what looked like quaint towns, past people who waved, their faces filled with worry as we waved back and moved on by. Just like the other states we'd been in, broken-down cars sat in the roads, the occasional older vehicle rolling past. No one bothered us here, and we didn't attempt to talk to anyone, though we might have to eventually as Hosea had only been able to provide us a ride and a day's worth of food. We both understood—their mission was to help as many vulnerable people as possible, and Tuck was capable.

Thankfully, the weather was mild, so much so that at one

point I took off my jacket and tied it around my waist. "Do you think this weather has to do with the solar flares?"

"Maybe. It's obviously affected the sky and so it's possible it affected the weather. But I'm also not well-versed in a typical Kansas winter."

I squinted into the sky he'd just mentioned, purple clouds floating over a lavender background. "Tuck... Hosea mentioned several solar flares hitting over the course of a day. Do you think that means they hit different parts of the world? Could this be a worldwide disaster?" *Might other nations come to our rescue? Or is the whole planet dark?*

"It could be. But all we can do right now is focus on getting home. It's the best way to survive. And then we hope more information trickles in from there. Once we're safe."

Safe. Was there even such a thing anymore? The beauty and quiet around me made me believe—for the moment at least—that there were still safe places where good people existed. "Hosea said things would get fixed eventually."

Tuck was silent again as though deciding how to answer. Finally, he said, "It will take at least several years."

I stopped, gaping at him. "*Years?*"

"At least."

He turned and started walking again, and I took up beside him, my legs like Jell-O. My head swam as a barrage of specifics wound through my mind. What would things look like after years with no power?

"What will people do for money?"

"They'll have to trade things of value."

Things of value. That phrase inspired a whole slew of unsettling half thoughts. What did I have of value now? My ribs felt hollow as I considered Tuck in my peripheral vision. He could work anywhere for the things that were now important—food, water, shelter...safety. He could come back to Topeka and find Hosea. His options would be limitless.

We need people with special skills.

It was me who would have no way to earn a living anymore. No one was going to trade me something precious for my voice, not when they were trying to survive. Birdsong was worth as much as my singing. I felt dizzy. Some of this had already occurred to me, and I'd begun to accept that my career would be put on hold. But I'd never imagined that *on hold* meant years. Would it even be salvageable by then? Who could even say?

I started humming again to shut out the unanswerable questions zipping through my mind, our feet hitting the pavement, providing a soothing cadence, my breath coming easier after a while.

Day Eight

We camped that night, so exhausted I was half-asleep before my body hit my sleeping bag, and the next day we started out again at daybreak, the Oklahoma sunrise coloring the plains in silvery-white light.

After a few miles, we saw a farmhouse in the distance, and Tuck came to a slow stop as he turned to shield his eyes from the glare and look at the property. I stopped too, and it took me a moment to pull myself from the semitrance I'd been in as I walked, focusing on the slap of my shoes on the road rather than the emptiness in my stomach and my growing thirst.

"It looks like a small farm," I said. "If we can sneak into the henhouse, would they even miss a couple of eggs?"

Tuck thinned his lips. He didn't like the idea of stealing, I could tell. But I also knew that he'd put survival above egg theft. Especially as eggs could be replaced for those who owned chickens.

"There might be a creek on their land or some other water source," Tuck said. "We could fill up our water bottles."

I gave a nod. We'd been refilling our bottles wherever we

could when they ran out and then boiling the water before drinking it. But we'd finished the last of our water earlier and would need to find some soon.

Tuck turned toward the dirt road that led to the house a good quarter mile off the road and I followed.

"Let's go through those trees so we can get a better view of the house before we just walk up on it," Tuck said, and then without waiting for me to answer, began moving in the direction of the evergreens. The copse of trees wasn't very thick and so it didn't take long to make it to the edge of the tree line.

Tuck began walking slowly, and I all but halted, watching as he carefully removed his backpack and then leaned through the break in the trees where the house was visible.

I went to join Tuck but halted when I heard a click and saw Tuck freeze and then raise both hands as he stepped back. I sucked in a breath as my pulse rate jumped.

Tuck took another few steps backward, a…child appearing in front of him, holding a raised shotgun. The kid—who looked to be no older than twelve—stepped forward, one eye squinted as he gestured with the shotgun for Tuck to step back. Tuck did and the kid's gaze swung to me and then back to Tuck. "What do you want?"

"We'd like to speak to your mom and dad if they're available," Tuck said. "We're not here to hurt anyone."

"What do you want with my mom and dad?" the kid demanded.

"Just to—"

"Kyler?"

"Over here, Dad!" Kyler called. "I caught some trespassers!"

The sound of footsteps over soft ground quickly approached and a moment later, a man wearing a dark green beanie and a brown jacket, appeared. His eyes swept the two of us as he took the shotgun from his son and took over pointing it in our direction. "Who are you?"

"Sir, I'm Tucker Mattice, and that's Emily Swanson. We're walking to California, and we were hoping you could spare a couple of eggs, or…well, anything really."

"Sorry. But we have a full house here and won't be giving away any of our food." He used the gun to gesture behind us. "Now move on."

"Okay, have a nice day." Tuck began to turn. To give up. My mouth dropped open. What were we going to do now? Catch a squirrel with our bare hands? He probably could. But I didn't want squirrel. I wanted those eggs.

I used my arm to nudge Tuck aside as I stepped forward. I plastered a big smile on my face. Nova's smile—the smile of the girl who knew how to get anything she wanted. Not the wavering concession speech of a man who was trying so hard to live his life on the straight and narrow that he couldn't bear the thought of stealing a couple of eggs or talking his way into a warm house. But I had no such compunctions. I was starving and tired. "We're here to trade," I said. "Nothing comes for free in this world, not anymore. At least for now. We're well aware."

The farmer's eyes did a brief sweep of the two of us before he let out a short laugh and nudged his son. "Go on back inside." Kyler looked briefly indignant but then turned toward the house. His father sized me up again. "No offense but doesn't look like you have much to offer."

Tuck went to step back in the position where he'd been, and I quickly put my arm out again, holding him back. "Information," I said.

The man paused, and he turned his head slightly. I saw the spark of interest in his eyes and jumped in to take advantage of the opportunity. "Sir, we've been walking for over a week now. We first spent the day with Sheriff Goodfellow in Silver Creek, Missouri, and then we spent some time with a man who walked from St. Louis. Yesterday we were in Topeka where some military members have set up a camp for…refugees. We've gained information about what's going on from there to here, and also specifics about one of the big cities. I imagine you've been chomping at the bit, so to speak, as you've waited for information that hasn't come. No mail. No garbage pickup. No aircraft overhead. If you have an older vehicle, maybe you drove to a store nearby, or maybe a neighbor did and reported to you that no one knew anything there either. If it wasn't emptied out then, I can almost guarantee it is by now."

I could feel Tuck's gaze on me, and he'd leaned back slightly as though to give me more room to talk.

"The most important thing to know is that we have news you're going to want to hear, and quickly. It pertains to your safety and that of your neighbors as well." I wasn't lying on that front. If Isaac was right, in short order, there were going to be a lot more people on the road. And that even meant backroads. I hadn't really let myself consider the details of that too much because it was frankly terrifying, but in that moment, I realized that, so far, we'd walked in relative safety, but that might no longer be the case.

The farmer's eyes had narrowed as I'd spoken, though the level of the firearm had lowered so that it was now aimed at the ground. I could only hope that was a good sign that meant he was at least considering my offer. "What is it you want to trade for this so-called vital information?"

"Dinner. We'll take anything you can spare."

"What else?" he demanded.

"Fresh water now and to take with us."

"Hmm."

Tuck interjected, "Sir, that's all—"

"And a place to stay tonight."

I heard Tuck let out a low hiss of air as though I'd gone a step too far, and I braced, waiting for the man to tell us to get lost.

"Dinner'd be whatever's at risk of spoiling and needs to be eaten or thrown away. You can sleep in my barn, but I can't

allow you to stay in the house while my family's sleeping. I'm
sure you can understand."

"That's great. Yes, we accept. Thank you," I said, the words
flowing out on one long breath of relief. *Oh my God. Dinner. A
chair to sit in and a fork.* I wanted to weep with gratitude.

I gave Tuck a giddy look over my shoulder and we followed
the farmer as he led us through his front yard and into his house.

thirty-one

Tuck

I had to hand it to Emily. She'd come through on the fly. Why hadn't I considered bargaining with information? It was just about the only commodity we had, and she'd thought of it, and suggested the trade with a charming smile, even with a shotgun pointed squarely at her midsection. Once again, she deserved my respect and my gratitude. She'd earned it in this case because here we were, sitting in the comfortable living room of a farmhouse, the soft cushions of a couch beneath my ass. Damn, it felt good.

"My name's Tom Pritchard and this is my wife, Jane," the farmer said, extending his hand toward the woman who'd joined him on the couch across from where I sat. She was about the same age as Tom, fortyish I'd guess with long blond hair pulled back into a bun and kind blue eyes.

"Emily, right?" Tom asked, looking at Emily, who'd sat down in an easy chair to my left.

"Yes, Emily Swanson."

"And Tuck?"

I nodded.

"Oh, forgive my manners. Can I offer you a glass of water?" Jane asked.

"That'd be great," Emily said.

"Thanks," I added as Jane stood and left the room.

"We're from California," I told Tom. "Our plane crashed in the wilderness in Illinois. Like Emily said, we eventually made it to a small town named Silver Creek n Missouri, and then walked or caught rides from there to here. We've mostly taken back roads, traveling during the day and camping at night."

Jane came back into the room carrying a tray with a pitcher of water and three glasses and set it on the coffee table.

"Their plane went down, Jane."

She'd started pouring but now paused and looked up at us. "Oh my. You're lucky to be alive."

"They've been walking and camping since then," he told her before looking back at us. "This isn't the best time of year for camping."

"No, it's not, especially with very limited supplies. But we have to get back home, and as you've probably noticed, the only vehicles that are running seem to be pre-1980 models."

"Sure did. If the power doesn't come back on soon, those are going to become real valuable."

"They already are valuable, and probably getting stolen left and right. We've hitched a ride a couple of times, but everyone is being very cautious, which is understandable."

He gave a nod, his craggy features troubled. Jane handed a glass of water to each of us, and we all drank. The preteen who'd held us at gunpoint wandered in with a boy who looked to be just a couple of years older and they stood by the stairs. "Kyler, Luca, you go on. This is an adult conversation."

The boys' faces dropped, but they turned to leave the room.

"Actually, sir," I said, "they're your boys, but if I can be blunt, you're going to need all hands on deck for what's heading your way."

Tom Pritchard glanced back at his sons, who had stopped and were looking at their father eagerly. He sighed and gestured that they should stay in the room. "Call Uriah too."

The older of the two boys leaned toward the stairs and called their brother, and a minute later, footsteps sounded and a boy who looked to be about sixteen or seventeen descended into the room.

I told him the short version of what had happened to us so far and included what I'd talked to Sheriff Goodfellow about.

Tom and Jane exchanged looks, their expressions registering the same stark disbelief that mine had when I'd been told about the outage extending all the way to Pennsylvania, and possibly beyond, and about the fires and the likely exodus, that so far seemed to be a trickle but would pick up as food and water disappeared. "My God," Tom murmured, running his hand over his sparse hair. "Okay. What else?"

I gave them a brief description of what Isaac had told us about his experience, and then what we'd learned from Hosea, leaving out that 90 percent statistic that I still couldn't believe was accurate. There was no reason to terrify people unnecessarily. "The grid won't be back up for a long time, potentially years. People are going to be coming from the cities and eventually, some of the towns," I said. "We've seen foot traffic pick up quite a bit. Right now, it seems like folks heading specific places— namely to family—but I'd imagine that soon it will simply be people escaping hopeless situations. Like Emily said, the stores are emptied out by now. In a few weeks, most pantries will be dry. I don't know about everywhere, but in these parts, farms will eventually be in possession of the last of the food. And that eventuality is fast approaching if it's not here already."

Jane took Tom's hand between them, and the three boys moved closer to where we were seated.

"Your chickens will become more precious than gold. I'd work with neighbors you trust to have them guarded around the clock. I'd also gather your neighbors and form a perimeter. Moving as many of your garden plants inside and starting to preserve seeds. Families will come here looking for help. There'll be children, and babies. You'll have to turn them away because if you don't, your own family will die. Some won't ask, some will be prepared to take, and you'll have to be ready for that too."

Tom glanced at his sons and then met my eyes. "We have ammunition."

"Are you ready to shoot a hungry mother who's trying to feed her toddler or a child the same age of one of your sons?"

Jane let out a small sound of distress, and Tom scrubbed a hand down his face. "I'm not telling you what you have to do—I'm only telling you to be prepared."

Jane gave a jerky nod. "Yes. We understand."

"How soon do you estimate?" the oldest boy named Uriah asked.

"Isaac was among the first to leave the city. He was alone and kept moving. If you'd been on his route, he'd already be to you."

"We've seen some travelers out on the road, and a few have come this way, which is why Kyler was on the porch watching for trespassers when he spotted you. But…"

"I don't know exact timing, but I'd estimate you have about a week until the numbers increase. Whether that's a little or a lot depends on many factors." Routes from cities. The locations around them where folks might stop first. If I were these people, I'd sit down and calculate it all out, but we'd given them the information. The rest would be up to them, because we'd be gone by morning. Tom seemed deep in thought, and I figured it was a good bet that he was already doing some calculations. He looked at his oldest son. "Uriah and Luca, go see the Bensons, Ortizes, Perkinses, and Hillmans. Tell them to meet here at ten a.m. tomorrow morning."

"What if they ask why?" Uriah asked.

"Tell them you don't know, but that your dad has some information he'd rather share in person."

Uriah and Luca left the room, and a moment later, the front door opened and closed.

"I'm gonna go guard our road from the porch again," Kyler said enthusiastically.

"Just make sure to stay on the porch," his mother said. "Come get your father if you spot anyone."

"Yes, ma'am." The boy skipped out of the room. To him, at least for now, this was an adventure, and I hoped it'd remain that way, though I was all but certain it would not.

Tom turned back to us. "The families I sent Uriah and Luca to are the neighbors I trust the most. We all have different resources. That will be important."

I nodded, glad I was right that he was already planning.

"Okay," Jane said, the word breathy and filled with worry, "we'll get a plan underway in the morning. Right now, I'm going to go to the shed and start bringing in some pots to put in the back room. It'll be our temporary greenhouse." She stood, and I thought her legs trembled a bit. What we'd said had obviously scared her, and I was sorry for that, but I also wasn't because if they weren't scared, they weren't living in reality, and they wouldn't do what needed to be done.

"Can I help?" Emily asked.

"You can help by collecting the eggs from the henhouse," Jane said with a wobbly smile. I sensed she needed a bit of time alone and couldn't blame her for that. She was a mother with three children and she'd just learned that hordes of people would likely be arriving on their doorstep in the weeks ahead, not to mention that the situation was going to last several years. I still felt slightly dazed when I thought about that. Staying on the move was helping me cope, and ensuring it settled little by little.

"Sure. Of course," Emily said with a smile.

"There's a basket in the kitchen near the backdoor," Jane said as she turned away. "And thank you." Jane exited the room quickly, and Tom watched her with a frown.

"Emily, while you see what the girls left for us, I'll show Tuck to the room you'll be sleeping in."

"We're really perfectly happy in the barn, sir. We have sleeping—"

"Nonsense. I said that before I spent a few minutes with you. You've given us invaluable information and you're obviously good folks. We have a guest room and I insist."

I met Emily's eyes as she stood, hers flaring slightly with something I couldn't read. Discomfort, perhaps, and I could only assume it was because we'd have to figure out a sleeping arrangement. I didn't mind taking the floor though. In fact, I'd been sleeping on the floor by choice since getting out of prison. And after bedding down on the hard ground, a portion of carpet would be a luxury.

Emily headed toward the kitchen where Tom pointed her, and then he helped me bring our backpacks and gear up the narrow set of steps. The room was small and cozy, a handsewn quilt covering the double bed, and a few more carefully folded over a quilt stand next to the dresser. "I'll get you a few candles and a lighter," Tom said. "There's a bathroom in the hall and water in the bathtub, but the plumbing obviously isn't working, and our water stopped running days ago. I hate to ask you to use the woods out back but—"

"Sir, we've been using the woods for a week. We're grateful for the bed, and the roof over our heads."

Tom nodded. "It's going to get bad, isn't it?"

He was looking at me man-to-man, a father with a family

to protect and a community of neighbors he cared for. "Yes," I said honestly. "It's likely going to get very bad."

I spent a few minutes arranging our stuff and setting up an area near the end of the bed where I'd sleep. Then I went downstairs and, finding the house empty, walked through the kitchen toward the back door to look for Emily and help her gather eggs if she needed it.

The chickens were situated a few hundred feet behind the house, a cobblestone path leading from the back door to the red coop. The sun shone down, and for the first time in a week, the sky appeared somewhat normal, fluffy white clouds dancing amidst a purply blue. I spotted Emily inside the pen, her back to me as she reached inside the coop and retrieved the eggs, setting them gently in the basket next to her on the ground. As I moved closer, the scent transported me back to the chicken coop on Honey Hill Farm, Emily's golden hair shiny under the sunlight. A yearning filled the space between my ribs so suddenly that it made me suck in a breath. I hadn't felt a longing for home like that in years.

Or maybe I just hadn't allowed myself to. But now, standing here, breathing in the animals and sunshine and the fresh, open air, and seeing her among it all, the way she'd once been, I let myself feel it. Let myself remember what it'd felt like when a home like this had been mine.

Emily opened the gate and walked through, her face breaking into a smile when she saw me. Pleasure radiated inside me. *It always felt so damn good to make you smile.* And the moment made me remember exactly why.

I met her near the gate. "Walk with me?"

"Haven't we done enough of that?"

I chuckled. "A stroll. Just to check out the property."

She smiled and then shaded her eyes as she looked across the back field. "It is pretty, isn't it?"

"It is." We turned and meandered across the grass, and then stepped onto a flagstone path that led to a firepit surrounded by portions of tree stumps fashioned as seats. Emily sat down on one, closing her eyes and tilting her face to the sun, a ray of light washing over. She was free of makeup, her long hair held back in a ponytail, and she looked young and fresh and beautiful. She looked more like the Emily I'd once known, and because of it, my heart squeezed. I remembered the way I'd stared at her across our family campfires or through gaps in branches as we grasped oranges in our palms...the way I used to fantasize about planting my lips on hers. I let myself stare at her now the way I had then, my gaze moving over her luminous skin, to her light brown lashes which were thick and feathery, and down to her pillowy lips. And even when she opened her eyes and focused her crystal blue gaze on me, I couldn't look away. I swore the scent of orange blossoms tickled my nose and that yearning stirred again. "You always did wear sunshine well."

Her eyes grew soft, and her lips parted as she took in a deep breath, closing her eyes again. She tilted her head back a bit more. And for a few minutes she was silent, but I didn't mind because it gave me even more time to study her to my heart's content, to reacquaint myself with each freckle and feature. Perhaps it was pointless, and even unwise, but drinking her in felt like feeding a different kind of hunger, and one that had gone mostly unacknowledged but was there all the same.

"Before we started on this journey, I'd forgotten what quiet is like," she finally said, opening her eyes. "I didn't realize how loud the world had become. My world anyway. And I... I'll miss the hustle. It will be hard giving that up. But this has reminded me to seek out the quiet sometimes too. It's reminded me what peace really feels like."

I stepped over to the tree stump seat next to the one she was on and sat down. "Hey, Emily?"

She turned to me. "Yeah?"

"I owe you an apology too." I squinted out to the fields and the rolls of hay behind her for a moment and then met her eyes. All day, I'd been thinking as we'd walked, going over everything that happened since we'd crash-landed in the middle of Nowhere, Illinois. "I'm sorry for what I said, about you being a sellout. You worked and climbed and didn't give up, just like you took control of a speeding horse and buggy. I was wrong and I'm sorry. You didn't end up where you were because of anything other than your talent and tenacity."

Her cheeks flushed and she smiled, and it was almost shy. "Not that it matters now. All that... It's over."

The sun shifted, hitting my eyes and I squinted at her. "You still have the telethon," I said. "And the marathon..."

I'd said it to make her smile and it did, but the smile didn't last. "Do I? That's beginning to feel like a pipe dream too."

"That was my point. You're good at making pipe dreams a reality."

"It might not be up to me," she said. "But I would like to find some way to help. Or maybe perform. Even if it's only for a few people. Or... I don't know. Military bases once they get set back up. *If* they do." She sighed. "Maybe there'll be an opportunity for me to be useful too."

I watched her. Ah, she felt useless and without value. And I had certainly contributed to that. Hell, at the time, I'd believed it. But I didn't believe it anymore. Emily was brave when she needed to be. She had gumption and nerve, and she was quick on her feet. She had the charm I didn't and enjoyed putting it to use. *Little Showboat.* "I guess we'll see when we get there," I said.

"Yeah, I guess we will."

thirty-two

Emily

We enjoyed an incredible dinner of vegetable stew and bread baked over the firepit, and for a brief few hours, the world felt almost normal, if a bit primitive. I'd spoken to Tuck earlier about appreciating the quiet. And the simple but delicious dinner with Tom and Jane and their boys made me realize too how little time I'd made to slow down and enjoy what was now so precious: good food, kind people, a feeling of safety, and later, a warm bed and walls surrounding me.

I'd had all those things, and never really paused to appreciate any of them, so focused on attaining goals that were somewhere beyond where I was in that moment. I would have done anything to snap my fingers and fix the current state of the country, but even if I could, I would take lessons from this experience. It'd only been a week, and I already felt changed in ways I was sure I'd be discovering for a long time to come.

Jane opened a bottle of wine, and we shared it as Tuck and

Tom talked, Tom pointing things out here and there around the property. I sighed, the alcohol and the fire making me feel warm and woozy. I looked to my right where I could see their garden off to the side of the house. "Is anything still growing?" I asked.

Jane followed my gaze. "A few things. I brought them inside earlier like Tuck suggested. We also have a cellar of preserved food. If we're very careful, we can make it until spring."

Spring. That word opened a small window of hope inside of me. Although...even when the weather turned, how would farms plant and harvest without trucks delivering the supplies they needed to do so? I'd grown up on a farm and knew that as much as the earth provided, we depended on gas to run our equipment, and a hundred other things that came from sources outside our operation.

"Is this farm how you make a living, or did...do you and Tom do other work?"

"Nope, this is our business. We're considered a specialty farm. We grow pumpkins and horseradish, primarily."

"Did you grow up on a farm?" I asked.

"No. No, my father was a lawyer, and I grew up in the lap of luxury in Chicago, actually. Tom and I met and married there. But it's been eighteen years since we moved."

"You just picked up and left Chicago to start a pumpkin farm?"

"Seems like a strange choice, right?" She laughed, but I didn't sense any offense. And honestly? It might have seemed like a strange choice last week. But certainly not now.

"But we love it. It's simple, and most days are slow, but once you live a life like this, you begin to understand how all those things you used to believe were real, just...aren't. I don't think we were meant to live in a rat race. How many people spend their lives going to jobs they hate only to barely pay their bills?

Coming home to stare at a television set that rots their brain while eating food that makes them sick?"

I thought about that. I didn't disagree with her. Even if that particular existence, for the time being, wasn't likely being lived by anyone. Now the Midwest was in survival mode. But I got her point because I hadn't wanted that life either. I never had. I had wanted *more* than that. I wanted to be rich and famous and adored by millions. I wanted to eat organic produce and grass-fed animals. Who didn't, if they had the choice? Who wanted to worry about bills or money or losing their property the way my parents were?

And I *could* see wanting to be surrounded by the great outdoors. I liked nature. I'd grown up in one of the most beautiful places in the country, natural beauty all around.

"What did you do before this?" I asked. We were skating around the fact that the world was changing drastically, but honestly, I needed a few moments—at least that—to pretend that life was somewhat normal. We'd been stranded. We were on a road trip and depending on the kindness of strangers tonight for a meal and a roof over our heads.

"I was a corporate executive, and Tom worked in finance."

"Wow. You really did live the rat race."

"Oh, we were deeply entrenched in the rat race. We were rich by most standards. Young and fashionable. We were invited to all the right parties. We wore all the best brands. And we were miserable, numbed out on pills, and on the verge of divorce."

"So, you decided to give it all up and move out here in the hopes of saving your marriage?"

"In a nutshell. It wasn't just our marriage that needed saving though. It was we as individuals. We had everything society had told us would make us happy, and yet we were miserable. *Why?* What were we missing? We needed to figure it out. And then I listened to this radio show about a couple who moved to Maine and bought a blueberry farm, and they seemed so happy. At peace in a way I'd never known anyone to be. The next day, I looked up farms for sale and this one was listed by an older couple with no children who had decided to retire and downsize. Pumpkins, I thought. Pumpkins it is."

"Just like that?"

She smiled. "If you understood the depth of my misery, you would understand the lack of fear. The decision was made in desperation, but it's been the best thing we ever did."

I took that in, not as surprised as I might have been had I heard the same story a few weeks ago, especially in light of what I'd been thinking about regarding happiness and gratitude and taking simple pleasures for granted.

Jane and I were both quiet for a few minutes as we sipped our wine. I stared at Tuck, deep in conversation with Tom as they now stood nearby, Tom pointing into the distance. Tuck wavered through the flames, his shifting form somehow making him all the more beautiful.

"He's very handsome," Jane said. I glanced at her to see her eyes on Tuck right before she gave me a smile.

"We grew up together," I said, turning my gaze back to him. Funny how his form was still familiar to me even though he'd grown from a teen to a man in the time we'd been apart. He still had that particular stance though, and he still cocked his head just so when he was focusing on something. Or someone. "I used to watch him through windows like this when I was a little girl." I'd had such a *deep* crush on him.

"You're a beautiful couple."

"Oh. No. No. We're just...friends," I settled on. Was that the right description of our relationship? Yes, yes, I thought so. We'd grown closer in the past few days, an understanding developing between us, forgiveness being sought by both.

"Oh. Really?" She frowned. "I didn't get that impression. You seem...close. He watches you constantly." As if he knew we were talking about him, or to prove Jane right, Tuck glanced over, his eyes finding mine.

"Tuck and I are complicated."

She took a drink of wine. "Situations like the one we're in tend to clarify things rather quickly."

I let out a breathy laugh. "Maybe. Or maybe things just get more muddled." I took a sip of wine as well and looked back over at Tuck, the fire crackling between us making him seem like nothing more than a memory. "You know how you think that if your childhood crush showed up, you'd realize he was just that and nothing more?" I murmured. "And you even think that maybe you had really bad taste back then that has nothing to do with the woman you became?"

Jane smiled. "Yeah. Sure, honey. It's usually true. I used to have a thing for the Karate Kid. He was it. He was the goal."

I laughed, but it turned into a sigh. "But then, you see the boy you used to dream about, and even though you're years older and everything about you has changed, and even though you're in a town full of the most beautiful people on the planet earth, he still makes you feel the same way you did back then— even more—and part of you hates it so much, and part of you doesn't at all."

I glanced over at Jane, but instead of looking sad for me, she was smiling. "I wouldn't be so quick to hate that. If the way he looks at you is any indication, he feels the very same way."

I practically stumbled up the stairs behind Tuck an hour later after Jane and I finished every last drop of the bottle of wine. I wasn't exactly drunk, but I was plenty tipsy. Tuck set the candle Jane had lit for him on the dresser and I fell onto the bed and let out a moan of pleasure. "Beautiful mattress," I whispered. "I love you."

Tuck gave me a crooked smile, sitting on the edge of the bed and removing his shoes. Then he placed them by the door and sat down on the floor where I now saw he'd rolled out his sleeping bag. I came up on my elbow. "Tuck, you don't need to sleep on the floor. There's plenty of room in this bed."

"It's fine, Emily. I'm good down here."

"Oh shut up. We've been walking for a week and sleeping on the ground. I'm not going to *not* share this bed. If you sleep on the floor, I will too in protest of you giving up a mattress, which is just dumb. No martyrs allowed."

"I wasn't being a martyr. I was being polite."

"You? Polite? Please. Why make such a drastic change to your personality now?"

"Funny." He still looked a little torn but stood and walked to the bed and sat down. "Are you sure?"

I patted the pillow next to me and scooted over. "Very."

He lay down, a sigh escaping his lips. We both got under the covers, and I turned his way. The moon was shining in through the open window above us, the candlelight flickering and again, I felt vaguely like I was in a waking dream, the blurriness of the wine only enhancing the sensation. I let my gaze move over the beautiful proportions of his profile. I itched to reach out and run my finger over his brow and nose, down to his chin and jaw, outlining the movement of my gaze. He turned his head and looked at me, our gazes catching and though I felt plenty woozy, I still felt the charge that sparked in the air.

I got the sense that his muscles had tightened slightly but couldn't say how I knew. A subtle shift maybe, or something else I was too tipsy to distinguish. What I did know was that the almost indiscernible movement of his body made my own respond. My nipples pebbled and a distant throbbing took up in my blood, made heavy and slow by the alcohol.

He blinked as if suddenly taken off guard, and then tipped his head back to look up at the moon. I did too, only able to see half of it from where we lay. "It seems like it's peeking in at us," I whispered.

He let out a soft chuckle and I smiled sleepily, my eyes already half-closed. The bed was so warm and comfortable and there was a roof and walls protecting us from harm. Tuck and I were so close, and I could smell the scent of his skin, making me feel equally comforted and excited. Candlelight flickered, and oh, how I wished I could stay in the moment for longer than a single night. Clouds floated past the moon, dimming its light, and I stared up at it again feeling a moment of uncertainty as if the laws of nature had changed and the moonlight might blink out like the rest of the world.

"The whole world feels different," I whispered, my words slurring. "Not just the power, but everything seems so uncertain." I lifted my arm and waved it toward the window. "I mean the planet itself. It's like whatever catastrophe shut everything down also made the earth unstable. You know like it might just start crumbling all around us." And it made me want to reach for him, to grab on and hold tight. Because I had this feeling that even if the world crumbled, somehow Tuck would figure out a way to survive. The comfort I'd just felt took on a shade of fear, and I scooted closer to him.

He turned toward me, so our faces were only inches apart. "No, Em. Whatever's going on, the earth will be okay. This planet has survived shifting plates and ice ages, volcanoes, tsunamis. The earth will be fine and so will we."

"Will we, Tuck?"

"I promised you I'd keep you safe, didn't I?"

I felt the ghost of a smile hover over my mouth. "Yeah, but even you can't protect me from everything."

My words blended together. I couldn't feel my lips anymore. And the last thing I heard before I drifted off to sleep was, "Watch me."

Day Nine

I'd woken tangled with Tuck, his breath soft against my temple, and something decidedly hard against my belly. My body had come instantly awake even if my mind was still half-asleep. I'd felt Tuck stir, and I'd known the moment he realized the situation, scooting out of bed so quickly he'd practically fallen off the side. I'd felt momentarily offended, and definitely frustrated, and pretended to keep sleeping until he'd shaken me "awake," saying we needed to get on the road.

We left the Pritchards before the sun had fully risen, our breath pluming in the chilly morning air. I looked back only once, trying to memorize the place where, for a moment in time, I'd felt safe and welcomed. And I said a silent prayer that their family would be okay.

Around midday, Tuck scored us a bag of almonds from an abandoned car, and we counted them out by the side of the road, Tuck pouring my half into my open palm. I popped one in my mouth, moaning as I chewed. Tuck's eyes lowered slightly and then he looked away. He'd been quiet for much of the day so far, and perhaps a little tense. It was fine. I had a lot on my mind too, and I lost myself in the music in my head, melodies and lyrics flowing through me like a waterfall. Part of me wished I had something—anything—to write them down on, but another part knew that I wouldn't forget. These weren't fleeting notes that I was trying desperately to catch. These songs were already deeply ingrained as if they'd existed inside me all along, and it'd only taken a worldwide catastrophe and a multistate walk to jar them loose.

Plus, the slight hangover I had didn't exactly make me feel chatty. As much as taking the edge off my current circumstances had felt good in the moment, I decided I wasn't going to drink my way through this.

We finished the almonds and drank some water and started walking again. Hours later, the sun drifting low, Tuck stopped and held the map up, swearing softly.

"Please don't tell me we're lost," I said, looking around. We'd walked through a small town earlier and then into a park that had dog-walking paths and bike trails. But it seemed that we'd suddenly found ourselves in a stretch of woods that I'd hoped would let out onto a main road, but as of yet, had not. I put my hand on my forehead. "Oh my God, you got us lost."

Tuck turned toward me, jaw tight. "Emily, do you want to lead the way? Maybe you could do a better job."

"Maybe I could," I bit back. I was hungry and thirsty, and I just wanted to lie down in a cozy bed again and instead I was tromping through some muddy woods. And I'd woken up pressed against Tuck and wanting him to kiss me so badly I still ached with it. And he hadn't spared me more than a few words over the course of an entire day. And to add insult to injury, now he'd gotten us lost. Wonderful.

He turned, focusing his full attention on me. "Yes, you probably could," he said. "Hell, if you don't need me anymore, then maybe we should part ways."

"It's probably for the best," I shot back, even if the very idea of parting from Tuck practically turned my insides to water. We came together, the heat of our sudden fight drawing me, and seeming to do the same to him.

He turned his head slightly, shutting one eye as though in consideration. "Then again, you have something I want and so I'm not going to let you go quite yet."

Our breath mingled, bodies so close I could feel his heat. I wanted to be tangled with him again. I wanted to feel his hardness pressed against my stomach. And I wanted him to want me with the same white-hot intensity.

"I do?" I asked breathily.

He brought his face close to mine and then leaned toward my ear. "I want that almond you saved in your pocket." He drew back and then his face blossomed in a grin, and though I was hyped up on anger and sexual frustration, I couldn't help bursting out in laughter.

I pushed him away and dug the almond from my pocket.

"Never," I said, beginning to bring it to my mouth, my tongue extended. But he caught my wrist, and I let out a sound that was halfway between a laugh and a scream as he spun me around, fake fighting for the singular almond.

"Give it here," he said, and I laughed again, tripping over something on the forest floor and flailing backward, landing on the soft backpack I was wearing and wheezing out another laugh.

"Never!" I repeated, attempting to bring the almond to my mouth again. Tuck lowered himself on top of me and grabbed my wrist, halting the almond near my mouth. We wrestled, fighting for the almond as I laughed and squirmed, the grin on Tuck's face wolfish with excitement.

He pinned my arm and went toward the almond with his mouth as I laughed and struggled, both of us panting and writhing in ways that were dialing my sexual frustration up to a hundred. But I couldn't deny that I loved it. Fighting with Tuck had always been thrilling, and apparently, I'd never grown out of it. And, if his flushed face and rapid breathing were any indication, he felt the same way. He bit off the almond and I let out a gasp of outrage before he brought his face up, the piece of almond between his straight white teeth. I lifted my hand, realizing he'd split it in half.

"Humph," I said, and popped the other half in my mouth, both of us chewing and smiling stupidly at each other. "Consider that your payment for helping me get home," I muttered.

"Paid in full," he said. Then he chuckled and got off me and held out his hand to help me up.

"Good, now get us out of—" I spotted something over his shoulder. "Oh my gosh, Tuck, look."

He turned, peering at the spot where I'd pointed. "A tree house."

I moved around him, hopping over a rotting trunk and rounding a feathery fir, its branches tickling my cheek as I passed. The ladder looked sturdy and didn't wobble when I shook it, and so I looked over my shoulder at Tuck who had arrived on my heels. "I'm going up."

"Careful," he said.

I quickly climbed the ladder, and then crawled into the small space that was a platform surrounded by four short walls that you could hide behind or look over. Just beyond, I could see a row of roofs, proving we weren't so lost after all.

A cardboard box sat near the corner, and I moved toward it as I heard the sound of Tuck ascending behind me. I looked inside the box and let out a sound of glee.

"What is it?" Tuck asked.

I pulled one of the items out of the box and held it up. "Crackers," I said and then removed a couple more things. "Spray cheese," I squeaked, close to crying with joy. "And marshmallows. Beautiful, glorious marshmallows."

thirty-three

Tuck

"You're kidding." But I could clearly see she wasn't. *Holy shit.* We'd come across a bounty. I'd been ravenous all day in more ways than I wanted to think about, not able to satisfy any of my myriad cravings. Walking had been a constant torture considering my serious case of blue balls.

I hadn't even realized how much I was suppressing my attraction to Emily while Charlie was around. Because the moment he went away, and even in the midst of danger and uncertainty, I couldn't stop thinking about what it'd be like to kiss her and feel her softness beneath me.

Emily ripped open the sleeve of crackers and shoved one in her mouth. Then she tossed one to me and leaned her head back as she squirted the cheese into her mouth.

I laughed and she gestured for me to do the same, so I tipped my head and opened my mouth. Emily grinned as she squeezed a generous serving of cheesy goo onto my tongue. Oh God, that was so good. Not as good as the dinner we'd eaten the night before with Tom and Jane and their family, but it'd been a long twelve hours with only a handful of almonds to fill our bellies, and so this was an unexpected windfall. Before I'd realized we'd turned in the wrong direction somewhere, I'd been thinking about snares and wondering how long it'd take to catch something for dinner.

"Wait," I said, knowing how easy it would be to gorge ourselves on this. "We need to ration. Who knows if we'll find anything to eat tomorrow."

She nodded, her mouth too full to speak for a moment. "I know, I know. Okay. Just one more squeeze."

We each enjoyed another mouthful of cheese and a few crackers and then regretfully packed them away in my backpack. But it was a relief to know that we had something for tomorrow too. Emily lay back on the wooden floor of the fort and smiled up at the canopy of trees. The sun was setting, the resplendent yellow sky filtering through the tree boughs. Everything looked mildly smudged and slightly out of focus as though we'd found ourselves in a make-believe forest. I lay down next to her, our hips touching as we stared upward. "This light," I said, "it reminds me of the hayloft at Honey Hill."

I didn't look at her, but I heard her mouth move into a smile. "Magical," she said. "That's how I think of Honey Hill Farm. That's how I remember it."

"Golden," I added. I felt unexpectedly choked up. "My memories of those years are gilded."

She did look at me then, and I turned toward her. "It's the first time you've talked about Honey Hill to me."

Our faces were so close. I had this urge to pull away, worried that my body would act on its own accord regardless of what my mind told me was best. But I'd spent the day struggling to move my mind from the way Emily had felt snuggled against me the night before and couldn't seem to do it anymore. It was exhausting because all I wanted to do was relive the memory of how we'd fit together so perfectly, how silky her skin was, and how, even though the only shower we'd taken in a week had been far too short and extremely frigid, to me, she still smelled like sunshine. "It's hard for me to talk about Honey Hill," I admitted. "It...hurts."

Her eyes filled with empathy. *This woman.* She was made up of so many different shades. One minute she was irritating me, the next turning me on, and then she looked at me in a way that pierced my damn heart. It was difficult for me to understand her sometimes because I was so black-and-white. And she fascinated me too, just the same way she always had. She was silly and reckless and reactive and strong and fearless and gentle and sweet. And I never knew exactly which version of Emily would appear and it made me crazy, but I also couldn't get enough.

The sun lowered, the hush of coming night falling over the woods. Emily reached out and used her thumb to smooth the space between my brows. I blew out a slow exhale, relaxing my face. I hadn't even realized how tightly I'd been holding myself until she touched me in just that spot.

"I thought you were angry," she murmured. "When your mother died."

I blinked, surprised by her words. What had been on my face that had reminded her of my mother's death? Her expression was wistful, slightly sad.

"But you weren't mad," she said. "You were sad but also... you were afraid." She paused, and I couldn't move, caught in her gaze, rendered mute by this version of her. *Sweet. Tender.* "I'm so sorry I didn't see that. I thought you were angry...at life, at me, at everything. And so, when I didn't get an immediate response, I ran from you. I left you alone because I thought it was what you wanted."

I wasn't sure what to say. But I felt captured in her gaze. *Seen* when I hadn't experienced that for years, and certainly hadn't known enough to miss it. And maybe it meant all the more that it was her gazing at me with such knowing depth. Clearly, I cared far more about her opinion of me than I'd allowed myself to believe, mostly because I'd assumed she found me lacking. The gentleness in her eyes made me want to fall into her and never come up for air. I hadn't felt that type of kindness in so long. I reached out and put my hand over hers, needing so desperately to touch her. "I didn't even know what I wanted, or needed, back then, Em. How could you have known?"

She sighed. She was so beautiful, especially now, gauzy light shifting over her face. She'd expressed regret about that time, but I had regrets too, ones that I hadn't even seen clearly until very recently. "In that car on the highway outside Springfield," I murmured, "you said you'd survived me leaving you once before." She frowned slightly and tilted her head. "I did. I did do that, Em. I left and barely said goodbye. That wasn't right. It's not what a good friend would have done." I understood now too why I'd sensed something unsaid when I'd denied lashing out at her in the wake of my mother's death. She'd agreed, but I knew now that she would have preferred that to the stony silence I'd given her instead.

"I should have written to you, Tuck. I should have called. I could have reminded you that you were wanted and loved. Instead, I decided to pretend you no longer existed. It was a coping mechanism, but it didn't work quite as well as I hoped it would."

I felt so damn close to her, my throat full with the knowledge that I'd earned something back I thought was lost to me forever. Emily. My sidekick, my friend.

"Do you remember when I asked you to the prom?" she said.

The prom? "No. When did you do that?"

"A few months before you moved to LA." She looked up at the branches above, one finger twisting in her hair. "I had this stupid fantasy that if we went to the prom together, we'd have this moment on the dance floor where you'd wrap your arms around me and look into my eyes and... I don't know. Somehow it would set the whole world back in place and we'd return to those magical, golden days."

I hadn't expected that. I hadn't even realized she'd been thinking much about me at all during that time. She'd seemed so focused on her music and all her friends, living the life any beautiful seventeen-year-old girl should live. I'd distanced myself because I had no role in that sort of carefree existence. My life was falling apart as I watched each piece of my legacy dismantled and sold.

She turned her head, her gaze moving over my face. "You were in the barn working and I gathered all my courage and asked if you were going to the prom. You told me you didn't have time for stupid dances and then you turned away."

My chest deflated. "Shit. I'm sorry, Em." I did remember that now. It had hurt me because I'd misunderstood it. "I didn't know you were asking me to go with you. I thought your question was an indication you didn't see what I was going through."

"Maybe it was, partially anyway. Like I said, I thought you were angry and so I didn't know how to approach you. I was confused and hurt too. And I was also seventeen. But see, Tuck, it was just a moment, a moment where either of us could have reacted differently—better maybe—but we didn't, and so life moved forward the way it did. That's what life does in the wake of our choices, good, bad, or in-between."

My heart warmed. I appreciated the grace she was extending to me. I realized she was relating that moment, and perhaps several others between us, to that dreadful night Abel died. "Life moved forward with no dance-floor moment," I said. "The one that would have righted everything."

She turned her body and rested an elbow on the floor, supporting her head in her palm. "Do you think it's too late to try it now?"

"To dance?"

"To dance *the* dance."

"Here?"

Her lips were so close, and there was a tiny smear of yellow cheese on the corner of her mouth. The need to lean in and lick it off and taste her was so strong, I almost moaned, swelling to life, my body so needy. "Well, maybe not here," she said. "I mean, we're horizontal right now and there's no music. But…in general. Do you think there's such a thing as creating a moment that rights everything that's gone so horribly wrong? If one moment can ruin everything, maybe one moment can fix it too."

The way she was looking at me, as if life itself hinged on my answer, made my breath hitch. And for some reason, whereas I would have immediately dismissed the whimsical idea before right now, something inside was tempted to say, *maybe. Maybe there is such a moment, a few seconds that undo every wrong. Maybe.* Only Emily could do that—help me see possibility and hope where before I'd seen none. Only her.

And right then, it felt like a form of magic. It felt like—together—we could find that moment if it existed at all.

The sudden boom of gunfire made us both startle, and I got on my knees, peering over the wall of the tree fort, my heart hammering. The noise had come from a short distance away, probably someone hunting in this small section of woods. "We should go."

"Darn. I was hoping this was a good place to camp."

"We're essentially in someone's backyard," I said. "There's a neighborhood right over there. And if folks are hunting nearby, it isn't safe. Also, if there's danger, we'd be cornered up here." I turned and started down the ladder. "We'll camp somewhere safer that's close by and start off again in the morning."

We put our backpacks on once we were on the ground and turned back the way we'd come. The sky dimmed another few shades, turning from gold to amber to twilight blue. It was a chilly night and our breath gusted from our mouths as we moved through the damp forest. We walked for thirty minutes or so, winding back through the park, toward the road where I was pretty sure we'd taken a wrong turn. A glow appeared between the break in some trees, and we slowed. "A fire," Emily whispered, her teeth chattering slightly. The sound of a harmonica met our ears. "Music," she said, the longing in her voice was deeper than it'd been when she'd mentioned the campfire.

We had matches, but lighting a fire was always risky, depending on where we were. It would draw others even if it was a necessary risk.

"They're laughing," Emily said. "And I hear women."

"That still doesn't mean they're safe." The way her voice rose hopefully though, told me she was excited by the possibility of more social contact. I'd seen the way she'd lit up each time there was an opportunity to experience fellowship and conversation. I'd always been a loner, happy to be left in my own head, while Emily flourished in a crowd.

"It's a good bet, Tuck. Come on." She pulled me closer, and we looked around the trees where we could see four people sitting on two fallen logs situated around a blazing fire. There were two women, a young man, and a teenage girl. I let out a slow breath. I could likely take all of them on if they threatened us. Unless they had a weapon. But I didn't see one anywhere.

"A guitar," Emily said, breathless. It wasn't hard to hear the longing in her voice. Music was her gift, but also, it had always filled her own soul. Emily needed music like she needed air. I'd known her since she was a baby, and it'd always been the case.

"They might not want us to join them though. Everyone is rightfully suspicious right now," I said. Because regardless of the longing in her eyes, her safety was still my job.

"Leave this to me," she said as she pulled me from the trees.

The man stood when he saw us, his stance tense, expression wary. "Hi," Emily said with a smile as she set her backpack down. "We were hoping we might join you." She reached into the front pocket. "We have marshmallows," she said, holding up the full bag like a hostess on a game show, displaying the grand prize.

The man's shoulders relaxed and the women who had leaned together sat back where they'd been and smiled. "Come get warm," the older of the two women said.

We took a seat and introduced ourselves. "It's nice to meet you both," the older woman said. "I'm Prisca, and that's Vincent and Martha and Ady."

"Where are you heading?"

"Home to Denver. We were on a cruise when the lights went out," Prisca said.

"A cruise? Oh my gosh, what happened?" Emily asked.

"Well," the man named Vincent said. "We were still close enough to port that the backup generators got us back to Galveston, Texas. We were lucky in that regard. We heard there are others out there who were too far away to make it back, completely stranded in the dark."

My mind conjured a dark ship sitting in the middle of the black ocean, no running water, no flushing toilets. Limited food. What a fucking nightmare.

"You were very lucky," I murmured.

The woman named Martha reached over and took Ady's hand, and the girl gave a tremulous smile in return. There was something in the exchange that I didn't know enough to understand, but I'd noticed it and figured that perhaps they hadn't been as "lucky" as they'd hoped. "We've made it this far and we're hoping to be home in the next week, depending on whether we can hitch rides. Well, you're traveling too. You probably know all about that. Where are you coming from?"

Emily handed Ady the bag of marshmallows, and the girl smiled, taking it and removing one marshmallow and passing it on. Then Emily gave them a brief breakdown of what we'd been through, skipping over the worst parts as I assumed they'd done too. Perhaps it was a new unspoken rule that where there were marshmallows and a campfire and friendly souls, the bad in the outside world should be left behind. All of us knew that it would be waiting for us as we set off on our travels again in the morning. And to face it all again, brief respites were necessary. What we did know now, was that Texas was in the dark as well, all the way to the Gulf of Mexico. We weren't heading in that direction, but the knowledge made me even more certain that California was likely dark too.

"You look familiar," Ady said shyly to Emily as Vincent handed everyone sticks from a pile they'd obviously collected earlier.

Emily smiled as she took one of the sticks and skewered a marshmallow. The others had already done the same and the sweet scent of melting sugar rose in the air, the smell bringing with it nostalgia. *How many times had I roasted marshmallows as a kid, and then burnt my tongue on the hot gooey inside?* "Do I?" Emily asked. And then she shrugged. "I must just have that kind of face."

The girl smiled but looked unconvinced as though she was trying to place this pretty country girl with the long blond braid and winning smile.

Emily nodded over to the guitar as she turned her marshmallow over the fire, the outside turning golden. "Who plays?" she asked.

"I do," Vincent said. "Or, well, I'm learning. It's funny, I strapped that on my back as we started off, thinking I'd ditch it somewhere once I was sick of lugging it, but..."

"The music has been important to us." Martha smiled at Vincent. "Even from a beginner. Do you play?" she asked Emily.

"I do." I could practically feel Emily vibrating with the hope that they'd ask her to play, and so when Martha picked up the guitar and leaned around the fire to hand it to Emily, I was relieved on her behalf. Emily took it, running her fingers lovingly over the strings and then stood, walking to a spot near the front of the fire where she had room to hold the guitar without bumping anyone. She sat down on a smaller section of fallen tree and began to strum.

I felt the collective stilling as everyone realized how good she was, that dreamy look coming over her face that I recognized well.

She began to sing, and from my peripheral vision, I saw Prisca and Vincent lean forward very slightly, pulled toward her in a way I'd seen others react as well. The song was filled with soul and sadness, and I knew immediately it was one of her originals. Or maybe I'd heard it long before, floating on the breeze and mingling with the scent of citrus.

Did you hum it once, Emily? When you were just a girl, your head full of musical dreams?

She met my eyes through the flames, and I felt a lump form in my throat. I felt briefly hypnotized by the fire and the music, my heartbeat growing loud in my ears. The moment felt ancient and new, and scary in some way I couldn't even define. And yet despite all my churning emotions, I couldn't look away.

I was captured, by her beauty, but mostly by her spirit, and maybe it was me or maybe it was her, but I hadn't seen her shine like this even when she was outfitted in sequins and glitter. She'd shrugged off the nails and the hair and the shimmery makeup, and yet somehow, she glowed all the brighter for it.

I was falling... God, it had happened quickly. Or maybe it had happened far too slowly. But either way, it made me feel both breathless and terrified. Like one of those ships floating alone in uncharted water.

Emily tipped her head slightly as though she'd sensed the

minute change in my demeanor as I'd realized the depth of my feelings for her.

The night had descended, and a trillion stars blanketed the sky, the moon sitting on Emily's shoulder as though it too was leaning in to listen. Her voice was rich and velvety and though I didn't look around—couldn't pull my eyes from her—I knew everyone else was as awestruck as me.

Every corner holds a story, every room a memory
Now the silence only echoes with where you used to be

Can we ever be ourselves again in that perfect place and
    time
The wishes and the daydreams when your promises were
    mine

I'm searching for a way back to the place I used to know
Because happiness can crumble fast and pain goes oh so
    slow

In the loneliest spaces, where the darkest shadows gather
I'd find you there, and I'd stay if you'd rather

If I could go back, I'd find you in the dark
If I could go back, I'd find you in the dark

Later, as the fire began to die, our bellies full of marshmallows, Emily strummed one last chord, the quiet of the night falling flat in the wake of her dwindling voice. Prisca yawned and Martha smiled down at Ady, who had fallen asleep on her shoulder, a gentle smile on the young girl's face.

"That was incredible," Vincent said quietly. "We'll never forget it. I mean it." He sounded slightly choked up as if she had just shown him that there were still good things in the world, and he'd clearly needed the reminder.

Emily looked tired, but peaceful and pleased and we said good-night to them as Emily and I made our way to a spot next to a grouping of pines. Our eyes met in the dim light of the stars and without discussing it, we zipped our sleeping bags together and then climbed inside, our jackets under our heads like pillows. She scooted toward me, and I wrapped her in my arms. "That was beautiful."

She snuggled closer. "Thank you."

Maybe the silent agreement to sleep together the way we'd done the night before was easier with the others sleeping nearby, because it offered an element of safety. I wanted her with a desperate aching neediness. But the fact that strangers were close provided limits that would be easy to break had we been alone. But even so, I knew in the last two nights we'd crossed a line, and that if one of us didn't put a halt to it, it was only heading in one direction from here.

Day Ten

Again, we woke in each other's arms and then left the others sleeping there in the early hours of dawn. Later, the sun, high in the sky, we heard the rattle of an old car approaching, and stepped off the road, weary from walking and needing a rest anyway. But when a tiny old woman and old man trundled by in the rusty car, Emily ran back to the road and started waving her arms. They came to a slow stop, obviously having seen her in their rearview mirror and we both ran to where they were parked.

"Hi," Emily greeted breathlessly, producing that Nova-esque smile. "Can we catch a ride?"

The old woman looked her up and down and then glanced

back at me. "Where ya headed?" she asked, obviously having assessed that we looked mostly harmless.

"As far west as you're going," Emily said.

The woman hitched her thumb toward the back door. "Hop in."

Emily grinned at me, and I opened the car door so we could both slide in.

We exited the vehicle hours later, having crossed the rest of the way through Oklahoma and into New Mexico, the sunset brilliant over the snowy desert mountains. The old couple, who had been waiting for power to come back on or information to arrive, had finally grown tired of waiting and decided to drive to a daughter's house about an hour from where we got out. We wished them well and began walking.

That tension that had been ramping up between Emily and me for days now—hell, maybe for weeks, even if I hadn't acknowledged it at the time—was thrumming between us. The few hours in the car, our thighs touching, Emily's head on my shoulder as we rocked down the road hadn't helped matters.

"It seems like there are more people walking today," Emily said.

"Or maybe it's just the area," I answered, though I'd had the same thought. And I suspected the people we'd told the Pritchards to look out for—who would be streaming out of the cities and towns once things got desperate or dangerous or both—had started to multiply.

There was some snow on the ground here and the sun glittered off it, the landscape somehow both stark and rich, and we stopped for a moment to drink it in.

"Should we look for somewhere to camp?" Emily asked, our eyes meeting briefly before we both looked away.

"There are some ranches way out there." I pointed into the distance. "We could see if anyone is willing to put us up for a night, although I'd expect a no at this point. People will be rightly hoarding, not sharing."

"There's at least some shelter out that way among the rocks. How far do you think that is?"

"A few miles. Come on, if we start walking now, we can make it there before dark."

We set off, walking about a quarter of a mile, when we heard a sound behind us, and turned to see a horse trotting straight toward us.

"Are you kidding?" Emily said. "I was just wishing we had another ride."

As the palomino got closer, I saw she was wearing a bridle but no saddle. She didn't seem wary of people, ready to walk right by us when I took hold of her reins. She shook her head back and forth for a moment but then stopped and stood waiting for me to take the lead.

"Are you here by providence?" Emily asked as she pet her cheek. "Poor girl," Emily said, running a hand down her nose. "There's not much grass on the ground here, is there? Are you hungry? Who would have let you go?"

"She's probably just lost," I said, but I had to figure something bad had happened to her owners if their animal was wandering alone.

"Well," Emily sighed. "There's no way to find her home so I guess she's a free horse now. Should we remove her bridle?"

"Yeah, but I think we should bring her out there," I said, squinting in the direction we had been headed, toward the ranch far beyond. "There have to be other horses, and maybe that's even where she came from before getting loose. Are you up for a ride?"

She gave me a skeptical look. "The last time I was involved in a horse ride with you, I almost died."

I chuckled. "There won't be any death-defying acrobatics this time. Probably."

She grinned and cocked her head, the dwindling sun out-lining her in a hazy glow, the breeze lifting the pieces of hair that had come loose from her braid. And I knew that no matter what happened here, and for the rest of my life, when I thought of this journey, I'd see her just this way.

I led the horse to where there was a rock that I could stand on and then held on to her, pausing to make sure she wasn't going to bolt, and then pulled myself up and over. The horse shifted, but seemed mostly unconcerned with having a rider, and so I took my backpack off and gestured for Emily to do the same. I tied them together and then draped them over the horse so they wouldn't fall off. "Ready?" I asked Emily as I reached my hand out to her.

She stepped up onto the rock and then I gripped her arm and she let out a surprised gasp that turned into laughter as I lifted her, and she landed behind me. Emily wrapped her arms around my waist, her body pressed against my back. "Ready," she confirmed, her breath warm on the nape of my neck.

We trotted toward the open desert, nothing but the sky and the mountains in front of us. The red clay ground met the pinkish orange sky, pearly light shining through gaps in the clouds and creating spotlights on the snowcapped hills. It was so stunning that all I could do was stare, our bodies swaying as the horse carried us forward, Emily's soft sigh behind me let-ting me know she was as awestruck as me.

We trotted at a leisurely pace for a few minutes, the sun low-ering and a deep blue joining the swashes of color.

"No death-defying stunts," she murmured at my ear. "But what do you say we make it across this desert sooner rather than later?"

My heart rate quickened. The ranch I'd spotted was barely visible now in the lowering light and I didn't want to be in the middle of the desert when the sun went down. But I knew Emily was suggesting an all-out ride for more reasons than safety. She wanted a thrill. And why not when those were currently in such short supply. "Hold on tight, Showboat."

Emily pulled in a breath, her arms clamping tightly around my waist as I dug my heals into the horse's sides and her trot moved into a gallop. I leaned forward and so did Emily, following my lead. The horse seemed eager to run, not holding back in the least, the wind whipping her mane back and making me squint and laugh. Behind me, Emily laughed too, her body hot and soft against my own.

We raced across the hard-packed earth, the sun's flame being quenched by the icy stars. The world didn't matter. None of my problems or regrets could keep up. It was only us, wild and free, laughing with abandon, blood pumping furiously through my veins, and Emily's arms holding me like she'd never let go.

We all might crash and burn, but for that moment, for right then, we were young and alive, and we had already come so far that I believed nothing could stop us now.

The sprawling house came into view, a modern-looking barn off to the side and a corral where I saw five or six horses milling about. I pulled on the horse's reins, and she slowed, her mane falling back into place as her gallop slowed to a trot. I could feel Emily's heart racing against my back, her laughter fading, quickened breath still warming my ear. "Tuck," she murmured, and I wondered if she even knew she said my name.

My body felt alive, but so did my heart and my soul. She'd always done that for me when no one else could. And I didn't even know exactly how, but I'd craved it, needed it, and I'd had no idea how much.

The horse came to a halt, bending her head to nibble at a patch of dry grass.

Emily grasped my shoulders and then climbed around my body to face me, her core pressed to mine as our eyes met, breath mingling. She leaned forward gently as my body hardened, and I let out a small sound of pained bliss. I wanted her. I wanted her so desperately I was quivering with it.

We breathed together for a few stilted moments, eyes searching, her pretty lips parting. And then I couldn't hold back another second, suddenly feeling like I'd barely managed to hold on all my life. I wrapped my hand around the back of her neck and pulled her forward and then I met her mouth with mine.

thirty-four

Emily

I let out a strangled sound of relief and pleasure as his tongue swept into my mouth, claiming me. Him. The man who'd kept me safe as the world around us crumbled. The boy I'd loved all my life. Tuck.

I writhed, our hearts crashing against each other's chests, small sounds of desperation coming from the back of his throat each time I slid against him. The Tuck I'd just raced across the desert with was the Tuck I'd known, the one who'd looked to me to draw him out. He'd only ever needed a small push, the tiniest of nudges to release some of the pent-up pressure he held inside. And I'd loved it. Loved the way he'd trusted me. Loved the way he made me feel necessary. We'd always balanced each other, and I wanted to weep with the knowledge that we still did.

"Em," he gritted, breaking from my mouth, breath coming out in harsh gusts against my cheek. "Em. I'm going to—"

"Not here," I said, my own voice filled with the heady arousal pounding between my legs. We'd find a camp, and we'd spread out our sleeping bags. We'd have the whole night. With a shiver of desperate anticipation, I quickly swung my leg around him, scooted back, and then dismounted the horse. He jumped down easily too and turned toward me, smoothing a few pieces of hair back from my face. He looked slightly drugged and maybe feverish as well, and though I appreciated the horse for the thrilling ride she'd just given us, I needed to get her to a safe spot so we could pick up where we'd just left off. "Do you think that's her ranch?" I asked, pointing next to us where the other horses roamed, nibbling on bales of hay sitting in various spots around the corral.

Tuck's vision seemed to clear, and he tilted his head slightly as he watched the horses. "There are bales of hay all over. And their pen is open," he said, pointing to where I now saw a wide-open gate.

He took the horse's reins in his hand and began leading her to the corral. "Why would they leave their gate open?"

"Possibly because they left and weren't sure they'd return and wanted to give the horses a way out when the food was gone. Or at least, that's what I'd do," he muttered.

I removed our backpacks from where they'd been draped, and Tuck took off the horse's bridle, rubbing her down with his hand before she wandered over to a bale of hay. There was a water trough near the fence that appeared connected to a rain barrel, that another horse stood drinking from.

Tuck paused and looked around, obviously considering what to do with the bridle in his hand. "The stable door is open," I said, pointing across the way. We walked through the corral, and into the dim stable, the last of the light illuminating the entrance, but casting the back in shadow. Tuck set the bridle down just as I spotted something taped to the wall on my left. I removed it, read quickly, and handed it to Tuck.

"It's a list of the horse's names next to descriptions," he said. "'If you take one of our horses, we beg you to please treat them well. They are loved.'" Tuck lowered the note. "They did leave, then," he said. "Temporarily, at least."

I briefly wondered why, but realized I didn't have to. All over the country, people were either trying to get to safety, or attempting to make it to the people they loved. As this ranch was far away from any major metropolitan area and somewhat tucked behind some hills, the owners wouldn't have to worry much about safety, especially if they were armed. They'd have a good view of anyone approaching from all directions, and they'd have time to prepare. Of course, it was possible they'd run out of food and been forced to head out to search for some, but I thought it was more likely that they'd left to find a family member. It made a lump form in my throat to consider the choices people had had to make, willing to leave safety behind for love.

We left the stables and walked around the front of the house. The front door was locked, but when we rounded the corner of the house and found a side door that led into an attached garage, Tuck turned the knob and pulled it open. He stood there still for a moment, his body blocking the interior. "You've got to be kidding me."

"What?" I asked, moving around him and stepping inside. I let out a giddy laugh of disbelief, turning to look at him with wide eyes before bringing my gaze back at the classic yellow car.

"It looks like there was one parked next to it," I said, nodding to the empty spot where a canvas cover like the ones my dad had used to protect his cars had been discarded. "Whoever lives in that house had to have taken one of the cars and left."

He moved around the yellow car and then tried the knob on a door that likely led into the house, finding it unlocked too. "Hello?" he shouted inside. Only silence returned, though he still shouted *hello* one more time to the same result. "Look," he said, walking toward a pegboard on the wall where a singular key was hung. "Holy shit." He plucked it off the board and held it up.

"Do you think it'll work?" Had we really gotten this lucky?

"There's only one way to find out." He opened the driver's side door, and I quickly rounded the car and got in on the passenger side as he was turning the key in the ignition. It rattled, and sputtered, and when it caught, rumbling to life, I let out a gleeful squeal as I clapped my hands together. "It runs! Oh my God. Tuck."

He met my eyes. "We'll write down the address. We'll return it as soon as we can."

"They have a car," I said. "And who even knows if they'll be back."

"Still," he said.

I smiled. "Still." Doing the right thing mattered, even now. And why that made me feel powerful when perhaps it should have done the opposite, I didn't even know.

He turned off the ignition and then I ran my hand over the dash and peeked at him sideways. "This classic car brings back memories," I said. "Of that old dusty loft you found peaceful for some reason."

He opened his mouth to say something but then merely smiled, that secretive one that had always made me want to pin him down and force him to tell me what he was thinking.

He slid from the car and pocketed the key. "So, then we'll stay here tonight and leave in the morning. But I do want to check the house more thoroughly and make sure this is what it looks like. Wait here for a few?"

I nodded and then he disappeared through the door, returning about five minutes later and beckoning me inside. "All clear," he said. "There's an itinerary for a middle school trip to DC on the kitchen counter. I wonder if they took off to find their kid."

God. The stories to be told from this disaster. I'd seen so many awful things on the road, the worst side of humanity showing itself, but I'd also been struck by the fact that when the lights went out, the first thing human beings did was reach for those they loved.

I wondered if years into the future, people would say, "Where were you?" And no one would have to clarify, "When?" Because everyone would know exactly what the asker meant. *Where were you when the lights went out?*

And I had this overwhelming feeling of gratitude, even though my personal answer to that question would likely give me some amount of PTSD for many years to come. *I was on an airplane. We made a crash landing.* The gratitude was for the fact that when we crawled from the wreckage, I was with Tuck. And there was no one better to find at my side.

I heard a sound outside but realized it was just one of the horses out back, letting out a soft whinny. "What if the people who live here are gone now, but return?"

"We'll hear them coming. They have a car."

"Good point." I came to stand in front of him and our eyes met, the moment weighty and full.

He tilted his head, his gaze moving over my face. And there was something sort of assessing, and sort of soft in his eyes that made a small shiver run over my skin. Whatever he was thinking made him smile in that secretive way of his, and I very suddenly loved that secretive smile when I knew thoughts of me were behind it.

And though I'd been needy and desperate and ready to have sex while seated on a horse just a short time before, now that my blood had cooled and rational thought had returned, I felt a little nervous too. Tuck looking at me the way he was made me feel giddy, but also young and a little bit shy because God but this man meant so much to me, and he always had.

"If you, ah, have to use the bathroom, we should go outside now before I lock up. There won't be plumbing in here."

"I'm good."

"Okay, me too." He pointed at the staircase, a beam of muted light coming in through the large window overhead. "Go ahead and pick a room. I'm going to make sure all the doors and windows are secured and check to see if they left any weapons behind."

I nodded, and our eyes lingered, and it was clear that we both knew what we wanted and understood exactly what was going to happen between us. To me it felt destined, like I'd finally arrived at a place I'd been traveling to my entire life. My skin prickled with anticipation and for a moment I found it difficult to draw in air. For a moment I was afraid. But of what, I couldn't exactly say. It felt like holding something precious and delicate that, left unattended, was very likely to break. Or disappear. "I'll just...ah..." I waved my hand toward the stairs.

"I'll find you." He smiled and it was sweet. It was the smile of the boy he'd been, and it caused a flurry of wings to take up under my rib cage. I turned and ran quickly up the stairs.

I poked my head into a primary bedroom, and a child's room, both obviously lived in, the drawers open in the primary as though the couple had packed in a hurry.

The room at the end of the hall appeared to be a guest room, and I set my things down in the upholstered chair in the corner and then turned to the dresser where there were a couple of candles and a lighter. This family had done as so many others had probably done as well—they'd placed candles in all the rooms, they'd lit fires in their wood-burning fireplaces, and then they'd waited it out, thinking it was just a winter outage and the lights would be back on shortly. Especially in a more remote place like this, it might have been several days before they realized something was very wrong.

I lit the candles and the wicks flickered to life, mixing with the final glow of the sunset through the sheer curtains on the window.

The door to the attached bathroom was open slightly and I went inside and tried the faucet just because but the only thing that came out was a few brown dribbles.

But when I pulled back the shower curtain, I saw that they'd filled up the bathtub before they'd left. "Yes," I murmured. I plugged the sink and then used a cup on the vanity to scoop some water from the tub, using as little as I thought I needed to clean up.

A washcloth and a minute amount of their bodywash served to clean the road dust from my body. I twisted to dab at the wound on my hip, the one that hadn't bothered me for days now, noting that it was almost completely gone. This odd feeling of disbelief overcame me to know that so much healing could happen when you weren't even paying attention. And I had this sudden appreciation for my body that I'd never had before. Not because of the way it looked or performed, but because of the way it could *heal.* And hope blossomed, the belief that it wasn't only our bodies that would mend from the tragedy befalling the world, but so would our spirits. In time.

I hummed as I took my hair down and used my fingers to work out the tangles. I could hardly remember what it felt like to have clean, blown-out hair. "Ouch," I yelped when a finger got caught in my hair. I lowered my hand and saw that the last piece of my fake nail that had been glued to the bed of my thumb had lifted at the corner and snagged some strands.

The small remnant came off easily and I watched as the final piece of Nova dropped into the empty waste can next to the sink. I stood there for a moment, staring down at that tiny fragment of a different life, a different me. And I was surprised that that girl with the glamorous nails and luxurious hair extensions already felt so distant, the false parts of her dropped piece by piece on lonely back roads and in dewy fields as I was both lost...and somehow found.

I'd truly believed she was my ticket to happiness and so I'd embraced her even if that costume had never *quite* fit, not as uncomfortable as the last formal dress I'd worn, but a touch itchy nonetheless even if I couldn't figure out *why* when to the naked eye, I looked so damn perfect. I wondered now how long I would have been able to keep up the facade of Nova, wondered if I would have taken a similar route as Jane Pritchard, numbing with pills and wondering why I was so unhappy if all my dreams had supposedly come true.

It was a sad sort of thought because while a part of me felt free, and even confusingly saved in ways I couldn't untangle now, it was also a goodbye. To a thousand dreams that had come true for a moment but wouldn't last. To bright lights and cheering crowds. To the superstar I might have been.

I went back into the bedroom, where I found a T-shirt in one of the dresser drawers. I hoped it was simply one someone who had stayed in this room had left behind and would never miss. But as far as a pair of underwear, I was going to be a brazen thief because even someone else's clean ones were a luxury I could not pass up. I slipped the T-shirt over my head and then returned to the primary bedroom where I opened the top drawer and found the absolute bounty of an unopened package of cotton bikinis, size small.

"Oh sweet Jesus," I breathed, bringing the plastic to my lips and kissing it. "Oh thank You, God." I ripped the package open and pulled on the baby pink pair of underwear and then ran back to the guest room. I tossed the rest of the package of underwear into my backpack, threw myself on the bed, and then lay there grinning up at the ceiling. "Thank you, house owner, whoever you are. I will pay this forward."

"Pay what forward?" I sat up so quickly I gave myself a head rush, bringing my hand to my temple and cringe-laughing.

"Nothing," I said. "All secured?"

Tuck set his backpack down on the floor next to the chair. "Yeah." He closed the bedroom door and locked it, and that small click made my tummy squeeze. "All secured."

We stared at each other in heavy silence for a few seconds before I waved toward the bathroom. "There's water in there," I said. "In the tub. If you wanted to…clean up or—"

"Great. Yes. That'd be great." He picked his bag back up and went into the bathroom, closing the door behind him.

I lay back on the bed, trying to calm my nerves as I again gazed at the ceiling. God, my heart was thumping with both excitement and fear. I vaguely wondered if this is how it would have been if Tuck and I had dated in high school. If the cascade of tragedies that had occurred in the wake of his mother getting sick hadn't happened…if his mother had never died… Would we have snuck out windows at midnight? Would we have made out in the back seat of cars? Gone to that prom together and then rented a hotel room afterward and lost our virginity to each other?

It seemed like such a faraway possibility, and also one that *should* have happened but had been lost, caused by some wrinkle in time. And I felt this sense of wonder knowing maybe those disruptive wrinkles eventually smoothed, and when they did, what was lost, was found.

The door clicked open, and Tuck exited, dropping his backpack on the floor. His gaze slid over me, lingering on the pink cotton between my legs, barely showing beneath the hem of the T-shirt that had risen when I'd lain down. And I swore I could feel that glance touch my tender flesh, a buzz of electricity flowing from him to me. His eyes moved down my legs, and I saw him swallow. "Em," he said, his voice thick. "I, ah." He stuck his hands in his jean pockets, and I sat up, concerned by the doubt I heard in his tone.

"What's wrong?"

"Nothing's wrong. I just…you should know that it's been ah—"

"It's been a long time." My breath released, tenderness gripping my heart. He was worried because he hadn't had sex with anyone in a long time.

I stood, going to him and then placed my hand on his chest. "I understand."

He shook his head slowly, his expression so vulnerable. "No, Em, I'm not sure you do."

I lifted my hand and then ran my thumb over his flushed cheekbone before I brought my mouth to his, kissing him softly, just once, and then lowering my lips to his throat. "Yes, I do," I whispered. I trailed my hand down his T-shirt and then lifted the hem and dragged my fingers lightly over the warm skin of his stomach. His skin was velvety, and the sparse line of hair tickled my fingertips. I smiled against the dip at the base of his throat, and he let out a low groan.

My heart soared, and I felt electrified, and I knew that he was telling me that he was worried about things being over before they started, but honestly, I felt desperate too. To discover him, to explore, to satisfy a desire that it felt as if I'd carried all my life, beginning from those first flushed moments staring at his features in a photograph in my girlhood room.

I took a tiny step back and lifted his T-shirt, bringing it up and over his head. I took a moment, just one, to let my eyes roam his smooth, muscular chest and then brought my hand out and laid it over his heart. I'd known his body once, every dip and swell, because I'd memorized him. I'd watched as he picked fruit, and lifted bales of hay, and waded in the creek running through our land. But he'd become a man since then, and I had so much to rediscover. I felt greedy and hungry and breathless with need, overwhelmed by the weight of this moment.

He groaned when I lowered my mouth to one of his flat nipples, weaving his fingers into my hair. "Even this, Em, I... God."

"I know," I whispered, and then I went down on my knees.

He let out a small sound that made me smile. It was surprise and gratitude and uncertainty and desperation all mixed into one. And it was the first time I'd ever seen Tucker Mattice willingly hand over full control to anyone.

I unbuttoned his jeans and dragged them down over his straining erection, swallowing as I reminded myself that I would have time to explore him later. This was for him, and it meant that we could take our time after this.

God he was beautiful though. Big and hard and perfectly formed. I ran a finger along a vein and then licked the drop of moisture from his tip. He made another sound of desperate anticipation, and I gave him a small push so that he staggered back and fell into the upholstered chair behind him. Then I pulled his jeans farther down around his ankles and he kicked out of them so I could push them aside. I positioned myself between his thighs, meeting his stunned eyes once before I lowered my head and took him in my mouth. He bucked his hips, and I swirled my tongue, taking one long suck as he gave another helpless thrust, making incoherent sounds of pleasure.

I felt powerful and wonderful and, though I loved fighting with Tuck, I also loved pleasuring him, and never in my life had I felt this intoxicating mix of physical and emotional reactions to any man.

I bobbed my head, sliding up and down on his shaft faster and faster until he let out a growl and another thrust, pressing my shoulders so that my mouth disengaged with a pop. He had his head thrown back and he dug his fingers into my shoulders as he came, his abdominal muscles straining and tightening with each wave of pleasure.

Then his muscles went lax, and he sunk into the chair, bringing his hand to his hair as he raised his head. "My God. I told you," he said, voice laced with a smidge of embarrassment. "I'm surprised it took that long."

I breathed out a small laugh as I picked up his T-shirt and swiped it over his lower stomach. Then I leaned forward again, kissing the spot I'd just cleaned and dragging my lips around his naval.

"Earlier, when I mentioned that hayloft where you found peace, what were you thinking?" I propped my chin on his stomach and looked up at him. He still looked drugged and satisfied and very, very beautiful, candlelight caressing his features in both shadows and highlights.

"How do you know I was thinking anything?"

"Because I know your expressions, Tuck." I ran my short fingernails over his hip and felt the beginnings of another erection stir at my breasts. His eyes went sort of dreamy as he looked down at me. "Even now. I know when you're keeping secrets."

I brought my other hand to the opposite hip and scraped my fingernails over his skin and then leaned up slightly so I could do the same to his inner thighs. I watched as he stiffened into an erection again even though the evidence of his recent orgasm was still drying on his lower stomach. I wrapped my hand around him, and he let out a hum. "Tell me," I cajoled, giving a slow stroke.

"Oh God, Em. Uh, I was thinking about how you always liked to disturb my peace. A lifetime thorn in my side." He smiled but it was fleeting. When he met my eyes, I saw the earnestness in his expression. "I never could dig you out. Time hasn't changed that, and I don't have any desire to try."

My heart gave a kick. *Tuck.* He could be so sweet when he wanted to be. And oh I loved hearing his secrets.

He put his hand on mine and forced me to halt midstroke. He began to sit up, his stomach muscles bunching. "And do you want to know what I'm thinking now?"

A thrill whirled through me. "Yes."

"I'm thinking that if I don't get inside you, I might die, and there's a bed right behind us and I mean to make use of it. Is that okay with you?"

My mouth went dry, nipples pebbling, and all I could do was

nod. His eyes moved lazily to my chest and stayed there for a moment. And then he stood up, pulling me to my feet as he walked me backward, both of us laughing as we tumbled down.

thirty-five

Tuck

I hadn't known lust like this. I tried to tell myself the arousal coiled around my muscles and pumping through my veins was only natural considering how long I'd been celibate, but I knew very well that was a lie. Sure, that was part of it. But mostly, it was her. No one got me going like Emily. No one brought out my emotions like her. No one else both pressed my buttons and turned me on. No one stirred my soul like the woman beneath me. I wanted her desperately. But I also needed to keep her safe. "Before this goes too far... I need to check for condoms."

"I have an IUD," she murmured. And then she pressed against my aching erection, now standing at attention even though I'd climaxed not five minutes before.

I swallowed back a moan. And the knowledge that I didn't have to worry about coming inside her sent a bolt of excitement through my body. But I took a breath. I didn't want this to end too soon. Somewhere beyond the lust was this vague fear that we were on borrowed time. Like a shooting star speeding through the galaxy—hot and dazzling—but destined to burn out. Something told me I needed to relish every blazing moment. I barely wanted to blink. I breathed her in as I kissed down her throat, the moment slowing, her muscles softening beneath me.

"It was always leading here with us, wasn't it?" she asked breathily, her words slurred with passion.

I nuzzled her neck, rubbing my lips over her skin as I brought my hand under her T-shirt and cupped her breast. She moaned softly when I began rubbing my thumb over her nipple. *It was always leading here.* And I knew she didn't mean to this ranch house at the end of the world, but here, *us*, limbs wrapped, mouths melded, moving together.

"Yes," I confirmed. "Always."

I pulled her T-shirt over her head, and then stared down at her naked breasts, shimmering in the candlelight. When I met her eyes, they were tender, her lips curved as she watched me, obviously pleased by what she saw on my face. *It was always leading here. Yes.* The phrase repeated, pounding through my blood. I felt the truth of it to my soul. And you couldn't fight fate. We'd tried, hadn't we? And yet here we were. *Always* meant always.

Emily was still looking at me, and I wondered if she too was having a hard time closing her eyes, needing instead to witness every second of this long-awaited moment. *Keep your eyes open*, my heart whispered. *You've missed far too much already.* "God you're stunning, Em." I wanted her to know that, to feel it. To understand that to me, there was no one more beautiful than her. There never had been. That truth had haunted me, even if I hadn't admitted it to myself. But now it brought nothing but joy.

Her smile melted into a sigh as I lowered my face and licked at her nipple. I worshipped her breasts for long minutes as her pants grew louder and her hips came up off the bed, her core seeking mine. She ran her hands through my hair, her short nails scoring along my scalp.

"And you light me on fire," I grated. Sometimes my instinct was to draw away from the burn, but fuck I craved it too. I was hot and throbbing again, desperate to feel her clasped around me, to make her mine. *Finally.*

That fate again, pulling, driving my need.

This—us—could only be destiny. It felt so damn right. A certainty, but also a return of some sort, a rewind that I'd never imagined was possible. How many times had I wished I could go back to those bright, beautiful days with her when life made perfect sense? It felt like I'd somehow miraculously managed to do that, even if this was the future, not the past, an astonishing paradox of time.

Our eyes met and held, expressions becoming serious as if we both suddenly sensed the intense gravity of this moment. I knew I did. And though the paradox was miraculous, it was also startling. And scary too because it demanded a surrender, and lowering my guard had never been a strong suit of mine. I felt a strange tumbling, a reeling inside as though I'd both snapped back into place and found myself in a distant land. I let out a breath and gripped her, her eyes softening as she gripped me back. The next kiss was slow and long, our mouths and tongues exploring leisurely even as my blood pumped swiftly and my heart quickened. I needed it, the pause, the anchor that was her mouth and her hands and the soft press of her skin. Needed to come to terms with this dreamlike reality after weeks of fear and hardship where hypervigilance was a necessity. Relearning how to sink into a moment and get lost in this newfound pleasure.

She met my eyes again, searching them before she smiled and flipped me over. I laughed with shocked surprise before she leaned up, a wicked smile tilting her lips. She took my hands and held them over my head. "Say uncle," she said.

I laughed again. She'd known. She'd seen me overthinking, even here, even now, and she'd quickly put an end to that. "Never."

She reached down and moved her underwear aside and then lifted, hovering over me so that my tip was just grazing her entrance. All thoughts fled and like the few intense moments on the chair, her mouth working magic on my body, I reveled in utter mindlessness. I could feel her wet heat and it nearly drove me wild. She did a small twist, pressing down very slightly so that I barely parted her folds.

"Uncle, Emily. Christ." My words slurred.

She laughed, taking me slowly into her body, inch by inch until she was fully seated. I looked at the place we were connected, the sight making me impossibly harder, my head falling back on a moan, completely at her mercy. She leaned forward, and again, she took my hands where they still rested over my head and whispered in my ear, "I win."

I let out a tortured groan and she started moving. "I love it when you win," I said. "Please win some more." Her laughter ended in a small, pleasured gasp, her hips rotating faster.

I hooked my leg under hers and rolled us over and she laughed again as her back hit the mattress. But when I pulled out of her, she made a sound somewhere between loss and outrage and I couldn't help the chuckle even though I was desperate to get back inside her. I removed her underwear as quickly as possible and tossed them aside. "These were in the way." Then I moved over her and surged back inside, our moans of pleasure mingling. I pulled out slowly and then pushed back in, pressing gently until she gasped and purred my name.

I watched her face as I thrust slowly. Lips parted, gaze heavy, golden waves splayed over the pillow and candlelight flickering over her flushed skin. I felt drunk with pleasure but also entranced by her beauty, once more shocked and overwhelmed by the fact that this was *Emily* beneath me, legs hooked around my hips, hands moving over my biceps as I held myself above her. "You were my first kiss. Did you know that?"

She caught my gaze, warmth glowing in her eyes. "And you were mine," she said, the whispered words dissolving into a sigh as she bit her lip and tipped her head back when I pressed my weight lightly in the spot that had elicited the same reaction before. "Oh, Tuck, God, don't stop."

I didn't ever want to stop. I wanted this to go on and on and on. But my body had other ideas, blood pumping furiously, muscles tightening. Emily's sweet little gasps of pleasure were only driving me higher, her head moving back and forth on the pillow. "I...oh—" The pads of her fingers ran up my ass and then she bucked once, letting out a small scream as she came. Her display of pleasure sent me over the edge, and I groaned out my orgasm, gasping her name, the bliss sparkling through me and leaving me feeling loose-limbed and woozy.

The surroundings materialized slowly, the unfamiliar room wavering in the candlelight. Outside the wind blew and somewhere far away an owl hooted. The past was gone, the future was burning, but we had this, the here and the now, nestled in a desert hideaway.

"I can't feel my feet," I muttered after a moment into the side of her neck.

She laughed, and it caused me to slip out of her on a small flood of moisture. "That's okay. As long as other parts of you are in working order. We can do without your feet for now."

I chuckled and rolled to the side so I wasn't crushing her. She pushed me slightly and I turned onto my back, and then she snuggled into my side, propping her chin on my chest.

She was quiet for a few minutes as she nuzzled my skin. "I've been thinking about my IUD. Who will remove it for me when the time comes?"

"Hmm. I don't know that whole process, but there will be doctors who'll start seeing patients as soon as possible. I'm sure some already are." Their treatment options would be limited, and surgery would be out of the question once all remaining fuel sources had dried up. But I had no doubt that medical professionals who were at all able would help those who needed it.

She'd watched me as those fleeting thoughts moved through my mind, and she reached up and used her thumb to smooth what must be a crease between my brows. "It will work out. Let's leave all that behind for now," she said. "I know it will have to be dealt with...that and a lot more. But for now, Tuck, I just want this." She tipped her face toward my skin and kissed the spot below my shoulder, feathering her lips there for a moment. "You and me."

I wanted the same thing. I wanted that so much. Just her and me, escaping from the chaos of the world. For as long as we could. "Me too," I said, kissing the side of her forehead and remembering what I'd found before I'd come upstairs. "I have something I'd like to show you. Or...well, give me a few minutes and then meet me downstairs?"

She gave me a confused smile and rolled to the side so I could get up. I pulled on my jeans and shirt and headed to the living room.

It only took me a minute to light the room's array of candles that had been arranged on every surface. From the brief walk-through of the house that I'd done, I'd seen that the family who lived here—the Garcias—had set a candle or two in every room. But this was obviously the one they'd spent the most time in before leaving. This was where the majority of the candles were, and also where I'd found the item I wanted Emily to see. Or...experience.

I heard her soft footsteps descending the stairs and pushed a button. The soft strains of Edwin McCain began playing just as Emily rounded the corner, her eyes lighting up. "Oh my gosh," she said. "You found a CD player."

I glanced at the small battery-operated piece of equipment.

"They must have dug it out of storage," I said. "There's dust in the crevices. And the most recent CD is from 2003."

She smiled as she approached, candlelight flickering over her expression as the singer sang about who he'd be for the woman he loved. "I haven't heard this one in a while," she said.

"It's from a collection of love songs from the nineties. Not exactly our decade but I thought maybe we could have that dance."

Her eyes met mine. "*The* dance," she whispered. "The one that will make everything right."

"Maybe even temporarily," I said. "Even that." The dance that should have been but never was.

She took a step toward me, and I offered her my hand, both of us watching as our fingers laced together slowly. I pulled her close and she tipped her head back to look at me. "Even that," she agreed.

I brought her body flush with mine, so much more familiar even in the last hour, though I'd known her all my life. We swayed in the candlelight, and the dance felt beautiful and somehow sad too, both a reclaiming and a reminder that time was so fleeting and that all too soon, this moment would be a memory. But I was determined to gather as many as possible, fleeting though they might be, because deep in my heart I had this feeling that I'd need to cling to them later.

Emily lay her cheek against my shoulder, and I turned my face so I could breathe in the scent of her skin. The song came to an end, and we danced to the next one, and then the next, collecting as many moments as we could. And when the music began to slow, the batteries dying, we both stopped moving, staring into each other's eyes as the last drawn-out note faded into silence. Emily lifted her chin and looked up at me, her eyes sad, though her lips were tipped. "I imagined we would have rented a room in the hotel and gone up there after the prom."

"What would we have done there?"

She kissed my neck, her lips lingering. "How about I show you?" she whispered against my skin.

We got back in bed, sharing our memories and laughing about pranks we'd pulled and fights we'd had. Then we made love again, exploring each other leisurely until the candle burned out.

We stayed at the ranch in the middle of nowhere for three days, a brief respite from the uncertain world, a celebration of survival, and a sharing of hearts. We ate food from the pantry, but took as little as possible, mindful that this family might return. Hoping that they would. We tended to their horses and replenished what we could from the stable. We made coffee over their firepit and watched the sun rise behind the hills. And we danced in candlelight. Those hours were sweet, and dreamlike, and I knew no matter what came next, those three days would forever be seared into my soul.

My Emily. My wildflower. The thorn in my side. A silken-voiced troublemaker. *Little Showboat.* She was kind and unpredictable and slightly wild, even if she'd let herself be tamed for a while. But for that stretch of time, she was completely and utterly free. We both were.

We cleaned up their house, and then Emily wrote a note, leaving it on their kitchen counter next to the school trip itinerary. I stopped and read it as Emily did a final check of the rooms upstairs.

Dear Garcia Family,
Our names are Emily and Tuck and we stayed here for three days.
We cared for the horses and ensured that they're all healthy and injury-free. We also added one more to your herd, a palomino that we found walking alone on the road that we named Providence. She was quickly accepted by the others and they're all doing well.

We hope you reunited with your son and that the three of you are home and reading this together. We pray that you are.

We are taking the car in your garage, and if there is any way to return it, we promise to do that. And if there's any way to pay you for the rental and the mileage, we vow to do that too.

(I also took a few feminine items, and hope with all my might that the world is such that I might replace those someday soon.)

We want to thank you for the three days of peace your home brought us as we'd been traveling since the solar flare hit. Our journey was filled with challenges and setbacks, and we saw the worst of humanity on display. But we also saw the best, and I hope you saw it too. It's what we have to hold on to now in this new, chaotic world. And if this journey has made anything clear, it's that that is how we'll all survive. With the kindness of strangers, and the help of our friends.

And though you didn't grant permission ahead of time, I hope you'll extend forgiveness, and accept our deepest gratitude.
All our best,
E & T

thirty-six

Emily

Day Thirteen

I wiped the tears from my eyes as we drove away from the ranch where we'd spent three magical days, looking over my shoulder as the horses grew smaller and smaller.

"You okay?" Tuck asked, pulling me against him and kissing my temple.

I nodded, swallowing heavily. "I just worry about the horses."

"They'll be okay. The Garcias left them enough food for many months."

Would that be enough though? The world was breaking down by the day. It'd taken us nearly two weeks—even with a number of rides clear across states—to make it from Illinois to New Mexico, but we'd left directly in the wake of the solar flare hitting. We'd had several days—at least—where much of the world was at a standstill as people just waited. We'd entered

that pause—because of Tuck's instincts to get on the road—
and because of it, we had probably moved much more quickly
than others who hadn't.

And I was worried about the Garcias too. Perhaps it was ir-
rational, but I'd come to think of them as extended family. I'd
lived in their home. I'd passed by the family photos on the wall
and seen the love reflected there. I'd practically sensed their
panic as they realized the scope of the disaster and counted the
hours that they didn't hear from their only child, halfway across
the country as society collapsed.

I had to try my best to push those imaginings aside though
because they'd only end up breaking me. We'd heard story after
story as we'd traveled, and *everyone* was panicking. So many
were trying to get somewhere. People were doing everything
possible to protect themselves and those they loved in any way
they could. I turned toward Tuck, breathing him in and finding comfort in his scent and his solid strength beside me.

Even the back roads were more crowded now and it was
slow going, even in a car. We passed several men siphoning fuel
from the cars, watching us with narrowed eyes as we went by
as though we might stop and challenge them. And that made
sense being that we were in a vehicle that would only keep running if we had a continued supply of gasoline. Now that it had
obviously occurred to more people that there was fuel available in the deserted cars, I wondered how long it would take
until most of them were emptied out. I wondered how long
it'd take before people were fighting over the last of it to keep
their generators running, or whatever else they might have that
used gas and was still working.

Tuck looked concerned too as we passed by a couple with a
gas can and a hose, draining a Lexus SUV. "Things have pro-
gressed in the last few days," I murmured.

"Or regressed."

"Maybe we shouldn't have holed up for that long," I said. "But I can't manage to regret it."

"Me neither. I wish it could have been longer."

It could be, I wanted to say. *It could be forever.* But I didn't say that and neither did he. I hardly dared to dream that Tuck would stay with me, that he couldn't bear parting. And right now, there were a thousand unknowns and too many maybes that were bigger than us. I'd seen the way his eyes had lit up when Hosea mentioned helping abandoned children and others who needed assistance. Would he be pulled back on the road once he'd helped me get to my parents? There were so many things he could do now, and I wondered if staying with me would be enough.

That old familiar longing rose inside me, bringing a rush of fear. I felt like, in some ways, I'd been here before. Only now, it was far more complicated, and the stakes were higher.

I hadn't asked for promises and he hadn't offered any. Perhaps now was not the time for such things anyway.

I leaned my head back on the seat and stared out the passenger side window, mountains and desert moving past as Tuck went around a truck in the road.

What I did have to hold on to was that the bitterness between us had fallen away completely. We'd made peace. We'd made much more than that, but it was the peace I was going to attempt to take with me, even if I had to leave the rest behind.

But I didn't need to think of that. Not yet, and so I held out secret hope that we would find a way.

It took us a day and a half to make it to Arizona, only traveling by daylight. We stopped to siphon gas when we needed to with the gas can and hosing Tuck had taken from the Garcias' garage and put in the trunk, along with food, that we were still rationing, and water. I'd lost a significant amount of weight in the past two weeks. I thought about how the old me would have considered that a positive, and I wanted to grimace. *The old me*. This journey had transformed me, and I hardly wanted to think about what the next few years would do. Of course, that would depend on many factors, none of which were certain at the moment. For now, the entire country was just trying to survive, including us.

We made love at night, though not with the joyful abandon we had at the Garcias' home. The sex in the back of the car in the pitch black was needier, more grasping, even if we managed to laugh about the ridiculous maneuvers made necessary by the tiny space. I'd wondered about whether we'd have made out in back seats had life as we'd known it not crashed and burned and so I tried to enjoy the reclaiming of what I'd considered lost. A smoothing of another one of those wrinkles in time.

After just such a back seat interlude on the second night of traveling, I climbed out of the car, mostly naked, and pulled a sleeping bag from the trunk. I wrapped it around me and then scooted up on the hood of the car and lay back. After a minute, Tuck joined me with the other sleeping bag, and we stared up at the stars.

"We could be in California tomorrow night," I said. He'd shown me the route he thought safest on the map, and I'd been following the signs.

"If all goes well, I estimate we can get close before sunset. We'll play it safe and cross the California state line the next morning." I heard him look over at me but didn't turn to meet his eyes. "Home," he said softly.

So why didn't it feel like that? Of *course* it was home. I'd lived in Southern California all my life. My family was there. It was our destination, and we'd arrive in less than twenty-four hours if all went well. We should feel victorious. Sure, there were many unknowns, and a vast number of challenges before us. But we'd made it. We'd started out on foot two thousand miles ago and we were almost home! And all I could feel was sadness and fear. "Home," I finally repeated, turning to him.

His eyes were milky in the low light of the moon, and I could only make out the shadowy lines of his profile. "We did it."

He reached over and grasped my hand. "We did," he said. "Almost."

Almost. Such a big word in a time like this. I craved more. *Certainty. Predictability.* "What do you think it's going to be like there?"

"I'd imagine it's going to be like it is here. Los Angeles is my worry."

"Los Angeles. I thought we were going directly to my parents?"

"We are." He paused. "I'm going to bring you to them, and then I'm going to go to Los Angeles and check on my uncle." He was quiet again for a moment, and a pain shot through my stomach. "He was there for me when I needed him, even when I didn't deserve it. I owe him. He might be in trouble, and I owe him."

He owed him. To his mind, Tuck owed a lot of people. That had even been his motivation for helping me—and Charlie—get home initially. He'd owed it to my parents. It was his driving force. Repaying debts, making amends. And I wanted to be angry and resentful at him for that, but I couldn't. He was honorable and good. But I was deeply worried that his honor meant more to him than I did. "If your uncle needs somewhere to stay, you know, out of the city...bring him to my parents."

"Your parents might just have enough to get by—"

"Tuck." I squeezed his hand. "We'll make room for your uncle. And you too. You know that." And though I meant it, I also hoped that if Tuck's uncle was there at our farm, it would give Tuck even more reason to stay.

Pitiful, Emily. Desperately trying to give Tuck a reason to stay, other than just...you.

"I've also been thinking about my dad," Tuck said somewhat

haltingly. "We've been estranged for so many years but...he's still the man who raised me."

I could see his sadness and conflict. It was the first time he'd mentioned his dad since we started this trip. This new reality had changed perspective for everyone. Priorities had crumbled and shifted. How could they not? And Tuck had that deep thread of honor that wove through him.

"Florida's gotta be okay, right?" I said. "So much sunshine... and all that fishing..."

"There's no way to know. That's been the hardest part. Even behind bars, we were never this cut off."

I stared up at the twinkling stars, the sky so infinite above us. Yes, it was true we were cut off in so many ways, but in others, the world had expanded. There was so much to adjust to and relearn. I couldn't even wrap my head around it all.

"Let's get somewhere safe and then we'll see what's what."

"That's the plan," he said and then he gathered me in his arms. An uncertain plan, but a plan nonetheless. I lay my head on his shoulder as a star shot across the sky, brilliant and beautiful and gone too soon.

Day Fifteen

We crossed into California the next evening, a little earlier than we'd estimated, and camped near a reservation that was completely still and silent, no evidence of people living there at all, though we didn't enter the area.

We drove through Joshua Tree at daybreak, the sun a glittery yellow diamond rising behind the hills, pearly rays fanning over the desert. And it was so beautiful I nearly wept.

We drove around the city of Palm Springs, foot traffic now heavy even on the outskirts where many of the neighborhoods were primarily Airbnb's. I looked over my shoulder at a group of women carrying suitcases who looked both shocked and scared, and wondered if they'd been here on vacation and then hunkered down as long as they possibly could before packing their bags and hitting the road. So many stories. So much fear and tragedy.

We drove on, heading toward home. It felt so close now, and so very far away. That feeling intensified when we saw the fire. "Holy shit," Tuck said, slowing down.

It looked like the entirety of the San Bernardino National Forest was burning, the sky practically black as we crested a hill. My heart sank. As a native Californian I was no stranger to forest fires, but this, in the midst of the current desperation and lack of water, was nothing short of calamitous. Tuck swore and then turned back the way we'd come, finally heading north rather than south toward my parents' home in an effort to go around the fire. He unfolded the map, glancing at it as he drove on the shoulder of the road by necessity as both lanes were filled with vehicles. We drove on, my hands clenched at my sides as we veered away from what had looked like a valley of hell.

The sky cleared and the scent of acrid smoke dissipated as we drove by a sign for Temecula, the parked cars and trucks becoming more sparse on the stretch of road we were on. But when I reached down to the floor where I had a bottle of water, I felt Tuck slow and come to a stop. I sat up just as Tuck began reversing away from a row of cars that had been arranged to block the road up ahead. In front of the blockade of vehicles were men in hunting gear holding rifles and standing duty at the perimeter. "What is that? Would they not let us through?" I asked as Tuck turned around. "Should we try?"

"No. I doubt they'll let us through. Everywhere is being sectioned off into mini states," Tuck said. "Borders are being established."

"On main roads? They can't do that."

"Who's going to stop them? It's smart, Em. It's the only way anyone is going to survive."

"The military must have a store of gasoline somewhere? Even if it's taken them a couple of weeks to mobilize. This would be one of the first things they addressed, right? The inability of citizens to travel?"

"Even with gasoline, most of the military's equipment might not work. And any military that tries to knock down these borders will have a fight on their hands because knocking down these borders is sentencing the people inside to death."

I looked back at the road. He'd given similar advice to the Pritchards. He'd told them to create a perimeter and have neighbors take shifts guarding it. Protecting their food and water and livestock. And it made sense to guard your own property at a time like this. I just hadn't realized people would start claiming whole swaths of land, setting up roadblocks into any area that had resources a certain group decided to claim.

"What about the ones outside the lines?" I asked. What about travelers, like us?

He shot me a troubled look but didn't say more. I supposed I didn't need him to.

We backtracked an hour and took another route, only to find that one was blocked as well. This one however, had a large group of people standing in front of it, yelling at the men with rifles. At the back of the group there was a man and a woman with a double stroller loaded down with items, a baby and a toddler both crying from the seats. "Fuck," Tuck swore, banging his palms on the steering wheel. He pulled off to the side of the road and unfolded the map just as the loud crack of a gun made me jump and reach for Tuck, gripping his shirt.

The crowd in front of the barrier was screaming now, as were the men behind it. The people parted, and a man lay on the ground, and even from a distance I could see the blood spreading from his body. "They shot him," I said. "Tuck, they shot him."

Tuck dropped the map, backed up and then turned around

just as one of the women spotted us, raising her hand and yelling, "Hey! Hey! Help!" and began running toward our car. I watched her through the rearview mirror, the others turning too and beginning to pursue our car, but then stopping as we sped away.

The desperation was palpable. Those people were likely out of food, had no transportation, and were on the wrong side of an already-established line. *Parents. Children. Young women my age, alone.* I swallowed gulps of air, tamping down my anguish.

Tuck was looking at the map as he drove back around the big rig we'd driven past a few minutes before. "Goddammit," Tuck swore. "Both roads I was going to take to your parents' are blocked. We're going to have to go another way." He pulled over to the side of the road and I was quiet, trying to process what I'd seen at the barricade as Tuck studied the map. After a few minutes, he set it down and pulled back onto the road. I didn't ask what new route we'd take, trusting him as I'd trusted him to get me this far.

We drove toward the coast now, the only direction available. "Should we try the highway?" I asked. Maybe back roads had been safest once, and mostly empty in many locations, but perhaps the opposite was true now. I couldn't imagine what anyone would be trying to protect on a highway, especially one where the cars had been raided.

"Not in a car," Tuck said distractedly, his gaze constantly moving to the rearview mirror as if he expected to be chased down at any moment. "We probably wouldn't be able to make it through because of the parked vehicles, but even if we could, it isn't safe. We'd have to travel way too slow in a car and be vulnerable to attack. It'd be safer to go by foot, but we don't have enough provisions for that. We'll need to stock up first, at least on water."

Not having enough provisions also meant we wouldn't be able to backtrack to Arizona and attempt to get to the San Fernando Valley from the opposite direction than the one we'd taken. Truthfully, we might not even make it back the way we'd come considering the barriers that seemed to be going up by the hour.

Tuck continued to look extremely unsettled, and it scared me too. "This looks like the only route we can take, but moving north to your parents will mean traveling through Los Angeles," he said.

Los Angeles.

All this way, we'd avoided cities because they weren't safe. Tuck had planned to go to Los Angeles alone, but Tuck was strong and street savvy, and his instincts for handling danger were honed. Me, I was none of those things.

That was the old you, Emily. Haven't you held your own on this journey? Haven't you proven that you can be an asset too?

"Okay," I said, giving him a tip of my chin. "Then we'll check on your uncle together. And then move on to my parents' from there."

"We don't have another choice right now," Tuck murmured, almost as if to himself. And again, he banged his palms on the steering wheel and cursed under his breath.

We turned onto another road, and then another, finally catching sight of the City of Angels sprawled in the distance.

thirty-seven

Tuck

Day Sixteen

I pulled the car behind a furniture store in a strip mall that had obviously been looted, front windows broken and glass sparkling in the morning sun. I parked behind two dumpsters that looked mostly empty and shut the engine off. "We'll come back for it if we can," I told Emily, pocketing the key.

"What if someone hotwires it?"

"They might. But I think it's safer leaving it here than attempting to drive it into the city."

We took our backpacks from the trunk, stuffing them with the remaining provisions and then rounding the building. We looked out to the city beyond, or what we could see of it, anyway, from where we stood. Smoke rose from several spots, whether from fires that had broken out naturally for one reason or another, or from people who'd set them, I had no way to know. A set of pops met our ears and Emily looked at me in alarm. "Gunfire?"

Probably. "Let's go this way," I said, leading her in the opposite direction, away from the sounds. A distant human wail rose up, and then a few more.

Emily's eyes met mine, and my guts cramped. I fucking hated walking her into what I knew very well would be a dangerous landscape, and yet, what choice was there? I couldn't drive into a scorching wildfire burning out of control, one that, in the absence of water or planes to drop fire retardant, would burn indefinitely. I wouldn't drive around randomly, either running out of fuel or encountering one roadblock after another until so many popped up that we were trapped.

My choices were to head out into the desert, driving as far as a car could go in terrain like that and scavenge for food and water, hopeful that we'd find enough not to starve. Or we could make our way to my uncle's house, hopeful that we could stock up on provisions there and—with him—begin the journey on foot to Emily's parents.

Decisions needed to be made quickly at this point because everything was devolving very rapidly now and what was already bad would only get worse from here.

We walked through an industrial area, many of the buildings burned out, any businesses that had once operated here looted of everything. We stuck our heads in a Dollar General, the shelves utterly barren, and what looked like blood smeared across the floors. Next door, a Department of Motor Vehicles sat vacant, chairs overturned, and counters toppled. I assumed there'd been computers and phones present, but they were gone now and why anyone would take the time to lug those things away considering the circumstances was beyond me. Perhaps, in some cases, it was just human nature to *take* and that's what had happened here.

We continued on. This area of town had been completely

stripped. Even the cars sitting in the streets here had been emptied, doors, glove boxes, and trunks standing open, and even
some of the engines missing. No wonder very few people wandered the streets and the ones that did, averted their gazes and
turned quickly away. They knew at this point that information and help wasn't coming and that other people only rep-
resented danger.

"There's no smog," Emily murmured as we came to the top
of a hill with a better view of the city. I'd been so focused on
looking down every block and skirting doorways, that I hadn't
noticed the sky. But I looked up briefly now and noticed she
was right. Even despite the massive fire that burned miles away,
the brown cloud that typically coated Los Angeles in a dirty
haze was gone.

But before I could comment, a smell rose up and both Emily
and I put our hands over our noses. Emily coughed, tilting her
head toward me. "Dead bodies," she said, both of us familiar
with the putrid scent by now.

And when we turned the corner, we saw why. What had
once been a tent city of homeless people was now a pile of rotting corpses. "Oh God," Emily said, turning her face into my
shoulder. I wrapped my arm around her and led her in the opposite direction.

A man stood on a street corner, one hand raised, the other
clutching a Bible as a group of people stood before him. The
people started swaying as the man's voice boomed, "And there
shall be signs in the sun, and in the moon, and in the stars; and
upon the earth distress of nations, with perplexity; the sea and
the waves roaring; men's hearts failing them for fear, and for
looking after those things which are coming on the earth: for
the powers of heaven shall be shaken."

His voice faded as we moved on, and the screams and wails
we'd heard in the distance grew closer. The occasional noise

of an engine revving could be heard, and dog howls rose into the crystal sky.

It appeared that lots of people had already left.

But many had also stayed.

I'd heard once—somewhere—that on any given day, New York City had less than a week's worth of food for every man, woman, and child. If the same was true of other major metropolitan areas, Los Angeles had run dry a week and a half before. But even that was generous considering many would horde and leave none for others. In some places, people had gone hungry on day one and stores that sold groceries had been stripped bare within a couple days, if not hours.

As we walked, we discussed in low tones the best route to take to my uncle's house in Lynwood. From where we were, it would take about three hours to walk, and though I wanted to attempt jogging to get there more quickly, I also knew caution was key.

"We could try to make it to my condo instead," Emily said. "I have food there."

"My uncle's house is closer," I said, glancing toward the west where Emily lived. It was also where the majority of the smoke was rising from, and where I could hear engines gunning. My best guess was that it'd been taken over. "Plus, you don't have the keys to your condo, and we can't scale the building."

"It's all electronic," she murmured. "I don't know if that means it's wide-open, or inaccessible."

"Either way, we'd be shit out of luck."

We put our hands over our noses again as another block of bodies stretched before us. Goddammit, these poor people. They'd lived desperate lives on the streets, and then been the first ones left to die. Next to me, Emily swiped her eye and looked away. "What'd they die from?" she asked.

"Most lack of water, probably. Some needed medication. Violence. No way to tell."

The farther we walked, the more people we saw, some rooting through overflowing trash cans of food that—if there was any there—would be long-rotted by now. Just like Hosea had said, disease was going to spread quickly in a landscape like this, if it wasn't already. Awful scents of death and garbage and pungent, smoldering fires assaulted our noses and the sound of children and babies crying made us both wince.

"Tuck, look," Emily said, grabbing my arm as she stopped and pointed to the end of a wide street. I stared, taking a moment to make sense of what I saw. It was a pile of wreckage sitting in the middle of the road, a crumpled helicopter with a news logo barely visible that had obviously crashed onto the tops of several cars.

"Jesus," I muttered, wondering again how many aircraft had been in the sky when the solar flare hit and whether all of them had crash-landed like ours had. How many survivors were there and how many hadn't had pilots as good as ours?

We walked through a neighborhood of small family homes, where there were red and blue X's on many of the doors. I remembered back to news footage I'd seen of Hurricane Katrina and the houses with the X's spray-painted on them indicating a dead body was inside and wondered if that was the case here too. But authorities had marked the houses then; there were no authorities anywhere in sight now.

A man walked by us with a dead seagull in his hands and when I turned toward him to ask about the x's, he pulled out a knife as he whipped the dead bird behind him and screamed, "Get back!"

I raised one hand and grabbed Emily's arm with the other. "We don't want your bird," I said. "I was just wondering why there are x's on the doors."

The man blew out a rattly breath and took another step back, still holding the seagull behind him, which I assumed he was planning on eating. "Gangs," he said. "Turf wars. Downtown is the worst. They've already taken over hotels and restaurants. Those who fought back died. They control the streets and the food down there. Some of the smaller gangs are laying claim to residential areas. No homes are safe." He looked up the street as though thinking of his own home and then mumbled, "I gotta go. Good luck."

My heart had dropped as he'd spoken. Gangs were staking claim to homes? Whole neighborhoods?

I heard the rumble of an engine and turned toward the sound. The man stopped and looked back at us. "If you have anything of value on you, I'd hide," he said, and then he darted between two houses and disappeared.

Anything of value. That phrase had recently taken on a whole new meaning.

I pulled Emily onto a porch on the other side of the street, and we ducked behind the railing, our eyes meeting as the rumble grew louder. She blinked, features contorted with alarm as she grabbed my hand.

The vehicle passed by slowly, the sounds of male chatter accompanying the growl of the car. I raised my head a bare inch and peeked over the wooden barrier we were kneeling behind. A red classic convertible Ferrari was just rounding the corner, men holding guns sitting on the tops of the seats on both sides, their heads turning as they surveyed the area. One of the men tossed his cigarette right before another man said, "We've been through here. Let's go." And the car made a sudden turn, tires squealing as they disappeared around a corner.

"What the hell?" Emily breathed.

"The gangs that man just mentioned. Probably out looking for food and water," I said. Other than the cars and weapons they obviously already had, that was what was of value now.

We remained behind the railing for several more minutes, the roar of the car receding, before we left the porch. I looked over my shoulder and swore I saw the movement of a curtain.

Someone had watched us as we'd taken cover on their porch. A shiver snaked down my spine. I needed to be more careful. *Stay sharp, Mattice*, I could hear Hosea saying, the same advice he'd given me in prison, the reminder that had helped keep me from getting regular beatdowns. And worse.

Although if what the man in the car had said was true, they'd been through here already which had to mean these homes were stripped of sustenance. And the man clutching the dead bird suddenly made much more sense.

We started walking, and Emily took my hand. "Are there gangs in your uncle's neighborhood?" she asked. But she must have figured there were after the stories I'd told her about who I'd fallen in with when I'd moved here. I just nodded.

"Gangs will want to take over the areas that have the most resources though, right?" she asked. "Once the police aren't an issue and alarms no longer work, they'll target the wealthy."

"Yes," I agreed. "The power structure has flipped. But still, anyone who has anything at all is a target at a time like this."

"Even that man with the bird," Emily murmured.

On the outskirts of that neighborhood, the smell of death rose again, so strong and abhorrent that we were both forced to take an item of clothing from our backpacks and cover our faces. "It's a hospital," Emily said, her voice muffled. "Oh God, Tuck, I can't. We have to go around."

I took her arm and pulled her toward another street so that we could round the area and come out on the other side. I looked over my shoulder once when we got to the higher ground of the other block, and caught sight of a huge hole to the side of the building where bodies were piled. I swallowed down the vomit that rose in my throat and looked away, walking faster and pulling Emily with me. They'd created a mass grave beside the hospital for all the people they couldn't save. But what else were they going to do? There was no one to pick up the bodies, certainly no one who was going to expend energy digging graves. Maybe some of the families had done that somehow, but most simply wouldn't be able to. *Jesus fucking Christ.*

I had this intense urge to pull Emily somewhere and curl my body around her, to protect her from the sights and sounds and smells and anything that might threaten her in this hellscape, of which the possibilities were countless. But we only had a little ways to go, and so we moved forward, at a faster clip this time.

It was late afternoon when we finally entered the neighborhood where my uncle had taken me in when I was just a kid. The streets were trashed, corpses lying here and there. We looked at them vacantly, even if Emily still let out a small moan each time we came upon one. They no longer made us jump or cringe and that was a horror in itself.

"Hey, hello," a man said, coming out of an alleyway and rushing toward us. I pulled Emily and jumped back, holding my hand out, demanding he halt.

He stopped, holding his hand out as well. "I don't mean any harm. I don't." The last word emerged on a squeak, and he drew in a shaky breath as though holding back tears. "My wife and I got a baby, man. A six-month-old. Her formula ran out a week ago. There's none anywhere. No milk, nothing. We... Shit. Do you know anyone who has a baby? Who nurses? Please."

"I'm sorry. No."

The man hung his head, tears sliding down his cheeks and my gut wrenched for this father. "Tuck," Emily said, her voice barely more than a whisper. And I knew what she was asking, or suggesting, or giving permission for without saying more than that. I let out a slow breath, feeling both relief and the anxiety of putting someone before ourselves. It wasn't wise, and yet, we had hope, and a plan, and this man obviously did not.

"Come on," I muttered, gesturing for him to follow me into the privacy of the alley. "Do you have water?" I asked, because if he didn't, what I was going to give him wouldn't help. They'd all die anyway.

"Y-yes. We filled up our tub and all the sinks." I swung my backpack off my shoulder and removed two cans of condensed milk Emily and I had taken from the Garcias for the protein and the fat. I moved close and slipped the cans to the man and he gasped softly and grabbed for them, his eyes meeting mine.

"Thank you, thank you so much." More tears slid down his cheeks and he looked stricken with shock.

I leaned in closer. "Mix it with water to make it last longer. Then check veterinary offices. The pet food will be gone, but there might be some puppy or kitten formula. I'd go to the zoo as well and check there for the same. Do it quickly, tomorrow morning. And then get the hell out of LA. Bring any weapons you have. You might be able to trade a gun for some milk at a farm. It's probably the only thing valuable enough to trade with other than food."

The man was bobbing his head, his face wet with tears. "Thank you, thank you." It seemed like the only thing he could manage.

"Go," I said. "Now. Hide that and hide it well."

He stuffed it under his jacket and then put his hands in his pockets, giving us one last look as if we were visions that might disappear any moment, and then turned and walked quickly back down the alley.

"We shouldn't have done that," I muttered.

Emily smiled gently. "I know," she said. "But sometimes… I don't know, it feels like people are sent right to you. And we received more than our fair share of goodness too."

I took her in, my heart expanding. I'd thought her selfish and vacuous at one point and been completely wrong. Or…if she'd begun traveling down that road because of the people surrounding her and the life she lived, this situation had exposed the deeper parts of her. The girl I remembered who cried when one of the barn cat's kittens died, the one who'd tried to love me when I'd been unlovable. I took her face in my hands and risked a moment on this dangerous street to kiss her lips. It felt vital. It felt like it might be one of the only things powerful enough to give us the strength to continue on.

We exited the alley and kept walking, staying as far away from the people we saw on the streets as possible. We couldn't say yes to anyone asking for food again. To do so would jeopardize Emily more than I was willing to.

I couldn't help remembering the day we'd walked into Silver Creek two weeks and a million years ago. Then, we'd been worried, lost, but had been taken into a town just beginning to enact a plan of action. LA was already mostly hollowed out, the flood of people who'd called this city home streaming into the countryside. For a while anyway. I wondered how long it would take before most of those people were dead. Because the country had resources, but only so many. And we'd arrived at the point where few were willing to share.

We turned the corner onto my uncle's street and my heart sunk when I saw all red *x*'s on the doors. "Fuck," I breathed as we stopped in front of the chain-link fence. I grasped its handle, knowing the metallic scent it would leave on my palm. I'd entered this gate when I was seventeen years old, a scowl on my face and a broken heart. And he'd been standing on the porch, his shoulder leaned against the post holding up the small overhang, arms crossed and looking at me like he had my number. And he did. He'd watched me self-destruct and he might have been disappointed, but he'd never seemed surprised.

Because he'd been there.

But the *x* on his door told me he might not be anymore.

How will I ever find you now?

Still, I had to see. I had to know for sure.

"I need you to crouch down behind that fence, Emily," I said, turning to the wooden fence across the way that led to a park that was as old and broken down as it'd been when I'd lived here. Despite that, kids had played there, but it was empty now.

"No, I want—"

"I don't know if the *x* on the door means a death occurred or that gang members took this house over. If they did claim it, it might mean they did it randomly, but it also might mean they're still in there. Please."

Her eyes held mine for a moment, and whatever she saw there convinced her to nod and head for the fence. I watched as she ducked behind it and then I turned back to the house, opened the gate, and then walked up the short concrete walkway to the front door. I knocked, loudly enough that anyone inside could hear me, but not so loud that it echoed down the block and might attract attention. This entire street looked empty, but who knew.

When no one answered my second knock either, I tried the handle. It turned in my palm and I pushed the door open. The smell hit me immediately and my knees almost buckled at what it told me even before I stepped inside and saw my uncle's body in the recliner. A moan made its way up my throat, and I walked farther inside, putting a hand against the wall to brace myself for a moment. "Oh Jesus."

If I'd been here...

But no, then I wouldn't have been with Emily. And to think of her in that field alone with Charlie was unthinkable. Still, guilt was a vise, tightening around my heart. He'd died alone.

I pulled in a breath as I brought my eyes to my uncle's body again, noting the gunshot wound in his chest. There was no weapon in his hands, but I knew there had been. He'd fought to the end, I was sure, even if whoever had come in had had the bigger gun and gotten off the first shot. I held my breath and then approached his body and removed the cross necklace and put it in my pocket. "Thank you," I said. "I wish I'd told you sooner. Thank you for saving me. And I'm sorry."

I straightened my spine, stuffing down the sorrow that ripped through me like a thunderstorm. There was no time for that now. I did a quick search of his kitchen, but it'd been completely stripped of food and water.

There was nothing here.

When I exited the house, Emily was standing at the gate. "I told you to stay hidden."

"I was worried," she said, her gaze moving over my features, her brow creasing. "Are you okay? Is he—"

"He's dead."

"Oh, Tuck. I'm so sorry. What can I do?"

"Nothing. But there's one more house I have to check. It's a few streets over."

My guts burned, and my heart felt like it was lodged in my throat. So much savagery here. So many good people had died simply because they weren't willing—or were unable—to flee. And there'd been no one to help them fight. Out on the road with Emily, I'd begun to believe that maybe I could put my past behind me and reach for my own happiness. But being on this street was a reminder that I still owed a debt, and I'd barely made a dent.

thirty-eight

Emily

He was pulling away from me. Not physically, but mentally and emotionally. I remembered what it felt like; it'd happened before.

I didn't ask where we were going. I just walked the couple blocks beside him, allowing him time to come to terms with the fact that his uncle was dead. There wasn't the time for grief—that would have to be set aside—but acceptance would help. Or so I hoped.

We stopped in front of a small house that looked very similar to his uncle's, as did most of the homes in this obviously low-income neighborhood. A large red *x* marked this door as well and Tuck let out a staggered breath and hung his head. After a moment, he turned and looked around and then walked up to the porch, leaning toward the window and using his hand to shade his eyes as he gazed inside. I heard a groan come from his throat before he stood straight. "Let's go."

"Whose house is it, Tuck?" I asked quietly as we turned back down the block and began walking.

For a moment he was quiet, leaning toward an alley and peering down it before taking my arm and pulling me forward. "Abel's girlfriend's."

Abel.

The young man who'd robbed a convenience store and bled to death in Tuck's car, a crime that Tuck had taken partial responsibility for even though—to my mind—he shouldn't have. I looked up at him, his jaw set, expression blank. "Were they... were they both in—"

"Yes," he said, his voice choked.

"I'm so sorry. Tuck—"

"Come on. I know somewhere we can stay overnight. We'll leave for your parents' in the morning."

My heart sank. I saw him shutting down, returning to the man he'd been. Not angry like I'd once thought. Not bitter. *Helpless. Grief-stricken.* All this carnage, all this death, and now the vision of what had to be the dead bodies of Abel's girlfriend and young son had reminded him that he was still trying to make up for not doing what he believed he should have when presented the chance. For failing Abel, and in so doing, failing Abel's girlfriend and son.

And the thing was? It'd just so happened that he'd found himself in a world ripe with chances to pay that unseen debt. They were everywhere. I'd seen the relief on his face when he'd given the man with the baby our condensed milk. And I'd felt relief too. I'd wanted to give it to him. But for Tuck, it wasn't just an act of kindness, it was a small step toward the redemption he was still seeking.

Only I wondered when it would be enough, wondered how many lives he'd have to save to assuage the shame and guilt he couldn't let go of.

What I was beginning to fear—deeply—was that I wasn't enough to convince him to give it up.

I wasn't even sure it was right that I try. Because the world needed heroes now and their motivations didn't much matter.

"This way," he said, leading me toward an obviously abandoned laundromat. Only, it clearly wasn't abandoned recently. This place had been an empty shell for quite some time—a decade at least if I had to guess. I followed Tuck to the rear, and he looked around before opening the back door and pulling me inside. The large empty space was dim and mostly empty. Any equipment had been cleared long ago, the only remnant of what it'd once been a coin machine half hanging on the wall that said, "Detergent."

"No one's going to come in here," he said, turning to our right where there was a smaller room that had likely once been a manager's office. We entered the mostly empty space, a small window high up on the wall glowing with the final rays of sunset. There was a large metal shelf on one wall, and Tuck closed the door and then pushed the shelf in front of it.

"How long has this place been abandoned?"

"It closed down a year or so after I moved here. There was a for-sale sign up on the land for years, and I think it was purchased a couple of times, but it always fell through. I don't know why."

I put my pack down and then sat on the floor under the window, my back propped against the wall. I took out a can of beans and peeled the top back, tipping it and pouring them into my mouth before handing the can to Tuck. "Bon appetite," I said, attempting to make him smile.

He did, sitting down next to me and taking the can. "Are you okay?" I asked.

He was quiet as he chewed but nodded when he handed the can back to me. "I will be."

Will you, Tuck?

We took out a few crackers and we ate for a moment. As hungry as I was, the food brought no pleasure. I felt heavy with fear and sorrow. And I knew what these feelings meant. I remembered well the distant look on Tuck's face.

"What happened to Abel's girlfriend and their son wasn't your fault. Neither was your uncle's death. Evil men with guns are to blame for that."

Maybe Tuck's feelings for me weren't as big as his need for atonement. Maybe he'd decide his place wasn't with me and my parents. But even so, even if he chose to go out into the world and fight for others, I wanted him to find a way to let go of the guilt he carried, because it killed me to see him hurting and trying with all his might to find forgiveness from those who weren't alive to extend it. An impossible task. And too painful for any one person to bear.

He sighed. "They had no one to protect them, Emily. I'm talking about Cherie and Abel Jr. If Abel hadn't died that day, he'd have been there to protect them."

"If, Tuck. If. That's a losing game and you know it. *Everyone* made choices that day, and the days preceding it. The what-if game isn't going to bring anyone back. What if Abel had decided that staying home and taking care of his pregnant girlfriend was more important than committing a crime that might get him thrown in jail? Or killed? What if he'd decided to go out and get a job instead of robbing a store?"

"Stop, Em. He was desperate."

"His desperation and his choices weren't your fault. You didn't owe him anything."

"You're being judgmental."

"Sure, I am," I said. "That's what the what-if game is all about. You have to judge every choice made—fair or not, reasonable or not—if you're going to play."

He looked away and ran his hand through his hair.

"Aren't you even a little bit mad at him, Tuck? Aren't you

angry that Abel put you in the position he did? Even despite being young and desperate. He asked you for a ride and didn't tell you he was going to commit a crime. He set you up, Tuck, whether he thought about that or not."

Something passed over his face, a discomfort that let me know I'd come somewhere close to the truth whether Tuck was willing to admit that yet or not. Or maybe his anger at Abel helped fuel his guilt. God, he was carrying so much. "What he did wasn't right," he said. "But I can only judge what I did that day. Only me."

I got up on my knees and turned toward him. "Yes. But what you did then was influenced by so many things." I reached out, and put my fingers on his jaw, turning his face my way, demanding that he look at me. He didn't get to do this this time, retreat inside himself without letting me have a say. I was hurting here too. For him. For me. For the world and all the people suffering right now. And maybe this wasn't the perfect time for this conversation, hiding in the back of an abandoned laundromat while outside the world burned. But I wanted Tuck to be whole so that he could let go of the shame he'd been stubbornly holding on to all these years. He believed the only way he could serve the world was to sacrifice his own happiness, and I could tell that the particular dead bodies he'd seen today had opened a wound in him and reconfirmed that. And if that inner narrative was going to be interrupted by outside rationale, my time to offer a voice of reason might very well be dwindling.

"I know you regret not being there for Abel in the way you now see he needed," I said. "I get it." I lowered my hand from his bearded jaw and lay it on his arm. "But so many choices were made, and they weren't all yours. You're carrying all of them, every single one, and no one's shoulders are strong enough for that. You can't bring them back. Even if you save a thousand lives or do a million good deeds, they'll still be gone."

His head fell back against the wall. "I know that, Em. But

I finally have the chance to right some wrongs by putting my talents to use and doing something worthwhile, something necessary. Who would I be if I walked away from that?"

"No one's asking you not to help where you can," I said. *Just do it closer to home. Do it without leaving me again.*

The room had grown dim while we talked and now we were both in shadow. We'd need to sleep if we were going to wake up at dawn and begin journeying to my parents' farm. Tuck sighed and gestured for me to come closer. I did, and he wrapped his arm around me, pulling me against him and kissing my temple. "I'm sorry," he said. And though I wasn't sure exactly what he was saying sorry for, it broke my heart anyway.

Was Tuck planning to go to battle for a collapsing society in honor of the deaths he felt responsible for? Or was he using that calling as a way to avoid staying with me? Or a vague combination of both even he couldn't separate or explain? Suddenly, the words I'd spoken to him while standing at that substation weeks ago, before we had any real idea that we were walking into a changed world came back to me. *I'm standing here too, Tuck, among the ashes.* I'd meant it figuratively then, but it was literal too, wasn't it? And something I'd experienced before.

And once again, I was losing my best friend. But this time, I was also losing the man I'd fallen deeply in love with. Once again, his pain was bigger than his love for me.

thirty-nine

Tuck

Day Seventeen

We left the laundromat behind as soon as the sky had gone from black to platinum gray. The sound of engines roared in the distance followed by a pop, and a chill shuddered through me when I thought of what might be happening in all those downtown hotels that apparently had been taken over. Was anyone being helped or taken in? Or had those buildings all become magnets for crime and brutality?

"What are they doing down there?" Emily asked, obviously having heard the same distant sounds.

"They're surviving the same way they always have," I murmured. "Only now, the rules favor them."

Dogs howled, and my heart gave a sharp knock when I wondered who was feeding them. Even people who loved their pets were going to prioritize their human family. *Dogs can hunt if they need to*, I told myself. There was only so much I could worry about at the same time. If I let my mind run away from me, I'd reel off into Crazytown.

"Fuck," I hissed when we heard noise up ahead and looked around the corner. We'd taken this route here just the day before, but now part of it was blocked off by two cars parked hood to hood and a bonfire behind it where men with guns were conversing loudly, a cackle rising here and there. Beside me, Emily jumped when one of the men threw a bottle he'd been drinking from, and it shattered on the pavement.

"What will they do if they spot us?"

Maybe nothing. Maybe we'd get robbed. Or worse. "I don't want to find out."

Her eyes met mine. "We'll have to travel around."

"It'll take hours longer," I said. We leaned back behind the building, and I pounded it with my fist. "Fucking assholes," I gritted. "We're almost out of water. It was going to be just enough to get us out of the city and to a water source." I swiped my hand through my unruly hair. "Let me think for a minute." I started going over other routes we might take, but I was worried all of them might have similar roadblocks. The city was being taken over quickly, neighborhood by neighborhood, and now block by block.

We stood there, and I looked around, orienting myself, considering other places we might find some water. Where though, when the whole damn city must be hunting for the same thing? Emily suddenly grabbed my forearm. "I know a place where we might find some food and bottled water."

"Where?" I asked skeptically.

"It's a recording studio. It's this nondescript building in the middle of a nondescript block. Artists who use it like it for its privacy and the fact that paparazzi don't follow them there. Many of them record at night."

I gestured for her to hurry and get to the point. Each moment now was crucial if we were going to get out of here.

"Anyway, there's an entire room next to the booths that has snacks and cases of water."

"How far?"

"About an hour's walk from here."

It was a risk. We might encounter other blockades. But there weren't a lot of options and water was essential. I wanted to kick myself. I'd calculated and planned and determined we'd have enough to get in and out. I'd also hoped we might restock at my uncle's when we picked him up. But I hadn't anticipated having to take such long routes due to turf wars.

"Shit," I murmured when we heard another vehicle approaching on the street with the men and the bonfire. I put my arm across her and pushed lightly, and we both plastered ourselves against the building, our eyes meeting in the gray light of dawn.

And then suddenly there was yelling and noise and the sharp pops of gunfire. "Run, go that way," I hissed, and we both ducked and ran back down the block. I pulled Emily into a doorway when we'd gotten halfway and again, we pressed ourselves as close to the building as possible as the screech of tires came from the street beyond, the car turning onto the block where we were now hiding, tucked into shadow.

I held my breath as the car went tearing by, two bloody bodies crumpled onto the rear hood of a gold convertible, the driver—thankfully—focused straight ahead.

I blew out the breath I'd been holding and took her trembling hand. "Lead the way," I said.

It took us forty-five minutes to make the walk, despite having to hide from approaching vehicles twice, the sky lightening from platinum to pearl as we traveled. The block Emily had directed us to was as nondescript as she'd described, a number of ugly square buildings with weeds growing through the small, paved sections in front. They almost appeared like storage facilities that had gone unused for some time. She was right, those searching for necessities wouldn't likely bother with these. At least not until absolutely everything else had been looted.

We tried the front door, but that was locked. "There's a door in the back," Emily said, taking my hand as we rounded the structure. "And if not, we can break a window. There's no need to worry about alarms now," she murmured.

The back door was locked as well, but as she wiggled the handle, I noticed the shade move slightly on the window close by. I took her hand and pulled her so that we were on the other side of the door. "Someone just looked out of that window," I said. Before she could answer, the back door squeaked open, and I shoved Emily behind me as I faced the person emerging.

It was a woman. And she was unarmed.

"Layne?" I heard Emily say from behind me where she was obviously peeking out.

"I knew that was you," the woman named Layne said. "Oh my God. Come here. Are you okay?"

Emily stepped around me and Layne took Emily in her arms, and they embraced. "I can't believe you're here," Emily said after she'd stepped back.

"I'm assuming you came looking for food and water too? Who's your friend?"

"I'm so sorry. Tuck, this is Layne Beckett. She's an amazing singer. Layne, Tuck Mattice. We walked from Illinois where my plane went down."

"Holy shit, are you kidding me? No, of course you're not. Nova, the things that are happening in this city right now." She gave her head a small shake. "God, speaking of which, I've lost my mind. Come inside. Hurry."

We all entered the building and Layne closed and locked the door behind us, leading us through a dark room to a space beyond where light was emanating. "There are no windows in here, so it's safe to have some lights on. There were some battery-operated string lights and other mood lighting," she said, turning slightly and using air quotes. "Oh, and Leon Lee is here. He's your manager, right?"

"Yes," Emily breathed. "Oh my God."

"He's sleeping in one of the booths. We got here at three a.m., and he needed to get some sleep."

We entered the larger space, and I looked around at the carpeted bench seating lining the perimeter of the room. The floor was black, as were the walls, but the twinkle lights and other battery-operated lanterns and globes gave the place a peaceful glow. There were three recording rooms in front of this one, all of them with large viewing windows. Only one was open, the other two covered from the inside by black curtains.

Layne glanced at the watch on her wrist. "I'm supposed to wake Leon in thirty minutes. Can I get either of you something to eat? Water?"

"Yes, water would be great," Emily said.

Layne opened one of the benches and reached inside. "We've hidden all the supplies in these," she said. "In case anyone breaks in or whatever. Things are wild. I spend most of the day trying to believe this is even real."

She handed us each a bottle of water, and I drank several sips but then capped it again. We'd grown used to rationing at this point. Emily did the same and then we sat down.

"You can't be planning to stay here indefinitely," Emily said to Layne.

"No, no, we aren't. We're leaving tomorrow morning."

"Leaving for where?"

"San Diego." She looked back and forth between us. "You should both come. I'm sure Leon wouldn't hesitate to take you with him."

I frowned. "What's going on in San Diego?"

"There's a whole neighborhood in La Jolla that's been turned into a safety zone. Leon's been back and forth between there and here. He's the reason I'm not hiding in my apartment with half a bag of Doritos and the water remaining in my toilet tank, knowing I would have to go out into the streets soon, or die alone." She wrapped her arms around herself and drew her shoulders up. "It was terrifying, Nova. And I know your plane crashed, so you probably experienced worse than me."

Emily reached across and took her hand and squeezed it. "Please, call me Emily. And yes, we all have stories," she said.

Layne nodded, a jerky movement. "Leon helped Freddie and some others get there, which is how Leon knew about me. He's been rescuing the people he can."

"Wait, the San Diego thing," Emily said, obviously as unclear as me about what was there. "What do you mean a 'safety zone'?"

"It was actually organized years ago, luckily enough. There's a community up in the hills above the ocean that has been running a co-op. A group of rich retirees who own these Mc-Mansions with huge yards got together and decided one would grow grapes, the other vegetables, another would keep chickens. They had a farmers market just among themselves every weekend and are self-sufficient if they want to be. I mean, these people are rich enough that they don't even do any of the work themselves unless they want to. They have staff who live on-site now and take care of most of the labor. And there are pools in the majority of the backyards. They have water for years."

Ah, a group of crunchy Californians with time on their hands, money burning a hole in their pockets, and a desire to feel like they were living off the land. Well, God bless them because it sounded like they were ahead of the curve. "Leon's father was war buddies with one of the residents so that's how he has an in. It's grown a lot in the last couple of weeks as they've invited outsiders in. Leon made contact with a few strong men he knows who didn't have a place to go. He offered them a spot in the community in exchange for guarding the gates. So now they have security. There are a couple of doctors among the residents, which is obviously important. And they love that Leon has brought in some artists and entertainers too. They know how important the arts will be going forward."

Going forward.

"Oh," Emily said. "I see." She looked over at me, and for the first time in weeks, I realized I couldn't tell what she was thinking. I felt hollow inside. I knew there was a wedge between us, and most of me hated it more than anything I'd ever hated, and part of me clung to it because I knew it'd be necessary for my survival when we parted. And the fact that history was repeating itself didn't escape me either, which only added to my despair.

"How are you traveling there safely?" I asked. "There are barricades everywhere. Whatever path Leon took might already be closed." Things were unwinding rapidly. Nothing could be counted on. Even if San Diego was less than two hours away by car.

"Yes. There are four blockades set up that are allowing people passage as long as they don't stay. Guides will walk you through. They're not bad people. They're just trying to protect their own. Like I said, Leon's traveled the route a few times, so they know and trust him."

The door to one of the recording booths opened, and a man walked through looking sleep-mussed, his eyes widening when he saw Emily and me. "Emily? Holy shit. How the hell are you here?"

"Leon!" She practically ran over to him, and they hugged.

"My God," he said after they'd let go. "Did you just randomly find your way here?"

She laughed and wiped a tear from her eye. "We came here for the food and water," she said. And I had to admit the relief in finding these two people, even if I didn't know them. They were part of Emily's life, and damn, but it was good to know that decent people were still fighting through this. And even more than that, it was a relief to hear that whole zones were being formed, even now, to keep people safe.

Like Layne had said, that couldn't last, but for now, some who could, were making room rather than casting out.

Emily introduced me to the man who had once been her manager and I shook his hand. He looked between us. "You came to the right place. I'm so glad you remembered this studio, Emily. Did Layne tell you about the safe zone?"

Emily nodded.

"You should come with us," Leon said. "This will be my final trip."

Emily glanced over at me quickly and then away. "We... I can't. We're heading to my parents in the San Fernando Valley."

"San Fernando?" He shook his head and frowned. "Oh... damn. There were massive fires there when the event first happened. From what I've heard, the people there are living in makeshift camps and it's pretty desperate."

More fucking fires. Shit. My heart dropped and Emily's eyes widened. "Are you sure?"

"Yeah, but hopefully their community came together, and your parents are okay." He looked back and forth between the two of us. "Hey, listen, this safe zone in San Diego, I could make sure that they allow you a few family members too. Each resident was given a number of guest allotments. My father's old friend Merrick Winchester doesn't have family nearby and so he gave me his allotments and I've been trying to find as many as I can to fill those spaces. As long as we get there to-morrow, they'll hold spaces for your family to follow later." He glanced from me back to Emily. "There will come a point, and it's probably fast approaching, where all the spaces will be filled and they won't be able to feed or house anyone else, but for now, they have room and they're gathering a diverse community of people who have something to offer. Come with us, both of you."

"How would I get word to my parents though?" Emily asked. "Even snail mail doesn't exist anymore."

"There will be ways once things settle down," Leon said. "There are already teens here in the city who are delivering messages on bikes for a few scraps of food and some water. If there's a service that will help keep them and their family alive, humans will find it. There will be a way to contact your parents sooner than you think. Especially if you're in a location with currency, which you will be if you come with us. You'd be shocked at what people do these days for a loaf of bread."

Emily's brow creased at what he'd said, but then she gave a distracted nod. Leon hugged Emily again, and then he and Layne got out some food and laid out a little picnic as we all talked about the things we'd seen and the places we'd been, at least most of it. It was difficult to sum it all up, and I was distracted and hurting because I could tell by the way Emily's eyes kept drifting to the wall as she obviously considered something or another, that she was thinking about taking them up on their offer.

I'd thought I had at least the last short leg of this journey with her to her parents' house, but that might not be the case. And I couldn't decide if I should try to talk her out of this or encourage her to take these two people she obviously trusted up on their offer of a safe haven.

Because we didn't know exactly what was happening in the San Fernando Valley, and this might be an opportunity too good to pass up. Both for her and her parents, given they were alive and at least mostly well.

We finally closed the curtain on one of the small recording studios that still contained a few pieces of equipment. Leon was going to take the first watch, and then wake me for the second. Emily had said good-night to both Layne and Leon and let them know she'd decide before morning whether to go with them or continue on to her parents'.

We lay down on our sleeping bags on the floor, one of the small battery-operated lamps we'd turned on in the corner casting the barest glow. I could see the slope of her cheekbone, and I let my gaze run along it, feeling an ache so sharp that I swore it pierced something inside. Some vital organ that I could live without, but only barely. And I decided to make it easier on her.

"I think you should go with them," I said softly, my lungs deflating under the weight of my words. "I'll continue on to your parents, and if they're in need of a safe zone too, I'll bring them to you."

"But we were supposed to travel there together," she said, her voice little more than a whisper. "That was the plan. Since the beginning."

"We didn't know about this place in San Diego though, Emily. It seems…it seems like an opportunity too good to pass up." I paused. God, my throat ached. It hurt to say this even if I knew it was true. Because I wanted her to be safe more than anything or I'd cease to be useful at all.

She paused only a moment. "Yes, it's somewhere safe when there isn't much of that anymore. And my parents may need it too. They may have lost everything. They may be barely surviving."

"Right. And like Layne said, the community members in San Diego appreciate the fact that Leon's brought artists to join them too. Your voice, Em, your songs…don't underestimate how much people need music right now. If those residents recognize that value, they must be good, and wise."

Again, she was silent, and with each quiet breath, I felt the chasm widening between us. "I… I wanted that," she said. "A way to use my music to help. Even…a little."

"Yes," I said. *Tell me this is all wrong even if it seems right. Stay with me.* But that was only my selfishness talking and I wouldn't let that lead me. Not anymore. I'd already decided I was leaving.

"Will you go to Kansas and meet back up with Hosea?" she asked, her voice a whisper.

"If you and your parents are safe, then I'll go and help where I'm needed. We're at war now, Emily. That's essentially what it is. And Hosea and his team are doing good work for those who are most at risk now. They're making a difference and they'll only be more necessary as time goes on. They could use me."

She was silent for several heavy moments. "Yes, they've probably grown since we were there. They—they rescued so many abandoned children and youth. There must be so many more out there…waiting. And as far as my parents, I'm hopeful, you know, that they're okay. They have good friends. They're smart. They're away from major cities. If there were fires, hopefully their farm was spared. And if so, they have food. I think they're okay."

"I do too, Em."

"But even if they don't need a place to go, they'll be worried about me. They need to know I'm okay."

"I'll deliver the message."

"If nothing else, it could be a good rest stop on your way back to Kansas."

"Yes."

She was silent again and my pain felt all-encompassing, a heavy tarp weighing me down as I sensed the minutes that we had together filtering through an unseen hourglass. But I had to force myself to be glad about this unexpected development. It was hope in the midst of hell. How could anyone pass up a commune with plenty of food and water, overlooking the ocean with security at the gate? And if she didn't go now, and then later we found that her parents weren't okay for one reason or another, would there be a second chance? Not necessarily. Like

Leon had said, the point where they'd have to turn people away was likely fast approaching.

"You could come too," she whispered softly. "Instead of Kansas."

But I couldn't. I wasn't looking for safety. I was looking for purpose. I was looking to help those who'd been left behind the borders. To help the helpless. To balance the scales that had been tipped because of me. "I can't, Em."

She nodded and I could feel her sorrow. I took her in my arms, and she clutched me too, holding on while we still could.

We made love by the glow of the lamp, our hearts beating in tandem, staying as quiet as we possibly could so as not to be heard. And as we lay together afterward, breaths stilted as the sweat dried on our skin, I thought I felt the wetness of her tears on my chest and barely held back my own.

"This wasn't supposed to hurt," I murmured into her hair. "All this time, I was looking forward to saying goodbye to you, and now…" My joke fell flat, the pain in my voice belying the attempt at levity.

Even so, she let out a soggy laugh but gripped me tighter.

Hours later, when Leon woke me to take over the watch, the batteries in the lamp had died and the room was cast in darkness.

forty

Emily

Day Eighteen

Tuck had insisted on traveling with us to the first barrier we'd be crossing through on our two-day walk to San Diego. He'd suggested coming with us on the journey, but that would have meant backtracking several days to my parents, and I'd much rather he get there as quickly as possible. And if necessary, direct my parents to where I was.

"I've traveled this route several times," Leon reassured him. "We'll be there before sunset tomorrow. I got her." And then he patted his waist where he'd shown us the weapon he now carried.

The world already felt scary and unfamiliar, and that morning I felt brittle and on edge. I wanted to feel hopeful. I wanted to experience gratitude at knowing there was a safe place in the midst of all this madness, and that I was headed there now.

But the only thing I could focus on was the pain of knowing Tuck wouldn't be with me.

Morning mist swirled, birds wheeling above as the checkpoint came into view. The people who were guarding it had moved concrete roadside barriers into the center of the road and two men with hulking muscles stood in front of them, guns strapped to their bodies.

Tuck moved slightly closer to me as we approached, his protective nature ever present in his actions and the way he instinctively put his body in front of those he meant to block from harm. *Oh God. How will I say goodbye? This isn't right. Please tell me you can't let me go, that nothing means more than I do. That whatever happens, you'll return to me, and you'll stay.*

But I knew he wouldn't, because it wasn't true.

And part of me loved him all the more for the fact that he was going out into a dangerous world, hell-bent on helping others. I'd vowed that morning as we'd left the recording studio with backpacks of food and water that I wouldn't beg him not to leave me. Because truthfully? I knew he might very well honor my request if I begged him hard enough. But I couldn't let him remain with me out of obligation. It would eventually break my heart even more than it was already breaking.

Still, as Leon stood talking to the guards, who obviously knew him, I looked at Tuck, tearing up against my will. "Saying thank you for getting me to this point doesn't seem like enough."

"It's more than enough," he said, his knuckle trailing over my cheek. I turned into it but then turned away. I was barely holding on. If he touched me, I'd break.

"I can't believe we made it here," I said, voice as wobbly as the smile I attempted. "From that plane, all the way here. We did it. And now—"

"Now you're going to be safe. Everything is going to be good, Emily."

I nodded. And I saw the heartbreak on his face too, and it hurt so much I could hardly bear it. Leon said my name, and I looked up to see him and Layne passing around the concrete structures. I turned back to Tuck. "If my parents are fine where they are, then I won't see you anytime soon. But when this is all over, if you…if you're ever this way…" *Years from now, when the world is safer, when…* I didn't even know what to say or how to finish that thought. The world offered no guarantees right now, and I couldn't ask Tuck for any either.

"Ready, Emily?" Leon called.

I met Tuck's eyes as I tried desperately to hold back my tears and then he grabbed me, hugging me fiercely as I let out a quiet sob. Then he released me and turned away before I could see his face and began walking the other way.

I sucked back my sobs, a lump in my throat causing the air to squeak out on a quiet whistle.

Layne took my hand when I met up with them. "Are you okay?"

No. No, I wasn't okay. The whistle turned into a soft moan of despair, my heart shattering as a hundred things I needed to say but hadn't, poured from the cracks. I turned. "Tuck!"

He pivoted, racing toward me as we met in front of the barrier, him catching me as he said my name, holding me and stroking my hair. Tears coursed down my cheeks, and I could hardly find my voice. "I just want to say thank you again. There's so much, Tuck. I don't think you truly know. Thank you not just for getting me here, but for keeping me safe, for feeding me and protecting me and—"

"Em, of course. Em, don't cry." He sounded broken too, his voice scratchy, eyes filled with such sorrow.

"I just… What I really needed to say is that you're a good man, Tuck. You're honorable and fair and so, so good and you're going to save lives and rescue people. And that's a wonderful thing, Tuck. Such a valiant goal." *And I love you and something tells me I won't see you again and I can't live with myself if I don't say this to you now.*

"You're going to be fine," he practically choked. "You're going to be safe and happy and you're going to sing again because your voice brings people joy. The world needs that so desperately right now, Em. You're going to make a difference too. Remember that your voice is medicine, Em, as sure as whatever they've gathered to treat people within that safe zone overlooking the Pacific Ocean." He smiled, but it was so very sad. He smoothed back my hair and kissed my forehead, our hands running over each other, memorizing.

"I'm scared to be alone," I gasped. "But mostly, I'm scared to be without you."

He used his thumbs to swipe my tears. "No. No, you're brave and competent, more than you know. And you'll be safe with them." He inclined his head back to where Leon and Layne were waiting for me.

I gave a jerky nod and a small hiccup. "Promise me you'll be safe too. Please take care of yourself sometimes, okay? Promise me."

"I do, Em. I promise."

"We were good together, weren't we? We were a good team. I'll always remember that, for all my life. I'll never forget."

"Me neither. I'll never forget a moment of it."

"Emily," Leon called. "I'm sorry, but we have to get to the next checkpoint while certain guards are on duty."

I looked back and nodded, pulling in a shaky breath and swallowing down my sobs. Then I leaned up and kissed Tuck on his lips, allowing my mouth to linger before pulling away and then turning and running to Leon and Layne, their expressions filled with sympathy.

This time I didn't look back.

The next forty-eight hours were mostly uneventful, and I was grateful. Even fear didn't penetrate the grief, and I was thank-

ful for that too. The monotonous walking helped as I was able
to lull my mind and keep my thoughts at bay. It was when we
stopped that the sadness pierced, that the reality Tuck was no
longer beside me hit me like a blow.

Just before sunset the next day, we made our way up the
side of a rock cliff on a beach in San Diego. I used my hand as
a visor to shield my eyes as I looked out to the gray-hued sea,
sailboats swaying in a line. "What are they doing?" I asked.

Leon glanced in the direction where I was staring. "Keeping watch."

"Of what?"

"Of others trying to fish in their water."

I blinked as I turned away. *Their* water? Even sections of the
ocean were being barricaded now?

The sunset blazed, casting the sky in striations of red and orange. We walked through several quiet neighborhoods that felt
mostly abandoned, and then a looted business district.

"There it is," Leon said, pointing at the hill that rose up in
front of us, shimmering solar lights leading from the base to
the peak.

The ocean curved around from where we'd ascended, and
was closer now, the waves crashing just beyond, the glittery
spray reaching into the fiery sky.

"We're going to find peace here," Layne said, squeezing my
hand.

"Yes," I said, mustering a smile. But I feared that I'd never
find peace again.

forty-one

Tuck

Day Nineteen

The San Fernando Valley was a wasteland. Everywhere I looked were flattened piles of ash, whole neighborhoods burned to the ground. I drove slowly past what had once been a strip mall and was now nothing more than a heap of blackened bricks. Fear trembled in the back of my throat, and I braced as I rounded the corner of the street the Swansons lived on. A breath I hadn't realized I'd held gusted from my mouth, a wave of cool relief washing over me when their house came into view.

It's still standing.

Thank God. Thank God.

I turned off the car I'd located in the back of an auto body shop in Mission Viejo and hot-wired. It'd been a risk to drive through the outskirts of the city, but my risk assessment had changed since I'd said goodbye to Emily. I'd half expected to be blockaded or fired upon, but I'd gotten lucky, and the car had saved me a day of walking. I sat there for a moment, gathering myself. The Swansons' house was still there, but that didn't mean they were okay. In fact, now that I looked around, I was spotting clues that something bad had happened here. Bullet holes riddled the side of the burned-out car sitting across from where I was, and what I thought might be old blood was smeared across the street like a profusely bleeding body had been dragged.

I got out of the car and walked slowly across the street. A hawk's screech echoed through the stillness, and I looked up to see the bird gliding across the clear blue sky. A lizard darted from behind a rock, momentarily startling me before zipping away.

"Tuck?"

I spun around to find a man, outlined by the sun and holding a rifle, causing my heart to jolt. I put my hands up and squinted as my eyes adjusted to the bright light. "Mr. Swanson?"

"Oh, thank the good Lord. It *is* you. Jena said it was, but I thought she must be mistaken." He approached quickly and wrapped me in a bear hug. "Damn, it's good to see you. Are you okay? You look okay."

"Tuck!" Mrs. Swanson came running out of the house, obviously having been watching from a window while Mr. Swanson exited from the back and came around behind me.

Mrs. Swanson let out a cry and gathered me in a hug. "Oh, Tuck. You're here. Where's Emily?" Her eyes flared with fear, obviously afraid to ask.

"She's okay," I said. "She's fine. She wrote you a note." I took it from my pocket and handed it to Mrs. Swanson.

"Oh, thank you, God, thank you," Emily's mother said, looking over at her husband who gave her a nod, tears in his eyes. She opened the note and scanned it quickly, bringing two fingers to her lips as she read. When she was finished, she handed it to her husband. "Our girl is fine. She's good. I told you Tuck would take care of her," she said. She looked at me, smiling as tears shimmered in her eyes as well. "I told Phil there's no one better to be with Emily. No one." She hooked her arm through mine. "Come inside. I want to hear every detail about how you made it home."

The Swansons' exterior was riddled with bullet holes too, and a couple of the windows were boarded up. But the inside was undamaged and looked about the same as it had the last time I'd been there, what now felt like a hundred years ago. The Christmas tree that Mrs. Swanson had just been putting up when I'd been here last was still standing. My God, what day was it? The calendar had ceased having any meaning. Christmas had come and gone, and we hadn't even noticed.

I told the Swansons about our plane crash, and the journey home from there, not able to relay every detail lest it take four hours to tell, and also, because some of those details belonged to Emily and me alone. My heart twisted when I thought of the moments that would only ever be ours and I missed her with a ferocity that nearly brought me to my knees.

Their expressions shifted through several obvious emotions as I described what we'd gone through and what we'd seen: horror, shock, sadness, relief. "The entire country," Mrs. Swanson murmured. "It's what we heard but didn't think we could believe." Mr. Swanson took her hand in his.

"What happened here?" I asked. "There were obviously lots of fires just like in other places. But the bullets? The blood?"

"The homes left standing were attacked, including ours. We joined forces with the neighbors still here and fought back. There aren't many, but there are enough." She glanced at her husband again, something unspoken moving between them. "We had to. There was no other choice."

"Of course there wasn't," I said. "They obviously meant you harm."

"Whatever they wanted, they didn't get it," Mr. Swanson said. "We've since set up lookouts and have eyes on anyone coming or going. It's how I knew you were here."

"You did well."

"We did what we had to do," he said.

"What will you do now?" I asked.

He let out a long, slow breath, letting go of his wife's hand and running his fingers over his jaw. "We'll clear, and we'll rebuild. Several of the citrus trees made it through the fires and we'll begin grafting in the spring. If you have time, I'd love to go over the particulars to ensure I'm not overlooking anything. There's no room for error right now and almost all of the others who live here moved in after the citrus business began to die."

"Yeah, of course. I'd be happy to." I looked between them. "It's going to be a lot of work."

She gave me a wistful smile. "There are plenty of young people here, and they have children. We'll do our part, of course, but we do know our limits. We've made a good team so far, all of us together."

I felt a knot in my shoulder muscles loosen. They were taken care of. They'd made it this far, and I felt confident they'd continue forward. I was especially relieved to know they'd banded together with others.

"Will you stay, Tuck?" Mrs. Swanson asked. "You would be invaluable to getting a functioning citrus farm set up. We lost some animals, but still have chickens and several goats. We'll need to start breeding them as quickly as possible." She brought her hand to her forehead. "Oh, there are a million things to do. But what else is there now if we want to survive?"

"I'd love to stay and help with the labor, Mrs. Swanson, but I've been offered a position in Kansas, and maybe other places too. There are people in need of help everywhere now, and things are only going to get worse before they get better. Especially in the cities. There are groups of people with special skills, some military, some first responders, and others, who have backgrounds like me. They're forming teams and doing what they can for people in bad situations."

Her brow knitted. "That sounds very dangerous."

"Maybe. I'm up for it."

"I know. Yes, of course you are. And we're up for the work we have in front of us too. Thank heavens we have enough to start with."

I also had the confidence that they were up for the task and had plenty of willing hands and strong bodies. And weapons as well. If they didn't, well, that would be different, but they did. They had much more than most and they'd be okay. "I'd love to stay for a couple of days if you'll allow me to, and if you have the food to spare. I'll go over what I know about the land and the trees and anything else that might come in handy, and then I'll take off."

"We've pooled our food items in the old barn," she said. "And we're rationing for now, until we have more animals, and until the spring planting gets underway."

"Wise," I said.

She smiled and stood. "Come on, I'll get you set up in the guest room. You must be exhausted."

The guest room. *Emily's old room.* She'd be everywhere, and though I knew it would hurt, I also desperately craved having any part of her surrounding me.

We'd eaten a rationed dinner of canned franks and beans, corn, and sourdough bread cooked over a campfire, and afterward, I wandered out back to the patio. It seemed virtually untouched from the fight that had been waged for this property, though it had aged over the years and obviously gone untended as the Swansons put all their work and focus into keeping the orchard alive. Weeds grew through the gaps in the pavers and the edging had moved so that it was now misshapen. The furniture was rusty and the planters, once overflowing with flowers, were now merely dirt. The only thing that did work was the solar lighting that twinkled around the space. I took a seat on the short rock wall, my heart heavy as I looked around.

The back door opened, and Mrs. Swanson stepped outside, smiling as she came toward me. "I'm going to clean this up in the spring," she said. "It will be a nice space to gather again." She sat down next to me. "We had so many good times out here, didn't we?"

Something sharp pierced my heart, and though it hurt, it also made me smile. "I feel my mom out here," I said. "And Em too."

I pointed to the portion of patio where she'd always put on her performances for us. "I can still see her there and hear her voice. I knew, even then, that she'd be a star."

I felt Mrs. Swanson's gaze on the side of my face and turned toward her. "Oh...oh, you fell in love," she said. It wasn't a question; it was as though it'd been written on my face. And maybe it was. This was the one place, I supposed, where I couldn't have kept my feelings for Emily inside even if I'd tried.

Yes. I had fallen in love with Emily. Only, falling in love with Emily had been like finding a shortcut that led back home. The journey had been effortless because I'd already been halfway there.

God, I missed her. I ached with it.

Even though I hadn't confirmed what Mrs. Swanson said, her face blossomed in a smile. "You did. Oh. Then why? Why didn't Emily come back here with you? Why did you separate?"

"Right now? For the promise of safety. Neither one of us knew if you all were..."

"Yes, of course," she said. "You didn't know if we'd even be here." Her gaze drifted away. "So many have died."

We were quiet for a moment, letting that awful reality settle. "But long term?" she asked.

"I don't have anything to offer her right now. Even if— *when*—Emily makes it home, I can't stay here, clearing land and planting trees."

"There will be quite a bit more to it than that."

"I know, but you get my point. For six years, I was purposeless." I tilted my head, looking up at the night sky, stars just blinking to life. It stretched on and on, just like I remembered from my childhood. "I woke in the morning and ate breakfast and then worked out, read, ate lunch, dinner, went to bed and then woke up and did the same damn thing the next day. I have a chance now to be out there, serving others, making up for the lives that were lost because of me. Emily... Emily deserves someone who doesn't have the baggage I do. And I... well, I have the chance to offset some of what I did, and who would I be if I didn't take it?"

"A man who's decided he deserves some happiness. And some peace."

"Do I though? The people who were harmed because of me, and those who lost their lives, will never have happiness, or peace, so why should I?"

"Because, Tuck, you still have love in your heart and breath in your lungs. I'm sorry for what you've suffered. Sometimes I blame myself for what happened to you."

"What? Why? No. You had no part—"

"I could have talked to your father and begged him not to let you go to LA. I could have gone there myself and dragged you back and taken you in—"

"I wouldn't have let you. Please don't blame yourself. I'm the only one who should bear that burden."

"I love you though, sweetheart. And when your heart breaks, so does mine. You've always been the son I never had, and

Mariana would have wanted me to step in more than I did. I let her down, too."

"No, no. I don't want you to feel that way. Please don't. My choices are mine. I made them, and I'm the one who should suffer for them."

"How long should you suffer? Is there a time limit? Will you know when it arrives?"

"I don't know. Maybe."

"Or is it putting your own life in danger that you believe is the necessity? Or maybe sacrificing yourself altogether, *you* being the one to die this time instead of someone else. Will that balance the scales? Is that what you're after? Because if so, just know that you dying will kill part of us too. And Emily."

"I'm not suicidal if that's what you're asking. I'm just... I'm trying to find redemption."

I ran my hand through my hair. I was confused and my purpose, the one I'd been so set on, wobbled before me. Emily had made similar points in that laundromat in LA, but it'd been easier to dismiss what she'd said then with the stench of dead bodies all around us and the recent vision of those I cared about rotting in their living rooms.

She reached over and took my hand. "I understand that, I do, and, Tuck, you've done heroic deeds to help others who weren't able to help themselves. When presented the opportunities, you took them and I'm proud of you for that. But will serving strangers really bring you the redemption you're seeking?"

"Maybe not, but what else do I have?"

"You have the opportunity to earn grace every day by loving well and living with honor, and yes, by tending the earth too and rebuilding what has been destroyed. By doing your part to help a community who could use your labor and your knowledge. Perhaps you don't see the importance of those roles?" She paused but didn't wait for me to answer. "But beyond any of that, it sounds like you have Emily."

Emily. Just hearing her name made my heart twist with longing. "We were only meant to be temporary."

I looked away but again felt her stare. "Is it only that you believe you're not worthy of Emily?" she asked. "Is it really redemption you're seeking? Or is it love you're running from?"

I felt a soft clunk inside me. "What?"

She tightened her fingers around my hand. "It's scary, I understand. You lost so much, everything that you held dear and true. Your past and your future. It was all so suddenly gone. It's terrifying to put yourself in a position where that might happen again. To lay your heart on the line must seem like the riskiest thing you could ever do after the rug was swept out from under you once before. Perhaps it's easier to focus on your guilt, rather than your fear."

I sighed. Okay, she was right. I could admit that. The thought of handing my heart to Emily had me quaking. I could stare down the barrel of a gun, but I couldn't bear the thought of her looking at me with revulsion someday and walking out the door. "Even if I stay, what if Emily eventually decides she made a mistake? We went on this intense journey where we became close. We bonded. That was bound to happen, I guess. But what about some ordinary Tuesday when she looks over at me and realizes how much better she could have done?" *What if she takes her love and leaves?*

"I can't answer all these questions for you, sweetheart. I wish I could. But you're going to have to come to the answers inside yourself because that's the only place the truth exists. What I will say is this—you have a legacy, Tuck. That didn't go away because your mom died, or your father sold this land. A legacy is everlasting. You forgot that for a while. I hope you remember."

And then she gave my hand one last squeeze, stood, and went back inside, leaving me alone under the stars.

forty-two

Emily

Day Twenty

The tall wrought iron gate had presumably once been operated by a security guard who sat inside a small box and pushed
buttons to open and close it. Now, however, it was manned
by two large men both wearing camo and with rifles in hand.
They nodded at Leon when we arrived in front of it and pulled
the bolt before swinging it open. My gaze lingered on one of
them. He looked familiar. A stunt man from LA, I thought.
Hadn't he worked on one of Charlie's movies? It made sense, I
supposed, as Leon had told me he lined up the security detail
here in exchange for residency.

The street before us wound upward, those solar lights
brighter now that the sun had sunk lower in the sky. They
twinkled everywhere, lighting the way forward and, for a brief

moment, I dared to dream that this lovely place would come to feel like home.

The only house I could see from this vantage point was the side of a white mansion a little ways up the hill, half of it disappearing around the turn. But I knew there were more beyond, with gardens and swimming pools and henhouses and all the various features and amenities being used to keep this community safe and fed. The foliage around us was lush and fragrant, palm trees rising into the dusky sky. "It really is as gorgeous as you described, Leon," Layne said, her neck bent as she gazed up the hill.

"Wait until you see the rest," he said with a sideways smile.

We walked toward what looked like a gatehouse and when Leon knocked, a young man exited. "Hi, Leon."

"Hi, Asher." He gestured back toward us. "This is Emily and Layne."

"Welcome," Asher said before looking back at Leon. "Was that your final trip?" There was something in Asher's tone I couldn't quite discern. A note of caution, perhaps? Nervousness? It was hard to say, and I was too physically and emotionally exhausted to think much about it anyway.

"Yes," Leon said. "It's too dangerous to travel into Los Angeles now."

Asher gestured for us to follow. There were two dirt bikes sitting off to the side and Asher got on one and Leon mounted the other. "Your chariots await," Leon said. I smiled weakly.

"We'll go slow enough that you won't need a helmet," Asher said. "Just hold on."

Layne got on behind Asher and I propped myself on the seat behind Leon, and then they both turned the keys already in the ignitions and began slowly driving up the winding road.

I estimated there were about thirty homes in this neighborhood, and it only took about five minutes to get to the top, slips of stunning mansions visible through the trees as we rolled by. The dirt bikes turned into a driveway and came to a stop in front of a gorgeous white brick estate, an empty water fountain sitting off to the side. I hefted my backpack on my shoulder, the familiar movement causing my heart to constrict. It had been a constant for the last however many miles as I'd traveled with Tuck.

Tuck.

Tuck.

"Follow me," Leon said. "I'll show you where you'll be staying."

I hesitated, glancing around at the quiet night, lanterns flickering and the scent of night-blooming jasmine somewhere close by tickling my nose. I heard the dirt bike fire up as Asher drove away and then turned toward Leon and Layne and followed them to the front of the house.

"It's safe here," Leon said as we entered. "You'll have nothing to worry about."

We set our things down in the foyer. The inside of the home was as beautiful as the outside, marble floors and unlit crystal chandeliers sparkling in the candlelight scattered all around the vast foyer. Leon led us into a sitting room on the right with a soaring ceiling, and similarly lit by hundreds of candles. I almost startled when I noticed an old man standing near the window with blue velvet curtains. He smiled kindly and walked toward us, his cane tapping on the floor. "I'm sorry to startle you. I just realized how spooky I must look, an old man standing in the shadows. I promise I'm not as eerie as first impressions might suggest. Welcome to Cielo Hills," he said. "Hi, Leon."

"Merrick. I'm going to go get some water for me and Emily and Layne."

He nodded as Leon turned and left the room. "Please come and sit down. You must be so tired. I'm Merrick Winchester, and I insist you call me Merrick. This is my home and it's my honor to share it."

We approached the old man with the cane. Layne shook his hand and then I did too, his skin papery but his grip strong. "Thank you so much for allowing us here. The world, it's..." I was suddenly lost for words. Or...no, it wasn't that I didn't have the words, it was that there were too many attempting to fill my mouth all at once and my brain was too tired to choose just one: *terrifying, awful, tragic, lonely...*

But Mr. Winchester—*Merrick*—who was still holding my hand, gave it a gentle squeeze. "I know, my dear. We're very lucky. We wanted to pack this community with as many as possible, but there are only so many resources. We did the math and came up with a number based on the crops and the few animals we have..." He sighed. "Even so, rationing will be necessary as I've told every newcomer here. I hope you're prepared for that. So many are doing the same, I suppose, whether their land is miles wide or one square inch."

"Not everyone is calculating how much they can realistically share," I said as we all sat down. "Some are hoarding."

"Yes, it's base human nature, of course, to hoard. You always hope that in a moment like this, you'd act in such a way that your legacy would be honor, but you never truly know until it arrives, I suppose."

"It seems like you acted quickly to help as many as possible as soon as the event happened," Layne said.

"We had a community meeting the morning after the power went down. No one knew exactly what had happened, but we explored the possibilities and made agreements based on worst-case scenarios. In some sense, we set up this community with just such a disaster in mind. But none of us imagined something of this magnitude would actually come to pass. Before this, it had become somewhat of a group pet project if you will, a way to use the land with purpose. I like to think it's kept us young." A fleeting smile touched his face. "If we'd truly known what would happen, we would have done so much more." He looked away for a moment. "As a result, our resources will only go so far. Still, to lock ourselves behind a gate while others we might have helped suffered outside, was unthinkable to all of us."

My shoulders relaxed and I pulled in a full breath after what felt like a day of oxygen deprivation. These were good people. I'd arrived in a safe place after all. Thanks to Leon.

"I know I speak for Emily when I say we couldn't be any more appreciative. But...don't you all have family to fill up this community?"

"Many do. Some were close enough to make it here. Others were not. We were all allotted the same number of potential guests. Some who didn't need them gave their allotments away to others who did. We've tried to be very fair. And we've saved a small amount of space for family members who arrive at a later date. No one could stomach the thought of turning them away."

That must be how Leon had been able to secure a spot for my parents should they need it. My shoulders dropped a notch lower. In the back of my mind, this had almost seemed too good to be true, but it wasn't. These were just good people with big hearts and a solid plan.

Leon came back in the room with four glasses of water on a tray and set it down. Layne and I picked up a glass and both drank thirstily. "Thank you," I said when I set my mostly empty glass back down.

"Is your family here, Mr. Winchester?" Layne asked.

"I don't have children and the family I have is not close by. But, when Leon arrived pretty immediately after the event, I thought it must be fate. Here I was with a handful of guest allotments and Leon with nowhere to go *and* the capability of bringing other souls here who'd been abandoned in Los Angeles."

I glanced at Leon, who looked vaguely uncomfortable. "That was very generous." I was surprised he'd given his precious spaces away so easily. Perhaps Leon felt that way too, hence his discomfort.

"Leon's father saved my life in that jungle in Vietnam when we were only boys and paid the ultimate price because of his sacrifice. I didn't think there was a way to ever truly repay that debt, but then Leon showed up, and I wondered if his father had guided him to me and it was my chance to even the score," Merrick said as if hearing my unvoiced thoughts.

I felt a pinch in my chest. I related to questions of fate. We'd experienced so much of what I thought could only be that. And I was painfully familiar with men who felt they needed to repay a debt. It was a good quality; it spoke of honor. But I also knew it sometimes obscured vision. Thankfully, Mr. Winchester hadn't had to choose whether to leave others behind in order to settle a score he believed needed settling.

"It's almost like you're starting a mini government here," Layne said.

"It's essential," Merrick answered. "Or what we are fortunate enough to have won't last and none of us will benefit. Rules will keep us from sinking into anarchy."

I stifled a yawn.

"In any event," Merrick said, "there is plenty of time to get to know each other. You'll want to tour the gardens and meet all the others. But for now, Leon, why don't you show Emily to her room. Layne—"

Before Merrick could finish that sentence, we heard the front door open, and the guard speak to someone in the foyer. Then Freddie Halston was rushing into the room. Layne stood with a cry and ran toward him, both of them meeting in an embrace. "You're here. Oh, thank God. You're here," he said.

I looked away, my heart simultaneously rejoicing for them and grieving the loss of the person I wanted to embrace.

"I was getting so desperate. Then I ran into Leon and he got me here. I wanted to go back to LA with Leon, but he said he had contacts—"

"Shh," she said, putting her fingers to his lips. "We're together now. We're both okay."

He let out a gusty exhale. "Thank you, Leon," Freddie said as he and Layne parted. "From the bottom of my heart, thank you."

I stood. "Hi, Freddie."

"Nova!" His eyes widened when he saw me. "Oh my gosh. How—"

"There's lots of time to talk tomorrow. I think we could all use a good night's sleep," Leon said as he rose from his seat.

I agreed. As much as I wanted to see more of this beautiful place and meet all the residents who sounded so lovely, and hear what Freddie had been through too, my eyes were so heavy. A few minutes more and I wouldn't be able to keep them open. We all said good-night and Leon grabbed my backpack for me and led me upstairs to a bedroom. I barely took the time to look around. All I cared about was that it had a place to sleep.

I locked the door behind Leon and then tumbled onto the mattress. And yet, despite my exhaustion, I lay staring at the ceiling, sadness rolling over me in waves.

I'd made it to my new home—a beautiful, safe home the likes of which the whole world was looking for right now—and yet, I felt utterly lost.

forty-three

Tuck

Day Twenty-Two

A legacy is everlasting. Those words echoed in my head as I walked the property, taking stock of the damage and also what had been spared. Mr. Swanson hadn't had a chance to surveille every inch of his property, too busy in the last few weeks with fighting off invaders, and then basic survival. But if they were going to rebuild, they needed to know exactly what work lay in front of them, and what should be prioritized.

I stood at the top of the hill and gazed down at the land that had once been Honey Hill Farm. Somewhat miraculously, the old barn remained, but the house had been demolished and most of the land had been cleared long ago, including those lush trees. The development company that had bought the property from my father eight years before hadn't expanded its new neighborhood quite this far yet. Whether that was because of funding issues, permit problems, or any number of holdups, I had no idea. But I was grateful. Who knew if the unnamed executives who'd swooped up this land were still alive, but if they were, I was doubtful they'd even remember every inch of property in their portfolio. They had no connection to this patch of earth, not really, but I did and the Swansons did as well. I supposed, when you got right down to it, to claim it would be stealing. But it was hard to see it that way, and in any case, the world was different now.

I used my hand to shade my eyes, peering out at what now looked like wasteland. But I could envision what it could be because I'd seen it in its glory once before, and it continued to live inside me despite my own best effort.

I'd suggest to Mr. Swanson that they continue the new rows of trees onto this property. It would be smart to plant as much as possible and use every inch of the rich soil that still remained.

Feeding people was the priority now. Helping as many survive as possible.

A legacy is everlasting. That echo again.

And I'd come to understand what she'd meant. My grandfather had arrived on this very land with nothing and built a thriving life from scratch. And I'd thought this farm was my legacy, the house and the land and the business. But maybe a legacy didn't have to be a tangible thing. Maybe my legacy was my grandfather himself. He'd worked his fingers to the bone to create something from nothing. He'd held dreams and hopes and a vision that he strived toward every day. He'd had perseverance and a work ethic that surpassed most. He'd cared deeply about the earth, and about his family and the community.

Follow in his footsteps, my mom had said regarding my grandfather. *But also, forge your own. If anyone is capable, it's you, my smart boy.*

Oh, Mom. I miss you. I wish you were here.

But she was, wasn't she? Part of her anyway. Just walking

through this property, even as destroyed as many parts were, I saw her everywhere, her words flowing back to me like she'd never left.

And I could embrace her advice and learn from my grandfather. Or I could head out into an uncertain world, looking for strangers to give me the redemption I sought.

Perhaps my redemption was right here at home.

If I had the courage to stay.

Because Mrs. Swanson had been right about that too. I'd convinced myself I was being brave and honorable. But partly, at least, it was really that I was a coward. Terrified to love. Terrified to go all in and have it taken from me like it had been before, or so I'd thought.

Emily was the one who'd been brave. And I'd let her walk away. I'd seen the look in her eyes, and I'd *known* that she'd been waiting for me to decide to lay my heart on the line...or not.

I swore under my breath. I'd let her down. I'd let myself down.

And now, maybe she'd found not only safety in San Diego, but purpose and friendship. She was back among the people who'd once called her Nova. Maybe she'd remember who she'd been and who she wanted to attempt to be again—whatever that looked like now—and my chance had come and gone.

She'd be home once it was safe to travel to visit her parents, whether or not that was years away. But even if I stayed here in the San Fernando Valley, rebuilding what we could, would Emily want to stay?

Our moment had passed.

My stomach roiled. I felt sick. I hadn't fought for her. I hadn't responded to her attempts to break through to me, just like I'd done after my mother died. Again, I'd shut her out. I'd *wanted* to suffer, and so emotionally, I'd pushed her away. But in pushing her away, I'd hurt us both. What I should have said at that border near LA when we'd said a teary goodbye was, *Fuck no, you're not leaving with them. You're coming with me. We'll find our own safety, wherever that is.*

I walked the short distance to the old barn and pulled open the door. The squeak that emerged from the rusty hinges was familiar and for a moment, I felt like a kid, a head full of dreams and a heart brimming with hope.

Mr. Swanson's car had been pulled in here and the past and the present collided once again, the ringing of Emily's laughter echoing in my head. My heart. *Emily.*

I closed my eyes, grimacing as though I'd been hit. I felt like I had. Picturing her as we'd said goodbye still felt like a physical blow.

I let out a pained breath and turned away, my trembling fingers running over the dusty red paint. I wondered if this old thing still ran. If not, we should try to get it fixed. I'd add that to the list.

I walked over to the area on the far wall where three long folding tables had been set up. Here was all the food they'd collected from neighbors, items not just lining the tops, but sitting on the floor beneath as well. Boxes of crackers, pasta, lentils, rice, peanut butter... And several pieces of paper were tacked up on the wall above, the names of each person taking part in the rationing of this food listed, including allergies and other pertinent information. They'd done well here. The care and the love and the goodwill was obvious everywhere I turned.

A ladder still stood propped beneath the loft, and I gave it a shake, determining that it was still sturdy before climbing to the top. I moved on my knees over to the window where I brought my head back in surprise. *Well, holy shit.*

My old things were still here. Books were scattered on the floor, covered in a thick layer of dust. I moved one aside and read the titles, and then sat there with them on my knees as I shifted back through time to the boy I'd been. I'd loved knowledge, loved gathering information that would come in handy when I was running Honey Hill. Hosea had spoken of the now useful skills and attributes I'd gathered while making all kinds of mistakes and surviving the consequences of my own poor choices. But sitting there, staring down at those books, made me wonder if my grandfather had also had those qualities because he'd suffered hardships as well—perhaps of his own making, perhaps not. Maybe a combination of the two. Perhaps that kind of grit and fortitude could *only* be gathered after you'd hit rock bottom and managed to climb out, one foothold at a time.

A breeze of peace blew through me as I set the books aside, glancing at the folder underneath. I frowned at the unfamiliar item as I picked it up. But when I opened it, my heart lurched. It was Emily's folder and by the date written on the inside flap, I saw it was from the year I'd moved to my uncle's house. Had it been before? Or after? It could have been either since I'd stopped coming up here entirely in the wake of my mother's death.

I leafed through the pages, some sheets of music, others handwritten song lyrics. My heart constricted again at the sight of her neat printing, handwriting that I still recognized even after all these years. And as I began reading the lines, my breath hitched, and warmth infused my body. They were the lyrics to "Find You in the Dark," the song that had enchanted the world, and later, comforted a group of weary travelers around a campfire.

But "Find You in the Dark" hadn't been the original title. She'd first named it "To Tuck."

I dropped the folder, the papers falling out and scattering, and then wiped my dusty palms on my jeans as regret burned through me.

She'd tried to reach me and blamed herself for not getting through. She'd fought for me in the only way she knew how, and I'd dismissed her entirely each time she tried. *Oh, Em.* Love blossomed, so powerful that I felt like it might knock me over. Love for the girl she'd been then, and love for the woman of now, the beautiful, tenacious person she'd grown to be. She'd done it again in that old laundromat, trying so hard to reach me, and I'd practically looked right through her, so involved in hating myself that I couldn't hear a word she'd said. *I'm so fucking sorry.*

I looked out the old grimy window, picturing her where she was, hours away. And I knew with sudden surety what I had to do.

Wait for me, Emily. Don't give up on me yet.

forty-four

Emily

Day Twenty-Five

It'd been five days since Layne and I had arrived in Cielo Hills. We'd been given a tour of every beautiful property, including the gardens and the chicken pens tucked away in tree-covered corners. The residents were lovely and welcoming, seeming to take comfort in each new face that arrived, another person to care for. Another extended family member to grieve the downfall of the world as we'd known and loved it. A team of sorts with which to link arms and face what was to come.

The owners of these homes were all retirees, mostly senior citizens who took us under their wings and doted on us in any way they were able. They'd also gathered a wonderful group of employees who were now so much more than that, many of their own families sharing space with the homeowners.

Before the solar flare hit, this community was stunning and

luxurious, but now? Now it was an actual paradise sitting high on a hill, a gate at the front and unscalable cliffs surrounding it. I couldn't help thinking of it as one of those medieval castles overlooking villages where those not as fortunate suffered and starved. And so, while I was deeply grateful to be safe and fed, I could not stop thinking of those who were not. The visions were agonizing because I knew the pain and terror I was picturing was actually playing out everywhere across the nation.

In five days, Tuck had not shown up with my parents. Which I prayed meant they were doing fine, and Tuck was taking a short breather—one he deserved. If something was wrong, he'd have come to tell me. He'd never withhold news like that or risk me returning someday to find that they'd been gone since the beginning. And if my parents needed this sanctuary, they would have been here by now. I didn't let my mind wander further than that. I couldn't. I could only picture them there, on their property, surviving and rebuilding with the resources they had. *Thank God you didn't move. Thank God you held on to what you had.* The things the whole country was fighting for right now—animals, crops, land, and the know-how to tend it.

And the vision I conjured of my parents on their land brought me peace, but it also made my guts churn with longing. I was here, wandering through the gardens of others when I should be laboring on my family farm. It felt...wrong.

And I missed Tuck desperately. I felt hollow inside, like a vital organ was missing and I was just barely alive. Which, in the midst of paradise, felt deeply ungrateful. And yet, the feeling remained. My heart was twisted with too many emotions to manage. I stood on the cliff just past the house at the top of the hill and stared across the water, trying to picture Tuck. Was he still there in the San Fernando Valley? Or had he already left for Kansas? Surely he'd need at least a week to recover and gather what supplies he could before taking off again? Or, knowing Tuck, he'd be offering any help necessary to my parents and their community before he left.

I returned to Merrick Winchester's home and went in the side door, avoiding the front room where I could hear voices and some soft laughter. Layne had moved into the house next door where Freddie had a room, but they were here now, visiting with Merrick. But I didn't have any desire to socialize, I felt far too bereft. All I really wanted to do was sleep and shut off the deep loneliness and pain.

My eyes flew open, and I blinked groggily up at the ceiling, a sliver of moonlight offering the barest bit of light. Something had woken me—a distant crack. It'd sounded like gunfire.

There it is again.

My stomach tightened and I threw the blankets back and got out of bed. I knew that sound all too well. I'd heard it more times than I cared to remember in recent weeks.

My window faced the back of the house, my view mostly restricted by tall trees. And beyond that was the edge of a cliff that dropped down to the ocean. The gunfire—if that's what it was—had seemed to come from somewhere down the hill. I'd need to look out a front window to see the street outside.

I slipped out of my room, using the moonlight coming in the tall windows to make my way down the hallway. I didn't hear anyone else stirring from behind the other bedroom doors. If they'd heard the noise too, they were unconcerned.

It was probably coming from beyond the gate, echoing in the stillness of the night. Or maybe from the ocean far below.

I was paranoid. But then again, I had very good reason to be. We all did.

I padded down the stairs, my footsteps silent on the plush runner and when I got to the bottom, I heard tense voices from the living room.

I started to go in that direction, to see if someone else had heard what I did, when Merrick's voice grew louder momentarily, clearly distressed. I paused, suddenly on guard and moving more slowly now.

"Put the gun away, Leon. This is wrong."

My heart thumped with confusion and fear. I plastered my body against the wall. I could barely see into the large room with vaulted ceilings. Merrick was standing near the window and Leon was in front of him, a gun in his hand. *What is happening?*

"Asher came over the walkie-talkie," Merrick said. "There's been a breach. The others need—"

"Asher's been taken care of."

"Oh God. What did you do to him?"

"He wasn't harmed. He's just been temporarily restrained," Leon said.

I pulled in a breath, the air barely trickling down my throat. Asher was the young man who lived in what had been the guardhouse near the gate. He'd been restrained? By who? Who breached the gate? What was happening here?

"Leon, why?" Merrick gasped. "I welcomed you here. I allowed you to bring others."

"Consider your debt repaid."

"My God, you're a snake, Leon. I did owe a debt. To your father who was a good, honorable man. You can choose to be like him. I know you're afraid, but you don't have to do this."

"My father's dead. He died because he put others before himself, and if that's honor then what's the point? I'm not going to make the same mistake. The days of selflessness are gone. Now it's about survival. Not just for a month or even a few, but for longer than that.

"The others are on their way up the hill. They'll start from the top and make their way down. They're taking over the homes, even now. It will go quickly. No one will be hurt as long as they cooperate."

Oh my God. Leon had let armed men in the gate, and they were taking over these homes? Panic infused my veins causing my limbs to tremble. Other sounds met my ears now. Distant footsteps running. Voices from far away.

"The guards at the gate," Merrick said, his voice choked. "They let these people in? You said we could trust them. You said we needed them."

"Obviously you did. You created a government, Merrick, but you forgot that every small country needs an army."

"But why? You were safe. You were being cared for and fed."

"I'm creating space, it's as simple as that. I'm preparing for what comes next."

Creating space. What did that mean exactly?

Merrick let out a sound that was somewhere between a moan and a cough and Leon turned slightly so that I pulled in a breath and plastered myself more firmly to the wall.

"There are so many weaknesses here," Leon went on. "And no weapons. If not my people, this place would have been taken over in a few weeks. Sacked by a violent horde who wouldn't treat anyone with the dignity I will. How the fuck are you going to have a future with a community who will die off in a few short years? Then what, Merrick? All of you are such damn do-gooders. But a plan for the future is important too. Young people, strong people. Do you know how fucked the world is? No one needs to waste food on a bunch of senior citizens who can barely walk, much less defend the community. They do nothing for a world like this except use up resources. They'll be dust in the ground soon enough and we need those resources now."

Merrick took a few steps and sank down on a chair, his shoulders rolling forward.

"You're not such a spring chicken yourself, Leon," Merrick said, his voice weak.

"I'm a leader, however," Leon said. "I get shit done. I make the hard calls that no one else is willing to make."

My head was buzzing, lips quivering. My God, what Merrick had said was true—Leon was a *snake*. I'd hitched my wagon to a viper. He'd arranged with the guards at the front to let people he'd gathered come inside to take over these homes? Who were they? Desperate people he knew from the show business world who'd been offered a spot in exchange for *this*? Told they could die outside these gates or take this community over? Given maps and numbers and... *Oh my God.*

"You said they wouldn't harm anyone—"

"They won't," Leon said. "Not if it's not necessary. These aren't bloodthirsty killers. They're going to gather everyone and those considered...non-essential will be walked out the front gate."

Merrick's shoulders sagged further. "It's as good as killing them, Leon. You know that. And there's no such thing as a nonessential human being."

"Unfortunately, Merrick, that's simply no longer true."

The front door burst open, the sounds of a group of men entering the home and I startled, letting out a small squeak. My heart pressed against the wall of my chest as my stomach dropped. "Watch him," Leon said to whomever had entered the house. *Oh God.* I turned to run, but Leon had heard me and before I could make it to the staircase, he was on my heels. "Stop, Emily."

I skidded to a stop, looking slowly over my shoulder to see Leon standing there with the gun pointed in my direction. "I do not want to shoot you, but I will if I have to."

I turned toward him, my mouth dry, heart pounding. "You're not who I thought you were."

"I'm exactly who you thought I was," he said. "It's why you wanted me on your team."

I stood there, my mind filled with static, fear and disappointment cascading through my limbs. But maybe he was right. Maybe I'd liked the fact that he was a cutthroat businessman. I'd valued him for his dog-eat-dog attitude and ability to be callous. It'd meant he always got what he wanted and when he was working on my behalf, it meant I did too.

And evidently, he wasn't afraid to up the level of "cutthroat" depending on the circumstances.

He gestured with his gun. "You're valuable here, Emily. Don't worry, you can stay as long as you cooperate. Go on up to your room. I'll walk you there."

I glanced up the stairs toward my room. What else could I do? There was nowhere to run, and he had a gun on me. And I didn't think attempting to fight him was a good gamble. So, on shaky legs, I turned and ascended the stairs, Leon trailing behind. I suddenly wanted nothing more than to put a door between us and when Leon's hand stopped me, I sucked in a fearful gasp.

"The world is burning, Emily," Leon said. I glanced over his shoulder where a young man with a chiseled jaw wearing camo was turning down the hallway. "And this is a utopia. If I'd have told you every detail of what I planned beforehand, you might not have come. And that would have been a mistake because you'd have died out there."

He allowed me to shut the door and I leaned back on it, letting out a shuddery breath.

Outside, there was an exchange between Leon and the young man. I didn't hear every word, but it was clear that he'd directed him to guard my door. I flipped the lock, knowing that the flimsy thing wouldn't help me much if a muscled dude decided to kick it down. But it was better than nothing.

I heard sounds that told me the men with guns were beginning to gather residents from their rooms. Then, I supposed, it would be determined who could stay and who could go. I was relatively safe up here, already guaranteed I'd be one of the chosen ones who could stay. But how could I remain locked in this room without at least attempting to warn the others?

I unlatched the window and looked down at the dark yard below. It was too far to jump. I turned, surveying my room for a moment, weighing my options before I moved quickly to my bed. I ripped my sheets off and expediently tied them together, giving a yank to ensure the knot was tight, my eyes darting to the door handle that I kept expecting to jiggle.

My heart pounded as I opened the window as wide as it would go and then threw the knotted sheet down. It was a significant drop but even if the sheet didn't hold, I was hopeful it would slow my descent enough that I wouldn't break my leg.

I heard another scream and then a few cries and more sounds of alarm as people were led out of their rooms. I only took a moment to slip on the clean jeans and sweatshirt I'd been given and a pair of canvas sneakers.

With trembling fingers, I tied the end of the sheet to the leg of a massive wardrobe next to the window, my heart rapping against my breastbone. I sat down on the ledge, took a deep breath, and then swung my legs over. Then I turned onto my stomach, the ledge digging into my ribs as I grabbed hold of the sheet and lowered my body. For a moment I simply dangled over empty air, gritting my teeth so I wouldn't scream. *Please hold, please hold.* I went lower, my arms burning as I slowly descended.

And then the sheet gave, coming off the wardrobe above as I bit my tongue and went plummeting the rest of the way to the ground.

I hit hard, landing in a crouch with a staggered breath, and then doing a quick assessment of my limbs. *Nothing broken. You're okay.* I got up and then I ran around the side of the house and plastered myself against the brick. I exhaled in relief. I was okay. I was free.

From the room at least.

And I only had limited time to warn others—to let them know what was going on so they could...what? Escape? There was no escape. The only choices were to hide...or fight back.

I turned, running through the backyard, toward the property next door, where Layne and Freddie were. I ducked among the trees and headed toward my friends to warn them that our castle on the hill was being stormed.

forty-five

Tuck

The journey from the San Fernando Valley back to the border Emily had crossed with Leon and Layne took far longer than I'd hoped. There was really no traveling by car anymore—there were too many barricades to cover any ground. But I wasn't surprised that so many more had popped up in a few days' time—those who'd found a small plot of safety with even a few resources had staked their claim and erected whatever walls they were able.

By the time I'd made it to the spot where I'd said goodbye to Emily, the moon was high in the sky and, though I had plenty of food, I was running low on water. I took the tiniest of sips from my canteen, returned it to my backpack and then rounded the bend where the concrete barriers sat, a lone man patrolling, a rifle strapped to his broad chest.

As I moved closer, the burly man noticed me, standing straight, his fingers inching toward his weapon. I raised my hands and approached. "Stay back," he said, removing his gun, but holding it by his side rather than pointing it at me. He looked weary, his face slightly gaunt even if his muscles were still impressive.

I halted. "I was here a few days ago and the men patrolling let my friends pass through. I don't want to stay, I just need to get to someone who's in San Diego."

"No one passes through."

I let out a frustrated breath. "Please. If someone wants to escort me—"

"Not allowed." He raised his rifle and used it to gesture behind me. "Turn around."

"I have food," I said. "In the backpack. Granola bars and a few cans too. I'll give it all to you."

The man shook his head, and again, I sensed his fatigue and the fact that, whereas some might find satisfaction in the new-found power, he didn't enjoy this job. "I don't need your food."

I wanted to scream. I wanted to leap over this barrier and attack, to run around him despite his threats and take my chances. Emily was on the other side of that made-up line. I released a slow breath. Getting myself killed wouldn't do any good. I'd have to figure out a way around.

"But... I'll trade your necklace for passage," he said.

For a second his words didn't compute. Still confused, I looked down as I remembered that I'd put on my uncle's cross necklace before setting out. It'd been a last-minute decision, the hope that wearing this would mean a part of him was with me, and perhaps even guiding my way.

I removed the necklace, approaching slowly and holding it toward him. He kept eye contact, his gun lowering. The closer I got, the more I noticed how tired he appeared, with dark patches smudged beneath his eyes. Just like so many, this man had obviously been through some form of hell. And he'd found refuge behind this wall, but he didn't relish turning others away. That too was wearing on him.

The guard reached his hand out, and I put the necklace in his palm, his thumb sliding over the silver cross, his breath releasing on a sigh. "The things people are doing to survive…so much betrayal everywhere," he murmured.

My heart jumped and I swallowed. And for whatever reason, Leon's face popped into my mind. We'd both trusted him. There didn't seem reason not to. But what if…what if he had other motives for leading Emily to that safety zone on a hill?

I couldn't think that way without any evidence or it'd make me crazy. But I suddenly felt even more desperate to get to her. To make sure she was okay.

The guard turned away from me, set his gun down, and began putting the necklace around his neck. "Go," he said quietly. "They'll shoot at you if they see you."

So much betrayal everywhere.

I hurriedly skirted the barrier, jogging forward, toward Emily. *God, please let her be safe.*

forty-six

Emily

Thankfully, I'd been to Freddie and Layne's room and knew where it was. And it was also a relief that it was on the ground floor. I peered in the window I'd just knocked on, a flame flickering to life within the room, and the shadow of a person appeared in front of me. *Layne.* I took a step back as the window opened and then I put my finger to my lips, her brow knitting before her head turned toward a noise from the street.

Freddie appeared next to her, and Layne shushed him too. I gestured to both of them to climb out just as the distant sounds of people entering the house they were in could be heard from the front. "Come on," I whispered.

Freddie climbed quickly from his window, and then turned to help Layne out too. "What's happening? Who is that?" Layne whispered as I led them away from the back of the house.

"Leon's a Judas. This community is being taken over by his

people. They're armed and they're going to march everyone out the front gate, except those of Leon's choosing."

I'd said all that as one continuous stream of whispered words and now took in a big gulp of air as Freddie and Layne stared at me in shock. But the sounds coming from the streets in front of the homes and now inside many of them as well, told the truth of what I was saying.

"His choosing?" Layne asked, eyes wide.

"Young, strong, I don't know. They're his people. He's the leader here now. The guards at the front are loyal to him and let the others in."

"Fuck," Freddie hissed. "I worked with those dudes guarding the gate in LA. I always thought they were sketchy," he muttered. The low beam of a flashlight flickered next to us, and we all leaned back, using the fence for cover. After a moment it disappeared as though someone out on the street had shined it through the side yard. We waited for a moment, listening before Freddie met my eyes and then looked at Layne. "A number of us have been planning for something like this. There are many here who've been gathering weapons and supplies. Some had them in their homes and risked going back out for them. Other attained them in other ways."

"You were keeping that from me?" Layne asked.

"We didn't want to offend the original residents. You weren't here yet, but they wrung their hands even about arming the guards at the gate. They had a whole meeting about it and everything. And I didn't want to worry you, I know you don't like guns. But we might end up having some of the last food in the city. We might be very close to that point now."

He took a few steps and leaned around the fence quickly, surveilling the area and then walking back to us. "Come on, I'll explain as we walk."

We left the cover of the fence and started walking across an area of open lawn, finally moving behind a spread of trees and bushes where we could get lost in shadow.

"It was just a contingency," Freddie went on. "Me, the original staff, and some of the others who have been here longer than you, thought something like this might happen. Even two armed dudes at the entrance weren't going to cut it if a group of people worked as a unit to overtake them. We didn't expect it from within, but we figured there'd come a point where we'd have to defend this community and its resources."

Leon had essentially said the same thing. Only he'd used that belief to enact his own takeover. Freddie and whomever else he'd been working with here had done it to defend these people.

"Where are the weapons?" Layne asked.

"In the gardens. We need to get to the others before they're rounded up. Our best chance is to surprise them. Asher, who lives down in the old guardhouse, has been gathering ammo for weeks. We have a planned meeting place near the bottom of the hill."

"Asher's incapacitated, but unharmed," I said, repeating what I'd heard Leon say. "I'll get down there and help Asher. You and Layne start gathering the people you can. Many are probably already being guarded. Gather your own army." I gripped my clammy hands together. I was simultaneously relieved that others had formed a small army, had a tentative plan, and the ability to fight fire with fire. But it also sounded extremely dangerous. "This could get really bloody," I said, my voice shaky.

Freddie looked at Layne quickly and then back to me. "Some things are worth fighting for. We have the upper hand in that we all know the lay of this land and they do not. If we can surprise and incapacitate some of them, then maybe we can convince the others to drop their weapons. They've got to be weakened from lack of food. But...yes, it will be a battle. It's either that, or willingly leave, but that's certain death because there's nowhere else to go."

Only that wasn't true for me.

My eyes met Layne's in the dim light of the lantern hanging nearby. "Emily…" She put her hand on my arm. "I understand if this isn't your fight."

An ache pierced my chest. She knew. She knew how much despair I felt at the absence of Tuck and my parents. This wasn't my fight. There was only one place I would willingly die to protect. But it also *was* my fight because these people had taken me in and been kind to me and they were now facing betrayal and starvation. How could I live with myself if I didn't participate in helping them in some way? How could I ever look Tuck in the eyes again if I didn't exhibit at least some of the honor so important to him?

I'd learned so many lessons about valor and what it truly meant to have integrity in the last few weeks. I had learned who I wanted to be and the values I would put ahead of anything, even death.

"I'm sorry… I'm sorry I can't stay." My purpose wasn't here. And though I prayed with all my heart Layne and Freddie and the rest would be victorious tonight, my home was elsewhere.

"I know," Layne said. "You have somewhere to go."

I grabbed her hand in mine. "I'll help Asher. Then you fight," I said. "Fight hard."

"You too," she said. "It won't be easy for you to make it home."

"Some things are worth fighting for," I said. She pulled me to her and we embraced, holding each other tight before letting go.

I gave Freddie a quick hug too and then they turned and cut through the foliage. I ducked low and ran to the next house, climbing the pool fence and running quietly around the pool, then jumping the fence again on the other side. There was a high stone wall surrounding the garden at the back of the next house and I grunted in frustration. If I scaled every wall and fence from here down to the front gate, it'd take hours. If it hadn't been discovered we were gone by now, it most certainly would be by then.

I hesitated for a moment, and then turned toward the front, but spotted the sweep of a flashlight from that direction where they likely had at least one guard in front of each house. I couldn't risk being caught by one of them. I needed to get to Asher.

There was only one good option, and it would get me to the bottom of the hill quickly. I turned, running along the stone wall and heading toward the edge of the cliff. Behind the gates and fences was a small portion of trees, bushes, and foliage that was almost completely shrouded in darkness. It would take me just as long to step carefully through that lightless area. Instead, I squeezed through the back bushes that suddenly opened up to the edge of the cliff and before I could think about it, I stepped down onto the narrow ledge.

I'd spotted this trail as I'd stood staring out to sea, pretending that if I squinted far enough, I could catch sight of my home. The thought of it now spurred me on and I pressed my back to the rock, moving forward.

Distant noises reminded me to hurry. The element of surprise was going to be crucial. The fact that Freddie and the others had weapons when Leon had told his men they were unarmed was going to work in their favor too. Ammunition was going to be imperative.

The moon was just bright enough to see where I was stepping, back pressed against the side of the cliff as I moved slowly and carefully along the extremely narrow trail, moving down and then around, the path widening but not by much.

I caught sight of a solar lantern twinkling in the trees, here and there, and could hear the gentle breaking of waves on the other side of the cliff. I breathed in the scents of sea and earth, and despite my racing heart, I noted again how beautiful this place was, and felt a sweep of rage that Leon had betrayed these people for his own evil, selfish purposes.

Wind whipped, chilling me, even despite the adrenaline pumping through my body. Thankfully, winter in Southern California was mild, but not so mild on this particular night that the cropped jeans and thin sweatshirt I'd donned were enough to keep me warm.

The darkness concealed me, but it also made the journey treacherous and several times I lost traction, slipping for a moment, stopping, and regaining balance before continuing on.

As I moved, I pictured what was happening above. Leon and his troops would still be gathering the residents from the houses, two or more guards with guns making sure they didn't gain the upper hand. Maybe they'd even start separating those Leon considered of value from those he did not. Perhaps they'd begin marching certain people outside by daylight, leaving them to starve in the street, the action of the usurpers made possible by their hunger and fear. *I didn't kill them*, they'd tell themselves. *I just took their place. It was that or die. There was no more food.*

A muffled scream came from one of the gargantuan homes, and my heart skipped a beat. I didn't want to think about who might be screaming and why, and so I didn't because it would do me no good. But it did bolster my decision to try my best to give these people some sort of fighting chance.

I let out a sigh of relief when I stepped onto a larger portion of land, picking up my speed. The journey downhill less precarious, but the sounds of Leon's men were everywhere now, no longer attempting to be quiet as they went from home to home.

A burst of gunfire sounded from above, my heart jolting with each distant crack.

"Oh God," I said. Maybe the people Leon had arranged to take over weren't killers, but they still had weapons and if someone attempted to fight back, they were going to use them.

Who was going to try to escape? If you had nowhere else to go, escape meant death just as surely as facing down a loaded gun.

Based on my travel time and descent, I estimated that I was very close to the front gate. That was confirmed when I spotted the roof of the guardhouse.

I moved swiftly around the back of the small structure, and then stood on my tiptoes to look inside. There was just enough light cast by the lanterns nearby to see that Asher was tied to a chair. He spotted me, his eyes widening as he beckoned me for help by gesturing with his head.

I ducked down again and moved quickly among the shadows to the front of the building, peeking around. The guards were there, but their backs were to me. I kept my eyes on them, my heart thundering as I opened the door, praying it wouldn't squeak, and slipped inside. I released a gush of breath and then I ran to where Asher was, going down on my knees behind him and beginning to untie his bindings. "The guards are compromised. They surprised me in my sleep and tied me up," he whispered. "I was able to grab one of their walkie-talkies—"

"That was intercepted. This place is being taken over by Leon Lee and a group of armed men you might have heard being let in through the gate. They plan on evicting the elderly by force, if not others too. Leon says they're not planning on shooting anyone, but I don't know if that's true. They're unaware you have any weapons here though. Freddie and Layne are gathering as many of your people as they can. They said you know where to meet."

Once Freddie and Layne alerted a few, they could all begin spreading out quickly, already knowing the lay of the land, every row in all the gardens and each wall and terrace. Even the elderly were on their home turf whereas the invaders were not. It was a huge advantage.

The rope came loose, and Asher began freeing his hands. "I never trusted that guy," Asher hissed before bending forward to untie the bindings at his ankles. "He acted like he owned the place the first day he arrived. They'll be sorry they ever attempted this. Are you with us?"

"No. I'm not staying. I have somewhere else to be."

His gaze hung on me for a moment. "If you belong somewhere else, don't give that up. I won't forget what you did for me. For us. Thank you." Asher pried up a floorboard and took out a large black bag. He reached inside and pulled out a handgun. Then he stood and grabbed something off the top of a shelf and handed it to me. I took it. A key. "Do you know how to ride a dirt bike?"

I remembered the bikes that Asher and Leon had used to take Layne and me up the hill that first day. How was I going to get one of those past the guards though? "It's been a while," I said.

"Come on." Asher pulled in a breath and then unlocked the window at the back of the room. This window was older than the one I'd escaped from and didn't swing open. Instead, he raised it slightly, pausing when it let out a creak. I cringed and looked over my shoulder as though I could see the guards through the wall. But when I heard one of them laugh loudly at something the other said, my shoulders lowered in relief. Asher raised the window higher, pausing and then pushing it up enough that we could squeeze through.

He stepped aside and I crawled out a window for the second time that night, grateful that this one didn't involve a descent. Asher was right behind me and we both stood, listening again before he whispered, "I have my own bike that's parked outside the gate, behind some trees on the left." *Oh.* Outside the gate. It was where I was willingly heading, but the phrase itself inspired a ricochet of fear. "Wait for the two shots and then come down to the gate. I'll open it for you."

I opened my mouth to ask about the two shots but then realized what he meant. He was going to ambush the guards and kill them. Which was necessary. They'd betrayed the entire community. Instead, I said, "A bike is valuable. What if you need it." It was probably what they used to go out and obtain all the weapons and ammunition they'd been able to score while others searched for food. It was why they had a fighting chance now. Each vehicle was a matter of life and death.

He glanced behind him and then back to me. "Have you ever heard the phrase, 'burn the boats'?"

Burn the boats? What? "No."

His mouth gave a small quirk. "Look it up someday."

"I'll google it as soon as I can."

Asher smiled, and then turned, ducking around the building and into the foliage that ended near the front gate. I closed my eyes and hummed so quietly that no one who wasn't standing an inch from me would have heard. I waited, my hands gripped together until I heard a loud rustle, a pop, and then a yell that was cut off by another pop.

I walked quickly around the guardhouse and to the gate where Asher was already standing. In my peripheral vision, I saw the two guards lying in a heap next to each other but didn't turn my head.

Asher pulled the gate open, and I slipped through the small space. He closed it behind me and as he was closing it, I said, "Thank you so much. And good luck." It seemed so inadequate, but it was all I had.

"You too," he said and then he turned away, off to join the others. Off to fight.

I found the bike where he'd said it would be and then rolled it down the street, getting far enough away before swinging my leg over it and sitting down. Then I turned the ignition, the loud rumble in the midst of the silent night making me grimace.

I released the brake, the bike flying forward, wobbling momentarily as I emitted a high-pitched hiss, certain I was going to tumble off. But I gripped the handles, finding control and speeding off into the night. If I rode fast, and wasn't stopped, I could be home before morning.

forty-seven

Tuck

The guards at the next barrier were jacked up on tension and power, and I got the inkling they were itching to shoot someone and at the smallest excuse would do so. I backtracked about a quarter mile and then veered off to the side where I'd seen a few others walking earlier, making their way around the guarded area even though there was only desert in that direction.

Those walking sent furtive glances in my direction, clutching their packs tightly, some holding weapons down at their sides, the threat clear. Even those who weren't looking for trouble would protect what they had at all costs.

To my right was unforgiving terrain bereft of any sustenance and to my left a rocky embankment that led up to the guarded area, men with guns roaming the perimeter and watching from higher ground.

I took my water out and drank another small sip. I'd have to make this last until I made it to Emily, and it was going to be tight. I'd likely arrive parched, but I'd arrive. I wouldn't give up, because I was worried about what the guard at the first barricade had insinuated. Emily might be in trouble. But even if she wasn't, I had to tell her I loved her, and then I'd beg her to come back to her parents' farm. Or if she'd found the purpose she was looking for in San Diego, then I'd stay if she let me. I'd find my own purpose doing something local, returning each evening to her side, creating my legacy wherever she was.

Please don't be too late.

Please wait for me, Em. I don't deserve you. It turns out I never have. But please wait for me.

The click of a gun brought me from my thoughts, and I ducked and pivoted. A man with a shotgun was standing behind me, barrel pointed at my chest. "Drop your backpack. It's all I want." He was crying and shaking, and the gun wavered from side to side. "Haven't eaten in a week," he said.

I brought my hands up. "Whoa, hey relax, okay? We're all hungry. We're all trying to survive." I took off my backpack slowly and then set it on the ground. "I'll give you some of my food," I said. "But I can't give it all. You know that. I'm willing to share."

"You're not willing to do shit! This gun is convincing you to. The world has gone to hell, man. Fuck this! Toss your bag over now. Now!"

The gun shook and the man let out another sob, and goddammit, but I just needed to get to Emily. But this man was right, the world had gone to hell, and if I was going to make it to San Diego, I couldn't do it without food and water. The Swansons had offered to give me one of their weapons and some ammo, but I couldn't allow them to do that. I never would have forgiven myself if I left them without enough defense and they'd ended up needing it.

My brain was shuffling through my options. The man was desperate and unpredictable, but he was also going to be easy to overcome and likely couldn't hit a target that was still and directly in front of him. A loud pop startled me, and I dove to the ground, a bloody hole appearing in the center of the man's forehead, mouth falling open right before he dropped.

I jerked around to see another gunman scooping my pack up off the ground. "Damn thieves," he said, his mouth quirking as he held his rifle with one hand and unzipped my backpack with the other. He removed my canteen and then tipped his head back, glugging down the remainder of my water. *Mother fuck.*

He tossed that on the ground and then gestured with his gun for me to move along. I was vibrating with rage, ready to lunge at this man and take him to the ground, fuck the fact that he had a gun and was obviously a good shot. But Emily's face blossomed in my mind, laughing as she twirled her braid.

What good would it do to get myself killed now when the precious last of my water was gone anyway? Killing this man wouldn't bring it back.

"Get on," he said, ripping a pack of trail mix open with his teeth and pouring that back too.

I moved around him, and then walked past. There were thieves on this stretch of land, the only one accessible due to the many roadblocks. And why not claim this area that ensured travelers, some of whom had provisions, if you were willing to steal from others? No need to hunt supplies down when they came straight to you.

And it felt like a roundhouse kick to the gut that because of it, men like him were going to live while others died.

A dwindling rainstorm blew through the desert later that day and I used a leaf to collect enough to quench my thirst. Then I found shelter behind a large rock, sleeping fitfully in an upright position for a few hours before rising and traveling on.

Another roadblock appeared just before sunset, and I swore under my breath. How many fucking roadblocks were there between me and Emily? I still had at least a day of travel left, and while each roadblock brought me closer, if I came to a point where I could no longer move forward, I wouldn't have enough supplies to go back. As it was, I was depleted. I kept glancing at the sky, praying for rain as I imagined many others were doing as well.

There were four or five people, voices raised and arms gesticulating wildly standing in front of the guards patrolling this area of road that led to a higher elevation. The guards appeared unmoved, expressions blank. They were directing people to the right where only parched earth stretched around the rising cliff they were protecting. No one was getting through.

I began to turn, to walk back out toward the desert and go around when I saw a group of people behind the barrier who'd come close enough to see what the yelling and screaming was from outside their protective wall. Well, good for them for being on the other side. I hoped there was enough for everyone there, like at the Swansons'. I hoped they were sharing and that the bad rising from this situation was being balanced by the good. My gaze hooked on a face that looked familiar, and I hesitated, our eyes meeting. A woman holding a baby stood next to him, and in a sudden flash, I realized who he was— the man who'd begged us for help for his baby girl. The one I'd given the two cans of condensed milk.

Our eyes held, both of us seemingly frozen. He'd taken my advice. He'd left the city and found his way to safety and from the looks of it, just in time. He broke eye contact, turning away, the three of them headed up the hill toward the trees, the man glancing back once before pulling his wife and baby closer.

The other people who'd been begging for entrance turned back in the other direction, their quiet cries growing softer as they moved away. I took in a breath and walked around the barricades, taking several minutes to rest and gather my resolve before traveling through the area so desolate and lacking resources, it was open to all. Right now, however, I was the only one on this particular stretch of emptiness.

The sun dipped, clouds clearing, and I swore under my breath. There wouldn't be rain tonight. Up ahead, I heard a soft smack and paused momentarily before moving forward. I took a few more steps and then halted again when I spotted what looked like a backpack sitting on a rock next to a brambly bush. I turned, looking around for a person who might have left it there. But no one would do that, not in times like these.

I squinted up to the rocky plateau on my left and noticed a man at the top with a gun strapped to his chest. They were guarding the area all along here in case someone decided to attempt a climb. The armed man, however, didn't even spare me a glance.

I walked over to the abandoned pack, picking it up and then looking around again. The terrain remained desolate. I un-zipped the backpack and looked inside. There was a large bottle of water and several food items. I shook my head in wonder. *What is this?* And why would anyone leave it behind? Some-thing caught my eye, and I pulled it out, my heart clenching as I held it up. It was a label from a can of condensed milk and written over the logo were two words: *Thank you.*

I craned my neck, peering up again at the area being pa-trolled, the one that I could see extended much farther than this. *The man I'd helped had gathered these things and then tossed them down from above for me to find.* Had he tracked me as I walked? He had to have. My lungs tightened and my eyes burned. Then I sat down on the rock, emotion crashing over me in waves. The water eased my parched throat, and I wiped my mouth with the back of my hand, letting out a small wondrous laugh. The laugh turned into a shuddery breath, as I moved my finger over that label for condensed milk that had helped feed a hun-gry baby girl until her parents could get her to safety.

I tipped my head back and gazed out to the horizon, this

feeling descending. This inexplicable knowing that clogged my throat and filled my heart. It suddenly seemed so clear to me that redemption was everywhere, in every moment of every day. And so too...was mercy.

forty-eight

Emily

I flew along the shore, the only place I could think to ride the dirt bike where I wouldn't be met with blockades like the ones we had to pass through to get here. Once I encountered a mass of rocks stretched into the ocean, I accelerated up the embankment and drove on the highway that wound around the shore. Broken-down cars littered this stretch of road, but I maneuvered easily around and through, finding that only a handful of people were out, either siphoning gas, or traveling along the edge.

I was afraid to slow down. Afraid that if I did, someone would attack, causing me and the bike to skid along the asphalt only to leave me broken and bleeding by the side of the road so they could steal my ride.

It wasn't paranoia. It was reality and the state of the world right now.

The highway turned into a one-lane road, and that led into

a community, and the roadblock I'd expected appeared. It was the one we'd passed through on the way here. I drove around it, into the weedy desert terrain. Again, I was free to go as fast as I dared and so I did, racing across the hard-packed dirt, avoiding rocks and brambles, remembering the absolute thrill of a similar ride on a horse with Tuck, his deep laughter drifting to me on the wind.

I distanced myself from the rocks against the incline because I could see people sleeping there. Or maybe they were dead, bodies littered outside the cordoned-off zones. Perhaps more and more bodies would continue to pile up in spots like that as the days turned into weeks.

But I couldn't think about that. All I could think about was home.

Please be there, Tuck. At my parents'. I need to tell you I love you, even if you don't say it back. I need you to know even if you decide to go.

It was all that mattered now. Love was more precious than food or water, more important than those chickens worth their weight in gold. And I hadn't said it because I thought it mattered that he might not say it back.

If I rode fast and hard, even if I had to go around barricades, I could make it home by morning. *Please be there. Please—*

The dirt bike hit something as though I'd crashed into an invisible wall, throwing me backward violently as I screamed, and the bike came out from under me. For a moment I was airborne and then everything went black.

I woke with a moan, pain radiating through my head and down my spine. I sucked in a breath, and my lungs expanded, feeling raw and achy as though they'd collapsed, and I'd filled them too quickly.

What happened? Oh my God, what happened?

A man stood over me, the dirt bike next to him, and a rope hanging from his hand. "I'm real sorry," he said. "But I need that bike." *Oh God.* He'd heard me coming. He'd used the rope somehow to stop me. "I'm not a bad person. I'm a restaurant manager. Or I was. They—they looted it. Killed two of my employees. I hid under my desk. I—I just need to get away from here. To the ocean. Where there's food."

I wiggled my toes and then my fingers, relief trickling through me at the knowledge I wasn't paralyzed. I still felt mildly numb though and couldn't tell if I was in shock, or if a bone, or several, were broken. I couldn't manage to find enough breath to speak. I couldn't tell this man there were boats blocking any food that was in the ocean. Modern-day pirates that would kill him rather than let him fish.

"Please," I said, wincing as another sharp pain stabbed at the place behind my eyes. "Please don't leave me here like this."

"I'm a good person," he repeated. "But it's kill or be killed now. That's the way it is. I'm sorry. I'm a good person but I need that bike."

He paused as he peered down at me, our eyes meeting in the starlit desert. "You're pretty. And young," he said. "And I am sorry but look up at the stars and it'll be over soon."

And then, as though he'd suddenly decided he wanted no part of this, he flew backward, landing on the ground with a thud and a shriek of shock.

"Get the fuck away from her." *Tuck. Tuck's voice. How?*

And then he appeared, moving forward, hands clenched into fists, his face full of rage. *Tuck. Oh, Tuck. How are you here? Is this real?* His face blurred and I drifted, sighing out in wonder. I'd conjured him. "I was coming to you," I said, the words streaming together.

And then I heard yells and the sounds of a scuffle and the wet cracks of punches landing, and I tried desperately to pull myself from the stupor I was in, but the stars were so bright, and Tuck was somewhere nearby even though there was no way he could be. And perhaps I was dreaming, but if I was, why was I still in so much pain?

Then I smelled him, Tuck, and arms were wrapping around me, and a high-pitched moan released from my chest as he moved me slightly, his fingers pressing into my flesh. "I'm so sorry, Em. I've got you. You're okay. Let me see." He moved down my arms and then my legs, releasing a breath that sounded full of relief. "I'm going to sit you up," he said. "Remember when we used to play red rover, Em? And you would charge that line with all your might and then land on the ground so hard it shocked me. But then you'd get up. You always got up, you never stay down for long, do you, Em?"

I cried when he brought me to a sitting position, my head throbbing so hard I thought I'd pass out. And maybe I did because a moment later he was cradling me in his arms, his lips warm at my temple, and water at my lips. I took in several sips and then he brought the bottle from my mouth. "You're really here," I said, clutching at his jacket and his hair, running my hands over his face.

"I'm here. I was coming for you. I love you, Emily. I love you so much. And I'm so sorry I didn't say it because it's true and it's the only thing that's real. You're okay. You're going to be okay." Then he lifted me gently and set me on the dirt bike before getting on, so I was facing him. "Can you sit up?" he asked.

I nodded. I was so woozy, but my body seemed to be working, even if I was having a hard time stringing thoughts together. The dirt bike rumbled to life, and we began moving, the wind in my hair once again, but this time in the other direction. I lay my head against Tuck's heart, the beat steady and strong right beneath my ear. "I love you," I murmured. "I've always loved you."

"I love you too," he said again. "And I'm going to get you home and love you every day for the rest of your life."

"Promise?"

"I promise. Now, Em, tell me about that game we used to play, the one with the green bucket..."

"I made that up, and then I changed the rules whenever I wanted."

He breathed out a sound that was a laugh and a sigh in one. "I knew you did."

"Then why'd you play?"

"Because I secretly liked being kept on my toes."

"Hmm." I smiled. I was so sleepy, and everything hurt. "Then I have a lot of work ahead of me."

"We both do."

I drifted but then came to when Tuck asked me a question, slurring my answer and then melting against his chest. We rode over bumpy ground and then smooth, the glow of the sun making me squint when I opened my eyes and looked over his shoulder.

I heard gunfire somewhere very close by, and Tuck made a sharp turn, flying around a big rig and then speeding up as the rumble of engines roared behind us. Wind whipped, we leaned left, then right, streaking past cars and trees before the noise of the engines faded behind us and I felt Tuck relax.

Voices shouted here and there, screams rose, and I kept my face pressed against Tuck, trusting him with every ounce of my soul, one of his arms clamped tightly around my waist, and the other steering the bike.

The air grew still, the rumble of the dirt bike fading away as I cracked open my eyes and Tuck lifted me from the bike. His eyes met mine and he said the most beautiful two words in the English language, the ones I'd been waiting to hear from him for two thousand miles and also my entire life: "We're home."

epilogue

Tuck

Over a year had passed since that early January day when we'd arrived back where we'd begun.

It'd taken Emily a good couple of months to recover completely from the severe concussion she'd suffered in that desert in the middle of the night not far from the place where I'd hunkered down in the darkness to rest for a few hours.

As strange as it was, in some ways, that rope the man had stretched in her path as he'd heard her zipping through the desert and seen her headlights, had been another sort of miracle. Despite that I'd been terrified out of my mind to see her lying there seemingly broken and half-alive, if she hadn't been flung off the dirt bike right then, she might have flown right by me, and I'd never have known it was her.

I'd have continued on to San Diego, just missing her, and Emily would have attempted to make it home, perhaps encountering more danger…

Well, who knows what would have been. I had a long history of playing the what-if game, and I tried not to do much of that now. Because when I didn't think too hard about it, when I simply let the entire journey we'd undertaken swirl in my mind as a misty memory, every twist and turn seemed fated. Each challenge and every victory had propelled us forward in some astonishing way.

Not that I had a lot of time on my hands to sit and daydream anyway. Rebuilding the world was a full-time job, or at least, rebuilding our corner of it. I stood now, stretching my back from where I'd put a newly grafted tree into the ground and patted the dirt around it.

Our orange orchard now stretched as far as the eye could see, the same as it once had. From where I was, I could just catch a glimpse of the vegetable garden and the house Emily's father and I had built for Emily and me.

I began walking, examining the trees that had been planted last spring. They were doing well, but it would be a few years until they produced fruit. The trees that had been spared from the fires, however, were heavy with bright orange jewels. They sparkled in the sunlight and scented the air around me.

I moved a little farther into the grove, able to see our land stretched below me from this higher ground. The barnyard... the chicken coop...the garden that was continually being expanded as we were able to trade for seeds we didn't yet have at the farmers market a few miles from here. And up the hill a little farther were my bees and the honeycomb that Emily's mom used to make candles.

These days, I often found it necessary to simply stop and take stock of everything around me. Perhaps, in some ways, it was only now that I was fully grasping the immensity of all that had occurred. We'd been working so long and hard up to this point to create a life where we could count on continued survival, that sometimes I had to remind myself what the world used to look like.

My gaze moved beyond, to the outside world, and my heart gave a hollow knock like it always did when I thought about how many people had perished. Cities, that had become bastions of crime in the aftermath of the solar flare, were now empty graveyards. Criminals and predators had ruled over the wreckage for a time, but eventually, their reign of terror had ended when supplies ran dry. Then they turned on each other, their numbers diminishing further by the day.

The criminals who had managed to survive had come into the countryside to find a new set of victims, but we'd been prepared, they'd been depleted, and that battle had been over before it'd really begun.

In some places, I'd heard the military was reforming and beginning a cleanup, but I wasn't sure if that was true or not, or if it was, where they'd even begin. I'd also heard that the attempt to make repairs to the grid had stalled, in part because of the roads still blocked by inoperable vehicles, and a lack of workers.

We heard a lot of things from those passing through, but none of it could be corroborated, so we didn't worry too much about it. We had enough to concern ourselves with as it was.

Movement caught my eye, and I watched Emily step out of our house and walk in the direction of the old barn. *Where are you going, Showboat?*

I plucked a few oranges to drop off at our gate later for hungry people passing through. There weren't many travelers now, and the makeshift barriers that had once been constructed were mostly unmanned these days. Once, weapons and food had been the most sought-after commodities, but now, people looking for a home bargained with skills. We'd scored a doctor a year ago, a wonderful older man with a lifetime of knowledge. Just yesterday, we'd welcomed a woman who had been a math teacher and her daughter. They had been among the many who hadn't found safety or shelter, though they'd managed to survive. Their hollow, haunted eyes told us survival had come at a price.

We'd welcomed many such people.

Being part of our community would help. The regular meals would heal their bodies, and Emily's music would be part of healing their souls. I'd watched it happen before, gazes hung on her as her voice soared above the campfire, the notes somehow stitching closed internal wounds and reminding those who had witnessed ugliness and horror that beauty still existed in the world and that it was worth fighting for.

She'd written a treasure trove of music with every step we took on our journey home, songs that spoke first of anger and disappointment, then of understanding and love, and finally the reuniting of souls. And I listened to each one in awe, the miles we'd traveled coming right back and socking me in the gut. And I fell back in love with her all over again.

I set the oranges in the basket in front of our gate and then made my way to the barn and slipped through the door. I knew right where she was.

I walked past the car that had become unusable in the last few months since fuel could no longer be found, moving quietly toward the ladder that led to the loft.

My head cleared the high-up floor and there she was.

Emily Mattice.

She looked over at me and smiled from where she was lying under the window. "What are you doing here?" I asked as I crawled toward her. "We're leaving for the market in a little bit."

I sat down beside her and lay back, gazing at the small slice of blue sky that showed through the glass. We'd made good use of this loft while our house was being built and we still lived with Emily's parents. But now that we had our own place, and plenty of privacy, we hadn't had reason to come up here much.

"I know," she said. "This is probably the last time I'll come up here for a while." She ran her hand over her barely rounded stomach and smiled over at me. "Climbing ladders will have to be on hold temporarily."

I smiled back and lay my hand on top of hers, that same zing of fear and joy reverberating through me that I'd felt when she'd first told me about the baby as we lay in front of our fireplace. Only now, the joy was greater than the fear. This baby was an embodiment of hope in the future, and a living symbol of everything we'd been through to get here. He or she was more precious than the trees or the land or the seeds we planted in the ground. He or she would ensure that the world went on and, as a wise prophet had once said, was proof that life longed for itself.

"Do you think Gretel will have those caramels she brought last week?" Emily asked.

I smiled. She'd eaten so many of those, she swore she was never going to look at another caramel again. "If she was able to find more sugar," I said.

"Do you know that she brought them there in a Louis Vuitton purse?" Emily laughed. "She used it just like a brown paper bag. The purse was worthless. It was the caramels everyone was drooling over," she said, her voice mildly incredulous.

"Things have changed," I said with a chuckle.

She rolled toward me and propped her hands on my chest and laid her chin there. "Yes," she agreed. "Lots has changed. But other things have stayed the same."

She leaned up and kissed me and rubbed her nose over mine. "I love you."

"I love you too."

"Come on, Mattice," she said, as she got up. "Caramels await. And maybe we can find a few books to add to that library of yours."

I descended the ladder first and she followed, and then we exited the barn, strolling hand in hand through the orchard.

The cloudless sky stretched over the land, what, to us, was the whole wide world, our patch of heaven, and where our journey had ended, all woven together by a thread of love.

★ ★ ★ ★ ★

acknowledgments

When I first read the outline for *Heart of the Sun*, crafted by the team at Temple Hill, my jaw almost hit the floor. Not only was I immediately gripped by the intense story, but I had listened to an interview about the subject of an EMP event in the United States just days earlier and had been doing some basic research out of pure curiosity (and a bit of dread). I've learned to follow what I believe are signs and immediately expressed my interest and commitment to telling Tuck and Emily's tale as they traveled through a crumbling society. Thank you from the bottom of my heart to Temple Hill for trusting me to flesh out the fine points of your brilliant idea. And special thanks to Alli Dyer for helping me set the tone and offering invaluable direction as I set off on this journey.

Immense gratitude to Cat Clyne for taking this 140,000-word road trip/love story/breakdown of civilization and seeing every spot where improvements could be made and characters required polishing in that mess of a first draft. There were a lot of moving parts within this manuscript, and I couldn't have seen the forest for the trees without you. And thank you as well to Gina Macedo for sprucing it up even further and keeping track of the days and distance.

To Marion Archer, whose empathy knows no bounds. I am so lucky to have you.

Thank you to Kimberly Brower for too many things to mention. Mostly though, for always, no matter what, having my back.

To you, the reader, thank you for traversing the miles with Tuck and Emily. And with me as well, whether from my first book or just this one. My love and appreciation for each and every one of you can't be sufficiently put into words. And thank you too to all of you who spread your love of reading through beautiful art on social media. Your work inspires others to discover the love of reading, and the importance of that can't be overstated.

And to my husband: I'd walk a million miles with you, and then a million more.